PERPETUAL LIGHT

JORDAN K. ROSE

www.crescentmoonpress.com

Perpetual Light
Jordan K. Rose

ISBN: 978-1-937254-06-3
E-ISBN: 978-1-937254-07-0

Crescent Moon Press
1385 Highway 35
Box 269
Middletown, NJ 07748

Crescent Moon Press electronic publication/print publication: March 2012 www.crescentmoonpress.com

**for Ken,
the love of my life**

PROLOGUE

*"L'amore e dolcissima corrispondenza degli spiriti, che di
due anime ne compone una sola."*
~Guerrazzi
Love is the sweetest joining of spirits, when two souls become
as one.

April 11, 1667

The Abyss hovered, waiting to take me.

More time, I need more time. He's coming.

The raspy sounds of my own breathing filled my ears. With
each jagged gasp, pain shot through my body straight to my
core.

Pressure, cold and heavy, weighed on me. The Abyss
called.

Not yet.

The next breath held the scent of sun-kissed grapevines,
and I knew he was near.

"No. God, no." He sobbed as he lifted me into his arms.
"*Lucia.*"

My eyes opened.

Vittorio.

He was changed. His skin, tanned from years in the
vineyard, was now gray, and deep, dark grooves circled his
eyes. Gone were the beautiful green and gold flecks of his
hazel irises, replaced with the crimson glow of one who
walked in shadows.

He needed me.

The Abyss stretched forward, reaching for me, its frigid
tendrils swirling as souls trapped within its depths screamed
for salvation. Cold burns whipped across my aura as the

~ ☽ ~

angry void attempted to claim me.

No. Not yet. I concentrated on Vittorio, steeling myself against my bitter destiny. Another moment with him was all I needed.

Gazing into his eyes, I found his trembling soul, hidden within him. Without hesitating my power wrapped around him, hiding his presence from The Abyss.

Tortured and terrified, he stared back at me, unmoving, his heart hammering in his chest.

Calm, my love.

A scream pierced the air. The Abyss grew impatient.

My very essence quaked as the angry void surrounded me. But I called on my powers and captured his soul, holding it in the warmth of eternity, caressing it, loving him.

Drink from me. Drink and take my gift. Keep me with you forever. It was all I could offer, the only way I knew to keep him safe, to keep us together.

He shook his head. "I don't want to hurt you, *cuore mio.*" A single red-tinged tear rolled down his cheek.

No, you cannot hurt me. I will give you strength. I will give you the light you need. Drink.

I lifted my chin and pulled him to my neck, muffling his sobs against my skin.

His fangs penetrated my flesh, and he drank.

And The Abyss howled at my return.

~ ☾ ~

CHAPTER ONE

"Amor di nostra vita ultimo inganno."
~Leopardi
Love is the ultimate deception of our life.

Present Day
Providence, RI
La Moda Boutique

A familiar ache throbbed deep in my chest. The quiet, steady rhythm worked itself into a cadence that my heart tried to match. But it was too fast, too loud, too deep. My heart couldn't compete.

Stay calm, Lu. You can do it.

I swayed against a mannequin, and she teetered on her pedestal. With trembling hands, I gripped the window frame, holding on hard to reality.

Darkness loomed around me, stalking closer with every breath like an animal coming to devour me. Shivers ran along my skin as I swallowed back a scream.

In a sudden flash, brilliant sunlight reflected off the fresh fallen snow, creating a golden splendor. Its warmth bathed me, calming my racing heart and banishing the ache from my body.

The darkness receded.

"I'll be Home for Christmas" played in the background, its soft melody soothing me. Fully stocked clothing racks waited for the day's first customer. The scents of freshly baked gingerbread and coffee wafted in the air.

I took a deep breath.

~ ☾ ~

Dad stopped shoveling and waved. "You okay?" he yelled through the window.

"*What?*" Mom yelled back.

"Not you! *Lucia.* Is she okay?" he hollered, pointing at me.

"What is it, honey?" Mom dropped a wrapped package beneath the Christmas tree and hurried toward me. She pushed my hair back from my face, gently twirling the long brown spirals in her hands.

"Nothing," I whispered, briefly glancing in her direction. *Breathe, Lu. A deep breath in. Hold. Exhale.* After repeating the words a couple times, I had coaxed myself through the process.

The bells on the door jingled as Dad entered the shop. "Aren't your eyes bothering you?" He kicked slush from his boots then stepped inside.

My heart raced. "What?"

"Direct sunlight. It must hurt your eyes. The way they shimmer is something else, Lu. I'd swear they were glowing." He quickly stripped off his hat, gloves, and scarf.

Glancing down, I found my sunglasses in my hands. Unsure of when I'd taken them off, I shoved them onto my face with a vague sense of unease.

"Are your eyes bothering you, honey?" Mom's gaze darted from me to Dad and back to me.

"No. I'm fine," I lied. In the last two weeks, my eyes had gone from hazel-green to an almost iridescent emerald shade. I couldn't explain it and had spent most of my time trying to hide them, wearing sunglasses everywhere.

I ducked around a display table and straightened the handbags piled on top. Mom followed me, hovering.

I moved on to a rack of blouses, pretending to adjust the holiday bows she'd attached to the hangers. "The shop looks great. I like the ornaments and the train." Every year she decorated La Moda for the holiday, creating window displays to rival 5th Avenue. "The tree smells good, too." I smiled. "Christmas-y."

She watched me wearing *that* look, the one she always wore when she thought I was hiding something. The one that meant she was deciding the wording of her next question, the

~ ☾ ~

question that would get her the most information. Whenever she worried about me, she strategized like a commander preparing for battle.

I hunkered down and waited for the assault, hoping to evade the inevitable offensive.

Ours was the least complex game of espionage ever to be played. Nothing covert about it. She chased and I ran, dodging questions like a sparrow dodges a hawk.

"How've you been sleeping?" she asked, plugging in the tree lights. "Art, fix these. I don't want them flashing." She handed Dad the last string of lights.

"I've been sleeping fine." I marched to the desk to get to work on the inventory.

"Any dreams?" She straightened some jackets on a rack while Dad fiddled with the bulbs.

"No." I opened the file on the desk marked 'Inventory', pushed the power button on the computer, and organized the highlighters.

"No dreams? That's interesting." She folded a couple sweaters. "Not even about Vittorio?"

The Christmas tree lights stopped alternating and a steady glow illuminated the shop.

All my life I'd had vivid dreams, most of them sweet and pleasant, involving a vineyard in Italy and one man, Vittorio, my dream-husband. He was tall with dark, wavy hair and eyes that sparkled with flecks of gold and green. And his smile always melted my heart. 'Cuore mio', he called me, and loved me in a way I'd never experienced in my own life.

Until recently, I always looked forward to going to sleep, knowing I'd see him. But, lately, Vittorio hadn't appeared in any of my dreams.

"Nope." I shuffled the papers in the file.

Dad sipped his coffee, quietly waiting for his moment. Like any good husband and father, he always knew to keep out of it, even if he was equally as worried as she. Lingering in the background, he listened to the battle, waiting for the opportunity to swoop in and call a truce. A true diplomat, he never chose sides.

"Is this the complete order for Gemma?" I asked as the

~ ☾ ~

computer came to life.

"Mm-hmm. Any nightmares?"

The numbers on the page swam before me as I bit my tongue to keep from blurting out an answer that would have given her more information than she needed. *Deep breath in. Hold. Exhale.*

In the past two weeks everything had changed: my eyes, my dreams, even the way I felt in my own skin. Every morning I woke in a state of grief so overwhelming all I could do was sob. No explanation for the grief existed. Nothing sad was happening in my life, no losses, no disappointments, nothing. Just the dreams. The inability to explain my grief consumed most of my mornings, if not my days.

"Has the blond man made any more appearances?" She clicked the switch, and the desk lamp shined above me.

I shook my head and thumbed through the pages in the file.

The blond man, wicked as Satan, prowled my nightmares, stalking me the way a wolf hunts a lamb, hiding in the edges of my mind, creeping into my world one slow step at a time. I'd always been able to keep ahead of him, to escape to safety, enveloped in a void that echoed with his enraged screams. As though watching him from a safe room, I'd been forced to witness him act out his anger, leaping from the recesses of my thoughts to brutally attack and murder so many innocent lives.

To call the dreams "nightmares" didn't even begin to describe their intensity.

He hadn't haunted my dreams for several nights. But he hadn't disappeared either. Everywhere I went I'd taken to looking over my shoulder, my intuition piquéd by an unspoken omen. A foreboding. Someone or something hunted me. A darkness—no, an evil like nothing I'd ever known hovered just beyond my vision. Its presence loomed. I couldn't see him, but I knew he was there.

Forcing myself to concentrate on the work at hand, I entered the numbers from the page into a spreadsheet then blinked in surprise. "This is a small jewelry order, a third of the size of the usual one."

~ ☾ ~

"It will do for now," she answered. "I'm glad to hear the nightmares have stopped."

Without looking, I felt her probing gaze, the way it wandered over me, studying every fidgety muscle, gauging the depth of each breath, and anticipating every thought that moved through my mind.

I didn't react, just sat there, pretending to study the paperwork. She hadn't asked a question. No need to respond.

The nightmares were worse than usual, more frequent, more vivid, more violent. And, although I recognized the people in my dreams, I didn't *know* them—or maybe I knew them, but didn't recognize them. Whichever it was, I desperately wished never to dream of them again.

Mom moved on to the camisole display, arranging them by color and size. "So, you're sleeping well?"

"Fine." I tapped the keyboard, entering numbers as fast as I could.

Multiple theories on what was happening had occurred to me. Maybe I was possessed. This was my number one theory, considering the dreams and my recent paranoia. Two: maybe my eyes weren't changing at all, and I was imagining it. I kept telling myself that, but every time I checked, they still glowed.

My last theory was that I suffered from multiple personalities, and when I inhabited my 'other self' I was putting in funky contacts and living some weird life. But no matter how many times I jabbed a finger into my eye to draw out the contact lens, there was never one to remove.

So, theory number one seemed the only logical answer. Of course, when demon possession seems a logical explanation for your life, you know you've hit new a low.

"Are you staying for lunch?" Dad asked. "I'm starving."

Mom scowled at him. "It's not lunchtime."

He grinned and smoothed his hands over his sweater. "Lu should stay for lunch." Almost twenty years ago Dad retired from teaching and came to work in the shop with Mom, which left my overprotective dad free to tag along with me on a number of business trips.

Somehow, no matter how hard I tried to improve his fashion sense, he never lost the math teacher vibe. The

~ ☾ ~

button-up sweater over an oxford with casual pants was his uniform. He'd worn it for nearly forty years. I half expected him to grab a piece of chalk and begin writing equations on the wall.

"I'll get sandwiches at The Corner Bistro," he said, grinning.

I was fairly certain I was the only kid in history whose dad transferred to every school she ever attended, and taught for each grade level as she passed through them. He had only been my teacher five of the thirteen years—second and seventh grades and the last three years of high school.

It goes without saying, my homework was always in on time.

"Can't stay for lunch. I need to get to Gemma by two o'clock. Tempo's Christmas party is tonight, and the boss wants us all there by six." I printed the Gemma document and stuffed it into my bag.

"Ah, Tempo's big shindig." Dad grabbed a handful of gingerbread cookies off the tray mom had left for the customers. "That paying employer of yours throws a good party." He sat on the settee by the window. "You know, they should let you bring your parents."

"Arturo, shush." Mom removed three cookies from his hands, put them back on the tray, and moved it across the room. "Lucia doesn't want to bring her parents. Is Michael going to the party with you?" She ran her fingers through her dark hair, letting the big curls roll around them, then wiggled them loose.

"No. He has some business meeting he can't miss. What about the other orders? You said there were some inventory issues." I closed one manila folder and opened another, trying very hard to keep her occupied with work so she'd quit interrogating me.

Michael and I had dated for a few years. Sometimes we were more serious than others. Sometimes we were just friends, which was our current state. I hadn't been able to "pull the trigger," as Dad liked to call it. I loved Michael, but I wasn't ready for marriage.

"It's all there." Her fingers worked her hair again. Then

~ ☾ ~

she reached for mine, gently fluffing the long tresses. Her touch, so tender, reminded me of my childhood and the many nights when she brushed my hair. I closed my eyes for a moment, relaxing.

"What are you wearing tonight?" she asked.

"A burgundy velvet gown."

With a quick hug, she said, "Get pictures. You know I've always loved to see my little girl dressed up."

I squeezed my eyes shut, fighting back sudden tears. I'd have loved to have a family, a little girl of my own. But with all the traveling I did for Tempo, my lifestyle wasn't conducive to one. Worse than that, lately the nightmares had become so horrible I'd begun wondering if I was sane enough to be near adults, never mind children.

An hour later we'd finished the inventory, and I had just packed my bag, slipped into my coat, and kissed my parents good-bye when the door to the shop opened. A gust of wind whooshed in, carrying with it the scent of a freshly mown lawn.

With my back to the door, I knew exactly who had entered. He was the only man I'd ever met with that cologne. And, although I liked his cologne, I didn't like him. Maybe it was that annoying confidence, or his irritating ability to observe *everything*, or the inexplicable magnetism he had with customers. Whatever it was, he irked me to no end. I gritted my teeth and exhaled loudly, trying to clear my lungs.

"What's wrong, honey?" Mom asked.

"Nothing," I growled before wheeling on the new arrival. "What are you doing here?"

Peter glided into the shop, that annoying, cocky smile threatening at the corners of his mouth. "Jack sent me. I'm supposed to learn everything you know. I believe we have an appointment at Gemma."

Jack sent him. Stupid Jack. I'll...

Two weeks ago our boss Jack promoted me, out of the blue, to Senior Buyer. The company had decided to make an abrupt change in structure, adding a junior level. My lines, women's accessories, moved the fastest, selling at nearly double the rate of any others, so I was given the punishment

~ ☾ ~

of training the junior. Peter was my junior.

"Mr. and Mrs. DiComano, it's a pleasure to see you," Peter said. The lilt of an English accent seemed to color his voice, but the slight inflection faded as quickly as it came.

He stood directly in front of me. A light blue ring surrounded his midnight blue irises, giving the illusion of depth. He exuded a tranquil, welcoming charm. When he faced my parents, his smile broadened.

"Oh, the pleasure is ours." Mom walked toward Peter, her eyes fixed on his.

"Yes. Thanks for coming by." Dad extended his hand.

As they both reached for him, Peter's jaw clenched, freezing that dumb expression on his face.

"It's good of you to come," Dad said, his voice deepening.

I looked at Dad. The only other time I'd heard his voice drop like that was when he caught Billy Taylor kissing me in the stairwell at school. Needless to say, Billy did not take me to the prom.

My parents regarded Peter like warriors sizing up an enemy. I wasn't sure if they were sympathetic to my dislike or if they'd developed their own in the thirty seconds Peter was in the shop, but either way, I liked it.

I fixed my hair under my hat and didn't bother to hide my pleasure as I watched the faceoff. Thank God for parents.

My smugness vanished and shock took over when they suddenly began acting as though he was a rock star, their eyes wide, giant grins, heads nodding as if they were all telepathically communicating. No one should be this happy to see Peter. They weren't this happy when I arrived.

"What the hell? What's going on here?" I asked.

"Lucia, behave." Mom frowned.

Ignoring me, the three of them began chatting about the job with all its travel requirements.

"Peter, we know you'll keep her safe, won't you?" Mom asked, her tone more commanding than inquisitive.

Dad rested his hand on Peter's shoulder, keeping a firm grip.

"Yes, Mrs. DiComano, until my last breath."

"Are you kidding?" I asked. "I've been traveling since I was

~ ☾ ~

born. You brought me to the US from Italy when I was three days old. I haven't stopped since. I've traveled to third world countries alone and been perfectly fine. Now, you're asking *him*, my junior, to keep me safe? Have you lost it?" Peter shuffled to the left as I barreled between him and Dad. "Until your last breath? Give me a break."

"Lucia, you know I've never liked you traveling alone. Now that you have someone to look out for you, I feel better." Mom patted Peter's arm. "He's strong and smart. He'll keep you safe. And, I think he has friends that...well, they'll help." She plucked a piece of lint from his jacket, then squeezed his arm.

I grabbed her hand and pulled her away from him. She always liked people, but she didn't fawn over anyone but me, and she'd never responded this way to a stranger. "He's all of twenty-two years old. He's never been anywhere or done anything. I'm babysitting him, and he's not exactly a superhero who would scare off attackers." I motioned at Peter.

Taller than my five-feet-four-inches, though only by six inches or so, Peter was muscular, but trim. Certainly handsome, with fantastic blue eyes and blond hair, but he was still a baby, one I had been forced into grooming.

More unsettling, his skin often seemed odd, changing throughout the day. Usually, he started the day looking like he had the flu, but by the end he appeared to have recovered; the dark circles under his eyes faded, and his skin went from gray to almost luminescent.

Either he was weird or I was seeing things, which made me hate him even more. Mom should *not* like him.

His eyes twinkled, and the corner of his mouth ticked upward as he watched me guiding Mom away from him. I snickered, and that stupid, full-on cocky grin returned.

"We should get going if we're going to reach Boston in time to meet Elizabeth and Alexander before the party," he said. "Mr. and Mrs. DiComano, you have nothing to fear. Lucia is safe with me and my friends."

"I hope so." Dad's brows lowered.

"Yes, sir." Peter fidgeted with his gloves.

~ ☾ ~

Mom wriggled her hand from mine and leaned toward Peter. "Thank you." She kissed his cheek.

She could have knocked me over with a feather at that point.

"Be careful, Lucia. Remember, you are the light of our lives, always the light," Dad said, kissing my cheek.

"I know, Dad." If I hadn't heard him say that a million times, I hadn't heard it once.

Mom hugged me. "In your travels keep your eyes open, my girl. Pay attention to what's around you." She squeezed me tighter than usual. *"Ti amo, piccola mia."*

"Ti amo, Mom. Are you feeling okay?"

"Yes, honey." She stepped into Dad's embrace.

"Are you sure?" I asked, studying the two of them. Their eyes held something different. Relief? Their faces relaxed, tender smiles curving their lips.

"We're fine. We'll see you soon, honey," Dad said.

"Let's go, Lu. We don't want to hit any traffic," Peter said.

I spun to tell him to shut up and had to turn completely around. He was across the room, holding the door open.

"How did you do that?"

"Do what?" he asked.

"Get across the room that fast." I snatched my laptop bag and the Gemma file, heading toward the door.

"I don't know what you mean. I just walked the few steps."

"It's more than twenty feet," I countered.

He shrugged.

"Bye, honey," Mom said. "Take good care, Peter."

"La tenero al sicuro," Peter said as he opened the door.

I waved to my parents and closed the door, then reeled back to scowl at him. "You're going to keep me safe? I'm going to shove you in front of a bus." I stomped past him.

~ ☾ ~

CHAPTER TWO

The wind kicked up, blowing my hat from my head. Long, brown spirals shot in every direction. My shadow transformed into Medusa. "My hat!" I dropped my bag and the file, lunging for the mod cap. The soft corduroy brim brushed the tips of my fingers and tumbled downward. "No." I bent down to the dirty slush puddle where the hat should have landed. And stopped. The only thing floating in the murky water was a gum wrapper.

"You probably should have put the file in the bag." The English accent hung on the word "bag".

I turned on my heel. "Will you please shut the..."

That cocky smile appeared. "Do you want to put the hat on first or put the file in the bag?" He stood beside me, my bag hanging on his shoulder, the file in one hand, and my hat in the other.

"How did you do that?"

"Well, I guess that since I'm younger than you, I'm just faster, too." He handed me the hat.

"I hate you. Make no mistake: I hate you." I jammed the hat on my head and jerked the file from his hand. "Give me my bag."

He handed it over without another word.

"Where's your car? Never mind. I don't care. Meet me at Gemma." I walked around to the driver's side and opened the door.

"I took the train down. I'll ride to Boston with you." Without waiting for a response he opened the passenger door and sat in my car. "Get in." He closed the car door and opened the glove compartment.

I gritted my teeth. "I need to make a call." Slamming the

~ ☾ ~

door, I dug out my phone. Number three on the speed dial connected me immediately.

"Jack Paterson." The calm, smooth voice answered.

"Why is he here?"

"Lu." He sighed, and his tone became a little less relaxed. "He's your junior. You're supposed to train him, remember?"

"I never said I *wanted* a junior. I never said I *wanted* a promotion. And I never said he was welcome to chase me around like some nerdy high schooler. *I want him out of here.*" I growled the words into the phone.

"Lu, damn it, he's yours. You're keeping him and that's final. We're not having this argument again. Stay off the internet, do not interrogate him about his work history, and stop trying to dig up skeletons from his closet. For God's sake, I've never met anyone so opposed to being promo—"

I slapped the phone shut and let out a snarl of angry disgust. We'd had this argument daily for two weeks. I kept losing, and I hated to lose.

Son of a bitch. I may be stuck with him, but he's not horning in on my life or my territory.

The passenger side door opened. "Lu, get in," Peter said from across the roof of the car.

I spun around to face him. "Don't tell me what to do. I'm in charge." Too angry to control myself, I yelled the words at him. "*I* tell *you* what to do."

"Get in the car." There was an edge to his command that just rubbed me all wrong.

"Who do you think you are? *You* get in the car," I ordered and pointed my finger at him.

His handsome face changed. The welcoming, deep blue eyes narrowed to cold black beads. Anger ebbed in their depths. The smile vanished, replaced by a thin, straight line, accentuated by the constricted muscles of his jaw. He sneered, and I'd have sworn fangs flashed in his mouth. His hand on the roof closed to a fist.

The wind changed directions, carrying with it a repulsive vomity-mothball odor. I gagged.

He stared over my shoulder. "Get in the car. *Now.*" His lip hitched upward, flashing those strange teeth again.

~ ☾ ~

I fumbled for the door, glancing over my shoulder, expecting the evil from my dreams to attack. Before the driver's side door was open, Peter appeared beside me, ripping the keys from my hand and shoving me into the car. Moving too fast for me to register his actions, he'd managed to take the keys, toss me into the backseat, slide into the driver's seat, and get the car into traffic.

I lay stunned on the backseat, squinting at the sunroof, nearly blinded by the light. When the car stopped short, I rolled off the seat and landed on the floor. That's when my senses finally returned.

"What the hell?" I tried to right myself, which the erratic driving of that maniac made nearly impossible. My coat was twisted, my knee pinning part of it beneath me. I wiggled around, a shoe came off, the hat went under the seat, and, as I fought to wrench myself free, the sound of fabric tearing signaled the end of my favorite coat.

"Now look what you've done. This coat was specially made for me by Angelina Faustina. Do you have any idea who that is?" I rolled over, heard something crunch, sat up, and managed to get onto the seat. A dark purple strip of velvet hung down my side. My designer glasses lay in three pieces on the floor. *Oh shit. That was my last pair. Now what?*

I desperately tried to repair the lens, frame and arm, only half listening to Peter as he informed me, in intricate, infuriating detail, exactly who Angelina Faustina was, including her bizarre fetish for men with stumpy toes. Then he detailed my connection to her throughout the last four years. He was annoying, but the kid had obviously done his homework.

The car swerved into the breakdown lane, around a slower moving Camry. I slid across the seat, unable to keep from screaming.

He jammed the pedal to the floor. The engine revved, accelerating well beyond the speed limit for the on-ramp. I slammed backward and was briefly pinned by the force.

Borrow Peter's glasses. The words moved through my mind, but I'd have sworn they were not my own.

He wove the car in and out of traffic, passing on the left,

~ (~

the right, and up the middle. "Here. Wear these." A pair of plain black sunglasses landed in my lap.

I gawked at him, trying to decide if I should thank him, punch him, or laugh hysterically.

I slid the sunglasses on. "How do you know all that about Angelina?" I yanked on my hat. "Never mind. I don't need to know. Pull over. I'm driving." I unbuttoned my ruined coat and shrugged out of it while wiggling my foot back into my shoe.

"It would seem ridiculous for me to pull over on 95 North. I'll just drive us to Boston." Cars blurred past us as he sped down the highway.

I leaned into the front seat. "Let's get a few things settled: I'm in charge. You take orders from me, not the other way around. I don't appreciate you scaring the daylights out of me so you can have your way. You are never, ever to do that again. That thing you did with your eyes and mouth, don't ever do it again. You got that, tough guy?"

"Yes, ma'am."

"And one more thing. I'm not that old, jerk. Now pull over." I sat back and waited for him to stop the car.

"You're right. You're not that old. Thirty-seven is really just a baby." He glanced back at me in the mirror. No smile, just a matter-of-fact expression on his face.

"Don't get smart. Are you—"

"Before you ask me to pull over again, let's discuss Gemma," he interrupted. "According to my sources, you discovered Elizabeth at a trade show in Vegas about four and a half months ago. You liked each other instantly, laughing and spending most of your time together that week. You've introduced a number of her lines to both Tempo and La Moda. Am I right so far?" That damn grin had returned.

"I hate your smile."

He glanced in the rearview mirror, one eyebrow slightly arched. "Elizabeth has run Gemma jewelry for approximately fifteen years. She employs a number of her family members. Her husband, Alexander, handles the manufacturing. Her brother-in-law, Victor, manages procurement of materials. And her nephew, Bruno, is in charge of shipping and

~ ☾ ~

receiving. While Elizabeth designs most of the pieces, she also manages the sales end of the business."

I had to admit, his research was pretty thorough. I'd assigned him to study the designers, providing him the entire list of all eight hundred seventy six. Somehow, I'd neglected to tell him which ones were mine and that he really only needed to know those. My intention had been to keep him out of my hair for several days. But, amazingly, the next morning he was back with very, very detailed notes.

"Is there anything else you want to tell me about Elizabeth?" I asked. Part of me hoped he had some peculiar detail while the other part of me feared he did.

"Well, let's see. Her nephew, Bruno, has a, well... Are you sure you want to know?" His eyes twinkled in the mirror, brows slightly raised. "It's a bit strange."

My eyes widened. I hadn't met Bruno yet. I planned to meet him and his father tonight at the party. Would knowing something personal about him make it impossible to keep a straight face? Would not knowing eat at me all night? "Tell me."

"He likes to... Maybe I shouldn't. Sometimes it's best not to share." Peter concentrated on driving, making every effort not to notice me in the mirror.

"Just tell me. I can keep a secret."

"Okay. But no complaining when you can't look him in the eye tonight. He likes to wear pink panties." Now he checked the mirror. He said the words without even an ounce of expression. Perfectly straight-faced.

"You're an idiot." Annoyed that I'd fallen for his stupid prank and beginning to feel flushed, I lowered the window. Of course, driving at warp speed made the wind swoosh into the car. "Turn on the air conditioner." I rolled up the window.

"It's not a joke. He wears pink underwear." Cool air began blowing.

I leaned between the two front seats to adjust the vents. "How would you know that? Have you seen him in pink underwear? And, if you have, when?"

"You sent me to do research. I researched. You'd be surprised what you can find with the Internet at your fingertips."

~ ☾ ~

"Did you find a picture of him in pink underwear? Was that on the Internet?" I rolled my eyes. "Stop the car. I'll drive."

"We're almost there. Another fifteen minutes. I'm not stopping now."

The drive took us less than fifteen minutes, primarily because he took risks sane people wouldn't even consider. After taking back the keys and reminding him that *I* was in charge and, therefore, *I* would drive on the ride to the hotel, we entered the building.

The offices for Gemma were located in Chinatown in what appeared from the outside to be an old, run-down sweatshop. The inside was more modern. A few paintings and some sketches of jewelry designs decorated the interior's plain, white walls.

Elizabeth's office was a windowless conference room. A small desk at one side held her files and supplies, but her laptop sat on a large table in the middle of the room. An enormous painting of a vineyard hung on one of the longer walls.

Cyprus trees lined the sloping hills in the background of the painting. A few sparse clouds dotted the blue sky. The large building on the side looked like it could have been a winery and a home. Wine barrels stood outside one entrance while chairs and a table set for a meal waited under a tree at another. A small house sat on a hill in the background. My imagination wandered to the little house. I saw myself walking over the threshold, cooking in the kitchen, dancing in the parlor...

"Hello, Lu." Elizabeth smiled as she entered the room. Her long, silky black hair hung all the way down her back. She wore jeans and a colorful blouse. An ornate gold cross hung from her neck, floating in the ruffles of her shirt. Multiple bangles jingled on both wrists and an elaborate ring decorated each hand.

In spite of her lively greeting and attire, her appearance surprised me. I would have sworn she wasn't feeling well if it hadn't been for her incredibly cheerful personality. A gray pallor washed her skin and dark circles surrounded her eyes.

~ ☾ ~

"You must be Peter. I'm Elizabeth." She closed the door and rounded the table to where Peter and I stood admiring the painting.

"A pleasure to finally meet you. I'm looking forward to working with you." Peter shook Elizabeth's hand, grinning like he couldn't wait to tell her about her nephew and the pink panties.

She released his hand, and I thought I saw her roll her eyes as she ushered us to the table. "Let me show you what I created for you." She opened a thin, square velvet box. "The gold is 14-carat. The gems are garnet and citrine. Do you like it?"

The necklace was exquisite. Small, elongated beads formed the gold chain, and the looped design stamped into the beads almost created the shape of a star. Six stones, three citrine and three garnets, were set in a gold pendant at the bottom of the chain. The middle of the pendant had the same scrolled effect as the beads.

"Elizabeth, it's beautiful. I couldn't have imagined anything like it." She had offered to create the necklace for me when we met. Although I had been uncomfortable about it at first, she made it difficult to refuse her, accusing me of hurting her feelings, even suggesting we shouldn't do business together. She'd given me no choice but to accept.

"Let's see how it looks," she said, helping me with the clasp. "Oh, it's perfect. Look in the mirror." I caught a whiff of gardenias as she led me across the room. The light, sweet scent was her signature perfume.

The necklace lay against my skin, sparkling in the mirror.

The oddest feeling of déjà vu came to me. My mind raced, like it was rushing to place the memory, trying to remember the last time we had done this.

"Do you like it?"

"Yes. This will be perfect with my dress tonight. Thank you." I smiled, letting the memory slip away.

After replacing the necklace in its case, we got to work reviewing the orders. The Tempo purchases would all be in after the first of the year. The order for La Moda would be ready for delivery by next week.

~ ☾ ~

"Is Bruno still planning to attend the party?" I asked as I packed my laptop.

"Oh, yes. We're all coming," she said. "It's a family event."

"Great. We're looking forward to having you," I said, trying to control my jaw. A wild desire to giggle rushed through me when my eyes met Peter's. "Where is this vineyard?" I pointed to the painting and forced my mind away from the idea of Elizabeth's nephew wearing pink panties.

"Oh, it's in a small village in Tuscany. I forget the name. My brother-in-law painted it many years ago on a trip to Italy. Come. Let me walk you out." She stepped around the table, pausing when the door opened and her husband appeared.

"Good afternoon, Lucia." Alexander made a slight bow. His heavy Romanian accent and deep voice made him sound like a spy from an old movie.

"It's nice to see you, Alexander," I said. And that was no lie. He was the epitome of tall, dark and handsome, with eyes as black as coal and pearly white teeth. A leather tie held his long, black hair away from his face. His moustache and beard were trimmed close enough to show his defined chin. And he smelled wonderful. I could only describe the scent as spicy-licorice. Really, he just smelled yummy.

"I'm sorry to interrupt. Elizabeth, our next appointment has arrived." His gaze quickly moved from her face to Peter's and back.

Peter nodded. "We were just leaving," he said. "It was nice to meet you both. Lu, let's get going." He guided me toward the door.

"Yes. You should get going so you can prepare for the party. We'll see you in a few hours." Elizabeth led the way back to the lobby.

They walked us to the car, standing very close as Peter and I argued over who would drive.

"Just get in," Peter said.

Knowing that I'd never been able to keep an emotionless expression when I was aggravated, and not wanting my newest designer to see me losing my temper, I faced Peter and leaned into his chest. "No, not until you promise not to

~ ☾ ~

do what you did in Providence."

He stared down at me, his eyes narrowing slightly.

"The eyes. We've already talked about that," I said.

He closed his eyes. "Please, get in."

"Promise."

"Lucia." Alexander breathed my name, his voice low and calm. The spicy-sweet scent of his cologne filled my lungs. A mild feeling of euphoria overcame me. Drawn by the flicker in his eyes, like stars burning in two onyx gems, he held me captive in his sight. He smiled, and that thin line of white teeth shone. "Let Peter drive."

"Okay." He and Elizabeth escorted me to the passenger's side while Peter hopped behind the wheel.

"See you at the party," Elizabeth called as she closed the door, and the car sped away from the curb.

~ ☾ ~

CHAPTER THREE

The entire State Room of the Bay Tower was draped in white and silver, and hundreds of twinkling Christmas lights hung from the ceiling, giving the impression of falling snow. This year's theme, A Winter Wonderland, marked every inch of the ballroom.

Jewelry displays had been strategically placed around the bar, dance floor, and cocktail area. Each exhibit resembled a partially opened Christmas gift decorated with confetti and small ornaments. Models wore next year's fashions as they wandered through the crowd answering questions about the designs.

The band played a jazzy rendition of "Jingle Bells" while guests mingled. Tempo always hosted a fantastic Christmas party.

"How'd you manage those?" Marie asked, pointing to my sunglasses when Peter and I finally met her for a drink. She patted the stool to her left and moved her handbag onto the bar so I could sit beside her.

"I procured them for her," Peter answered. He stood beside me, watching the room in the mirror behind the bar.

"They're from the summer line. You like?" I tilted my head to the side to show the rhinestone-studded arms, careful not to lean too far to the left. All I needed was Marie to notice my eyes. She'd never let up with the questions and my night, actually my life, could be ruined.

"Yes. What about that necklace? Whose is it?" she asked.

"Gemma. There isn't another like it."

"How do you manage it? I know the dress is a Cho. The glasses are John Black's. Jewelry by Gemma. And all specially made for you. Amazing that you have such clout. I mean,

~ ☾ ~

you're good, but you're not that good," she teased.

Marie managed the women's clothing lines. Her favorite designer, Carlo Rico, had dressed her himself in a strapless royal blue gown. He always emphasized her voluptuous figure. Thankfully, Cho knew how to accentuate my athletic body, because standing beside Marie could be intimidating for any woman. Her perfect, cocoa-brown skin and dark eyes, combined with that figure, made her look like a bombshell waiting for action.

"You're just jealous," I said.

"You've got that right. But mostly because you found a hairstylist capable of taming that mane of yours. How on earth did you get it up like that?" She walked around me, inspecting the swell of curls bubbling from the back of my head to cascade down my shoulder.

"Magic," I answered, sipping my wine. A miracle was more like it. Two stylists worked together to control my unruly tresses. Since I'd been forced to remove the sunglasses during the hair appointment I'd kept my eyes closed the whole time, afraid they'd glow like radon balls sitting in my eye sockets, so I'd missed the how-to portion of the session.

"Lu, come with me. I want to introduce you to someone, a new designer I met in Santiago. Peter, you won't mind waiting here, will you?" Marie grabbed my hand and yanked me from my seat.

"Let me finish my drink. This is the first time I've sat down all night." I tugged her back toward the bar. "We'll come with you in a minute."

"*Only* you. He doesn't want to deal with a junior," she whispered.

I leaned toward her. "I'm not ditching Peter. I can't take any chances on setting him free tonight. He doesn't know enough not to stick his foot in his mouth," I mumbled.

"Can't you leave him with Jack?" she asked.

"No. You know *Jack* can't be trusted not to put his foot plus his entire leg into his mouth. I'm not leaving Peter alone."

"Fine." She cast a sideways glance at Peter then stormed off in a huff.

~ ☾ ~

"I don't think she likes me," Peter said.

"Don't worry about it. I don't like you either." I fought to hide a grin and had to look away from him. As much as I hated to admit it, he was growing on me. Even his stupid smile irritated me less.

"Ah, Peter, Lucia! I was wondering when I'd find you." Elizabeth's Greek accent laced the sentence, running it together like one long word.

I glanced into the mirror. "Hi, Eliza..." As I began to respond I noticed the man standing behind her and stopped short.

He was enormous. She'd told me her nephew was a big guy, but I had no idea she meant more than six feet tall and four feet wide and *very* muscular. Short, dark hair framed his chiseled face and black rings circled his dark brown irises. It was odd. There was something surprisingly alluring about him. He was not what I considered handsome, but he was beautiful.

"Good evening." He greeted my reflection with a slight incline of his head.

"Your mouth is open," Peter murmured.

I covered my mouth with my napkin. "You lied."

"Not a chance." He pretended to inspect his cufflink. "You can't stop thinking about it, can you?"

I couldn't. The thought of this guy in pink panties popped into my head and wouldn't leave. I giggled.

"What's so funny?" Bruno asked.

"Lucia, this is my nephew, Bruno. Bruno, this is Lucia DiComano and Peter Della Caccia, her junior," Elizabeth interrupted. She pursed her lips.

I swiveled my chair around to face them all and found it completely impossible to look at Bruno without grinning like an idiot.

"Why are you smiling like that?" he asked.

"I think she's happy to see you," Peter answered.

"Yes, it appears so. But why do you think that is?" Bruno stared at Peter. The cocky grin made an appearance, and Peter winked.

I giggled, again. But this time I wasn't able to control it. I choked, coughed, and wheezed. Then I laughed some more,

~ ☾ ~

completely losing my composure.

Bruno moved toward me so gracefully, it almost seemed he hadn't moved.

"I'm sorry," I said, snorting between laughs. I slipped off the barstool, and he caught me, wrapping an arm around my waist and placing me back on the seat.

When he touched me, an image of the ocean with rolling waves under vast blue skies came to me. The smell of the sea wafted around me. The giggles stopped, along with the coughing, and gasping. I felt like I was floating on the water while the gentle current rippled over my skin.

"Better?" he asked.

"Yes. Thank you. I'm not sure what happened. I'm...I apologize."

He stepped back and shot a disgusted look at Peter, who had a wild grin plastered on his face.

"Well, the party is wonderful." Elizabeth worked her way between the two men. "Bruno, let's find your father and uncle. Shall we? Peter, it was nice to see you again. Lucia, we'll chat at dinner." She looped her arm in Bruno's and guided him away from us.

"Of course. Enjoy yourselves," I called as they walked away.

"Pink panties." Peter whispered.

"Oh, shut up." I hopped off the barstool. "I looked like an idiot thanks to you."

"I told you it would be difficult not to laugh." He grinned.

I frowned. "Come on. I want to find Marie and meet her designer from Santiago."

He rolled his eyes and followed me through the crowded ballroom.

As we meandered through the clusters of people, we walked into the most disgusting stench I'd ever smelled. I stopped walking and tried not to gag. The miasma of funk reminded me of wet dog combined with the stink of an overstuffed, dirty ashtray. Then those two smells merged with that vomity-mothball fetor I'd smelled in Providence. I had never in my life smelled anything so repulsive. Spinning around to try to get away from the stink, I caught sight of Peter. He looked just as

~ ☾ ~

repulsed as I felt. The stench was incredible, but no one except Peter seemed to notice. The partygoers around us laughed and joked and happily carried on.

"I'm gonna puke," I said.

"Just hold on." Peter held me to his chest. The clean, fresh scent of cut grass flooded my nostrils.

"What cologne do you wear?" I mumbled into his shirt.

"I don't," he answered as he shuffled us away from the crowd.

"You don't?"

His only response was a growl that came from low in his chest and vibrated across my arm.

I glanced up to find him more menacing than he looked in Providence, brows crimped, jaw set, and lips forming a snarl. Three men stood in front of us, each with dark, cherry red eyes. They were absolutely disturbing. And the stench emanated from them.

The wet dog smell came from a man with bushy eyebrows. The furry drapes on his brow ridges hung nearly to his cheeks. The ashtray odor came from a tall, thin man who looked like a rat, and the vomity-mothball stench came from a short, blocky redheaded man.

"Peter. Imagine meeting you here," the redhead said through a thick Scottish accent. He fingered the sporran hanging in front of his tartan kilt.

The strangers glided toward us. Peter's arm tightened around my waist. The scent of the sea came to me when someone brushed against my back. I glanced over my shoulder to see Bruno standing behind me.

"Brian." Peter said. "Where is your master?"

"I am my own master," the Scotsman hissed. The popping sound of his knuckles cracking punctuated his declaration.

I gagged. "Peter?" My lunch was about to make a re-appearance.

"Lucia, it's always the same response. You need to toughen up." Brian laughed and stepped closer.

"How do you know my name?" I asked. A wave of nausea hit, and I ducked into Peter's open jacket, pulling his lapel across my face.

~ ☾ ~

Brian's laughter was cut short by Elizabeth's voice. She appeared between us and the fragrance of her gardenia perfume cleared away the funk.

"Brian, who are your friends?" she asked. Tension coursed between them. She stood directly in front of Brian, and her mien seemed to radiate, giving the impression that she was bigger than any of the men. Brian's mood altered, his chin rising as he eased backward a foot or two. "I hope you don't care too much for them. You and Samuel don't seem to be very good at keeping friends."

"Until later, lovely," Brian said to me. The three men backed away, melting into the crowd, taking their funk with them.

"Who was that?" I asked.

"That was—." Elizabeth stopped speaking and stepped back as Marie burst through the crowd like a firecracker.

"*Lu*. I need you." She shoved past Bruno and Peter without even acknowledging them.

"Is everything okay?" I asked.

"Come with me. I'll explain," she answered, wrenching me away from Peter.

"I'll be back," I called over my shoulder and stumbled along behind her. "Marie, what's going on?" I snatched my hand from hers.

"Nothing." She studied the crowd and all her concentration seemed directed at some unseen entity, as though she was waiting for a signal. "I just want to introduce you to that designer. His sister has a great line of belts and leather goods." She grabbed my hand again and crossed the dance floor.

"Are you sure?"

"I'm fine." Her voice sounded flat, mechanical, as though she'd been programmed to speak.

Her behavior was so out of character that I didn't want to refuse. "Is something wrong, Marie?"

She didn't answer, just headed down the hallway past the ladies' room, toward the emergency exit.

"Where are we going?"

"Oh, the designer wants to meet with you alone. He's out

~ ☾ ~

here." She motioned to the door.

"I'm not going out there. Are you sure you're okay?"

She walked back toward me. "Come on. It will be fine." Grabbing my wrist, she dragged me toward the door.

"Marie! I'm not going. You can tell the designer I'll meet him inside with everyone else." I jerked away from her.

"You have to come. He wants you now," she barked. Her brows drew together above her empty eyes and she seemed engrossed in something else. It was as if she had no idea what she was doing.

I backed away, but her tight grip made it impossible to escape. Practically leaning away from her on a forty-five degree angle, I still wasn't able to move her. She looked behind me and her black eyes fixed on someone in our wake. "We don't need you, Junior," she growled.

I whipped around to see Peter and Bruno charging down the hall. "Thank God you're here. I can't get away from her," I mouthed to them, exasperated by Marie's behavior.

Peter pried Marie's hands off my wrist. As we backed away from her, she ogled Bruno as if lost in a daydream, her head tilted back, eyes glazed. He stepped between us, blocking my view. The next thing I heard was Marie say, "Yes, out in the hall." Then she straightened her dress and walked past us to the party as if nothing had happened.

"What the hell was that all about?" I asked.

"I'm not sure," Bruno answered.

"Why don't we go find Elizabeth?" Peter asked, stepping closer to me.

"Good idea." Bruno said, his voice coming from the end of the hall.

"Where's he going?" I leaned around Peter to watch Bruno slip through the emergency exit door.

"Maybe there's a lingerie sale out there." Peter's hand pressed to the small of my back. "Let's go."

I frowned at him. "You're an idiot." There was something weird about Bruno, and not just pink panties. "I want to find Marie, make sure she's okay." I sidestepped him and led the way back to the party.

With a huff, Peter trailed me down the hall to the ballroom.

~ ☾ ~

CHAPTER FOUR

"Amore la spinge e tira. Non per elezion ma per destino."
~Petrarca
Love drives one not by choice but by fate.

When we returned to the ballroom, we found Elizabeth standing just outside the entrance to the hallway, eyes set into a hardened stare.

"What are you doing?" I asked.

In a slow and deliberate fashion, she turned her head, eyes still trained on the room. When her gaze met mine, her face softened to its usual pleasant expression. "Lu, let me introduce you to my brother-in-law, Victor."

When he stepped between us, my universe flipped upside down.

Vittorio.

My dream-husband stood only inches from me, even more handsome than in my imaginings. Gold and green flecks shimmered in the hazel undertone of his dark eyes, and his brown hair fell in waves around his face.

But there was something different about his smile. It held a tension that didn't exist in my dreams.

"It's nice to see you, Lucia." His deep, accented voice sounded exactly the same as I remembered. He wrapped his hand around mine, and my heart about stopped.

"I... I..." I shook his hand, unable to tear my gaze from his. We stood, holding hands for God knows how long before I noticed the comforting scent of sun-kissed grapevines.

He touched my cheek, and I nearly fainted. My eyes closed. That familiar ache throbbed deep within me, and my heart raced to match it. The realization that I'd found what I

~ ☾ ~

had lost, that my time had arrived, overcame me.

"How are you feeling?" he asked. I opened my eyes to find myself in his arms. His velvety smooth voice was all I heard. *Lucia,* cuore mio... The words sounded clear as day, but his lips never moved. *I've waited a long time for you.*

"What did you say?" I asked.

He never opened his mouth, yet the words had skimmed through my mind as his hand slid from my cheek to the nape of my neck. His eyes glittered, and my stomach somersaulted.

How could this be? How could he know about *'cuore mio'*? I stumbled back from him, frightened.

Elizabeth caught me. "Lu, everything is fine. We're here to help you." I looked from Vittorio to her. The band played, but the song sounded like background music jumbled with the low hum of hundreds of party guests talking and laughing, oblivious to our presence. The man who'd starred in my dreams stood in front of me, demanding my attention. I stared at him, barely able to breathe. *How can this be?*

"Lucia, they have all been trying to protect you," Vittorio said.

"From what?" My voice sounded firm, in spite of my shaking knees and trembling hands.

"There are others who want to hurt you. Elizabeth, Alexander, Bruno, and Peter have been helping to keep you safe," he answered.

"Safe from who? And why?" I jerked away from Elizabeth.

"Safe from Samuel and Brian and their underlings," Vittorio answered.

"Who are they and what do they want?" The pounding of my heart made it difficult for me to concentrate. I was truly frightened, but at the same time completely drawn to him. I should have walked away, just left, but I didn't want to. I didn't know why or what it was, but something kept me there.

"You have certain abilities they want." His hazel eyes sparkled, drawing me into their depths, and I'd have sworn I felt his presence deep inside me, a powerful energy hovering, barely able to contain itself, eagerness fraught with desire, need, and hunger.

"Now you're being absurd." I looked away from him,

~ ☾ ~

fearful that he was trying to possess me.

"Very well, then tell us why your eyes are changing," he countered.

"I don't know. Why don't *you* tell me why this is happening?" I adjusted my sunglasses. My temper flared as fear became anger, and the anger made me feel safer. "And while you're at it, why don't you tell me who you are?"

"Lucia, you know who I am," he said softly. "Look at me." It was a command, so tenderly spoken, yet so very stern that I had no choice but to look at him.

I looked up and he removed my sunglasses, then rested his hands on my shoulders.

"Am I not the same man from your dreams?" His expression remained inviting and gentle as he asked the questions, but somehow I felt his concern. A strong, almost dominating air clung to him, and yet, he was so very calm. "I know you remember me. What have you dreamt?"

My pulse pounded in my neck. I wanted to smack his hands away. It would have been the right thing to do, but I didn't. I couldn't, because I wanted to touch him. I wanted to lean into him, wrap my arms around him, feel his arms around me. I closed my eyes, trying to regain my senses. "I'm not telling you about my dreams. It's none of your business. Who are you people?"

"Lucia, I know what you've been dreaming—scenes from Italy, dreams of me and you, a wedding, a trip to Florence. These are things that really happened. They are part of our life together."

How does he know my dreams? How can he even exist?

The internal argument in my head nearly sent me to my knees. One voice screamed, *Run! Get out of here! He's a demon!* The other voice eased through me. *Finally. After all these years, all this time,* finally *I've found him.*

I shook my head, trying to clear out the voices. "Who are you?" I demanded, or at least I tried to demand. It was hard to be sure with the quiet voice within me answering for him. *You know who he is. He is yours.*

Vittorio's voice was nearly as soft. "Elizabeth and Alexander are friends of mine. They were the first to realize

~ ☾ ~

your existence. They found me so that we could find you.
Bruno and Peter are my sons," he explained. "Lucia, that trip
to Florence, that is what started this whole thing. That is
when this never ending existence began."

The Florence trip. One of my most beautiful dreams until
it became one of my worst nightmares. I hadn't told anyone
the details of my recent dreams, so how could he have
known? I stood motionless, listening to him. Fear crept back
over me.

He held my hand and my skin tingled, but I didn't pull
away. I liked the way I felt when he touched me. "Think about
the trip to Florence. We were separated, ripped apart, weren't
we?"

I nodded.

"What do you remember? What else happened?"

"There was a woman, a redhead," I whispered.

"Yes." His voice deepened and he inhaled a measured
breath. "Do you know what she was? You haven't gotten this
far in your memories, but if you concentrate it will come to
you."

The question perplexed me. *'What she was?' What kind of
question is that?* "I don't understand. What do you mean?"

"She was not human." The details of the dream surged to
the forefront of my mind, horrid details my conscious mind
had managed to hide flooded my vision. His terrified
screams, the gaping wound at his neck, blood pouring down
his chest. My own anguish, an almost unbearable intensity.
Not a dream but a nightmare, the worst imaginable.

He hesitated, watching me for a second, then added, "She
was a vampire."

My throat tightened. Tears built behind my eyes.

She'd bitten him. That redheaded bitch had bitten Vittorio.

The frightened little voice in my head took off screaming.
*VAMPIRES! VAMPIRES, NOT DEMONS! MORE THAN
ONE! NOT JUST VITTORIO! RUN!* My eyes bulged so wide
they hurt. *My God. What if they are vampires?* I swallowed
past the lump in my throat and stared at Vittorio, waiting for
fangs to appear, expecting him to lunge for my neck.

The calm little voice whispered, *He's right here, waiting*

~ ☾ ~

for me. Wanting me. He came to me. Finally. Finally, he's mine. I shook my head again, willing the voices to go away.

"Lucia, I know it seems unbelievable, but it's true." Vittorio's expression was familiar from my dreams. It was the one he wore when he tried to be as patient as possible with me. He reached for my arm, but I backed away, afraid if he touched me again he'd have some sort of power over me, and I wouldn't be able to break free from him.

A loud chuckle broke in the crowed room behind Peter and Elizabeth. We were at a party, celebrating. This was supposed to be a happy evening. People still talked and laughed, unaware that monsters walked among them.

The room swam for a second. *Vampires aren't real.* Delusional. I had to be delusional. That was the answer. The holidays. Work. Stress. That explained the dreams.

But what explains Vittorio?

"This is ridiculous." I looked from Peter to Elizabeth. "I've seen you both during the day. Aren't you supposed to be hiding in a coffin somewhere during the daylight hours?"

"Not all the old tales about vampires are true," Elizabeth responded.

"So, what's your story? Are you even a buyer? How did you end up at Tempo?" I asked Peter.

He smiled that damn smile. "We made the change in company structure happen so that I could guard you. I do have a background in jewelry. I've worked for Elizabeth for many years. Heirloom Jewelry, remember?"

"Yes," I answered, pursing my lips. "However, I've learned that Heirloom Jewelry closed more than fifty years ago." A quick Google search and I'd been able to figure that out.

"That's correct." Elizabeth stepped closer, her dark eyes unblinking, yet gentle. A soft smile graced her lips. "We closed the store and left the country for a period of time. We were searching for you. We came back to the states when we realized you were here."

I huffed at her. "Not one of you is old enough to have worked at that store."

"Oh, we're all old enough. Think about what we've been trying to explain." Her eyes widened a touch and she nodded

~ ☾ ~

as though it would make me understand.

The blood drained from my face. If they *were* vampires, they all could have been old enough to work there.

"I—I don't believe you. I don't believe any of this." I marched away from them.

"Lu, *wait*," Peter called as I rushed past the band and across the packed dance floor.

"Let her go, Peter. She needs a minute." Vittorio's voice carried to me, clear as day across the raucous party.

Startled, I stumbled into the wall. The scent of sun-kissed grapevines came to me just as Vittorio's arm encircled my waist.

"Lucia, take a moment to consider what we've told you." His heartbeat quickened as he held me to his chest and spoke the words against my cheek. "Recall your dreams. It will help you to understand. But then we must go." He moved effortlessly, weaving through the couples swaying to the music as though he could predict each duo's next step. The feel of his breath through my hair made me quiver. "It is not safe for you here."

I lunged away from him, only able to free one arm from his steady grip. "I'm not going anywhere with you. Let go of me."

Something flashed in his eyes, and he flinched, slowly releasing my other arm. His commanding presence intensified, centered on me, as if carefully testing my boundaries, but not crossing them. It was so evident to me that if he wanted to, he could easily push his way past them and force my compliance. I'd never experienced anything like him. His essence, not just his body, moved around me. Desire flared from him. He wanted me. But something stopped him, something held him at bay.

The gold and green flecks darkened to cold, black pools, and I recognized what shone in his eyes.

"You're...afraid of me."

"You're much more powerful than you know. And until you learn to control that power, you're too vulnerable to be left unprotected." He brushed a stray curl from my cheek, sending currents thrumming along my skin.

My pulse sped. *Right here, waiting for me, wanting me.*

~ ☾ ~

Finally. The familiar ache flared deep within my chest. My heart matched the pounding rhythm, and for a minute it was all I heard, all I felt.

"This makes no damn sense." *I must be losing my mind.* I ducked under a tray being carried by a waiter and dashed down the hall to the ladies' room.

~ ☾ ~

CHAPTER FIVE

I stood in the bathroom stall with my head against the door, contemplating everything I had just heard. How could vampires exist? This was ridiculous. How could any of them be...

Really, what the hell? Were they going to tell me that there really was a Santa Claus or that the Boogie Man lived in my closet? They hadn't actually done anything supernatural, so maybe they were all just crazy—some sort of weird cult. Maybe I was possessed and they were demons toying with me. *What if none of them actually exists? What if I imagined them? What if I'm losing my mind?* My mouth dropped open and I slumped against the wall.

Worse, what if they are vampires?

While I tried to make sense of the conversation rattling in my head, the bathroom door opened and closed. "Lu? You in here?" the mechanical voice asked.

Marie. Not this again. Where are my protectors now?

Peeking through the crack, I saw her leaning against the sink. She watched the door with vacant eyes.

"I know you're in there. You might as well come out."

She wasn't dragging me off to see some psycho designer. I didn't need this right now. There were more disturbing issues to consider—like my potential demon possession and the existence of vampires.

The stall door jiggled. "Come on, Lu."

"Go away."

The door rattled with the intensity of a storm. "He just wants to meet you." The latch gave way, and the door banged open. She lunged forward. "You're coming with me." Her grip was so tight her fingernails cut through my sleeve and into my arm.

~ ☾ ~

"Let go of me. *Marie?*"

She dragged me out of the stall, but I managed to twist loose before we reached the bathroom door. Stumbling forward, she fell to her knees. By the time she was up, I was ready. I hated to do it, but she left me no choice. I hauled off and punched her dead in the face. She fell backwards, out cold by the time she hit the floor. Three years of kickboxing had finally paid off.

"I'm so sorry, Marie." I ran from the bathroom.

When I reached the end of the hallway, my band of supposed protectors had dispersed. As if drawn by some sort of feral energy my attention landed across the room on Vittorio. He stood face to face with the stocky redheaded man, Brian. Two men raced past the bar toward the exit with Peter and Bruno in pursuit. I edged around the corner into the ballroom, scanning the crowd for Elizabeth and Alexander, but they were nowhere to be found. When I realized Vittorio and Brian had seen me, I ran past the band and headed toward the kitchen.

"Is there a back exit?" I asked one of the cooks.

"Yeah, over there," he answered, waving his spatula. "Go through that door. Take a left and the first door on the right leads to the stairs. Be careful of the supply boxes."

I bolted through the door into the hallway, and two things happened at once. I smashed into someone and a horrible acidy odor flooded my lungs, making it nearly impossible to breathe. I went down, coughing.

"Finally, Lucia. I have been trying to get to you all week," the man said in a thick German accent. "And now, you just run right to me. What a good girl you are." A sudden feeling of loathing overcame me, sinking into my gut. Sharp teeth glinted when he spoke, and his eyes blazed crimson under a halo of wild, blond hair. His ruthless tone terrified me more than the crazed expression on his face.

I said the only word I could manage to speak as the man from my recent nightmares leered down at me. "You?"

"Me."

He hoisted me to my feet and dipped his head to my neck. His long hair swept over my chest as he leaned close to me,

~ ☾ ~

sliding his nose across my skin, the intake of his breath the only sound he made. A cold trail streaked my skin from my chest to my ear.

Frozen in fear, I knew I should scream or run, but couldn't. A sneer warped his mouth, and his tongue darted across his lips. The veins in his neck throbbed when he traced my lips with his fingers. I jerked away.

Squeezing my chin, he dragged my face closer to his. "You are mine. I have waited many years, searching the world for you. Now, you will come with me."

"Hey, buddy, what're you doing to her?" someone yelled. The big, burly line cook from the kitchen lumbered toward us, a box under one arm.

"Help me!" I tried to free myself from the blond man's hold. "I don't know this man. He's hurting me."

"Oh, Lucia!" The German twisted me away from the cook. "You do know me. *Samuel*, remember?" He pointed to his chest then shrugged. "In no time, it will all come back to you. And even you will appreciate the irony."

"The lady doesn't seem to want you around. Leave her alone." The cook dropped the box and walked toward us with his chest pushed out, his arms at the ready.

Samuel smirked, tightening his hold, crushing my body against his. "Hmm. I don't think so. Does your shirt say Lenny? Yes, it does. Well, Lenny, I'm not going to let her go. So, what do you plan to do?"

"Buddy, I'm going to *make* you let her go." Lenny gripped Samuel's forearm.

Samuel tossed me aside and descended on Lenny before he could have realized what was happening. Using one hand Samuel wrenched the cook's head to the side while the other forced him down to his knees. His red, soulless eyes fixed on Lenny's neck, then two long fangs slid from under his lip.

Lenny crumbled to the ground helpless, spellbound by Samuel. The expression on his face could only be described as pure terror.

An icy chill sped down my back. Sweat broke over my skin. *Vampires. God help me. They're real.*

Samuel bit into Lenny's neck, ripping through his skin,

~ ☾ ~

shredding the muscles and blood vessels below. Bile coated
the back of my throat as I fought the urge to vomit. My legs
wouldn't move. I stood frozen in fear, witnessing the most
horrid event of my life. The sound of Lenny's gurgling breaths
soon faded to silence. The vampire leaned his head back.
"*Hmmm-hmmm*. Lenny was delicious." He threw the poor
man's body aside.

Horrified by what I'd seen and trembling all over, I
screamed and ran, only to find Samuel waiting at the back
door.

"Get away from me." I pivoted around heading toward the
other door, back toward Lenny.

"Oh, you're not going anywhere." Samuel stalked toward
me, backing me against the wall. Then his fists came up on
either side of my head, trapping me.

"What do you want?" My hands flew to his chest in an
attempt to stop him from stepping closer, my breath coming
in panicked gasps.

Lenny's blood dripped from Samuel's chin onto my dress.
"I've chased after you for so long." He leaned toward me, un-
phased by my attempt to block him. My arms bent, pinned
between us. He inhaled deeply and his eyelids closed. "You
smell delectable."

He smacked his lips, his tongue poking out like a serpent's.
Then he stared *into* me, and for a moment I felt like a
moviegoer watching Dracula seduce his prey. A cold pressure
descended around my body and a vile evil unfurled around
me. My knees buckled, and he dragged me against him.
"Gentle." My skin twitched beneath his fingers as though an
electric wire had been raked across my flesh. "I must be
gentle. Too rough and I'll lose you again." He kissed my
forehead. Pain seared through me, and I screamed, shoving
at his chest.

"Get away from me." My eyes burned as they filled with
tears. My heart pounded as the ache within me throbbed,
harder, louder than ever before. *He's going to kill me.*

"Tears? Did you care for Lenny?" Samuel laughed. "You
hardly knew him. Or are you frightened?" He pinched my
cheek then kissed me in the same spot, leaving Lenny's cold,

~ ☾ ~

wet blood on my skin. "Well, I don't want you to cry. I always pictured this reunion as one where you'd rejoice in me. You'd be as happy to have me as I am to have you."

He glanced toward the ceiling and shook his head. His eyes danced, cheeks flushed to a rosy hue, lips parted to expose bloodstained teeth and fangs as sharp as daggers. He licked his top lip. "I guess your happiness won't come until later. Or maybe it won't come at all. As long as I'm happy, I admit, I don't care if you are."

"You're disgusting. And you stink." My mind raced to Mom and Dad and Michael. *How can I die this way? How can I be* killed *by a vampire?* How?

He laughed so hard he had to back away to lean against the opposite wall. "Is that the best you've got? You can do better than that. You just don't realize it yet. You're able to hurt vampires with just a single thought. You don't know this, do you? They haven't explained it to you, have they? This is *superb.* I have you all to myself and I get to teach you everything I want you to know. Outstanding!" He moved with such speed, arm circling my waist and pinning me against him, that I had no opportunity to run. "Let's get started, shall we?" As I tried to wrestle free, he laughed. "You might as well quit. You're not getting away, and you'll only tire yourself with trying."

Knotting his fingers in my hair, he wrenched my head back to display my neck. His tongue slid along my throat, stopping just below my jaw, and my skin burned. *"Get off me! Help!"*

His smile vanished, and greed replaced his maniacal joy. All of his energy, every ounce of his attention, centered on my eyes, and that cold pressure returned. "You are mine." His putrid breath streamed hot on my face.

"No!" I shouted, pounding my fists against his chest and clawing his neck.

The air crackled with energy, descending upon me, a weight so heavy, so empty I could barely draw breath. My heart hammered in my chest, racing as if to outrun the cold. Heat built inside me, burning me from the inside out. Sweat dripped from my hair and ran down my neck into my gown. A black abyss closed in on me, holding me captive in its ice-cold

~ ☾ ~

grip. Paralyzed with fear, I no longer fought Samuel. I watched the blackness and waited to die.

The sounds of someone struggling to breathe, loud and jagged gasps, filled my ears. Then the breathing stopped, and the screaming began.

A soothing voice reached me. "Calm, Lucia."

My screaming ceased, but Samuel's continued. He howled and released me, doubling over.

"Run, Lucia," the voice ordered.

I ran, making it down the stairs and through the ballroom below, Samuel's screams rattling in my head.

"Hold the elevator." I shoved my arm between the closing doors. Four wide-eyed people standing inside scrambled away from the entrance. The two couples shuffled closer together, and the husbands put their arms around the wives.

A man with a mustache raised his eyebrows and clucked his tongue. "That's a dangerous thing you just did."

"I'm in a hurry." I jabbed the button for the lobby. My reflection in the mirrored wall caught my attention. Wild plaits fell lose, no longer contained by the multitude of bobby pins and hair spray. My eyes glowed, and blood smeared my cheek and neck. The slit in my dress that had originally stopped mid-thigh now went clear up to my hip. I looked like a possessed Cinderella racing home before midnight. When the doors opened on the eighteenth floor the other passengers rushed out, looking back at me, their eyes wide with horror.

I leaned on the button for the lobby. "Come on," I breathed.

The doors finally opened to the ground floor, and I all but fell into the foyer. A mob of people crowded the room, their raucous voices filling the cavernous lobby. The cacophony made it nearly impossible to think. *The exit. Where?* I needed to reach the door. I peered toward the entrance and found Peter. He surveyed the room, only occasionally glancing toward the door. His midnight blue gaze locked on me, and he stepped forward. A group of laughing partiers bustled to the side and blocked his way.

I ducked into the crowd, keeping my head down so my

~ ☾ ~

eyes wouldn't draw attention while I hunted for another escape route. When the side door came into view, I made a beeline for the exit, weaving my way between couples.

"Lu! Hi! Merry Christmas." An excited woman grabbed my arm and reeled me in for a hug.

I twisted out of her embrace, checking the crowd around us.

"Lu, it's me, Rita. From Lone Star Leathers." She bobbed back and forth, trying to stay in front of me. "You have to come to Texas. You've got to see the new line. You'll love it."

"Yeah," I said, searching for Peter.

From the corner of my eye, Bruno came into view. As he moved, the crowd stepped aside, allowing him to easily pass. I shoved Rita toward her husband.

"Hey!" she shouted.

"Get out of my way!" I jostled my way through the crush of revelers. Guests fell into each other and drinks flew into the air. But I kept going until I reached the exit. I threw myself into the door, forcing it open, and ran down the alley toward State Street.

"Lucia. *Wait.*" Peter's voice came from behind me. My breath caught in my throat, and I felt like my legs weren't working fast enough. He gripped my wrist as he spun me around to face him.

"Get away from me." I slammed my free fist up under his chin. His head jerked back, and I kneed him in the groin. With a groan, he doubled-over.

I turned and ran. A sharp pain shot through my ankle as I stepped off the curb. *Oh God, please don't let it be broken.* A horn blared. The lights of the truck blinded me. Everything went dark.

The cold black Abyss returned, threading its tendril-like fingers around me and squeezing. The weight of eternity bore down, suffocating me. I gasped.

My shallow, raspy breaths became louder and louder until I could no longer comprehend the sound. My own screams echoed in my ears, slashing the darkness.

I'm dying.

The sudden recognition that I'd done this already, that I

~ ☾ ~

knew what was happening, soothed me.

It's not over. I'll be back.

The pressure leveled around me, and I waited in the familiar blackness, not seeing or feeling a thing. I wasn't afraid. I knew the process.

The blackness swallowed me as it had done so many other times. I inhaled one last breath and waited for the screaming to end.

It wouldn't take long until I moved from this life into my next one. Scenes of my past lives flashed through my mind, and I watched, realizing I'd missed my chance to stop this unending hell. I'd missed my chance to save him, to free his soul, to finally fulfill my destiny. The Abyss called to me. My senses clouded. I could only watch and wait for my life to slip away.

~ ☾ ~

CHAPTER SIX

"E son come d'amor baci baciati, gli incontri di due cori amanti amati."
~Battista Guarini
Kisses, when given in love, are the joining together of two loving souls.

Familiar voices chattered around me. Machines beeped. A woman cried, but my eyes wouldn't open. I wandered through my memory, seeing events from this life—the past week and all its oddities, Mom and Dad, college graduation, learning to speak English...Then back to blackness. The Abyss.

I glimpsed scenes that were vaguely familiar—a boat ride, the Hollywood sign, colonial New England, a hospital room, a dimly lit tomb.

Old memories of Vittorio and life on the vineyard with Mama, Papa and Nonna zoomed through my mind, finally stopping on one memory that made me very happy; our wedding day, April 18, 1648.

The only light in the church came from the soft glow of candles. Smoke from the burning incense puffed in the air. The sounds of happy sniffles carried from the pews to where we stood. Butterflies fluttered in my stomach. We joined hands. They fit together perfectly. His fingers, warm and gentle, wrapped around mine. When he squeezed my hands, I glanced at him. The flecks of gold and green in his hazel eyes dazzled me. His mouth curved into a beautiful smile. "I do."

The words were spoken so confidently, without hesitation, no question of their meaning, no doubt of his commitment. Vittorio gave himself to me, entrusting me with his heart, his

~ ☾ ~

love, his soul. And I accepted the gift, eager to tie our lives together, eager to bind myself to him in every way. We had been made for each other. I gave him not only my love, but my life. My world was perfect because of him.

After enjoying a feast prepared by our mothers and Nonna, we danced until late into the evening. As our wedding celebration drew to a close, we said goodnight and headed up the hill to the little house that waited for us. The night sky glittered with stars, and the silver moon lit our path home. When we reached the threshold, he lifted me and carried me to our room, to share our first night as husband and wife.

I lay on the bed, awash in moonlight, watching him undress. He began with the shirt, slipping it over his head to reveal his smooth, muscular chest. Dropping it to the floor, he kicked off his shoes and started on the trousers. He bent to unfasten the buttons at his knees and his stomach muscles rippled, drawing my attention away from his hands. The muscles bunched and flexed, and my heart sped. Then he worked the buttons at his waist, and the trousers came off in one quick movement.

I had a moment to admire him before he came to me. My gaze moved along his body, taking in every inch. His tanned chest and arms were achingly familiar. I'd seen him without a shirt in the fields many times. But now, *now* I surveyed his body with new eyes, his wife's eyes.

The pulse point jumped in his neck. Strong muscles in his chest contracted with each movement, letting me know where one ended and the next began. His nipples were just a little darker than his skin and perfectly round. The small scar on the left side of his chest, a perfect line just above his heart, was still there, the result of a childhood swimming accident.

My eyes moved over his tight abdomen then lower, seeing parts of him for the first time. A strange and new excitement raced through me. I followed the trail of hair below his bellybutton down to his cock and forced my eyes lower, taking in his long, muscular legs. But my gaze went back to that hard muscle I'd never seen.

He grinned. "Do you like what you see, *Signora* Della Caccia?"

~ ☾ ~

"*Hmm.* I do." I leaned up onto my elbows.

He climbed onto the bed, straddling my body as he crawled toward me. His hands and legs brushed against my skin, sparking small currents of excitement. The look on his face was so different from any he'd ever worn. Adoration, desire, need, and love shone in his eyes, but now something new burned there as well: hunger.

My heart took off racing. Eight months I'd spent trying to convince him to do this before our wedding. He had managed to elude me, and now the moment I had been waiting for, begging for, was finally here. I was so nervous I could barely stay on the bed. Now that I thought about it, I realized I had no idea what to do, no idea how to please him. What would he expect? What would he want?

I hardly had time to worry. He kissed me, his soft lips gently meeting mine then moving down my neck.

The tension in my body betrayed my nervousness. "Lucia, *cuore mio*, just relax." His breath against my ear made me quiver. With tender kisses, he calmed my racing heart as he undressed me. If he was nervous, I couldn't tell. Reaching behind me he easily unbuttoned my dress. With all the buttons open, he slipped the bodice down over my arms, exposing my breasts.

Goosebumps rose on my arms and chest, and I didn't know if it was from a nip in the air or my own unease at being exposed.

I watched his eyes as they left mine and traveled down my body, only briefly returning to my face. It was his turn to see parts of me he'd never seen. I licked my lips then bit my left cheek between my teeth. My pulse raced and my hands fidgeted, moving from my stomach to the bed and back, smoothing my violet linen skirt over my thighs then scratching at the dainty lace trim.

His hand caught mine at my abdomen. Then with feather-light kisses beginning at my neck he left a trail to my breasts, letting his tongue tease me the whole way. My breath hitched at the feel of his hot mouth on my nipple. He cupped my left breast, squeezing with just enough pressure to force another gasp from me while his mouth sucked on the other.

~ ☾ ~

The sensation of his tongue on my body, his warm, wet mouth latched onto my breast, and his breath coming quick against my skin made me moan. It was a sound I'd never made. His eyes rolled up, and I saw his pleasure. A quick smile flickered across his lips as he eased away from my breast, letting only his tongue touch me. Deep breathy groans came from my throat, encouraging him. He sucked my nipple back into his mouth. I writhed beneath him, hands clutching his shoulders, squeezing him against me. He shifted to my left breast, giving it all the attention he had showered on the right.

His mouth moved lower, licking his way down to my waist. He slipped my dress off my hips, peeling away the last layers of clothing. My knees trembled, and I wished we had pulled the blanket over us. He kissed my hips and thighs, nibbling as he went. When he moved my legs to continue with his traveling kisses I stopped him. "Vittorio?" I reached for him.

"Yes, love?" he answered between kisses.

"Please, stop."

"Why?" he asked, looking up.

I bit my lip. "I'm... I..."

He smiled and crawled back to me. "You're still nervous, aren't you?"

"Yes. Are you?"

"A little." He snuggled in closer. "But I love you. I'm more excited than nervous." He kissed my lips again then slid his tongue along my neck to my shoulder, stopping only to say, "Seems a little funny, considering all the badgering you did to make this happen sooner."

I frowned, knowing he was right. I had always known he would remain honorable, never risking my virtue. No matter how much I pleaded, attempted to seduce him, or even tried to trick him into making love to me, I knew he'd hold out until our wedding. I knew with such certainty he wouldn't give in that my lack of knowledge on the subject never even occurred to me. The actual functions of lovemaking had never entered my thoughts. I just fantasized about having him, seeing him, kissing him, touching him. I didn't once consider what came next.

~ ☾ ~

He hooked his arm under my leg as he kissed me, bringing my attention back to him. This was the moment I'd waited for, the consummation of our love. Whether it was fear or excitement or the realization that his love was all I'd ever need or want from life, I couldn't say, but my heart beat with such fervor that I thought it would burst.

Hard and eager, he strained against me. When he moved into me he was as gentle as he could be. I dug my nails into his back and whimpered at the slight pain.

"I'm sorry, Lucia," he said in a rough, raspy whisper.

He moved slowly at first, working his way inside me. The pace quickened when he was able to move more easily. He moved faster and deeper. The pain vanished, replaced by an intense pleasure, something sweet, and fiery, and completely overwhelming. I'd never experienced anything like it. I moved with him. My body seemed to know what to do, how to please us both. He slowed and moaned into my ear.

I gasped. "Don't stop. Please, don't stop."

He slid back, barely keeping joined with me then entered me harder, deeper, keeping this rhythm until a rapture like no other took me. This time I dug my nails into him as I experienced sheer ecstasy. My back bowed and my head sunk into the pillow as I was overcome with pleasure. I could barely move to keep up with him as he continued to love me until his body shuddered and a deep groan told me he'd reached the same fulfillment. He repeated my name, his hot breath quick against my neck as his body slowed.

When we were able to move again, he rolled onto his back and gathered me into his arms. I cuddled close to him, resting my head on his shoulder.

He softly kissed my lips as he squeezed me a little tighter. "This has been the happiest day of my life, Lucia. We are bound together forever."

I sighed. "Yes. Forever." Moonlight softly lit our bedroom. I knew that I could never be happier than I was in that moment.

Closing my eyes, I slipped into my dreams.

*****

Vittorio and I lay under the tree in our spot, up the hill

~ ☾ ~

from the vineyard. The scent of orange blossoms drifted on the air, and the bright sun shone down. He ran his fingers through my windswept curls. The sensation didn't feel right. It wasn't soft and sensual. It didn't make me long to be in his arms. My head throbbed each time he touched me. I tried to move away from him, but couldn't. My left arm and leg were stuck in the air, hanging above me.

The oddest sound came from behind my head. *Beep. Beep. Beep.* I opened my eyes and found the source of the noise, a machine at the head of the bed. *What is that?*

"Arturo, she's awake." The woman's voice sounded like it came from somewhere in the distance. "Let's wake Michael."

A slight movement to my right caught my eye. A man sat beside the bed, his arm draped across my chest while his head rested against my shoulder. Little pads on my chest dug into me under the weight of his arm. A woman stood opposite him and leaned over me. "Michael? Michael? Wake up." She gently nudged her shoulder.

An older man moved behind her. "Hi, honey."

The woman kissed my cheek. "Lu, my girl, how are you feeling?" Her eyes glistened, and she gingerly touched my temple, lightly caressing away the pain.

She looked so familiar, but I couldn't place her.

Fear crept over me. Who were they? Where was Vittorio? I trembled. Tears rushed down my cheeks. My breathing became more rapid. The beeping grew faster.

"Arturo, something's wrong," she said.

"Filomena, she's been through a lot. Give her some time. Honey, everything's going to be fine." The older man crowded closer to us and smiled.

The sleeping man lifted his head from the bed. "Lu." He kissed my cheek. "Baby."

Who were they? How did they know me? Where was I? Where was Vittorio?

"Vittorio! Vittorio!" I screamed and yanked on the straps holding my arm and leg in the air. "Help! Please help me!" I swung my unbound arm at the younger man, slapping his face. "Get away from me! Someone help me!"

The younger man grabbed my free arm while the older

~ ☾ ~

man and woman steadied the slings holding my other arm
and leg in the air.

"Nurse! Nurse!" the woman yelled. "Lu, calm down, honey.
You'll hurt yourself."

"Help me!" I tried to wiggle loose from them, but before I
could get my limbs out of the slings, two women had rushed
into the room.

"Lu, you're in a hospital. You were in an accident. You're
safe," one of the women said to me. "I'm Linda, your nurse.
We're taking care of you." She stepped around the younger
man, fumbled with tubes in my arm, and pushed buttons on
the machine.

Another nurse grabbed my leg from the woman and held it
in the air. "She needs to stop or she's going to make this
worse."

"Lu, you're going to be fine. Try to stay calm. You need to
keep your arm and leg in the slings. They were broken in the
accident." Linda loosened her grip on me. The other nurse
repositioned my leg in the sling then helped with my arm.

"Get away from me!" I barked at the man who had been
lying on me.

"Lu, do you remember Michael?" Linda asked me.

I shook my head, glaring at him. *Where's Vittorio? How
did I get here?*

"Why doesn't she remember me?" he whispered, slumping
back into the chair beside the bed. He rubbed his hand over
his face and finally through his salt and pepper hair, opening
his eyes to watch me.

I stared at him, angry, unflinching.

"Lucia, do you remember me?" the woman asked, pushing
past the older man to stand near my head.

Big, dark brown curls framed her face. Tiny lines etched
the skin around her green eyes, and tears trickled down her
cheeks. Pink marks appeared around her nose after she
wiped a handkerchief across it. She pushed my hair away
from my face. My head throbbed, and I winced. "Honey?"

"I don't know you," I said, choking back tears. Who was
she?

She moved some of the wires running from my chest to the

~ ☾ ~

machine beside the bed. "You will remember. You always do."

My mind raced, trying to remember her, trying to understand what was happening.

The older man rested his hand on her shoulder. "Lucia, you're the light of our lives. Always shining."

The light of their lives? What was he talking about?

"How much longer is this going to go on?" The man they called Michael asked.

"It takes time," Linda answered. She squeezed my hand. "Lu, Michael is your boyfriend and these are your parents."

I scowled at Michael. "No, he's not. I don't know him." He was no one to me. I needed Vittorio. "He's a liar. I don't know him. I don't know him!" My voice cracked.

His face fell. Tears welled in his brown eyes. "Lu, we've been together for three years. Try to remember."

My trembling started again. "Get away from me! Where's Vittorio? Vittorio? Vittorio!" I tried again to get my arm and leg loose, but the older man and the nurse grabbed them. Michael held my right arm.

"We're going to have to sedate her again. Do you have the medication?" Linda asked the other nurse.

"In my pocket," she answered.

"Vittorio! Vittorio!" I screamed. "Let go of me!"

Linda reached into the nurse's pocket for the syringe and quickly inserted the needle into a tube.

I continued to struggle, screaming, "Vittorio! Please, Vittorio, where are you?" As my body became heavy, he finally appeared in the window of the door, anxiety marring his beautiful face. I closed my eyes, whimpering, "Vittorio..."

~ ☾ ~

CHAPTER SEVEN

Stars twinkled in the night sky, and the scent of roasted meat and baking bread filtered through open windows, flavoring the gentle breeze. The shadows of the buildings danced in the moonlight. Vittorio's strong, calloused hand closed around mine, and he settled me into the curve of his arm. A perfect evening.

"I'm so excited," I squealed. "I can't believe we're actually in Florence."

"Did you enjoy the opera?" he asked.

"I loved it. It was beautiful. I never dreamed of such costumes and singing. Thank you for taking me." I beamed at him.

"Well, it's not every day my wife celebrates her twenty-ninth birthday. Do you want to stop at the little shop down the street? We can get a bite to eat."

"Yes. I'm starving. And...maybe they'd like to buy some Del Torrente wine." I grinned. We were supposed to be here on business, not just for fun.

"Yes, maybe. However, let's not deal with business tonight. Let's just celebrate your birthday." He kissed me, rubbing his nose to mine.

We strolled down the street arm in arm, stopping at the fountain in front of All Saint's Church to make a wish. I leaned into him and wrapped my arms around his waist. "I wish that we stay together for all eternity."

"I wish to always deserve your love," he said.

"Of course you will."

He smiled. "I hope so. I don't want anyone else to have it."

"Don't be silly," I teased as we walked toward the shop.

There was a sudden movement from the shadows,

~ ☾ ~

streaking toward us. Then something slammed me into the church wall, smacking my head hard enough to blur my vision. When I looked up, a woman held Vittorio.

Long, mangy, copper-colored hair knotted around her face, and a tattered dress barely covered her body. Her eyes blazed red as rubies. She wrenched Vittorio's head back and with two long, sharp fangs she bit into his neck. He screamed and struggled to break free, but her fingers dug into his flesh, forcing his compliance.

When she lifted her head, eyes glazed with pleasure, his blood ran from her mouth. In disbelief I watched, unable to comprehend what I saw. Laughing, she tossed Vittorio over her shoulder and ran into the night. Her cruel laugh rang in the distance.

"Vittorio! Vittorio!" I tried to lift my head, but my vision spun into blackness.

I awoke on a bed with a nun and a priest sitting on either side of me, praying. Incense burned in the corner.

"Father, she's awake," the nun said, moving closer to the bed. "My name is Sister Marie." She held a cool cloth to my brow.

"Child, I'm Father Gabriele. You are safe for now," the priest said.

"Where is Vittorio?" I asked.

"Gone. Taken. Transformed." The harsh words came from a man in the corner of the room. He exhaled a loud breath and moved toward us, his boots clomping on the floor. "Your husband is now a creature of evil." He stood over me, his steel-gray eyes scrutinizing mine.

"What? What do you mean? A creature of evil?" My head pounded and the room spun, but I managed to sit up with the help of the nun.

"Vittorio was taken by a blood-drinker," Sister Marie whispered. Her worried gaze darted toward the door. "Kerina."

"There is no need to whisper and hide, Sister. Evil always knows we track it, hunt it, and conquer it. Do not cower. Do not give Kerina even a moment to think you fear her." The

~ ☾ ~

man wheeled around, and the light of the fireplace reflected off a great sword hanging from his belt.

"I am Maximillian and this is my wife, Elsa." He motioned to a woman standing at the foot of the bed. "We are slayers, hunting Kerina, the one who stole your husband."

I looked from them to Father Gabriele. "Father, where is my husband?"

"Lost to us. He dwells in darkness with the blood-drinker." Father Gabriele continued, rolling rosary beads between his fingers. "The slayers are his only hope."

"Blood-drinker?" I'd never heard of such a thing.

"Vampires. Ones who walk in shadows, hidden from the light. They are lost souls," Maximillian answered, his thick German accent becoming harsher. He stroked his long silver beard and mustache. The weary look in his eyes accentuated his haggard, wrinkled face. "We are Pharos of Redemption tasked with bringing the blood-drinkers to the light."

"Pharos? Redemption? What are you talking about?" Tears pooled in my eyes, blurring my vision. My life was turning upside down, crashing in on me. I needed my husband. Who were these people? "Vittorio? What happened to him?"

"She took him," Sister Marie answered. "Drank him." She made the sign of the cross. "God help him."

"He's dead? She killed him?" I choked. My heart ached, throbbing in my chest like a war drum. My breaths came faster. The pounding grew louder until all I heard was the wild beating of the blood coursing through my veins. "No. No." I crossed my arms over my chest and rocked back and forth.

"He is not dead, Lucia," Elsa said. "Quiet your heart. Listen to us." She moved around Maximillian, her cape flapping, revealing her sword, equally as large as his. Moving it aside she sat on the bed. "She has taken him for her own, created him as one like she. His lost soul wanders in shadows now."

"Shadows? His soul is lost?" My mind ran wild with images of Satan and Hell and eternal damnation. "My husband is a good man, a *good* man. He doesn't deserve this."

~ ☾ ~

Her dark brown eyes seemed to fill my senses, and deep inside them a flash, a spark of light called to me. A quiet serenity filled the room. My heart slowed to a strong, steady beat. The air cleared, and clean, fresh breaths filled my lungs.

Tranquility spread in my mind as she spoke, "You are like us. You are a Pharo sent to guide souls back to redemption. It is time to embrace your calling. Come with us and free his soul. Lead Vittorio to salvation."

"A Pharo? My calling? I'm a wife, a farm girl." I couldn't understand what had happened. My life had been simple. Happy. Perfect.

"Pharos are beacons to salvation. We light the path for lost souls and lead them to The Splendor," she explained. "You *are* like us. In time, you'll remember." The light within her called to me, reminding me that I had a higher purpose and that so many counted on me to embrace my destiny.

"How? How can I... Where is he? How can I save him?"

"There is only one way, Lucia. You must end his physical existence to bring him to The Light," Elsa answered.

I swallowed. "End his...*kill him*? You want me to kill him?" Deep within me the drumming returned, like a battle cry. My heart hammered, pounding an identical beat. "I love him. I can't kill him."

"To refuse your ordination will do him no good. It is an impossibility to deny what you are," Maximillian growled.

"I'm not a murderer."

"Instinctively, you will hunt him. You will find him. And when you do, you will kill him. This is your reason for existing." His face constricted, wrinkles crowding his eyes, and he turned from the bed.

"Lucia, it is our duty to rescue the souls. We give them the opportunity to return to The Lord, to experience Salvation," Elsa explained.

"I'm not holy. How is it my duty? I'm no nun. I'm only a woman. I don't have any special connection to the church or God or anyone." My head spun.

She held out her hand. "Take it."

I slipped my hand into hers, and as her fingers closed around mine, energy sizzled over my skin. It traveled up my

~ ☾ ~

arm and across my body, flowing freely into me.

I gasped and jerked my hand back, but her grip tightened. "Relax. It won't hurt you. Max?" She glanced over her shoulder at him and waited until he stepped forward.

"Fine," he said and grabbed my other hand. His power raced up my arm to join hers, and together they wove through me to my heart. The ache flared, beating a rhythm faster and deeper than ever, and my pulse matched it with ease.

"Your power is strong, Lucia. Don't fight it. Learn to use it. Bring him to The Light," she said.

"I don't know. I don't...I *can't* kill him." I couldn't. I loved him. He was my reason for existing. I could never hurt him. *Never.*

The Light within me grew. Hot energy pulsed out from me, and I saw The Light. Beautiful, brilliant splendor shone within me, outside of me, all around. It called to me, showing me the path.

There was no other way. I couldn't leave him to Kerina, to the darkness. I had to save him. I had no choice. Allowing him to live meant condemning him.

"Yes." Tears ran down my face. "I'll do it."

"At last," Elsa said. "Your task will be difficult, but you are stronger than you know."

Maximillian dropped my hand to face the priest. "Father, we will need the information you have on Kerina. Her lair, her hunting patterns, everything."

"Of course. Remember, Max, you are all always welcome to All Saint's Church. Sister Marie and I will help in any way," Father Gabriele answered.

*****

I coughed. Something touched my lips. Cold liquid, sweet and thick, dripped into my mouth. I moved my tongue to taste it.

"Drink, Lucia. Please, drink." His voice sounded distraught as he pleaded with me. "Lucia, you must drink. This is our chance. Please, please, don't leave me."

Vittorio.

I concentrated on the cold sweetness at my lips,

~ ☾ ~

swallowing deeply. After only a few seconds, I realized my body hurt, everywhere. But the pain didn't stop me from reaching up to secure his wrist to my mouth. I held it tightly and drank from him. My breaths came stronger and deeper. Heat raced through me. Every bruised muscle and broken bone itched.

A door opened and closed, footsteps approached. Then a panicked English voice asked, "Elizabeth, will she survive? We can't let her go this time."

"Yes, she'll make it," she answered from somewhere at the end of the bed. With a clouded sense of what was happening, I fought to follow the conversation, "Vittorio, there's no time to heal her completely. You must strengthen the bond."

The bond? A calloused hand brushed against my cheek. *Our bond.*

"Vittorio? Are you listening?" another man asked, and the scent of the sea swelled.

Vittorio wasn't listening to them. He was speaking to me. "Lucia, *cuore mio*, I am finally able to save you from this hell."

I swallowed, taking what he offered, thankful to have him.

"Vittorio? We're running out of time. Fortify the bond before it's too late!" Elizabeth unwrapped my hand from his arm as she pulled him away from me. I coughed, and blood sprayed from my mouth.

"You must ensure the bond. Now is your chance. You may not get this opportunity again," she said.

"I can't! What if I can't stop? I can't kill her. I saved her so that we can end this. I can't risk it." His voice sounded frightened, a completely unfamiliar tone.

"You must. You can do it. Bruno will stop you, if need be," Elizabeth replied.

Bruno sat opposite Vittorio, and the vision of swelling waves on the ocean came to me. "Do it now. We're running out of time. Her parents will be back soon."

Machines beeped in the background. Vittorio sat beside me on the bed. The sight of him brought me great relief. I had found my reason for existing.

"Forgive me, *cuore mio*." His cold lips kissed my neck then

~ ☾ ~

sharp fangs punctured my skin. I cried out and clung to him. "Relax, my love. Just sleep." His voice moved through my mind as I closed my eyes and faded into unconsciousness.

~ ☾ ~

CHAPTER EIGHT

In the darkness, the figure that lay on the floor appeared to be sleeping. Though when the torchlight glowed over him there was no mistaking he was dead. "Max! Come see this!" I called.

Max entered the cave with Elsa trailing him. He bent to examine the dead body. The man's throat had been ripped open, and he'd been drained of all his blood. "Kerina is not far from here. This man can't be dead more than a day." I'd come to accept scenes like this. He wasn't the first victim she'd left in this state. His withered body resembled a raisin. "Let's make camp here for the night. We will dispose of the body first. Then we can stay in the cave."

After we buried the man, I sat beside the fire watching the flames, imagining what it would be like to destroy the woman who'd stolen my husband. I hoped she went straight to hell the instant my blade pierced her heart.

"It is an unusual thing, what has happened here," Max said as he stoked the fire. I glanced at him. His face scrunched up tight, his "thinking expression," as Elsa called it.

"What do you mean?" Elsa held a stone in one hand and her sword in the other. Slowly, methodically, she sharpened her blade.

"The separation. I still do not understand it. A fledgling never leaves his creator this soon." Max spat into the fire, then scratched his beard, still pondering Vittorio. "It has been a mere five years since Vittorio was created and yet, after only two, he left her. He is not strong enough to be on his own."

"Maybe she left him," I suggested.

"No. No, that would not happen. She would not let him go without determining what talent he might have. He is too

~ ☾ ~

young to rule out any latent talents. Something strange has happened," Max said.

Max talked about the "latent talents" constantly, obsessing over what might lie ahead. Apparently, some vampires came with special abilities, like mindreading or the ability to control animals or whatever else.

"Maybe someone took him," I said.

"No. That can't be it. Kerina would have been killed in a battle like that. And, clearly, she is alive." He pointed to the shallow grave we'd just dug. "She must have learned how to control Vittorio from afar, not just call him, but control him." He paced back and forth in front of the fire. "Maybe their telepathic link is stronger than any other I've seen. That must be it."

"That's nothing new. All sires can call their children back to them." Elsa had progressed to polishing her blade. "Maybe she is able to control his fledglings. Now that would be a skill."

"Maybe, but it's unlikely. She can communicate with them, but only the sire can control them. No vampire can control another's children." Max stopped pacing to fiddle with his beard. "She must have figured out that he has no talents. A dud." He clucked his tongue against the roof of his mouth.

"*Hey*," I squawked. "I know he's a monster, but he's still my husband." I secretly hoped he did have latent abilities. Part of me hoped his talent was avoiding capture while the other part hoped it was accepting his own death. I couldn't bear the thought of hurting him, even though I knew that someday I would have no choice.

"Lu, you know he is not the man you loved. An abomination of nature, heartlessly killing innocents, he is no longer human. Remember what I have taught you." Max squeezed my shoulders. "Vampires are the dead who have been denied the grave. Undead humans transformed into monsters and damned to walk the earth for eternity, lost. You must destroy him and return his soul to God."

"Think of the good you will be doing for mankind. When we kill Kerina and Vittorio, we will be saving countless lives," Elsa added.

~ ☾ ~

"I know." My heart sank to think of him like this. But it was true—he probably had killed hundreds. Stopping him was my responsibility. I had to open his path for redemption. I knew what had to be done. But knowing didn't make it hurt any less.

The next morning we began the day in darkness. "Let's go. We only have a couple of hours. Kerina will be at her weakest at sunrise, prior to completing the transition for daylight hours." Max snuffed the fire and grabbed his gear.

The transition was simple for an experienced vampire, but sunrise was still the most vulnerable time for any of them. Although they were capable of going out in sunlight, they didn't look very appealing. I hadn't seen one yet, but had heard enough to know that they looked like the walking dead.

"Hideous," Elsa said, sticking her tongue out and drawing circles around one of her eyes with her finger. "Gray skin, deep, dark circles under the eyes. Although, some look better than others. Who knows why?" She shrugged.

The Apennine Mountains were Kerina's home. She never left Italy. We traveled east, pursuing her trail. The human remains she left in her wake all carried the same scent mixed with the odor of their rotting bodies. Max explained that the smell was Kerina's personal aroma, her individual scent. "Vampires each have a distinct odor. They smell of whatever they were most associated with at the time they were created." Kerina's odor was a combination of perfume and sweat.

"She smells like a brothel," Elsa explained. "She was probably a whore." The theory seemed to fit just fine to me.

That odor hung in the air, suddenly stronger, heavier. Kerina was close. I realized not one animal made a sound, no birds chirped, not even the hum of any passing bees. Dead silence prevailed on the mountain pass.

The low thrumming deep within me sounded like a battle cry in the distance. Max and Elsa walked ahead of me, still discussing odor distinctions.

"The vampire waits for us." I stopped walking. "To trap us." I was certain of it. The ache in my breast told me

~ ☾ ~

something was terribly wrong.

"She cannot..." The words died in Elsa's throat when Kerina sprung from a tree, knocking Elsa to the ground. Fangs flashed in her mouth and she bit into Elsa's neck. The speed of her movements caught me by surprise. I stood still as a statue, barely breathing, shocked. Elsa struggled to break free of Kerina's grip.

"*Lucia*," Max barked. "Focus!"

I drew my sword and crucifix and followed Max's lead. We charged Kerina. She threw Elsa down and scurried backward, laughing, taunting us. Max stood over me, chanting prayers as I worked on the gash in Elsa's neck, binding a tight bandage around her. The blood pumped out of the wound with each beat of her heart. I'd never seen so much blood, not even the night Vittorio was taken. My stomach turned, and I had to look away to breathe.

"Max? What do I do?" I asked, mashing the cloth to the wound.

"I'll be fine." Elsa's trembling hands squeezed the bandage tight against her skin, and blood seeped from the edges. "Give me my sword." Her voice came rougher than usual. Her eyes narrowed. "That bitch can't kill me that easily." She grinned, taking her sword in her hand and pushing herself to her feet.

Kerina laughed. Her eyes lit like they were on fire. Her stench was dreadful. I'd have buckled over if not for my overwhelming urge to kill her.

Max chanted louder and Elsa joined him. I stood beside her, watching Kerina, waiting for an opportunity to attack.

"Old man, you're sadly mistaken if you think that nonsense will stop me." Her thick Irish brogue distorted her words.

She'd been living in the wild for quite some time. Her torn and dirty dress ended above her bare feet. Clumps of mud, leaves, and blood matted her orangey hair, and dirt caked her jagged nails.

She marched straight to Max and ripped the crucifix from his hand. "Your god does not scare me. Your foolish symbols mean nothing to me." She crushed the crucifix in her hand, letting the dust slide through her fingers while she laughed.

~ ☾ ~

Max swung his sword at her. She moved before the blade struck, but not fast enough. He sliced into her, leaving a large gash in her side. Rage flashed across her face. Elsa moved quickly, swinging her sword at Kerina's neck but missing.

In spite of the blood oozing from her side, Kerina's movements lacked none of her original speed. She grabbed Max's blade, snatching it from his hand. Then turned his sword on him and with one quick flick she split him open, laughing the whole time. He dropped where he stood, gasping for air.

"Max!" I lunged toward him, but with barely a wince he stopped me, warning me to keep my distance. Kerina hadn't killed him, but he wasn't going to survive her attack. Then she turned on Elsa and drove the blade straight into her chest.

I stopped breathing, frozen where I stood, reeling. Now what? I needed them. Both of them. I wasn't ready to be alone.

"A pity to have to waste a meal," Kerina said as she yanked the sword out and watched Elsa's body drop to the ground.

Left alone to kill her, I stood stock still, glowering at her. All these years I'd trained for this moment and now I was terrified I would fail. Hot tears of anger, vengeance, and loss built behind my eyes. I swallowed hard and forced the tears away.

Kerina wheeled on me, laughing, mocking me. "Your Vittorio couldn't kill me. Your vampire slayers couldn't kill me. What makes you think you can?"

She walked in a semi-circle around Max, keeping her eyes on me. The wound in her side bled profusely. She noticed me looking at it and said, "Oh, this? It will heal in no time." And no sooner than she'd spoken the words the skin began to re-knit itself, closing over the wound. She continued to circle Max. The metallic smell of his blood permeated the air. She licked her lips. I knew she wanted to take him, but the threat of my sword kept her from him.

Her lips pulled back and her fangs protruded. The fire in her eyes burned for his blood. I remembered that look from the night she took Vittorio. All the fear in me simmered down. What bubbled to the surface was a desire for

~ ☾ ~

vengeance blazing hotter than the flames of hell, hotter than the bloodlust in her eyes.

"What do you mean my Vittorio couldn't kill you?" I stepped toward Max, matching her movements one for one. If she thought I'd let her have him before she killed me, she had sorely underestimated my wrath.

"He couldn't do it. He had his chance but failed. He nearly had me dead, but didn't finish the job. He's a terrible vampire." She laughed. She was laughing at my husband. Even though he had become a monster, I couldn't tolerate anyone ridiculing him.

"What do you mean he's a terrible vampire?" My grip tightened on my sword, knuckles whitening. A cloud of dirt puffed around us as I shuffled closer.

Max gurgled and coughed, choking on his own blood. The spark within his eyes, all that was left of his light, called to me, once again reminding me not to let emotion rule me, not to destroy my chance. I maintained my distance, for the moment.

She hunched, balancing her weight from side to side, then lurched one step forward, dropped back on her heels and grinned, baring bloodstained teeth. "I mean, he's a terrible vampire. He feels guilty about killing people. I keep finding him in the woods hunting animals. He's not ruthless. He has not embraced his power. In fact, he goes to *church* on Sundays. He asks God to forgive him." Her eyes widened. "Fool."

She stopped pacing behind Max. "Forgive him for what? He's never going to die. He doesn't need to worry about God. I can't make him understand it." She bent down behind Max, propped him up and tilted his head back to rest on her shoulder. "Ah, Max. It's been many years. I've waited for you to misstep. Finally, my day has come, and with it you brought me my lover's wife. I can't thank you enough." She kissed his cheek.

"*Lover?*" I asked, unable to hide my astonishment.

"Oh, I'm sorry. Did I ruin a secret?"

My blood boiled. I already hated her for stealing him, but to hear that she was his lover infuriated me beyond words. I

~ ☾ ~

shook with rage, yet my fingers molded around my sword as though it were an extension of my body.

"You're angry?" The grin on her face widened. "Poor Vittorio, he can't help himself. He is my fledgling and must do as I say." Her wicked smile quavered and her eyes shifted from me to Max.

He took a shallow breath. The light in his eyes flickered and faded. I knew what I needed to do.

As Kerina bent her mouth to Max's throat, I swung my sword with grim determination. His head fell forward as my blade sliced through his neck. He died before she could taste a drop of him.

I stepped back, waiting for her to spring, but she didn't move immediately. Eventually she dropped Max's body and bellowed, "How *dare* you?" Her scream vibrated down my spine, a slow, painful pulsing. My knees buckled, and I fought to remain standing. She touched the slash in her neck, smearing her own blood across her chest. My blade had cut into her neck when I'd decapitated Max.

She stood slowly and stalked toward me. "I'm going to drain you little by little so that your death lasts for hours. I'll enjoy watching you die, hearing you scream for Vittorio, *my lover*." She snarled and her tongue darted between her fangs.

I'd have already been dead if she wasn't injured. Anger radiated out from her, and I backed away. I felt as if her expression alone could have killed me.

She stumbled as she moved towards me. I had to make my next move count. One of us was going to die today. Her body began to repair itself, but this wound did not heal nearly as quickly as the other. Even vampires suffered effects from extreme blood loss. In short, rapid bursts she continued moving toward me, but she stopped and laughed when I flinched, taunting me.

However, her weakened state had slowed her reflexes and, apparently, her wits. Stumbling around, she resembled an intoxicated mountain woman.

The blood loss did not make her any weaker than me. As I swung my sword to finish the job, she grabbed the blade, trying to pry it from my hand, but I refused to let go, refused

~ ☾ ~

to fail now. She pulled me to her, hooking her free arm around me.

"You're mine. Just a few sips from you and I'll be good as new."

The ever-present battle drum beat a louder call, pounding out a constant rhythm. I closed my eyes and saw the light within, the light of eternity. It shined as bright as any star, blinding me. My breath caught. My heart beat faster, no longer keeping pace with the drumming.

She bent her mouth to my neck. The stench of sweat burned my nostrils. Her fangs pinched my skin and her lips closed on my throat.

Show her The Light.

My eyes opened, and I twisted my head, peering into her blood-red orbs.

"You. You're rea—" she began.

Letting go of the sword, I grabbed a silver-tipped stake from my belt and drove it into her heart with all my strength. She screamed and shoved away from me, staggering backwards and pulling at the stake, as if she could dislodge it and live. She fell to her knees, screaming, reddish tears streaming from her vacant, crimson eyes.

I swung my sword hard and fast. Her head spun off her shoulders and her body dropped to the ground.

~ ☾ ~

CHAPTER NINE

*"L'amore e una guida cieca, e quelli che le seguano multo
spesso si smarriscono."*
~Anonymous.
Love is a blind guide and those who follow him often lose
their way.

The blackness surrounded me, silent and cold. Suspended
in its grip, I waited to be released, waited to be set free to
accomplish what was expected. I listened to the blissful quiet,
knowing soon enough chaos would surround me and my
destiny would claim me.

Soon I'd awaken and be forced to find a way to complete
the impossible.

My mind spun through the events of the last several
weeks—Elizabeth, Peter's arrival, seeing Vittorio, Samuel's
attack... The confrontation with Samuel remained so vivid to
me I could smell his odor. The putrid-acidy stench lingered
around me, reminding me of how he had killed Lenny and
planned to take me.

My eyes opened.

No longer hooked to any machines, I stretched out on the
bed, rolling my ankles and wrists. Each joint ached from lack
of use, but, at the very least, I'd be able to walk out of here on
my own.

A cold wall of air moved into the room, carrying with it a
feeling of doom. The sudden realization that I was not alone
hit me.

"Who's there?" I bolted upright, inspecting the shadows.

"Hello, Lucia." Samuel's voice slithered from the corner of
the room. The venomous sound prickled in my ears. He spoke

~ ☾ ~

my name like it was a dirty word. He moved into the moonlight, and his eyes flashed red.

"How did you get in here?" My heart pounded. I remembered the feeling of his cold mouth against my skin. *I don't want to die.*

"The window, of course." He motioned to the opening behind him. The thin layer of snow coating the windowsill shimmered in the moonlight.

His heels clicked on the floor as he approached the bed. "I smell your fear, Lucia." He cocked his head to the side. His mouth dropped open as he scented the air and fangs glinted in the pale light. "It appears your guards are busy elsewhere. They must have thought your nurse would keep you safe. She was tasty, but not nearly as tasty as you're going to be."

I followed the wave of his hand to the body slumped on the floor. Linda's head flipped back on to her shoulders, barely connected to her neck, her eyes wide, horror forever frozen within them, her mouth warped to a permanent scream. Tear tracks ran through her once perfect makeup, leaving black mascara streaming down her cheeks. She had seen her demise coming and been unable escape it. Blood ran from her neck down her white uniform to pool in her lap. I bit back a scream, unwilling to give him the satisfaction of seeing my guilt, but I knew she'd died because of me, because I'd avoided him for so long.

I inched to the edge of the bed.

"All these years." He grinned as he surveyed me, his body swaying, almost trance-like. "Your eyes are brighter this time." He crept closer. A strange energy, like dark excitement, hummed around him.

I lowered one foot to the floor.

He raised his arms toward the darkened ceiling. "The light continues to shine." His voice reverberated around us, and he laughed. "Not for much longer, I'm afraid. You've had a good run, but we all know that everything must come to an end." He dropped his arms, straightened his shirt, and leapt the last few feet to my bedside.

"What do you want?" I demanded, stumbling off the bed to face him.

~ ☾ ~

He stood opposite me, the bed between us. "What do I want? You don't know? That part hasn't come to you? That's funny. I always thought it was one of your first memories. Guess not. *Hmm.* I wonder what that means." He paused, eyeing me. Then he smiled. "You still don't know all the details. You don't know your own destiny." He chuckled. "You have to start over each time, don't you? That's it. That's what makes your knowledge so limited, short-sighted even."

He turned his back and sat on the edge of the bed, silent.

I took a weakened step backward, praying my legs would hold out long enough for me to escape.

He turned around quickly. "You remember Vittorio, don't you?"

I froze, but didn't say a word.

He frowned. "You do. I feel your...love, I guess you'd call it, for him." He scratched his face, his thumb digging at the cleft in his chin. The sound of his nails scraping stubble filled the silence. "Can your bond with Vittorio be the problem? Is Kerina's child what's been getting in the way all these years? It can't be, can it?"

I silently shuffled toward the door.

"How could I not see it? How, in all these years, did I not realize that he was the difference? *He* was the one? I should have taken the burden from you, killed him myself. Careless. I was careless," he hissed as he launched himself across the room at me.

I spun for the door, reaching for the handle, but, just as my fingers scraped the metal knob, an ironclad grip jerked me backward. His arms encased my waist and chest. I screamed and drove my nails into his skin, thrashing to break his hold.

He bent me over the bed. "Where do you think you're going? We have unfinished business."

The stink of his breath saturated the air. I could hardly breathe but still managed to rasp out, *"Get off me."*

"Lucia, look at your nurse." He rolled me sideways to face the poor woman. "If you're not careful, you're going to have more deaths on your conscious. You see, she didn't have to die. If she hadn't come into the room to check on you, she'd

~ ☾ ~

still be alive. Do you want others to end up like her?" His lips touched my temple, and I didn't have to look at him to know he was enjoying this moment.

I didn't answer, unable to take my eyes off Linda. Her head, barely attached to her shoulders, slung to the side, and just above her clavicle, in a pool of dark red blood, lay a tiny gold cross. Like Lenny, she had died because of me. *Another one.*

"Do you?" he demanded, shaking me.

"No," I breathed out.

"Then keep your mouth shut." He bent me backward over the bed, my left arm pinned between us, the other wrenched up behind my back, nearly dislocating my shoulder. I couldn't move. His fingers knotted in my hair then jerked my head back, exposing my neck.

"Get off me! *Get off me!*" I tried to keep screaming but his mouth crushed my throat.

Excruciating pain shot down my neck and into my head when his fangs, like two thick needles, ripped into my skin. My heart pounded. He didn't just bite me. He tore open my neck. Blood oozed from the wound, soaking my chest. The distinct metallic odor coated the air. A wave of nausea rolled over me.

My head lolled to the side, his lips latched onto me, and I felt him sucking, the slurping sound adding to my horror as his voice slithered through my mind. "Ah, Lucia. Finally, you are mine."

My mind darkened as The Abyss descended upon me, pulling me in as it had done so many times. The sucking and slurping sounds coming from Samuel faded as the sounds of my shallow, raspy breaths grew louder and louder.

Suddenly, he released me, and I tumbled to the floor. Growls erupted and furniture banged about the room. My mind went fuzzy, weak from Samuel's attack, making it impossible for me to understand what was happening. The room appeared darker than it should have been. The glow of the moonlit window faded away from me.

Too weak to remain conscious, I finally gave in, returning to the cold blackness like a long lost friend.

~ ☾ ~

*****

"Come to me, my child."

The deep, dulcet voice came from the soft, heated glow in the distance.

All around me, The Abyss hovered without shape or presence, without time or space. No sound. No pressure. Nothing at all—just a hollow void edging the splendor.

Warmth pulled me closer to the aurora, wrapping around me with each step, cradling me safely within its embrace.

The air grew crisp as I moved nearer, each breath more cleansing than the last. The faint trickle of running water sounded in the distance. The scent of an early morning rain gently streamed, filling my lungs with purifying breaths.

Blazing and glorious light radiated around me, sparkling brighter than the sun, brighter than any star could possibly shine. As I staggered into the light, I raised my hand to shield my eyes from the brilliance.

I stopped, unable to see, suddenly frightened of what waited for me.

"The Light will not harm you."

I turned toward the voice.

"Lower your hand, child, so we may see each other."

My hand dropped from my face, and I saw him.

A deep contentment reached his dark brown eyes. "It has been many years, but finally our Lucia has returned." He offered his hand to me, and without question I took it.

The energy that moved along my skin didn't sizzle or vibrate. It was more powerful than that, an all-consuming strength that knew its own potency. Gradually, it surged across my flesh, through my muscles, to my heart then into my very soul. It spread through me, pounding out that familiar rhythm. My heart leapt to meet it but failed. I couldn't keep pace, couldn't match the cadence. My knees buckled, but he didn't let me fall.

"You have waited too long to come home. Your power is weak." His calm voice dropped. "The bond complicates your existence."

I recognized the tone of his words and looked away. Shame flooded me, heating my cheeks. "I'm sorry, Father."

~ ☾ ~

"Your foolish heart has led you astray."

I couldn't respond. There was no point in denying it. He knew the truth. We both knew.

"She cannot help what her heart does, Arturo," a woman said. She cupped my cheeks in her hands. "We knew you would lose your path. We knew the moment you met him he would change your destiny."

"Mother." She looked the same as she had when last I saw her. Big curls hung to her shoulders and dark green eyes twinkled above a demure smile. I hugged her tight. She kissed my cheek and squeezed me.

Father inhaled sharply. "That may be, Filomena, but she *must* complete her task. More than three hundred years she has strayed. This has given Samuel time to grow, to become more powerful, more cunning. He recognizes her value and, worse, her weaknesses. He wants her for his own. He plans to create her into one like him. She must return to her work." His eyebrow arched and he pursed his lips. "The time for avoidance is past."

"He'd have found me sooner, if he wanted me that way," I said. "He could have taken me anytime these past few weeks."

"You have been guarded. He could not reach you. Only now has he devised a plan that left you vulnerable. Knowing we have been called back to The Light, he took advantage."

He turned from us, and Mother frowned.

"Your father has been terribly worried. We've done our best to stay close to you, but for these last ten lifetimes you've been stubbornly ignoring him." She inclined her head toward Father.

"Lucia, since your incarnation of 1629 we have retained our human appearances and personas to remain as beacons for you. Yet you have done everything in your power to avoid your task, including disregarding your parents. A sin, you know." He watched me.

"Yes, Father."

"You must destroy him. You are a Pharo. You cannot continue to ignore your responsibility."

"I'm not—"

"*Lucia!*" he boomed. "*Don't.*" He raised his hands, then let

~ ☾ ~

them drop to his sides and he stepped closer to me. "You witnessed Samuel's creation. You are the only one who can stop him. It's your burden, yours and yours alone. Do you understand?"

It had been my burden for more years than I cared to remember, more years than I *could* remember. I never actually ignored my task. I always opened the path to redemption for the lost souls I encountered. I simply had not had the opportunity to guide *him* to The Light in these last three hundred plus years.

"You jeopardize many by delaying. You will practice, regain your discipline and your energy, and then you must destroy him."

"But Father—"

"No arguments this time."

"Arturo, let her—"

"No. Not another word. Not from either of you." His penetrating gaze settled on me, and I whipped away, taking a few steps from him. "She has already allowed him to create others, to strengthen his forces. In her human body she doesn't recognize the dangers, doesn't see what is so obvious to us. She's left herself few resources, none of which she can truly trust."

"She has—"

"*Filomena.* You know as well as I, none of them can be trusted. She is too enticing. As a human she is weak. Her subconscious struggles to release the information she needs. The memories come too slowly. She can't assimilate them fast enough to defend herself. Samuel knows this. They all know. It's the reason he so boldly hunts her." He pointed at me. For all his anger, he couldn't help the waves of love emanating from him, as if he'd draped a blanket around me and hugged me close.

"The others cannot protect her, not from themselves. When they realize what power they could wield if they controlled her, they will turn on her. They will create her into one of them." He stepped to the edge of the light, away from me, facing the darkness. "It will leave me no choice. *You* cannot do it. You could never do it."

~ ☾ ~

"Father, that won't—" My protest died in my mouth when the warmth I felt suddenly burned. There was no point in arguing. I had caused this. By avoiding my duty I'd put everyone at risk. I stared at my feet, ashamed of myself. I was a Pharo. Why hadn't I fulfilled my destiny?

"No. I could never hurt her." Mother squeezed my hand, and a tear rolled down her cheek. "Arturo, you know as well as I that her heart will always lead her to victory. She has a hero's heart, a warrior's courage, and the light of eternity."

"Victory at what cost?" Father stepped in front of me. He swept my hair back from my neck to examine the wound Samuel made. Turning my chin, his thumb passed over the exact spot Vittorio had bitten. In spite of the fact that the wound had healed immediately, Father had no trouble finding it, no trouble seeing the mark that branded me. "So many attempts, so many lives. You can't keep going this way. Eventually, you won't be allowed another chance. Soon, you'll be sent..." His voice trailed off. He touched my chin, bringing my gaze to meet his. "And if he creates you, if he makes you one of them, I will be left with no choice but to free you myself."

"Father, I can destroy him. I will. I promise. This time I won't fail."

"Lucia, my child. Why? Why did you do it?"

I had avoided them all these long years in an effort to dodge that question. Not because I didn't want to see them. Not because I didn't miss them and love them, but because the answer was so simple, so complex, so noble, and so foolish that I was afraid to admit it. But there was no reason to hide the truth.

"I loved him," I whispered. "I just truly loved him. I wanted him with me." My heart ached thinking about Vittorio. It was selfish. This I knew, but I couldn't help myself.

For a few brief moments, he'd given himself to me. I could have freed him, if I'd been ready. But, naively, I cowered from my calling, missing my chance, leaving him to suffer, leaving his soul to wander in purgatory never to be redeemed, never to feel God's light shine on him.

~ ☾ ~

"I know." Father sighed. "You still want him. I feel your desire for him. He didn't realize what he did when he strengthened the bond. He has no idea what lies ahead. When you go back, you must complete the impossible. You realize this, don't you?"

"Yes." The impossible. I couldn't free him when it only meant opening the door to salvation for him. How would I ever free him when his soul was bound to mine?

"Go, Lucia. Practice hard and do what you must. Free their souls." My mother kissed my cheek.

"I'll see you back in Providence." I turned toward The Abyss.

"No, my girl. We cannot return," Mother answered.

As though a knife had been driven into my heart I gasped, then spun to face them, looking from one to the other. "Why? I need you. I feel better, stronger when I'm with you." I clutched her hand. They were all I had. All I ever *truly* had. Vittorio didn't really belong to me. I couldn't go on without them.

"Child, I told you. Your avoidance—" Father began.

"*Delay*, Arturo. She was only delayed," Mother interrupted.

"Very well. Your delay has jeopardized many. We are two of the many. We can't go back and be safe. We are no longer able to chase you through lifetimes. You must resolve this situation this time or we may not see you again."

Never see them again? All these years I'd been looking at them, never truly seeing them. And now that I had them, they could be lost to me forever.

"We'll be here when you need us, Lucia," Mother said. "But you must strengthen your own power to get to us. You are only here because of our abilities. You're far too weak."

I blinked, trying to keep tears from forming. "How? How do I do it?"

"With every death there is light to replenish the soul. You must be that light." She blotted away the tears from my cheeks and then her own.

Father rested his hand on my shoulder. "You are a Pharo in the dominion of vampires. Become the Slayer you once were."

~ ☾ ~

"I don't think I..." Their expressions remained stoic as they watched the realization of my task come to me. "Yes, I can," I had no choice. I must succeed. "I'll do it."

I stepped toward the dark, knowing that this was my last chance to fulfill the destiny bestowed on me eons ago, and that if I didn't do it this time, I would never have another chance.

As I reached the darkness, Father caught my shoulder and pulled me into his arms. "We love you, Lucia. Be careful. He's far more dangerous this time."

*****

My vision faded from me, and I became aware that I was falling. I had been thrown out the window and was plummeting downward. The cold air stung my skin and made my eyes water. My hospital gown flapped in the wind as I flailed about, reaching for something, anything. "No! *Help me!* God, *no!*"

"It's all right, Lucia," Vittorio whispered into my ear as he scooped me toward him, cradling me against his chest. An undertone of anger ebbed in his words. His eyes blazed with fury, and fangs extended below his lip. I clung to him, tucking my face into his neck.

We landed on the ground and he sprinted to a waiting car, diving into the backseat. The door slammed shut as the car sped away.

"I'm cold," I said. The heater kicked on as he took off his coat and placed it over me.

"We'll be home shortly," he said, examining my neck. "He took quite a bit from her. The marks are small, but I'm concerned about the tissue below," he told the driver.

He surveyed the wound with that look I remembered so well from my dreams fixed on his face. His brows pulled together and his eyes darkened. He was still worrying about me, all these years later. I reached up to touch his cheek. "Vittorio, I'll be fine."

"I know." He took my hand in his and lightly kissed each finger.

Every soft kiss caused my heart to beat faster until it pounded wildly. The rapid beating made it difficult for me to

~ ☾ ~

breathe. I knew what I had to do. But I wanted nothing more than to stay in his arms, to let him love me.

"What is it, Lucia?" Little lines appeared around his eyes. He held me tighter.

"Vittorio, I ..." I choked on the words and tried to wiggle out of his lap, but he simply shifted me in his arms. A comforting presence encircled me.

"You're exhausted. Sleep, my love. We'll talk later."

A heavy wave of exhaustion washed over me, pulling me under. I closed my eyes and relaxed in his embrace. It was the most comfortable I'd felt in centuries.

~ ☾ ~

CHAPTER TEN

"Chi e ferito d'amoro strale d'altra piaga no teme."
~Guarini
He who has been smitten by the arrows of love is no longer
afraid of any other wound.

I awoke on a huge bed with four dark wooden posts ending
in carved knobs. Across the room, sunlight streamed in
through giant windows, lighting a sitting area consisting of a
leather couch atop a round oriental rug. Embers burned in a
large fireplace as wisps of smoke danced in the sunlight.

Vittorio's bedroom. His scent lingered in the air. The
sheets smelled of him, the room felt like him. The art on the
walls was his work.

Opposite from the bed, a beautiful mural of a vineyard
stretched across the entire wall. It was Del Torrente, my
family's vineyard. The view was from our house on the hill.
The harvest. Workers gathered around the press with baskets
of grapes in their arms.

The orange tree, where Vittorio and I sat each day during
our courtship, featured prominently. In the beginning, sitting
under that tree was where we spent our only private
moments together. The scent of orange blossoms came to me.

The mural on the wall to the right surprised me. It
comprised of six different portraits, every one of which I
recognized. In the biggest of them, I stared back at me. My
wild mane flowed out from my head, my green eyes intense.
The other portraits were smaller, different views. A couple
were profiles. One portrait showed me wearing a peasant
dress and a kerchief. I chuckled at that one, remembering
how I hated the kerchief.

~ ☾ ~

I pulled the soft down comforter around my neck and scrunched into a ball. The deep plum color reminded me of wine. Glancing back at the vineyard, I longed for those easy-going days. My chest tightened at the thought of what lay ahead. A tear rolled down my nose and dripped onto the blanket.

The bed moved as he lay down behind me. He nuzzled my hair and snuggled in closer to me, gently laying his head on the pillow. His arm curled around me and his lips touched my neck.

I wasn't sure if it was his body so close to me, his lips and breath on my neck, or his scent that made it happen, but my whole body tingled. Parts of me that I didn't know *could* tingle were stirring. I lay still, cuddled in his arms, trying to stay calm, but the realization that we had actually found each other was almost more than I could take.

We lay together in silence. It had been some three hundred sixty years since the last time we'd been able to do this. I was finally in the arms of the man I loved above all others, the man I had bound myself to for all eternity. This was where I belonged.

My moment of contentment ended when my purpose for existing rammed its way into my thoughts. The low thrumming surged inside me. My promise to set him free nagged at me, ruining my happiness. I didn't want to consider what I had to do. I wanted to bask in the accomplishment of finding him, consider the possibility of spending some time with him, loving him, but destiny called.

My heart sped. Breaths came faster, shallower. My mind raced. *How am I going to do this? I can't kill him. I can't.* The thrumming flared, pounding so hard it was all I heard.

I shoved the blanket back, wiggled out from under his arm, and sat up, panting and clutching my chest. "I can't breathe."

"Slow down. Take a deep breath." His smooth, deep voice broke through the pounding. He sat beside me and rubbed my back. "Exhale. Slow inhale. You'll be fine."

"No. I...You..." I huffed. "Can't breathe." I stretched the collar of my nightgown.

~ ☾ ~

He slid me to the end of the bed and bent me over, head to my knees. "Breathe, Lucia. One breath at a time." He worked slow strokes up and down my back.

The wild panting stopped, and my breathing slowed to match the movement of his hand. A deep breath in as he moved down my back and a full exhale as his hand slid to my neck.

I faced him, feeling his hand splayed across my back, fingers gently massaging my sore muscles.

He was waiting for me. In spite of the gray skin and the deep, dark circles under his eyes, he appeared happy. His beautiful smile dazzled me. The hazel ring around his hazel-black eyes glittered. I touched his face, running my fingers along his jaw line, enjoying the feel of his scruffy chin against my palm.

"Better?" he asked, his hand resting on the small of my back.

"Your eyes. They glitter just like they did when we were married." I leaned closer. His scent swirled around me. "You smell like home," I whispered.

"Actually, *you* smell like home." He leaned to my neck and inhaled. "Like orange blossoms and honey." His lips tickled my skin as he spoke the soft Italian words.

"I do?" I leaned back and smelled my wrist. "I smell like..." I paused to inhale, "...the hospital." My nose crinkled. "I could use a shower. Where'd this come from?" I asked, straightening the pretty white nightgown I was wearing. The lace-trimmed sleeves bunched up my arms and the lavender satin ribbon crisscrossing over my chest had come untied, leaving my left breast partially exposed.

"That is from me. You complained about the bloodstained hospital gown, so I did the husbandly thing and bathed you. Then I dressed you. That last part was your idea." The devilish grin on his lips sent a zing of excitement coursing through me from my heart straight between my legs.

"Stop that." I glanced away as heat rose from my neck to my cheeks.

He laughed, deep and sexy, and my nipples hardened.

"Vittorio! Stop that." I knotted the ribbon at my neck and

~ ☾ ~

crossed my arms over my chest.

"What? All I did was laugh." I shifted uncomfortably and curls fell around my face. "You're so beautiful, just as you were in Italy. You haven't changed a bit." His gaze washed over me, finally settling on my eyes.

He loved me. I could feel it, feel him all around me, filling the space between us. Guilt squeezed my heart. He trusted me.

"Vittorio, there's something I have to do." I looked away. "To you. And it's not very pleasant." I dangled my feet off the bed.

How had I killed vampires in my earlier lives? Did I like any of them? If I did, how the hell did I do it? I didn't just like him. I loved him. *How* was I going to kill him?

"I know what you have to do. I understand." He reached for my hand.

I leaned away and slid off the bed. "You can't possibly understand." I walked to the wall then padded back to the bed. "I have to..." He cocked his head to the side and watched me. "I have to...What I have to do is really, really not...nice," I finished somewhat lamely, crinkling my nose.

"That all depends on how you do it." He fluffed a couple pillows and laid back.

"What?" I stopped walking.

"How you do it will determine whether it's benevolent or not." He laced his fingers behind his head, glancing upward. "There are ways to do it that would be quick and fairly painless. And then there are ways that would not. Those would be the...not *nice* ways." He lay on the bed, relaxed.

Confused, I paced back toward the wall.

"You're worrying for no reason, not an unusual trait for you. It's amazing how you haven't changed in all these years." He turned his head to follow my pacing.

"How wonderful for you. It's amazing that you haven't changed either. Still an overly confident pain in my ass. Do you even know what I'm talking about?" My hands fisted at my hips and every muscle in my body tightened as anger shot from my head to my toes.

He smiled. "Yes."

~ ☾ ~

"No. I don't think you do. I have to kill you. *Kill* you. I have never killed anyone. Certainly not someone I lo..." I stopped short. It wouldn't be right to tell him how I feel and then kill him.

"You love me. I knew it." He grinned, sending fire shooting to my bellybutton and lower.

"*AAAHHH!* Why are you doing this?" I marched to the bed. "Don't you understand? What is wrong with you?" I slammed my hands on the mattress and frowned at him.

"Lucia, I know exactly what you have to do." Faster than I could register, he sat on the edge of the bed, pulling me between his legs. "I know you must kill me. I'm well aware that because of me, you have not been allowed to rest." His hands held my waist. "From the instant I learned what was happening to you, I began searching for you. For more than three hundred years I have searched, preparing for the moment we would meet, knowing what you'd have to do." His eyes darkened slightly.

I squeezed his shoulders. "You *want* me to kill you?"

His voice deepened. "I didn't say I wanted you to do it today. When you're ready, I'll be ready. We'll get there together." His head dipped and he blinked his eyelashes against my cheek. I squirmed, same as always. "Besides, you couldn't do it today if you tried. You don't know how to call the power or control it."

"How do you know?" My hands slid to his chest.

"The last time I saw Samuel, he was feeding from you." His fingers caressed my neck where Samuel had bitten me, and I winced. "One would think that if you could have called on your own abilities, you would have." Little worry lines appeared around his eyes as he frowned. "You really are defenseless." He turned my chin to examine the bite. "There's no mark, but he ripped the muscles below. That's why it's sore."

Beneath my palms, I felt his chest vibrate as a low growl rumbled.

"You must practice." He moved me to the side and stood.

"What? How?" My stomach grumbled, and we both looked down.

~ ☾ ~

"First, you'll dress and eat, then we'll practice. The shower's behind the door on the right." He pointed. "Clothes are behind the door on the left. Elizabeth built a wardrobe for you. I'm sure you'll find something you like. When you're ready, come downstairs. I'll be in the kitchen." He kissed my cheek and left me alone.

I stood staring after him. *Practice? Practice killing vampires? How? How does one practice killing something? You either kill it or you don't. And what way is nice? A stake, an ax, lethal injection?* How? I flopped onto the bed, my face sinking into the pillow.

~ ☾ ~

CHAPTER ELEVEN

When I was clean, presentable, and no longer felling like I reeked of my hospital stay, I headed toward the kitchen, coaxed along by the smell of onions and pancetta sautéing, my stomach gurgling the whole way.

The house was beautiful with hardwood floors and high ceilings. The second floor hallway was shaped like an open square with the stairwell coming up the middle. It reminded me of an old plantation house with rooms along two sides and windows on the others. Artwork hung on the walls, pictures of Italy, ocean scenes, the view from Vittorio's bedroom, and, of course, me.

I found Vittorio with a dishtowel over his shoulder working at the stove. "*Mmm*. It smells great," I said.

The gourmet kitchen, any cook's dream, had a sub-zero freezer, six-burner gas stove with a grill and a double oven. The exhaust system looked like it could actually suck the stove up. Brand new pots hung from an overhead rack. The cabinets were made of cherry wood, some with glass fronts to display plates and glasses perfectly. It seemed comical to me that a house of vampires would have a fully stocked kitchen.

"I'm making a frittata for you," Vittorio announced, flipping the omelet with the air of a master chef.

"I can't believe you cook." I cleared my throat in an effort to hide a giggle.

"What? Of course I cook," he answered, as if I'd just said the stupidest thing he'd ever heard.

"*Why?* What do you eat that's cooked?"

"Nothing." He caught the frittata, placed the frying pan on the burner, and checked the heat.

"He can only cook three things," Peter interjected as he

~ ☾ ~

and Bruno entered the kitchen. "Frittata, beans and sausage, and rice pudding. He doesn't have the slightest idea how to cook anything else. Do you even know how to make toast?" He threw a loaf of bread across the counter.

Vittorio caught the bread with one hand, reaching for a plate with the other. "Hey, a human could survive on those three dishes. What can you make?"

"Nothing. But I'm not human," Peter answered.

Bruno shrugged out of his jacket then tossed it on a chair. "I know how to make cereal. If you're left with me I'll keep you fed."

I laughed. "Thanks. But I don't eat cereal."

"Well, then you'll starve if you're left with me for too long." He pulled out a stool from the buffet bar and sat down. This was the first time I'd seen him in the daylight. He looked tired, just the same as Peter did during the day, with gray skin and slight circles under his black-brown eyes. He resembled a giant teddy bear, even with the exhausted appearance.

"I'm quite sure I can fend for myself in the kitchen." I watched Vittorio. The three dishes he could make had been his favorites. The irony that he'd mastered preparing them now that he couldn't eat them stung. Just one more reminder that everything had changed since we'd last been together. I squeezed his arm as I walked around him. "What should I do?"

Peter pulled out the stool beside him, motioning for me to join them on the opposite side of the bar. "Oh, nothing. You have to let him cook for you. He's been practicing for centuries."

I slid onto the stool beside Peter. "Practicing?" *For centuries?* I let out a low whistle. He'd always been a perfectionist.

"Yes. I'm quite talented in the kitchen." Vittorio returned to preparing my breakfast, slicing bread for the toaster.

"Where are we?" I asked.

"Still Massachusetts. Danvers, more specifically," he answered.

"So where are Elizabeth and Alexander? Do they live here, too?"

~ ☾ ~

"Yes, they live here. They're tying up a few loose ends in Boston. They'll be back this afternoon," Bruno answered. "We've all lived together in some capacity since the search began. Sometimes we've split if we needed to check more than one area. But, usually, we're together."

"I see." It didn't surprise me that Vittorio had been searching for me. Our bond drew us to each other. But the fact that the other four had so loyally stayed with him, that was a surprise I hadn't expected.

Peter mentioned something about the upcoming Super Bowl and the three of them bantered about the game. It was like watching any family gathered around the kitchen having breakfast. The fact that this family wouldn't be eating didn't seem to matter. Their bantering had moved on to the two brothers vehemently arguing over which teams would make it to the big game.

"When do I get to hear about how Peter and Bruno came to be?" I interrupted.

Vittorio finished washing a bowl and checked the frittata. "Peter, do you want to explain your story?"

"Sure," Peter answered, turning to me. In his perfectly pressed khakis, argyle V-neck sweater and loafers, he looked like he had just stepped out of a J. Crew ad. "Vittorio found me in a field." He removed his glasses to clean them. His blond hair was flawless, not a single strand out of place. "I had fallen from my horse. I think I hit my head, because I don't really remember much of anything prior to waking with Vittorio and Elizabeth. So, since I was—"

"How old were you?" I touched his hand.

"Nineteen," he answered, grinning. "As I was saying—"

"What year was it?"

"1871. Are you going to let me tell you the story?" He huffed and rolled his eyes. I thought I noticed a hint of the British accent. "Or do you just want to ask a series of questions and hope you get all the info?"

"I'm sorry. I won't interrupt again."

"Okay. So, I was in a field, having fallen from my horse. The field had just been mown. I vaguely remember the sound of the clicking blades in the distance. The smell of freshly cut

~ ☾ ~

grass is the last thing I remember from my human life." He smiled.

"Oh, so you really don't *eat* grass. But do you all smell the cut grass? I smell it all the time."

"Yes, he's just a country boy." Bruno reached around me to ruffle Peter's hair.

I paused a moment, waiting, then cleared my throat. "Can I ask questions now?"

"Yes," Peter answered, leaning on his elbows.

"Where were you living when Vittorio found you?"

"England."

"That explains the accent."

"I told you, you weren't hiding it well," Bruno interrupted, all the while balancing a chef's knife on his finger.

"Yes, that does explain my accent. I hid it for the Tempo job. I didn't want too many questions when we were trying to keep you safe. But now we're free to use our regular accents," Peter explained, using the accent and snickering at Bruno.

I sipped my coffee. "What do you remember of your human life?"

"Nothing, really. I remember the horse, the sound of the mower blades, but nothing else. I think I hit my head pretty hard."

"Do you really know anything about jewelry?" I folded a napkin in my lap.

"Yes. I was serious about Heirloom Jewelry. We needed to make an income, and jewelry worked. We've had that company in a few different countries. We moved whenever we thought you were in another location, using the company as a façade."

Bruno leaned into me and grinned.

They'd uprooted their lives over and over, and to what end? To find the one who'd kill them all? I forced the thought away and nudged Bruno with my elbow. "So, what about you?"

"Where to start? Let me see..." Bruno also had a British accent. The only difference was his cockney English was more difficult to understand. I wasn't even sure if every word was truly English and sat staring at his mouth, concentrating on each syllable.

~ ☾ ~

"Watch your accent, Bruno. She can't understand you." Peter thumbed toward me and raised his eyebrows.

"Oh, sorry. I forget. You're new here." Bruno repeated the last thing he said with a much more restrained accent. "I was born in 1864 in England. Peter found me in 1882."

"Peter created you?"

"*No*," both Peter and Bruno answered. They gaped at me with wide eyes.

Vittorio topped off my coffee and slid the cup toward me. "It's a difficult and grueling process to create a vampire, Lucia. A young vampire, like Peter was, might not succeed. I created Bruno, too." The change in his tone matched his solemn expression. A heavy, sad feeling hung in the air.

"I was a sailor," Bruno said, drawing my attention. "Peter found me by the docks." His eyes darkened. "My father had beaten me and left me for dead." He glanced at Vittorio, whose expression remained set and serious. "If I hadn't been created, I'd have probably died that night. And if, by some miracle, I'd survived that beating, then it would only have been to return to a father who would have killed me some other night. I'm thankful for my new life."

"How old were you?" I asked, the coffee going cold in my stomach.

"Just eighteen. That was actually my birthday. I don't remember the exact date, but I remember my father laughing at me. I remember the sound of his rotten voice when he wished me a happy birthday before leaving me bleeding and broken on the dock."

"I'm sorry, Bruno." I patted his arm. To think his father had treated him so poorly made tears well in my eyes. Considering his size, I could only imagine that Bruno had always been a gentle soul, too good-hearted to fight his own father, even to save himself.

A lopsided smile appeared, though it seemed forced. "Thanks."

The glimpse of a sadder moment in his life made him seem too vulnerable. At some point, I'd be forced to do what his father had tried, but failed. I'd be forced to kill both Bruno and Peter. I drew in a ragged breath, shoving the idea from my mind.

~ ☾ ~

Vittorio placed the frittata in front of me. It looked and smelled wonderful and helped to ease my heartache. My mouth watered. "Has anyone ever tasted anything you've cooked?"

"What are you trying to say?" He cut a piece of frittata and held it to my mouth.

"Nothing. I'm just wondering if I'm the only woman you've ever cooked for. That's all." I hesitated less than a second and took the bite.

If I hadn't been sitting directly across from him, I might have missed what happened. In the blink of an eye he flinched, ever so slightly. The reaction was immediately followed with, "No. I have never cooked for another woman."

In an instant, I knew he wasn't being honest or, at least, he wasn't telling me everything. He had never been able to lie to me, so there had to be more to this story. I leaned away from him to study his face. He reached out to touch me.

"No." I raised my hand, stopping him. "Tell me. I want to know." My mind took off like a shot. All I could picture was him seducing woman after woman. I glanced at Bruno, remembering him influencing Marie at the party, and assumed this "vampire voodoo" was something all vampires used. I jumped straight to the idea of Vittorio making love with everyone he bit. The thought of his mouth on anyone else, even for a meal, infuriated me.

I concentrated on his features, measuring every little movement he made, but feeling so betrayed I couldn't see straight. "Tell me." I pushed my chair back from the counter as anger bubbled within me.

He took a deep breath and sighed. "Lucia, I'll tell you everything, but I'm not sure this is where I should start. You should hear about my whole existence before you consider this part. You're narrowing me down to a very, very small period of time." His voice was soft and gentle as he tried to convince me that his infidelity didn't matter. He reached for my hand, but I stepped away from him.

The anger shifted, and rage sparked inside me. The longer he waited to tell me what I wanted to know, the hotter it burned. "Tell me." My heart picked up speed. How could he

~ ☾ ~

have been with other women when I was searching for him, when my soul would not rest until his did? How could he be so untrue to me? Tears brimmed in my eyes.

"Lucia, my love for you has never lessened. You have always been the only reason my heart beat." Panic laced his words, cracking his usual smooth, velvety voice, and worry flashed in his eyes.

"You've been untrue," I said.

"I could say similar things about you. You've been with other men since our life together."

"How many?" I forced myself to look at him, to face the man who'd cheated on me. "How many women?"

His left eye narrowed below furrowed eyebrows and he leaned toward me, smashing his fists onto the counter. "Do you think it's easy for me to think of another man holding you? Do you know what it took for me not to kill Michael? I couldn't be left alone at the hospital. I wanted to kill him for all the men who had ever touched you." Now, bitter resentment cooled his voice.

Resentment. How dare *he?*

The countertop cracked under the weight of his hands. His expression turned to stone, as cold as the marble breaking between us.

How could he actually think that these things were even remotely the same? I turned away, unable to look at him. The first twinge of power rushed along my skin. My cheeks tightened, my eye watered, and my breathing quickened. I didn't know what, but something hummed around me. Whatever it was, the force was wild and powerful, waiting to be unleashed. I stormed out of the room before it broke free and I did something we'd both regret.

They followed me into the living room like a cloud of anxiety. Only Vittorio was brave enough to get close. He caught my arm and stood in front of me. Tension shone in his face, and the glitter in his eyes faded. His brows pulled together. "Don't be angry. You're scrutinizing the wrong thing. If you have any reason to want to kill me, it's that I'm a vampire. Under the circumstances, the fact that I may have had a relationship outside of our marriage should not

~ ☾ ~

motivate you." He tucked a stray curl behind my ear and slid his fingers along my cheek. "Think about it, Lucia. I have had to handle you loving many other men. It killed me, knowing it was happening."

He was right. How could I be angry with him? His fingers skimmed back and forth across my forearm. My shoulders drooped. I rested my head on his chest. "I didn't know about you or our destiny when I was with them."

"I know." His arms wrapped around me.

"*And* didn't I leave them all when I remembered you? I must have. Didn't I?" I looked at him.

"Yes. You did."

"So I never knowingly cheated on you. I never purposefully betrayed you, never willfully broke our vows." My hands flattened over his chest, and I felt his heart pounding.

"No, you didn't."

I shoved out of his embrace and whirled away from him. Blinding sunlight poured through the window. The power rushed across my skin. My breaths came faster, shallower.

I wasn't going to be able to let this one go easily. The thought of him holding another woman, whispering in her ear, kissing her, loving her, enraged me. I spun around to face him. "How *could* you? You can't even compare yourself with me. You've been aware of me all this time and you still loved someone else. I don't know if I can forgive you. I'm not sure I even *like* you right now!"

He stumbled away from me, fear rippling off him. "Lucia, my relationship happened before I learned what was happening with you. I didn't know you were coming back."

I stalked toward him. "How do you expect me to believe that? You watched me die in Italy. You knew I was coming back."

"*No*. I didn't know you were coming back. I had no idea that was happening until years later."

Beyond trying to contain myself, the urge to smash something over his head overcame me. Hatred—no—*fury*. That's what it was. Wild fury blinded me. I lunged toward him with my hand pulled back, fist ready to fly. A current of energy ran across my body like a bolt of lightning across the sky.

~ ☾ ~

He collapsed to the floor, screaming. The sound was monstrous, the most dreadful noise I'd ever heard. *"Lucia! Please!"* The sight of him writhing in pain made my heart ache as though it was being ripped from my chest. His back bowed and every muscle in his body constricted. Hands balled into fists, he gasped for air and my own lungs clenched in sympathy. His face contorted, but his empty, soulless eyes bulged wide open, black as night. Red tears leaked from the sockets, leaving bloody streaks down to his temples. He groaned in agony as he tried desperately to breathe.

I froze in place, terrified. He was dying right in front of me. *I* was killing him. I backed away from him, confused, wanting to stop it, but had no idea *how*. I cowered against the wall, hoping that if I stood far enough away, my attack on him would end.

"Lucia, stop it." Peter rushed to Vittorio's side.

"I don't know *how*," I cried. I didn't know what was happening. I couldn't control the power. It worked on its own. It was then that I believed Vittorio's words from the party. I was more powerful than I knew. And I was terrified.

Bruno lifted me, carrying me from the room. "Lucia," he said. His hypnotic tone fascinated me. "I want you to sleep." The scent of the sea washed over me. My head sagged and I felt myself being carried away.

~ ☾ ~

CHAPTER TWELVE

Alone, in the dark, the sound of Vittorio's tortured screams still rang in my ears. I bolted out of bed and ran to the door.

What have I done? I fumbled for the doorknob. *What if I killed him?* But his hand dropped onto my shoulder, stopping me.

"I'm fine." He pulled me into his arms.

I sobbed, tears soaking through his shirt down to his chest. "I'm so sorry. I didn't mean to hurt you."

"Shhh. I'm fine. Don't cry. I understand why you were upset."

I tried to kill him, and he's comforting me. And I'm letting him. This doesn't bode well for me accomplishing my task.

The reality was that what needed to be done terrified me. *How am I going to do this? I'm not a killer. How the hell did I even end up in this mess?* However noble the cause, hundreds of years later I was not the warrior I had been. This time around I was too soft.

"Let's lie down." His tone held no hint of distress. "I'll tell you what you wanted to know. It's probably best for me to get this out in the open so you don't lose your temper again."

He carried me to the bed, depositing me in the same spot I had just vacated, then pulled the blanket over me. I rolled onto my side, facing him as he turned on a bedside lamp. The only sign of what he had recently endured showed in his eyes. They were duller than usual, tired looking.

"Lucia, since I was created there have been two other women in my life. Intimately. The first, you know about. Kerina. She was my creator. I had no choice but to do as she bid me. Thankfully, I broke free from her not long after my

~ ☾ ~

creation." His voice, although low and calm, wasn't his usual. His accent crowded his words. "The second and only other relationship was with a vampire named Desiree. We spent only a short time together. It happened about fifty years after you died. I did not know of your existence at that time." His last sentence came out in Italian and he didn't speak another word of English as he bared his soul.

"I was not the man you have always known. I was more..." He hesitated. "I was bitter at my loss and angry that I did not die with you that day. Desiree was ruthless, but she taught me a number of things about vampires. We spent twenty or so years together." His voice faltered as he tried to explain.

Tears streamed down my face. "Twenty years is not a short time." I swallowed the lump in my throat. Vittorio and I had only been married for eleven years.

"It is to a vampire. And to a Pharo. I'm sorry. If I'd known—" He pinched the bridge of his nose, closing his eyes for a moment. "Do you want me to continue?"

"Yes." I needed to know the story, even if it hurt.

"I never loved her. She was a companion, one that fulfilled a need for me at that point in time. We were intimate, but not as you imagine. It was never a loving encounter." His gaze didn't stray from mine, and his eyes shone with sincerity. I knew he spoke the truth.

"Eventually, Elizabeth and Alexander found me. They had learned of your existence, your destiny. They explained what was happening to you, that you were searching for me. I left Desiree immediately to find you. I would never, *never* have been with her if I'd known of your existence. Please, please forgive me, Lucia."

His pleas broke my heart. I didn't have enough memories to know if I'd ever seen him this way, but what I saw now was too painful to watch. The guilt and disgust were more than I could stand. "Vittorio, of course I forgive you," I whispered. "Please stop berating yourself. I can't stand to see you this way." I pulled him to me and rolled onto my back. He followed, and I slipped my arms around him. "I think we only have a short period of time together. We can't spend it feeling terrible about our pasts."

~ ☾ ~

"I love you, *cuore mio*." He kissed my lips.

When he pulled away I moved with him, my lips meeting his and parting, my tongue slipping into his mouth. I slid my hand to the back of his head and pulled him toward me, hoping to make him forget Desiree. To make him think only of me.

He kissed me back, tempting me with his tongue. Hunger pulsed in his kiss. The need for him to love me as he had done so many times before overwhelmed me.

Even with the blanket between us, I felt him hard against me. I wanted him to touch me everywhere. I wanted to feel him inside me.

"Vittorio, make love to me," I begged between kisses.

He stopped kissing me. His eyes lit with more than their usual glitter. "Lucia, I want to make love to you. Lord knows I do. But there are things you need to know about me, about us, about this whole situation."

"What?" I asked breathily as I lured his lips back to mine. We kissed for a few minutes and I nearly forgot my question.

"I can't explain it here. We have to stop. I...I have..." he tried to explain as I nibbled his ear.

Desire arched between us as he brought his lips to mine again. His kiss bordered on dangerous. I sensed the animal desire in him as he moved against me. His arms closed around me, making it impossible to move. His legs pinned mine, and his hips pushed down on me as his mouth kissed a trail to my neck. My pulse pounded against his lips, and he moaned.

A slight sting began in my neck. "Vittorio?" His hips thrust into mine, and I moved with him, grinding my body against his. I wiggled my hands free and untucked his shirt from his jeans, scratching my fingernails up his back. I wanted him. God, how I wanted him. "Vittorio, please?" I tried to free my legs to wrap around him.

He didn't respond. Instead his legs held me in place, trapping me beneath him as he licked my neck, slow, yearning licks. His fangs pinched my skin, and his tongue worked greedily at the pinprick openings.

"Vittorio?" My pulse jumped as my heart hammered in my

~ ☾ ~

chest. "What are you doing?" I squeaked, barely able to catch my breath.

He was off the bed, standing near the couch before I even realized he'd released me. "Lucia, we can't. You have to know more before we can do anything else." He exhaled a ragged breath through extended fangs. "I need a minute or two." He rested his hands on the mantel, his head bowing to face the floor. "I'll start a fire and we can sit on the couch and talk."

I watched him for a second, studying the rapid rise and fall of his chest, the sound of his breath escaping past his fangs, and the way he moved as he started the fire. I knew in spite of being a vampire he was still my husband, still the same man I'd loved and married. Still my Vittorio.

I slid off the bed and padded barefoot to the bathroom. There were no marks on my neck, not a clue that he'd drawn any blood from me. All that remained was the hickey that had formed. I looked like a teenage girl getting home from a hot date.

When I returned to the room he was leaning against the window frame, staring out at the night. The roaring fire spread a romantic glow about the room. I sat on the couch in the toasty warmth, waiting for him to join me. "What do you want to tell me?" His image in the window glass appeared crystal clear. I smiled wryly. *Vampires really do cast reflections.* Another myth proven untrue.

His luminescent skin glowed in the moonlight. The dark circles under his eyes were gone. Only the sorrow within them detracted from his usual allure.

He shifted, and his pensive expression reflected back at me. "I love to kiss you. I always have. It's always excited me. The only difference is now it's a bit more perilous." He watched my reflection in the window.

I liked the idea that he loved to kiss me, but I'd felt his desire. It was more urgent, stronger than any man's I'd ever felt. I knew I might not be safe in his arms.

"There is so much for you to learn, so much for me to tell you." He sat beside me on the couch, his face an emotionless mask. In spite of the fire, the room's temperature dropped. His presence around me became a heavy pressure, dragging

~ ☾ ~

me under.

I touched his chin, turning his face to me. "You might as well start at the beginning."

"The memories I share with you will be intense. You'll feel my emotions, though I'll try to buffer them."

"What do you mean?" I folded one leg between us.

"Did Max explain that a vampire sire and his progeny have a telepathic link?"

"He did." At last, one point I could admit to remembering.

"With our bond, we share a similar connection. We can't hear each other's thoughts, but we are able to share memories."

"You're not going to bite me, are you?" As much as I wanted him, and even though I'd offered myself to him once, I wasn't feeling good about another bite.

"No. No more feeding. Not for either of us." He sighed as he scrubbed a hand over his face. "We already have the blood bond. All you have to do is open up. Let your aura free."

"I have an aura?"

He smiled. "You really don't remember anything from your previous lives, do you?"

"Not really."

"Well, you have an aura, and it is not free." He kicked off his shoes. "You keep it sealed up tight as long as you can." His grin widened.

"What's so funny?"

"You have dreamt very little beyond our lives in Italy, right?"

I squirmed on the couch, suddenly uncomfortable, like a naughty kid who hadn't done her homework. "How did you know?"

"When you sleep, your aura is free. I'm not sure if you don't know how to keep it contained or if you purposefully send it out, but, whatever the reason, you fly free when you sleep." He chuckled.

"What's so funny?" I frowned. "And what am I doing when I'm flying free?" I waved my hand in the air.

"You visit me." The look on his face made my stomach flip. "Tonight will be your first lesson in controlling your aura.

~ ☾ ~

You'll need to relax and let me lead you; let my presence into you so that I can show you. You must learn to use this skill to master your own powers." His fingers traced a line down my jaw.

"Your presence? Is that your aura?"

"Yes. Aura, presence, spirit, being, essence: they're all just different words for the same thing."

I sat back, holding his hands in mine. "I have a few questions. First, how do you know what my powers are? Second, how do I let you lead? Third, how am I going to master my own abilities? I don't even know what they *are.*"

"You have the power to visualize death and share that vision with a vampire."

"What?" I stood and walked to the window. *Visualize death? Share it? Who am I? The Grim Reaper?*

"That is your power. That's what you unleashed earlier today. You're not strong enough to follow through with delivering a death, which is why Bruno was able to intervene, but eventually you'll be unstoppable."

I thought back to the day's events. His face, twisted in agony, was all I could remember. "I have no idea how I did that."

"But you will. And then you'll be able to call on the power and project it." His reflection appeared behind me in the window, and he slipped his arms around my waist. "Once you master your power it will become the kind way of killing a vampire. Quick and painless." He kissed my hair, then rested his chin on my head.

"Okay," I mumbled, still thinking about him writhing on the floor. It wasn't pain I'd seen on his face. It was fear. Death had hung over him. I had taunted him with it. *When you're ready, I'll be ready.* His assurance from this morning repeated in my thoughts. He certainly hadn't been ready today. And, now that he'd had a taste of it, how would he ever be ready? *What will I do if he doesn't willingly meet his end? I'll have no choice but to force it upon him. How will I ever be ready?*

"You feel my presence around you. I can tell. Your aura responds, reaching for me, but you never let it out. Tonight,

~ ☾ ~

you'll come to me while you're awake." He knelt at the fireplace and stoked the flames, throwing a couple more logs onto the blaze. His spirit moved around me, testing my boundaries.

Little by little my body relaxed. "I feel what you're doing."

"Good. Once you learn this step, I will teach you to guard."

"What's that?" I returned to the couch and sat in the corner, my head reeling thinking about everything I needed to learn.

He replaced the fireplace poker. "It's a trick to keep your thoughts hidden. Lucia, I may not be the only vampire who can see your memories. You may also be sharing them with..."

"Oh my God." I swallowed and felt a stitch in my neck. "Samuel." I knew enough to know that Samuel's bite, although forced, had opened the possibility of a bond forming between us.

Vittorio's eyes darkened. The muscles of his jaw hardened, forcing his lips into a tight line.

~ ☾ ~

CHAPTER THIRTEEN

We lay together on the couch, his arms around me, my head tucked under his chin. "Relax, Lucia. There's no need for you to be so nervous."

"I don't understand what you're going to do." I squirmed, trying to find a comfortable spot.

"I'm simply going to show you a memory, share my experience. Nothing else." He rested his head on mine and inhaled. "Open to me, allow me to show you." Our legs tangled together, and he pulled me closer to him.

I slid my hand down his back, took a deep breath and held it for a few seconds, then exhaled. His scent filled my lungs. A couple more breaths and my heart rate slowed. I cuddled in closer to him, my cheek to his chest, listening to the pulsing beneath his skin.

His heart beat a slow, steady rhythm.

"You'll like this one," he said.

The air changed around us. We no longer felt separate from each other. It seemed as though we were joined as one. Inside me his presence hovered, powerful, nearly overwhelming. He held me engaged in each memory, but safe at the same time, allowing me to experience his memories as if I were there, as if they were my own. When I felt like I'd be overcome by the experience, he was there, holding me close, sheltering me from his emotions, numbing the pain.

*****

"No. Vittorio can be the winner," Lucia said. Her soft voice carried over her shoulder as she headed down the row of grapevines, away from me.

"Oh, no, Lucia." Rinnaldo caught her arm. "I don't think you should just give him a victory. It would mean nothing to

~ ☾ ~

just hand it to him." Rinnaldo winked at me and steered her back to our waiting companions.

She frowned, eyebrows pulling together to form a crease above her upturned nose. Long lashes surrounded her beautiful green eyes as she glanced from face to face, looking for someone to intervene. The left side of her bottom lip tucked in. A telltale sign. She knew she'd been caught.

I'd known her since she was born, watched that same expression play across her face hundreds of times in these fourteen years, but in the past few weeks something about her had changed. She wasn't the little girl trailing after me yammering about some ridiculous happening. She was different. The sound of her voice put my stomach in knots. I found myself hanging on her every word and having to force myself to pay attention to my work.

When her gaze finally met mine, I bit my tongue to keep from telling her she was right. It was all my fault. *And I love you.*

I could have finished the row, should have. Instead I'd spent the last half hour listening to her very detailed story about making sausages and lentils and how every good wife is supposed to know how to cook. Too caught up in the idea of her cooking for me, I completely forgot to check her work on this row. I couldn't say for sure if she'd secured even one tie. She blinked and nibbled her lip, and it took all the will power I had not to touch her, to kiss away that frown.

"I agree," Arturo said, waving her to him. "I've always thought Vittorio was lazy. I think a contest is what we need to prove his worth. Come, ten feet should be enough. You'll check the ties on the vines for ten feet. Whoever finishes first is the winner." Arturo positioned himself behind her at the vine, wearing a smile so big he could barely speak. "When we learn which of you works the slowest, we will know who is to blame for not completing this work."

"Vittorio, are you ready?"

"Yes, Arturo." I faced the vine, trying not to laugh. I knew she'd be angry, if she thought I was laughing.

"Lucia?"

I stood with my back to them, fussing with the vines and

~ ☾ ~

pretending to prepare for our contest, all the while straining to hear her voice, knowing she was squirming with dread. More competitive than any man I'd met, but smart enough to know when she was out-matched, she knew this wasn't going to end well. And they'd taunt her for days. We'd all tease her.

"Papa, I don't want to do this," she mumbled.

I peered over my shoulder, but couldn't look at her for more than a second. She clung to her father batting those pleading eyes, and I nearly backed out of the little competition, completely swayed by her sweet little pout.

"I wouldn't want to either. He's faster than me," Arturo said, spinning her toward the vine.

The other farm hands stood by us, laughing mercilessly.

"If she actually beats you, Vittorio, I'm telling the whole town," Carlo said.

"Yes, including your parents," Paolo added.

"*Papa*," she whined.

"Lucia, you can't back down from the challenge. You're the one who blamed him for the unfinished work," Arturo said.

"Maybe it was my fault. Maybe I was talking," she whispered, side-stepping her father.

"Then maybe you deserve this," he said, guiding her back into position.

"Ready? One, two, three. Go!" He shouted and hustled her down the vines, barking orders and inspecting four ties to her one.

"Papa! Stop yelling!"

"Move it! Move it! You're missing some! Go! Go!"

As they reached the end, I turned back to the vine and began checking them, moving as slowly as I possibly could, raising each hand as if a hundred pound weight dangled from my wrist.

"You win!" Arturo announced, holding her hand above her head.

"Stop it. Look at him!" She pointed at me, her breath coming fast.

I huffed and shuffled a slow step closer to them.

"You were right. I knew he was lazy." Arturo wiped the sweat from his brow.

~ ☾ ~

"You're only teasing me. You didn't even try," she said, hands on her hips.

"Oh, no, Lucia. You are so fast. I could never keep up with you. It was impossible to even see you moving. You were like a streak flying down the row." I continued to check the vines, moving faster than she or Arturo ever moved, finishing in half the time it took them.

I stood in front of her grinning. She rolled her eyes and tried not to laugh, sucking in her cheeks like she always did when she couldn't control them. A light breeze blew her soft brown curls and the scent of orange blossoms carried in the wind. My heart ached with sweet longing.

*****

His memory faded from my vision, though his presence within me stayed, gently caressing.

I sighed. "I'd forgotten about that day. I dreamt of it years ago."

"Yes, it's what made me remember. You were so nervous, and your father thought it was hysterical." He laughed.

I rolled my eyes and fought to keep from smirking. "So did you."

"That was the day I realized I was in love with you. And everyday thereafter, I watched and waited until you were old enough to court." He pecked a kiss on my lips. "They were two very long years."

"If I recall correctly, on my sixteenth birthday you followed me around like a puppy the entire day." I giggled.

"You didn't make it easy to discuss the topic." His lips tickled my ear, and a playful warning rumbled.

I squeezed myself closer to him. "Show me something I don't know. Something from your life without me."

His presence cooled and the memory wove to darkness.

*****

My eyes flipped open. *Where am I?* I lay perfectly still, trying to gain my bearings. The sights, sounds, and smells came at me all at once, everything registering simultaneously. The sound of chirping crickets filled the cave. I smelled the stink of sweat and perfume combined with the stench of decaying bodies. In the dark I saw everything: the individual

~ ☾ ~

specks of dirt on the ground, the dead bodies crumpled against the wall of the cave, and the hand that lay draped across me.

I knew instantly, this was not Lucia. The dirty, jagged nails did not belong to my beloved; this was not the delicate hand of my wife. *Who is this? Where is Lucia? What has happened? God, help me!*

Her body moved behind me, coming closer. She ran her nails down my arm and I jumped to my feet, backing away from her as a growl ripped from my throat. *How did I move so quickly? How is this happening?*

I didn't have time to formulate answers. She sprang on me, forcing me to the ground. Her teeth tore into my neck, ripping my throat open. Staggering pain shot from my neck up the entire side of my face, blinding me. I screamed and struggled to push her off, but she was stronger than me. I couldn't break free. She held on, drinking my blood. When she lifted her head from my neck, her eyes burned into mine. She sat up, straddling my chest. "You are mine. I have created you."

Her cruel, hideous face dripped with my blood, running from her mouth down to her chin. Her laugh rattled in the cave. "Finally, my own. My own child to do my bidding."

What's happening? What does she mean? I wrestled my arms free and tried to flip her off me. But she didn't budge. She was far stronger than any woman I'd ever met. *God, help me. What is this monster?*

She licked her lips and without so much as a warning her presence seized my soul. Her depravity moved within me, her voice twisting inside my mind, *I am your mistress. You are mine. Do not bother trying to fight me.* She rocked back. "You will do as I wish, and for now you will love me."

*****

His memory faded, shielding me from what happened next. I kept my forehead against his chest, not wanting to think about what she had forced him to do and unable to look at him. His arms tightened around me, and his cheek rested against my head. "I'm sorry," he whispered. I only nodded, unable to say anything. We lay quiet.

~ ☾ ~

I remembered how Kerina mocked Vittorio for not hunting or embracing his power. Anger boiled in me, again. He squeezed me. "I'm sorry, Lucia."

"She told me you were a terrible vampire, weak. Explain what she meant."

*****

Candles flickered on the altar, sending shadows dancing along the walls. I knelt in the pew.

"Father, forgive me for my existence. Finally, Lord, please bless Lucia. Keep her safe and let her never doubt my love."

Her vile presence touched my soul like a rotting black finger poking at a baby. *The She-Devil is here.*

"What are you doing?" she growled from outside the church. "*Come.*"

I walked to the door. "Forgive me, Father, but I hate her."

"What is wrong with you?" she snarled. "You're wasting your time. *We* are the gods. There is no one to hear your foolish prayers. Embrace your powers. Rejoice in yourself."

Anger rose within me. We'd had this argument many times over. And still she would not, could not accept that we were evil, unworthy of even begging The Lord's forgiveness.

"We are not gods. There is only one God! We are monsters! Abominations! Evil creatures!" I growled the words and struggled to keep from slamming my fists into her face.

She laughed at me, her laugh cruel and cutting. "You are a foolish man. You are immortal. That fact alone makes you a god. Why can't you just embrace your gifts? Enjoy what I have given you." She led me into a darkened alley. "Come. We will hunt. And this time you *will* hunt."

"No. I will *not*."

"You will hunt because I tell you to hunt." She shoved me against the wall. "I'm tired of your childish behavior. You are a vampire. I didn't create you just to chase you around, forcing you to feed. You *will* learn to hunt for yourself."

A low growl rumbled from my chest.

"Shut up. Your growls don't scare me, child." She walked to the end of the alley, watching and waiting for her next meal to appear. A young couple came into view. "Come. I will take

~ ☾ ~

the man. You can have the woman. She's smaller. You should
be able to handle her."

She didn't give me a chance to respond. Instead she
bounded into the street, grabbing the man. She dragged him
into the shadows and began feeding, leaving the woman
screaming in the night. I couldn't move. I didn't want to take
the woman. I didn't want her.

"Damn it, Vittorio." Kerina returned to the woman,
bewitching her. "Silence," she hissed at the woman. Instantly,
the woman's screams ceased. "Take her."

"*No.*"

"Take her, now."

Against my own desires, I moved to her side. The terrified
woman trembled as I held her in my arms. A sensation I
couldn't explain overcame me as I watched the pulse beat in
her neck. I never spoke aloud but I heard my voice calling to
her, encouraging words both seductive and enchanting, the
likes of which I'd never spoken to my own true love. Her
heart pounded against her ribs, strong and wet, and the sweet
scent of her blood filled my nostrils. She surrendered to me,
begging me to take her.

Lowering my mouth to her neck, I sank fangs into her
skin. Her blood, so sweet, quenched my raging thirst. I had
managed to control it until this point. But the taste of her
heated blood in my mouth unleashed my need. The bloodlust
overcame me. My body flushed as her blood moved through
me, filling every one of my weakened cells. I felt alive,
excited. I drank, drawing long and hard on her neck, enjoying
every mouthful. I listened as her beating heart slowed while I
drained her.

When her heart stopped, and there was no more blood for
me to drink, I pulled my lips from her neck and realized what
I'd done. The terrified expression, forever frozen on this small
woman's face, horrified me. I had put it there. Her last
breaths were spent in my arms, in pure terror. *I killed her. I
am a monster.*

Kerina stood beside me, smiling. "Good. You see? This is
what you were meant to do. Come. We'll return to the cave."

I held her a moment longer. My first victim. The first

~ ☾ ~

person I'd ever killed. How could I have done this? What kind of creature was I?

Come, Kerina's voice screamed in my head.

I dropped the woman to the ground and ran to follow Kerina.

It was days before I could leave the cave. I didn't trust myself to be near anyone, fearing I'd kill again.

I refused to hunt with her and had begun to realize my ability to block her mental intrusions. Infuriated, she'd increased her physical attacks in an attempt to force my compliance. In brute strength and speed she remained my equal, and, oftentimes, she was more powerful than I. At one point, she tried dragging me from the cave.

"*No.*" I twisted from her grasp, forcing her off me.

She fell, springing up to attack me. With each advance she made I learned more, studying her every move, painfully learning how to avoid injury and becoming stronger, preparing to someday defeat her. We fought until she gave up. "Fine. Stay in the cave." She stormed off to terrorize some other poor victim.

When she left, I wandered the woods, knowing there hadn't been a hunter in the area for weeks. I listened to the sounds of the forest and watched the owls hunt.

It occurred to me that I could hunt with them. I hunted the large animals, feeding on deer, wolf and wild cats. They didn't taste as good, but I could survive. I *didn't* have to hunt humans.

I can see Lucia again. I won't hurt her. A weight lifted from my chest. My heart beat, filling me with happiness for the first time since I lost Lucia. A reason for existing came to me. *Lucia.*

When I returned to the cave, Kerina waited for me. "Where were you? I told you to wait in the cave."

In my excitement, I naively answered her. "We don't have to hunt humans. We can hunt animals."

"I will not eat animals and neither will any child of mine. You will hunt humans." She pointed to the pile of decaying bodies against the wall. "I've brought you a meal. Now, you will feed." She dragged a sobbing man to my side. "Take him."

~ ☾ ~

Another command from that monster.

My temples throbbed as I fought to resist her order. "Let him go! I don't need him." Pressure descended around me, within me.

Take him. The words pulsed in my head.

"*No.*" I glared into the eyes of pure evil and stood my ground.

The man cried out, "Please, don't hurt me." He clung to my hands, begging for his life.

"You *will* take him." As she yelled at me, the man murmured The Lord's Prayer. His sobbing mumbles were nearly incomprehensible. If I hadn't prayed those same words as often as I did, I would not have been able to understand him.

Her will pushed against mine, forcing my hands to lift the terrified man off the ground. I could not let her control me. My fangs descended, mouth watering at the scent of his fear-seasoned blood.

No. *I will not be forced to kill.*

I left the cave, running as fast as I could to escape her, wishing to be free of her. But in the morning I returned, forced to do so by some invisible power. I may have been able to hold out against many of her orders, but I could not resist her call. No fledgling could resist his master's call. This I'd learned quickly. Kerina made sure of it and proudly taunted me with the fact. I *had* to return to her.

"Well, at least I still have some control over you." She fumed and stomped past me, making sure I saw the body of the man I'd abandoned the night before. By the condition of his throat I knew she'd been cruel to him.

My nails dug into my palms as I balled my fists. *Why hadn't I tried to free him?*

Two humans huddled in the back of the cave, whimpering as they clung to each other. She grabbed one, dragging a girl over to me. "*Feed.*"

"*No.*" My answer was absolute. I knew now I could hold out against her orders.

She lifted the girl. "Fine. If you don't want her, I'll take her. But, I'll take my time enjoying her while her mother

~ ☾ ~

watches. Then I'll take her mother."

The girl screamed and reached for her mother, desperately trying to cling to safety.

My gut doubled up, and I lunged for the child. "Why? Why must you do this? You don't have to hunt them."

Faster than I was able to move Kerina brought the girl's throat to her mouth, ripping her neck open and drinking like a savage while the mother screamed, begging for her daughter's life.

I raced to the mother, intent on saving at least one of them, but Kerina anticipated my move. Dropping the girl, leaving her blood to spill on to the cave floor, Kerina reached the mother seconds after me and wrenched the screaming woman from my arms.

Like a fool, I jerked the woman back, but Kerina did not relinquish her grip. The woman's wild screams of terror stopped as abruptly as a door slams against the wind...

*****

Vittorio's memory spiraled into blackness.

I looked at him, watching as he stared over my head into the night. Having to relive the memories brought back a flood of emotion that he'd managed to control or at least push down deep so that he didn't have to think of it. I felt his disappointment in himself. A self-loathing so cold and bitter it burned.

"Eventually, I decided to hunt with her. I couldn't tolerate her tormenting me," he admitted.

"How often did you hunt? How often do you feed?" I asked. All creatures required sustenance. He had to feed. I knew that plain as I knew *I* had to eat. My mind grappled with the idea of his need versus the terror of a poor victim held hostage and forced to die in agony. And the importance of my destiny became obvious.

"The answers to those questions are very different." He wiped his hand over his face, rubbing his eyes as though to gouge away the memory. "When a vampire is new he must feed more often than a mature vampire. At that time, we hunted daily. When she left me alone, I hunted in the woods for animals. It was amazing that I had such will-power not to

~ ☾ ~

feed with her when I was young."

"Now? How often now?" The image of that small girl screaming for her life flashed in my mind.

He glanced at me, a slight smile softening his expression. Sadness still hovered behind his eyes. "Hmm, less often. Maybe once or twice a week. That is all I need to sustain myself. But, if I'm going out during the day, I feed more often. It's always easier to blend in when we've fed. When we are out and about during the day we may feed a couple times."

I had seen Elizabeth and Peter during the day for long periods of time. Elizabeth had looked normal, beautiful in Vegas. How often had she fed to keep that appearance going? And from whom? She didn't strike me as the animal-eating type. Peter always had the gray day appearance in Boston. He must have fed less than her. But how often?

The idea of vampire feeding rolled around in my mind. I'd always known what they ate. But the idea of them eating to appear beautiful seemed far less acceptable than consumption for existence. "So... you feed to look good?" I tried to keep my voice even.

His fingers played in my hair. "Less to simply 'look good.' More to fit in." His eyebrows raised and he frowned. "You know what we look like when we aren't well fed. Imagine a human's response to seeing that."

He did have a point. I'd seen them in varying stages of not "looking good" and I hadn't particularly liked it. Anyone else would think they had some sort of contagious illness. Or might even guess what was really happening.

Vittorio's fingers traced tiny circles on my back. "When I know I will be tempted by something, I hunt daily to avoid the temptation."

"What would tempt you more than usual? Doesn't your desire for human blood tempt you consistently?" I asked.

"No, not every human is tempting, and some are more than others. It's like if you went to a restaurant. You'd never order something you don't like, but you wouldn't be able to resist something you loved." His eyes fixed on mine. Flecks of gold and green flared in the firelight.

~ ☾ ~

"So, everyday you walk around looking at a menu of people to taste?" I asked, unable to hide the sarcasm.

"No, don't be silly. I don't require human blood daily. I often hunt animals. Although, I admit to enjoying human treats." The corners of his mouth curved, revealing that devilish grin.

I pushed back from him to study his response. "You're kidding me, right?" My voice shot up several octaves. "You don't really think of us as treats, do you?" How could he? How could he have such little respect for us? My mouth hung open, utter shock consuming me. Had he become like Kerina?

"I should have explained to you that, as a vampire matures, he masters the ability to feed without killing his prey." He pulled me back to him, gently stroking my cheek then pushing my hair back from my neck. My skin flamed where his fingers touched me.

"Don't you think the person might be a bit freaked out by a vampire attack? I'm not sure leaving him alive is a better alternative." I wiggled away to study his face while he explained.

Mischievous, that's how he looked. The smile, the playfulness in his eyes. "They don't remember the experience. A masterful vampire can make them think they experienced ecstasy during the encounter, leaving them happy." His voice now carried that familiar confidence as he feathered kisses from the corner of my mouth, along my cheek to my ear, stopping long enough to nibble my earlobe.

I pictured him walking up to some woman, shaking her hand and introducing himself, then biting her neck. She'd have an orgasm, and Vittorio would leave her standing there completely disheveled, but happy.

"Are you able to make your meal have an orgasm?" I asked, sucking in my cheeks. I actually thought that didn't sound too bad.

"I am. But I'm not biting you. You are far too tempting. You are the reason I feed daily. I'd love to drink from you again. But I don't think I could control myself," he said, sternly, gazing deep into my eyes. "If the others had not been with me in the hospital, I probably would not have been able

~ ☾ ~

to stop. I'm sure I would have killed you." The undertone in his voice betrayed him. He knew I was never truly safe with him.

We both knew it.

A twinge of sadness jabbed my heart. I was never truly safe with him. And sooner than I wanted to admit, he wouldn't be safe with me either.

My head rested low on the pillow we shared so I was eye level with his neck. I imagined myself in his arms, head back with his lips caressing to my neck. I wondered what it would feel like, whether it would hurt. It reminded me of my run-in with Samuel and how painful that had been. I reached up to touch my neck.

"Lucia, let me see you." He turned my chin up to face him. "It does hurt for a few seconds, but then it feels very, very good, when it's done well. Samuel is a vicious vampire. He *meant* to hurt you." He leaned down and kissed the invisible scar from Samuel's bite.

I closed my eyes while he softly comforted me, making small circles that covered the entire area. He knew exactly where it was sore. His lips on my neck felt so good. My mind wandered to a memory of him making love to me. A smile spread across my face and he laughed into my neck.

"So you liked that, did you?" he asked between kisses.

"You saw that?"

"*Hmm.* You're still open to me."

"Still hanging around out there." I waved my hand above the couch.

He shifted his head on the pillow so that our noses were only inches apart. My eyes nearly crossed as I looked at him.

"The only thing I want to do more than make love to you is drink from you. At any point, either of these two desires could be number one. They are both primal needs, which is why the lovemaking is so dangerous. Many times vampires equate lovemaking and feeding. They often occur together." An excitement, or was it anticipation, emanated from him. "I've waited three-hundred-sixty years to hold you again. The scent of you, the feel of you in my arms, the taste of your kisses—all these things drive me wild. As you saw, I can

~ ☾ ~

barely control myself." His hand roamed from my shoulder, down my arm, on to my hip and then my thigh. "I need for you to know certain things before we make love. I have to do the right thing."

I grinned. This speech reminded me of the day he told me he hadn't kissed me because he wanted to marry me. I remembered how I felt when he did finally kiss me. That memory left me imagining what it would feel like to finally make love to him again.

~ ☾ ~

CHAPTER FOURTEEN

I rolled over and found myself alone in bed, still wearing my jeans and sweater. Embers glowed in the fireplace. Sunlight streamed through the window onto the empty couch where we had lain. Vittorio was gone. I lay back down, snuggling into the down pillows and comforter.

I had just begun to reflect on his memories when I noticed the painting above me.

I lay back on the pillow to study the image. Vittorio had painted me on the ceiling above his bed. My hair was wild, my eyes mesmerizing, as if they were real, and the expression on my face...very seductive. The painting stopped at my shoulders, which were bare. Thank God he'd stopped there!

The bedroom door opened. "Your breakfast." Vittorio glided in, carrying a tray.

"What am I doing on the ceiling?"

"I like to look at you, if you must know." He bumped the door shut with his hip.

I sat up. "How long has that been there?"

"Many, many years." He placed the tray on my lap. "Bruno insisted that you try his cereal." He frowned. "I also brought rice pudding, coffee, and juice."

"Thank you." The smell of cinnamon and cream rose from the freshly cooked pudding, making my mouth water. I scooped a spoonful of creamy custard into my mouth and savored the sweet, cinnamon-y delight. "It's delicious. Have you really practiced cooking for centuries?"

"Yes." He added a splash of milk to my coffee. "I wanted it to be perfect."

"Well, it is." I leaned toward him and puckered up. "Of course, practicing only three dishes for centuries, I'd expect

~ ☾ ~

them to be outstanding. It never occurred to you try any others?"

"Food, human food, has no appeal to me or any vampire, really. And we don't keep taste-testers around." He raised an eyebrow.

"But you run a business. It didn't occur to you to test some new dishes on your employees?"

"Are you trying to be difficult?"

I smiled. "No. I'm just saying that I'm probably going to get bored with frittata, sausage and lentils, and rice pudding every day."

"I have a gourmet kitchen and, last I recall, you were an outstanding cook. I'm sure you'll do just fine down there." He hitched his thumb toward the door.

"Wait a minute. This is the twenty-first century. The woman doesn't have to spend it in the kitchen." I scooped another bite of pudding.

"I'm aware of the women's movement, love. But, seeing as you're the only one who eats, you'd only be cooking for yourself. I don't expect you to rustle up a dinner for me." He emptied the small glass of milk into the cereal bowl.

The image of him feeding popped into my head. He held a beautiful woman in his arms, caressing her, gently kissing her neck then biting down. She moaned in ecstasy when his mouth began working her flesh.

My breath caught in my throat, and I choked, coughing rice pudding onto the tray.

"Lucia. I was kidding. That's not—"

I shoved the tray at him and jumped off the bed, running for the bathroom. I slammed the door shut and clicked the lock just as he grabbed the handle.

He jiggled the knob. "*Cuore mio*, let me in. You have the wrong idea," he said through the door.

I leaned against the wall, coughing and gasping, tears rolling down my face. He was mine, and I didn't want to share him. I *wouldn't* share him.

"*Cuore mio*, open up. You don't need to be upset. What you imagined won't happen. I love you, only you."

"But I can't...not like other women can." Sobs wracked my

~ ☾ ~

body as I thought about him holding someone else, enjoying her.

"No. No you can't. It's not safe for you or me." He remained quiet for a long moment. "But I don't have to feed from other women. Open up."

I unlocked the door, and he stepped inside.

"I can feed from men when I need human blood." He wiped my cheeks with his thumbs.

"I have no right to stop you from—"

"You have every right. You're my wife. If you're not happy with something, then we'll discuss it. We'll fix it."

"I'm not happy with my destiny," I buried my face in his chest. "But you can't fix that."

"No, Lucia. I can't fix that," he whispered as he held me.

"I don't want to kill you. I don't think I can. I don't think I can kill anyone."

"You're not ready, but you will be. You can't run forever. Besides, you're already making strides."

"What?" I looked at him.

"I saw what you imagined. You were open until you panicked." His lips curved. "You'll be able to do it, when the time comes."

I tucked my head back down. I didn't want to do it. I didn't want to kill him or anyone else. There had to be a way out of this.

"Get cleaned up and meet me downstairs in the parlor. We're going to help you practice calling your power." He pushed me back from him and stepped around me toward the tub. "I'll start the bath. Why don't you finish your breakfast? Please eat some of Bruno's cereal. He's in the kitchen now betting Peter that you loved it. You don't want to disappoint him, do you?"

I walked back to the bed, listening to the running water, unable to comprehend how he could be so damn calm about all this.

*****

The scene in the parlor was odd, to say the least. Sunlight beamed through the French doors, sending prisms of light across the room. Five vampires, each one of them gray, sat

~ ☾ ~

around watching TV and talking about Christmas, not one of them indicating any fear, or even interest, for what might happen. If I hadn't known, I never would have guessed they were waiting to take turns being targets as I practiced calling on the power to kill them.

"Are you sure this is a good idea?" I asked Vittorio as I entered the room.

"Positive." He pulled me onto his lap on a loveseat by the window. "You have to learn to defend yourself."

"Everything will be fine, Lucia," Elizabeth said. She and Alexander sat on the couch, flipping through a magazine together. Peter and Bruno each reclined in chairs, providing colorful commentary on every commercial they watched.

I didn't bother to argue. They seemed pretty well set on being tortured today.

"Let's get started," Vittorio said.

The TV screen went black, the magazine landed on the end table, and four vampires moved to the edges of their seats, staring at me expectantly.

I swallowed hard, desperately trying to find the courage to unleash The Abyss on any of them.

Vittorio gave directions while I stood by his side, trembling. "I'll stand in front of her. The rest of you should be out of her line of vision. I think if only one of us is visible she will have better control."

In a flash, the room emptied, leaving Vittorio and me facing each other. "*Wait.* How long do I have to do this? How will I stop? Where are they going?"

They returned to the room as if they'd never left.

"We'll be listening in the next room, Lucia." Alexander glided toward me. "You won't have long with Vittorio before we intervene. You just need to be able to summon the skill. We'll help you work up to controlling it from there." When he exhaled, the spicy licorice scent washed over me. I closed my eyes and inhaled. Instantly, I stopped shaking, and my heart slowed.

"You can do this," Alexander said.

"I know. I'm just not sure I *want* to do it."

"We shouldn't waste any more time. Let's begin," Vittorio

~ ☾ ~

said. They left the room again, and he turned to face me.

With my cheek pinched between my teeth I stood in front of him, trying to summon the desire to hurt him. Gray as he was, he appeared beautiful to me, making it impossible for me to even try. I turned away from him. "I can't." I clasped my hands behind my neck, wishing this whole situation away.

"You must. It's the only way. You must be able to defend yourself." He caught me by my shoulders. "You must set me free," he whispered into my ear. "You've promised me this. You can't fail us."

My head drooped forward. I knew I needed to do it. I had to learn to control myself and prepare to do what was necessary, no matter how painful it was. I turned around.

He cupped my face. "It will be fine. You're only practicing, and Alexander and Bruno can stop you."

"How do you know? What if they can't?"

"You're not strong enough to be unstoppable. Not to mention you don't actually want to do it. So, you're willing to quit." His encouraging smile amazed me. How was he so brave? Why wasn't he terrified of what we were about to do? He rested his forehead on mine. "It will be fine, *cuore mio*."

"Can't I just wait a few months then put a stake through your heart?"

"You forget. Killing me is only part of your task. If I thought you'd be able to do it then deliver my soul to redemption, I'd say yes. Not to mention I'm much stronger than you. There's no chance I'm letting you put a stake through my heart." He crammed his hands into his pockets. "I want salvation, just not enough to lie down and die. You'll need to master your power to complete the job."

"I could cut off your head," I offered with a frown.

"Not happening. Stop stalling. It's not easy for me to stand here, waiting for your attack, so let's get going." He stepped back and dragged his fingers through his hair.

I huffed, swallowed hard, then every possible thought other than The Abyss crossed my mind. I couldn't make myself think about the power no matter how I tried. While I thought about shoes, New Years Eve, influenza, and my hair, Vittorio stood, patiently waiting. I tapped my foot and looked

~ ☾ ~

around, unwilling to make eye contact with him.

"You do know that I can out wait you on this and any other issue, right?" He sighed. "Just focus on The Abyss."

I didn't respond, just kept looking around, avoiding him.

"Well, if you must be provoked..."

I glanced at him. His eyes were black as night. His face held no emotion. My eyes widened, heart pounding as I stepped away from him. *What is he doing?*

As sure as he was standing in front of me I felt him inside me, hovering, waiting. His presence was powerful, awesome. I waited for him to order me to attack him. But instead of commanding me, he showed me something, someone I didn't want to see, ever. Her savage red eyes glowed against pale skin, and long, golden hair hung over bare shoulders. It was Desiree. She reached for him, moving into his arms.

In an instant, anger pulsed through me. Of all the things he could have shown me, he chose her. How could he do this?

I fumed with rage. Jealousy seared through me, shooting straight to my head. The image of The Abyss, a powerful black void, appeared in front of me. I struggled to breathe, inhaling as deeply as I could, but getting very little air. The black, crushing darkness closed in on me so that my breathing ceased altogether.

I couldn't see. I couldn't feel. My body didn't exist anymore.

In the distance, I heard screaming.

"Lucia. *Lucia*," a voice called. "Sleep."

I awoke disoriented, unable to recall the exact details of what had just occurred, but knowing Vittorio had been in danger. Elizabeth sat on the edge of the couch, holding my hand. "Where's Vittorio?"

She smiled and the couch moved behind me.

"I'm here." He kissed my neck.

I turned to him, surveying the damage. He looked awful. It was late afternoon, a time when he should have looked better, healthier. He should have appeared human, yet his skin was grayer. The deep circles under his eyes sunk into his face. His irises were still dark, nearly black. I touched his cheek. "I'm

~ ☾ ~

so sorry," I whispered as the tears began.

"Stop crying. I'm fine."

How am I going to do this?

I closed my eyes and rested my cheek against his, enjoying the feel of his bristly chin and the idea that it was real, normal, until Elizabeth said, "Okay. It's my turn, Lu."

My eyes popped open, and I leaned back from Vittorio. "No."

"Yes. You have to practice." Elizabeth tugged my arm so that I had to face her.

"I can't hurt you."

"Yes, you can. It will give Alexander a chance to save me." She let her hair fall loose.

I couldn't understand why in the hell she wanted to go through with this, why she felt compelled to put herself in this position.

Alexander squatted in front of me, resting one hand on me and one on Elizabeth. "Lucia, we're going to make you practice whether you like it or not. You have to learn to defend yourself. There will be a time when Vittorio is not here, when we may not be here, but Samuel and Brian will be. You must be able to defend yourself or you will become Samuel's slave. Elizabeth will be fine. I won't let you kill her." His lips parted, revealing a line of perfect white teeth. "I stopped you from killing Vittorio, and I don't even like him half as much as I like her." He chuckled and pulled us both from the couch to stand opposite each other in the middle of the room.

Her big brown eyes beamed at me. Beautiful, silky black hair framed her pretty face. She smiled her most dazzling smile. "Go ahead, Lu. It will be fine."

Again, I could not bring The Abyss. My only thought was of the rapid pounding of my heart. I couldn't summon the image. I had no inspiration. Nothing about her provoked me to hurt her.

"Lu," she said, her voice dark, nearly possessed. Her pupils brimmed with crimson.

I gasped. She stepped closer to me, her fangs exposed.

My breathing quickened. All I could hear were my rapid,

~ ☾ ~

shallow breaths. I lurched back from her.

In one blurred movement her hand shot out, clamping onto my wrist, and she dragged me forward until I was pinned against her body. Entwining her fingers in my hair, she pulled my head back and bowed her mouth to my neck.

I blacked out.

I awoke on the couch, again, my head resting on Vittorio's thigh and my feet on Peter's lap. Elizabeth and Alexander were gone.

"Do you think she remembers anything?" Bruno asked.

"Subconsciously, yes. But otherwise, no." Vittorio gathered my hair away from my face.

I opened my eyes.

He smiled at me. "Good job."

"Is she dead?"

"No. But she's not feeling her best. Alexander took her upstairs to rest." Deep within his eyes flecks of gold and green reflected, as if trying to break through the effects of what I'd done to him.

"Is he mad?"

"Of course not. You're doing a great job summoning the skill. We know that when you're angry or frightened you can call the power to you. We need to work on control." He slid out from under me and left the room.

When the sound of pots and pans being placed on the stove reached the parlor, my stomach growled. "Excuse me."

Bruno pulled Peter and me to our feet. "Come on. Enough forced practice. Let's go try Vittorio's sausage and lentils." He lifted me and zoomed into the kitchen, dropping me on a stool. I swayed and nearly toppled over, but Peter caught me.

"Bruno, you might want to be more careful." As he stood with his arm around me, Peter glowered at Bruno.

"Sorry, Lu." Bruno patted my shoulder a little too hard and shoved me into the counter.

Peter swatted at him and frowned. Bruno jumped back, palms up, mouth open as if struggling to understand what he'd done.

"It's fine." I waved them both away. "It didn't feel like we

~ ☾ ~

were moving, but I guess the ride threw off my equilibrium."

Elizabeth and Alexander appeared out of nowhere. "This is the problem with men. They never think about what they're doing. They just *do*." Elizabeth brought me a glass of water. She placed the butter on the buffet bar and sliced a couple pieces of bread. Black pools had replaced her brown eyes, and the circles under them made her look like she'd been punched. Twice. Looking at her, my eyes flooded with tears.

"I'm *fine*." She rushed around the buffet bar to hug me, squeezing me tight, giving no impression that I'd hurt her or that she was frightened or angry.

I couldn't understand.

"What do you mean 'we just *do*'?" Alexander asked from across the kitchen. He sat on the counter, perusing the mail.

"You know what I mean. You never think about what you're doing first. You just do it, assuming you're right." Elizabeth straightened the canisters on the counter and wiped up some breadcrumbs.

"When have I ever done that? Just because Bruno does it, doesn't mean the rest of us do," Alexander said.

"England," she said, ticking off the locations on her fingers. "Massachusetts in the 1700's. Hollywood. Texas. Do you want me to continue?"

"No, darling. I think you've made your point," he said, flatly.

Elizabeth stood up tall and tossed her head back in a silent victory.

As Vittorio heated my meal, Bruno tasted a spoonful. "Ick," he said, nose crinkled, tongue sticking out.

Vittorio grimaced. "I thought you said this dish was the best of the three."

Bruno laughed. "It is the best. I don't know how she can eat *anything* you cook."

"You just don't like food." Vittorio's typically rock solid confidence wavered.

"I'm sure it's fine," I said. "Since I'm the only one who eats, I should be the judge."

"I don't know. We might need a food-tester to be sure you're safe from food poisoning," Bruno suggested.

~ ☾ ~

I giggled as I watched Vittorio squirm.

Alexander shuddered behind the Boston Globe. His sobering mood shot through the light atmosphere of the kitchen, causing it to evaporate instantly.

"What is it?" Elizabeth walked over to him and peered at the paper. Her mouth dropped open, then snapped shut. "*Oh.*"

"What?" Vittorio placed the heated meal in front of me. His eyes narrowed slightly.

"Lucia's picture is in the paper. They're looking for her everywhere. They think she killed that nurse," Alexander replied.

"What do you mean?" I dropped my fork, splashing sauce from the plate across the counter, and jumped from my seat. Elizabeth and Alexander were huddled reading the front-page article, but I ripped the paper from their hands. A picture of me from the party with the caption "**Fashion Guru Decapitates Nurse!!!**" took up the entire top half of the page.

I dropped the paper, feeling off balance, woozy. "How can they think I killed her? Her head was barely attached to her neck. How could *I* have done that?" My voice cracked. It was bad enough to sneak out on Michael, but to leave a dead woman in the room made everything a thousand times worse. "What am I going to do? How could I possibly explain how she was murdered? My God, they'll send me to jail for the rest of my life."

Vittorio stood behind me with his hand on my shoulder, reading the now crumpled article in his hand. "Lucia, you have to stay hidden. You need to learn about your abilities. Please, please, stay calm."

"Stay hidden?" I paced toward the buffet bar, my palms smashed to the top of my head. "I can't do that. This isn't happening. I could never murder anyone. I don't *believe* this." The image of that poor nurse stuck in my mind. Her head flopped to the side, mouth warped, eyes empty. Blood stained her white uniform down to her waist. The way her body had been twisted, she'd looked like she had been tortured.

~ ☾ ~

I pulled the paper from Vittorio's hands to read the article, my eyes widening the longer I read. "They describe me as psychotic. They actually have a statement from one of the people in the elevator. 'She looked like a crazy woman. Her clothes were torn. Something strange with her eyes. I can't be sure, but it was like they were glowing. I was afraid she would attack *us*.' There's a quote from my boyfriend, Michael, 'She's been so confused these past couple weeks. She didn't know any of us. We think she had a psychotic episode. She's really a wonderful woman, the love of my life. I can't believe she's done this. I feel terrible.'" I balled the paper in my hand and slammed my fist onto the counter. "He actually thinks I killed her. I don't believe this is happening to me." I stared into the room, no longer seeing any of them, mouth agape, and now utterly speechless.

My whole life had flipped upside down in the past couple weeks, and I thought I was managing it fairly well until this moment. Now, I realized some small part of me deep inside had been holding on to the other side, holding on to Michael and my parents and the possibility that I'd wake in my own bed with my old life. Part of me believed I'd go back to them. My stomach turned and became suddenly hollow. The three bites of lentils and sausage rolled around, rising in an awful wave of nausea.

Seeing the article brought that little belief to the surface, and drove home the point that everything had changed. There wasn't going to be a chance to go back. No more Michael, no more Mom and Dad. The pit in my stomach turned to ice.

Tears welled in my eyes, my throat tightening. Another family taken from me, ripped from my heart, more victims of my covenant with fate. An overwhelming sadness gripped me. My life was not my own. It belonged only to fate and to destiny and, maybe, to Vittorio.

"Lucia." Alexander pried the paper from my hands, passing it to Elizabeth. "You have to calm down. You don't know how to control yourself. Remember what happened to Vittorio yesterday." He stood in front of me with his hands on my shoulders.

~ ☾ ~

"Don't make me fall asleep again." The sadness gave way to rage so hot it burned. My words came out like a challenge and I squared my shoulders, ready to fight off any attempt to "calm" me.

"I won't, as long as you keep control of yourself." His full attention was directed at me, his tone unwavering.

"Lucia, you cannot worry about this right now," Elizabeth said. "Remember your destiny. You must master your abilities."

Then it hit me. Where were they when Samuel snuck into my room? Why hadn't someone been with me? If someone had been there, that nurse would still be alive.

From the corner of my eye I saw Vittorio leave the room. "Where are you going?"

"For a walk." The door banged open then slammed shut.

"What's his damn problem?" I shoved a stool out of the way, wanting to hurl it at his head.

"I'll go see." Peter left the kitchen at full tilt.

I leaned back against the counter, arms crossed over my chest. "Why wasn't someone with me that night?"

"We *were* there, Lucia, all of us." Alexander's fingers worked a repetitive pattern on Elizabeth's neck as if she was the one needing to be comforted. "Samuel's attack was well planned and he will stop at nothing to have you. He continues to create more children to command. That night he unleashed eight new vampires in the hospital. We had all we could do to keep them from killing hundreds."

"Vittorio was watching you in your room when the attack occurred. I called him out because we needed help. They were coming up the stairs and elevators. They had attacked a number of people. Alexander and I couldn't keep up with fending off the fledglings. We needed his help to stop them and to alter the victim's memories afterwards." Bruno leaned against the cabinet. His broad shoulders heaved as he sighed.

"He left your side to join the fight. Without him, many others would have been killed. We were lucky that nurse was the only fatality." Elizabeth squeezed Bruno's arm as she moved past him.

"Samuel snuck in through the window after Vittorio left

~ ☾ ~

the room. He was only with you for a few minutes before we sensed your panic. Vittorio returned to you immediately, leaving us to manage the last few," Alexander said.

"He feels terrible." Elizabeth's head dipped and she sighed as though in defeat. "We all do. We should have seen what was happening and taken you from the room sooner." Tears glistened in her sad eyes.

My stomach growled.

Bruno slid the plate toward me. "Lu, why don't you eat? Your dinner's getting cold. It won't do any good to waste it."

I was too angry, too frightened, and too confused to argue with him. I took a bite and chewed angrily. I didn't know how I was going to get out of this. No matter what happened now, there was no way I could go back. I was *not* going to jail.

What about Michael? How could I possibly leave him believing I was a monster, that I had killed that poor nurse? What would he think of me if he did see me again?

Everyone thought I was a murderer, but I hadn't killed anyone. Yet. The fact remained that I was supposed to kill vampires. My very reason for existing. How was I going to accomplish that?

I only managed to eat a few bites. "I'm going to bed." I pushed the plate away and stomped out of the room.

This had to be my worst life. How could any of the others have been this bad?

~ ☾ ~

CHAPTER FIFTEEN

By the time I finished in the bathroom, I wasn't as angry as I had been going in, but I still wasn't happy. The extra time spent washing my hair did ease my throbbing headache, though.

The only light in the bedroom came from the crackling flames in the fireplace. Vittorio lay in bed, waiting for me. He pulled the blanket back and patted the empty spot beside him. My eyes followed the sweep of his arm, glimpsing his chest and the gold chain and cross lying against his skin before returning to his face. His eyes were still dark, but his expression was gentle, less irritated.

"Where did you go?" The edge persisted in my voice even as I climbed in beside him.

"To walk in the woods." He pulled the blanket over me.

"Why?"

"I needed some air." He scooted closer, draping his arm around my waist.

"What did you need air for? You're not the one in trouble. Do you even really breathe?" I asked, still annoyed with him for leaving.

He rested his head in his hand as he looked down at me. Brown, wavy hair circled his fingers. Sparkly flecks of gold and green glittered in the depths of his eyes, and his lips curved to reveal a smile that left me disarmed. *God is he beautiful.*

"This whole thing is upsetting to me. If it wasn't for me, you wouldn't be in this mess. You may not even exist, or maybe you'd have a happy life with Michael." His body stiffened, muscles hardening. Even his lips pulled into a tight line.

~ ☾ ~

An arctic blast seemed to blanket the room. Then, as quick as it came, it dissipated. He pulled me closer, sliding a leg over me. I knew he was certainly upset that I'd been accused of murder and he had left me unprotected. But I also recognized the jealous look on his face instantly. The way his eyes narrowed, the barely perceptible twitch of his left brow, and the set of his jaw.

I sucked my cheeks in, not wanting to add to his irritation. But the idea that he was jealous seemed funny. I had walked through time, dying and returning over and over, searching for him. I was the accused murderer whose life was not her own. In spite of all this, he was jealous. I couldn't help but laugh.

"It's not funny," he said.

I laughed even harder.

"I don't see the humor in it."

"I do. I can't believe you'd worry about Michael."

"Of course I do. Why wouldn't I? He is your boyfriend. You do love him." The vibrating brow froze in a downward slant.

"Yes. He is my friend, and I do love him. But it's very different from the way I feel about you. I don't know what will happen, but I do know I won't leave you. I'll do what I have to do for you," I said, trying to reassure him. "You're my husband. You're the one I'm committed to saving." I rolled onto my side and put my arm around him.

He kissed my lips and sighed. "I never should have left you. I can't believe I let Samuel get to you." He squeezed me tight, his body curving around mine as though to cocoon me away from Samuel and all the dreadful things that had already happened, and the ones that had yet to occur.

I didn't want him to begin the self-reproach that I knew was coming. I changed the subject, trying to sooth his agitation. "Don't worry about it. Just don't do it again. Let's not talk about me anymore. I want to hear more of your story." I *wanted* to stop thinking about my stolen life and work on achieving my goal. Something needed to keep me grounded.

"What did we cover last night?" He stretched a bit, shrugging his shoulders as if to force his body to relax. His

~ ☾ ~

conflicted feelings played across his face; the absolute joy to finally be together again, fear that he'd hurt me, and shame. He'd done many things neither of us would be proud of in the three hundred sixty years he'd spent without me.

"Umm. Oh, we got up to the orgasmic meals." I grinned at him, trying to sooth his worries. "I still want to know about vampires in church, and I want you to tell me what you did after I died." An involuntary giggle escaped me. It was a strange feeling, talking about my own death, when it had already occurred. I mentioned it like I was asking what he did after I left for work, as if it was just a casual comment.

"Hmm. It's not so funny to me," he said.

"I'm sorry. I know it must bother you but—"

"Of course it does," he interrupted. "I can't help but feel guilty for it. The idea of you suffering kills me. I wish I'd saved you the first time."

"Oh, Vittorio. You couldn't. You didn't know how." I ran my hand up his chest. "Now that I'm here with you I don't feel badly at all." My fingers looped in his gold chain. "Well, outside of the utter terror I feel about having to kill you, the fear that I might accidently kill someone else, the idea of Samuel and Brian getting me, and the fact that I've lost another family...I feel pretty good." It was a long list of exceptions and the best option that I could see was to laugh about it, at least a little.

He groaned and rolled onto his back, obviously unamused. I thought it was going to take me hours to bring him back from the edge. "Lucia. I...damn it." I didn't have a chance to respond. He leapt out of bed and stood across the room leaning against the window frame, muscles rippling from the tension.

I followed him to the window and slid my arms around his waist, gently kissing his back. "I'm sorry. I shouldn't have joked that way. I didn't mean to make you feel bad." I trailed soft kisses across his skin, raising goosebumps as I went.

"I know you didn't. But none of it is even remotely funny. I can't tell you how horrible I feel about what keeps happening to you, about our first life together, about you missing out on your current life, about Samuel and Brian and, finally,

~ ☾ ~

knowing that you have no choice but to kill me." Emotions charged his voice: sadness, anger, jealousy, and fear. All of it drenched his words.

I slipped under his arm to stand in front of him, keeping my hands on his waist. "We can't change the past, Vittorio. It is what it is. We have to go forward. We have to figure out how to address the future. *Whatever* may come. Please, stop beating yourself up over it. This constant atonement doesn't make it go away. Come to bed and tell me more about your life without me." With my palms flat on his chest I gave a gentle push.

He didn't budge. The room temperature dropped.

"Vittorio?" I moved closer to him.

He became distant, withdrawing within himself. Silence filled the space between us.

When I stepped back toward the heat of the fire, he moved.

Holding my face in his hands, his eyes roved over me, almost frantic. "Promise me you won't think so lightly of this situation." He searched for the answer, deep inside my heart. The intensity of *him* frightened me. His voice, deep and serious, resonated inside me, "Promise me."

"I promise," I whispered.

He exerted complete power over me, holding me spellbound. His presence inside me expanded until he possessed nearly every inch of me. He moved slowly, touching parts of me that no one had ever touched, seeing pieces of me that I'd never shared with anyone, until finally he settled. As he gently caressed me, holding me to him, softly, tightly, lovingly caring for my entire being, I relaxed.

This was how he told me about the rest of his time with Kerina and the freedom he found after her death. When we finally moved from that spot in front of the window, I knew what had happened during his early years without me.

The memories started in church, All Saint's in Florence, the place where it all began. The taste of festering, bitter anger laced the memories, so raw that my body ached from it. Tears streamed down my cheeks as I considered what he'd endured.

*****

~ ☾ ~

Shadows danced on the walls of the church, cast there by candlelight. Burning incense clouded the air. The scent sickened me. At one time it brought me great comfort, joy. Now, *now*, it just reminded me that I'd never see God's kingdom, never hold my wife again, never be free of this horrible existence.

I couldn't kill myself. I didn't know how, and even if I did, wouldn't God consider me to have forsaken him? Would he forgive me? *I am cursed, damned to walk this earth for all eternity. Damn Kerina. Damn her!*

Deep in thought, I didn't notice someone else arrive for confession. He pulled back the curtain and stepped into the booth. I jumped from my seat and advanced on him. "I'm next." Shoving him back, I entered the confessional. As I sat down and drew the curtain to conceal myself I let out a small breath. *Control yourself.* Growling and flashing fangs at humans wasn't wise.

I slid the panel to the side, revealing the shadow of Father Gabriele. He faced the door, waiting for my confession. His profile appeared the same as usual. And as kind as he'd always been, still I worried how he'd react. "Forgive me, Father, for I have sinned. It's been one week since my last confession." The words flew from my lips.

"Yes, my son. Tell me your sins."

"My heart is filled with hatred, Father."

"What causes this?"

"My mistress. My existence," I hissed.

"What do you mean, my son?" He turned to face the screen between us.

"I should not exist. My life should have ended. Father, help me." My words came harsher than I intended. "I should have died. But she changed me, made me what I am."

"What...are you?" His voice dropped, and the chair creaked behind the screen as his silhouette leaned closer.

"I am evil. I must die. *Help me, Father.*" My plea, barely a whisper, pained and pathetic, rushed from my lips.

"My son, all of God's children deserve to live. As I've said before, I cannot help you die. I *can* help you to find peace in The Lord."

~ ☾ ~

"Peace? I do not deserve to exist." My fingernails cut into my fisted palms. Anger pulsed through me as I thought about my own existence. *I hate myself.*

"What have you done that you do not deserve to exist?"

"I have killed."

Silence hung like a black curtain between us. His breathing changed, breaths coming more quickly, and his heart beat faster. He reacted the same way each time, and yet he never ran from me. I could almost hear him thinking about what to do, wondering if he was safe.

Try to stay calm. You can't upset him. "I will not hurt you, Father. I need your help."

"My son, I *will* help you. Who have you killed?" His tone returned to the calm, fatherly one I'd heard so many times.

"Strangers. No one I knew. But they were all someone's family."

"Of course. And you have killed this week?"

"Yes. I didn't mean to do it. I didn't want to do it. I had no choice. I couldn't stop myself. She forced me." My hoarse voice choked on the words.

"Who?"

"My mistress. She created me, Father. She controls me. I— I cannot explain it better than that. I don't understand it myself. Forgive me, please." My shoulders heaved and I covered my mouth, startled by the loud sobs escaping me.

"My son, your pain is always the same. You must release this hatred. Love in God. Let the Holy Spirit fill you." Father Gabriele commanded as though he had the power to send the Holy Spirit into me. "I tell you this each time."

"I cannot." I wiped my face, scrubbing my sleeves over my cheeks to erase the bloody tear tracks. "The Holy Spirit will not come to me. I live by killing. I survive because others die." It was the first time I'd admitted this to him or even myself.

He sat silent for many minutes and I shifted uncomfortably in the stuffy confessional. *Why does he not speak to me? Is he tired of hearing my confession? How can he abandon me? What is he thinking?* "Father?"

"I...I'm here, m...my son."

He's frightened. Does he know?

~ ☾ ~

He lightly tapped the screen between us. "My son, come with me to the rectory. I want to see you."

I sniffled and cleared my throat, trying to regain my composure. "No. Father, that is not wise."

"I know who you are."

"You do not know me, Father." *You have no idea what I am.* I exhaled, trying to stay calm.

"The blood-drinker took you outside this church just two years ago," he whispered. "Is this correct?"

How does he know? Should I answer? What will he do? Now my breath came faster, my pulse quickening.

"My son, we saved Lucia."

Lucia. My Lucia! My heart raced as heat rushed through my body. "Yes, Father. It was me."

"Vittorio, you have been coming to me every week for the past month, making nearly the same confession each time. Child, what is it you seek?"

The words caught in my throat, nearly strangling me. After a long moment I was able to control myself enough to say, "God's mercy. I want to be free from this, Father. I want..."

"What is it?"

"I want my life back. I want Lucia." My sobs were uncontrollable. I knew I could not stay. He was not safe with me if I couldn't restrain myself.

I ran from the confessional into the street. For hours I ran, until the light of the following day, thinking about what he told me, that he knew who I was. He knew my Lucia. I needed to learn what he knew of her. I couldn't go back to the vineyard, but I needed to know what happened to her after Kerina took me.

The sounds of her screams, "Vittorio! Vittorio, please!" still rang in my ears. Years later, her terrified screams haunted me. When I slept, I heard her voice, crying for me to return and hold her.

The next afternoon, I returned to the church. Keeping in the shadows to avoid suspicion, I watched parishioners come and go. Maybe he wouldn't recognize me if I came during the day. Everyone believed that we only came out at night.

Father Gabriele knelt to pray at the altar. He seemed a

~ ☾ ~

kind old man; he'd saved my Lucia. I knelt in the pew behind him, bowing my head in prayer, not taking my eyes off him. He stood and walked past me. I froze, unable to speak. *What if he is frightened? What if I kill him? I need to speak to him. I need his help, his answers to my questions. Speak to him!*

I listened to his footsteps as he walked toward the door, opened it and stepped out. Coward that I was, I missed my chance. I lay in the pew and cried.

Why, God? Why has this happened to me? What have I done to deserve this? I'm begging you, please forgive me. Please, free me.

"My son," he whispered. Too self-absorbed, too emotional, I hadn't heard Father Gabriele return. He sat in the pew with me. "Vittorio, let me help you."

"How, Father? How can you help me?" I raised my head, expecting him to run, to scream when he saw the bloody tears streaming down my gray skin, the dark circles beneath my eyes and the fangs descending from beneath my top lip.

"Through Our Lord. You must turn to him for help." He sat beside me with confidence, showing no sign of fear.

"Aren't you frightened?"

He placed his hand on my shoulder. "You are not like the others. None have come for help. None have confessed their sins. None have turned to God."

"My guilt is so...overwhelming. Hatred is all I feel." I sat up to look at him. His gray hair was thin, and the deep wrinkles on his face only added to his gentle demeanor, giving me hope. "Tell me about Lucia." I leaned closer, one hand on the pew in front of us. "Tell me what you know of her."

"We rescued her from the blood-drinker, but she only remained overnight. Her horror was unmanageable. She refused to believe that you had been killed. She thought she would have known if you'd died. I guess she was correct." He looked directly into my eyes, undaunted by my haggard appearance.

Amazing. I've never seen a human look at me without terror.

"Where did she go? Back to the vineyard? Did her parents

~ ☾ ~

come for her?" *Tell me she didn't try to go alone. What if another of my kind captured her?*

"She did not go back. She left with Maximillian and his wife, Elsa. They are the slayers who have been tracking the one that took you. Now, Lucia tracks with them."

"*No.* God, no. She can't do this. It's too dangerous for her." *What have I done? I can't let her do this.* "Father Gabriele, where are they? I have to know. I have to lure Kerina away from them. She will kill Lucia."

He shook his head and sighed. "I don't know where she has gone. I think they tracked you into the mountains. But, Vittorio, she has sworn to save you, sworn to set your soul free."

My head pounded as if my brain would explode. "She is not strong enough. I can't see her. I can't control my urges. I can't trust myself not to kill her. My desire for her is nearly uncontrollable." My vision blurred and my stomach turned. She was in danger, had put herself on a course with death. *How can I save her?* I squeezed my temples, aiming to stop the excruciating pain, to clear my vision.

"She is not the same woman you knew. She is stronger, driven, angry. She will stop at nothing to save you, to avenge you." He reached out to touch my shoulder. "Vittorio, you must turn to God for guidance. Let him help you."

"Where was he that night? Why did he let this *happen?*" I howled. "*Why?*" My voice thundered in the empty church, bouncing off the ceiling and coming back to us. I pointed at the crucifix, wishing He'd answer me. *What do you want from me?*

I slumped to my knees, resting my head on the back of the pew in front of me, and fell silent. I could think of only one thing, only one way to keep Lucia safe. "I must kill Kerina. Then I will leave this country, flee from Lucia so I can't hurt her. That is the only way to ensure her safety."

"In all these weeks of confession you have not been able to kill Kerina. How will you do it now?"

"I don...I don't know." Tears formed again. He was right. I hadn't been strong enough to do it. "I *have* to kill her. I have to be free from her. She controls me, forces me to do evil, to

~ ☾ ~

kill. She will force me to kill Lucia. I can't let it happen."

As I sat sobbing in the arms of the priest, the bravest man I'd ever met, *she* called for me, *Vittorio*. Her evil, twisted voice wound its way through my mind, stinging me with every note.

I hate her. "I must go, Father Gabriele. She calls and I must return to her." I lifted my head from his shoulder.

"Go, my son. Do what you must, but return to this church whenever you can. Sister Marie and I will help you find your way back to God."

I ran back to Kerina, bracing myself for a fight. She would be angry, incensed that I had spent time in the church. I couldn't let her learn about Lucia or the priest. *Tonight I will break free of her. She will command me no more.*

She met me at the entrance of the cave.

"Where have you been?" The cave reeked of her foul stench.

"Out."

"*Where?*"

"*Out.*"

She sprang at me faster than usual, striking my face when she reached me. Her nails scratched across my cheek, ripping my skin open. I fell against the ground and she jumped onto me, clawing and punching. We rolled around on the cave floor until I landed on top.

As if transformed into a rabid animal, her eyes flared and her lips tightened over her fangs. I pulled my fist back, ready to smash her face. In the blink of an eye, she changed. Her face smoothed, eyes wide, fangs disappearing. "Vittorio, please. Let's not fight." She appeared so small and fragile.

My mind raced.

What am I doing? I can't hit a woman.

She's no woman. She's a monster. Hit her.

"Vittorio, I'm sorry. I don't want to fight." Her soft voice sounded sweet and sensual.

I blinked to be sure she was the same woman. *How can she be so gentle?* I dropped my fist and rolled back, staring at her.

Immediately, she pounced on me with a rage-fueled

~ ☾ ~

strength. She bit me, tearing my skin open. "*Fool.* Stupid *child.* You cannot beat me. I took you once, and you are mine forever," she screamed and laughed as I reeled back from her blows and crashed into the wall.

I bolted toward her, infuriated by my own stupidity. Attacking her with a new ferocity, I struck as hard as I could until I sent her sprawling backward to smash into the wall. Blood gushed from her head, and she bounced back, but I was ready. When she reached me, I spun to the side and caught her by the neck, twisting and pulling. Her bones cracked, and her blood ran through my fingers. Her screams abruptly stopped. I dropped her limp body to the ground and relished a bittersweet sense of triumph.

I am free.

*****

Vittorio shifted, sliding one arm around my waist as he held me immersed in his memories. I leaned into him, not bothering to even try to stop the tears, and needing him to hold me.

"Lucia, I left her, thinking she was dead. It was Father Gabriele's words that inspired me to escape. Knowing that you had traded your life on the vineyard to try and save me gave me the strength to leave her."

I compared Vittorio's memory of the fight with what Kerina had told me. He had been too kind, too naive as a fledgling to realize what he needed to do to be free. He wasn't really a killer at that time. He was still too human. Even now he didn't understand what had happened.

The final memory he shared was from years later and brought on a feeling of desperation so overwhelming it flooded every other emotion from me. My heart thudded heavily against my chest, and I barely kept from crying out.

*****

Nine years had passed since that horrible night in Florence and not a day had gone by that I hadn't thought of Lucia. Each evening, after the sun had set in the horizon and the stars lit the darkened sky, my mind replayed our last moments together. Her soft squeal of delight at the opera. Her sweet kiss at the fountain. The way she nestled against

~ ☾ ~

my body, snuggling into me for warmth. My wife. My only love.

I can no longer resist my need for her. I must find Lucia.

Father Gabriele said she had come back to the church months ago, but he'd had no word from her since then. She killed Kerina years ago. I'd have never believed my Lucia strong enough to defeat Kerina, but then, I'd have never believed our lives would become so distorted, so horrific.

I tracked her scent, the sweet aroma of honey and orange blossoms, all over Florence, into the mountains and back to the cave, but I did not find her.

Now, I roamed the mountainside searching for her. Only three days ago I picked up a trace of her along the hillside and followed her scent to the ledge, where it ended. I ran back to the hill but found no evidence of her. How could this be? She couldn't have vanished. I returned to the ledge, confused. Then I noticed the tracks. Wolves. On my first pass through this area I had been driven to find her, consumed by the knowledge that she was near. I'd tracked her through this wooded area where animals roamed and attached no importance to the scent of the wolves. In fact, I didn't even notice them.

I traced the steps she took to find...*Oh, God. No!*

Her broken body lay crumpled at the bottom of the ravine. In the pit of my stomach my entire being twisted. I jumped from the ledge, a drop that seemed to last hours until I landed, and each step toward her poor, broken body seemed an eternity.

Blood had dripped from her mouth to dry in a dark line down the side of her cheek. Her cracked lips bled. Dust caked in the tear tracks running down her face. Her shallow breathing was barely audible, though her chest shuddered with each breath.

"No. God, no." I carefully pulled her cold, frail body into my arms, trying not to cause her any more pain. "Lucia."

Her beautiful eyes blinked open. Even as the light behind them faded I was drawn to her, unable to look away.

My heart pounded. She was dying, soon to be gone from me forever. "I don't want to hurt you, *cuore mio.*" I blinked

~ ☾ ~

back tears as I pushed her hair away from her face. The pain should have been agonizing when I moved her, but she didn't make even a sign that she was hurt.

A comforting warmth surrounded me, moving through me. She slipped her arm around my neck and held me. My heart slowed.

I pressed my lips to her neck and felt her last breath leave her body. Then her eyes closed in eternal sleep.

"*No!*"

I howled for hours, tormented by my loss. I held her all night, rocking her body, begging her to return. "Please, Lucia. Please, you can't leave me."

When the first light of dawn broke, I carried her body to a place beneath a tree and buried her. "May God's perpetual light shine upon you, Lucia."

Losing her was the worst experience of my entire existence. I thought I'd lost her that night in Florence, but this was not the case. I'd truly lost her this night, the night God stole her from me.

*****

When he released me from this last memory, my legs buckled, and I nearly fell to the floor. He caught me and carried me back to the bed, where we lay together as I stared at the image of myself, considering all that I had learned. He lay on his side watching me, his presence pensive and comforting.

After several minutes, he broke the silence. "Lucia, Kerina never explained any of the gifts to me. She never told me I was capable of saving anyone from death, never explained that we did not have to kill or force this dark existence on to others. She didn't believe in the idea of only taking what you need to survive. She ravaged, a true glutton, taking all that she wanted." His words dripped with disgust.

He paused a moment and a tender smile appeared. "Maybe she never knew that I could save someone," he said softly. "I don't know. Maybe she couldn't. Maybe she was too rotten to save anyone."

A familiar air of protection moved around me, holding me tighter to him. "If I had known, if I'd understood, I would

~ ☾ ~

never have let you die that day in the ravine. I would have saved you so that you could set us free. I would never have allowed you to suffer like this," he murmured.

"I know, Vittorio." A tear ran down my cheek as I thought of all the years he had endured, believing that he could have saved us both if he'd only known how.

He kissed my lips. Deep within me, the ache pulsed. I closed my eyes. From the moment I went into The Light to see Father and Mother, I knew this time would come. I touched his cheek. "Vittorio, I'm so sorry."

"No, *cuore mio*. It wasn't your fault. There was nothing you could have done." He kissed my head and tucked me closer to him. "We had no choice."

The ache surged. My chest tightened, and my breath hitched in my lungs. "You don't understand. You don't remember." I sat up and looked away.

"What? I remember as if it happened only yesterday. I just showed you the exact memory." He sat next to me. "What's wrong?" His arm circled my waist and he pulled me into him.

"Vittorio, there's more to that memory. You just don't realize it." I slipped out of bed and paced in front of him. Telling him would change everything. His guilt for not saving me was tremendous.

When he learned what really happened, he might never forgive me.

~ ☾ ~

CHAPTER SIXTEEN

"Amor non lega troppo eguali tempre."
~Gozzzano
Love does not temper with equal force.

"You don't *really* know what I'm supposed to do." The drum beating inside me made it difficult to think. I couldn't bring myself to look at him. Pacing around the room, I finally paused in front of the fireplace. An occasional flare from the dying embers sparked.

"Lucia, I know you must free me. We've discussed this already. You've been reincarnated ten times to find me, to kill me." He knelt in front of the fireplace and tossed a couple logs on the fire, stoking it until the flames roared and heat poured into the room. "Stop worrying. I understand. I know what a Pharo does."

The pounding beats sped. I stood behind him, afraid to be away from him. "More than ten times, and not just you." My eyes glazed until the orange and yellow glow from the fire blurred.

He turned from tending the hearth to look at me. "What?"

I closed my eyes, unable to face him. "I've existed for thousands of years, not hundreds."

"What?" He stood. "What are you talking about?"

"I didn't become a Pharo because of you. I've always been a Pharo," I said, finally looking at him, forcing myself to see the heartbreaking confusion appear on his face.

His mouth dropped open as his eyes widened. "What do you mean? Not...No." He stumbled away from me.

Momentarily frozen in place, watching his befuddled response, I could only nod the confirmation.

~ ☾ ~

He grabbed his stomach as though I'd just punched him.

My heart pounded as I rushed toward him, wanting to take it all back, to erase everything that had *ever* happened. "Vittorio..."

"Samuel hunts you because of me." He backed toward the couch. "He wants to possess your power. He thinks he can rule all vampires if he controls you." He sat down, leaning on his elbows. "I've endangered you, led him right to you." He clutched his head between his hands. "What have I done?"

I knelt in front of him, pulling his hands from his face. "No, Samuel hunts *you* because of me. And he *could* control all of you if he captured me."

His brows creased and he looked past me. "I...I don't understand this. What are you supposed to do? I thought you had to kill me to redeem both of us."

The words spilled from my lips. I wanted him to understand, needed him to grasp why I'd allowed this to happen. "When I met you in Italy, I fell in love with you. Before meeting you there was never anyone I loved, no one to claim my heart." I touched his chin, bringing his gaze to mine. "I lived each life, did my duty, died, and started again. Then you came along and everything inside me changed. When you were taken and created, I couldn't bring myself to kill you. I couldn't lose you." I squeezed his arm.

He stared at me in silence, emotions flickering across his face. The energy in the room pulsed around me. Confusion. Fear. Sadness. Anger. He stalked to the window. "You let me live."

"Yes."

"That day in the ravine, you could have killed me, but you let me live." He watched me in the glass.

I stepped toward him. "Vittorio, I—"

He spun to face me, fangs extended, eyes black as The Abyss. "You could have given me salvation, but you let me live."

"I loved you. I couldn't—"

"You could have saved me." He charged me. I backed away, putting the couch between us. "You *chose* to condemn me to this life." His voice boomed. "You didn't love me. You

~ ☾ ~

couldn't possibly, or you'd never have done this to me." The couch flew into the wall, cracking the plaster. His ardor churned in a wild torrent. He ripped down the mantel from above the fireplace.

He's wrong. It wasn't like that. "Vittorio. I wanted to be with you. I want you with me forever. I can still bring you to The Light." I reached for him, my power prickling along my skin, The Abyss hovering, just outside my grasp, beckoning me to call on it.

"*Don't.*" The wooden mantel slammed into the wall above the fire, and flames shot out from below. "You condemned me to walk in shadows. I created others. I *killed*. All because of you." Like a wild beast he charged toward me and I forced myself to stay still. "You could have stopped me from doing these evil things. Instead, you were *selfish*." He screamed the words at me. Gripping my arms, he picked me up so my feet left the floor.

My heart hammered and my body trembled. His anger consumed him, terrifying me. In all our time together I'd never seen him like this. "No." I shook my head, tears welling in my eyes.

"Selfish." He threw me across the room onto the bed and stormed out.

I lay motionless, staring after him. Outside the room, the sounds of his anger rattled the quiet house. Glass shattered, plaster cracked and sprayed to the floor, he howled in anguish. Finally, a door slammed, and silence returned.

I lay, sobbing. I loved him. I hadn't sought to condemn him; I just couldn't bear losing him. All of the heinous things he'd done, he'd done because of me. I was to blame for his torment, for his lost soul, for the shadow within him.

What should I do next? Stay and wait for his return, hoping he'd forgive me, even help me? Should I go to meet Samuel alone? *Am I ready?* My power barely acknowledged the danger of Vittorio's rage. I couldn't go alone.

I needed Father and Mother, but I didn't have the strength to get to them.

Trapped, weakened to the point of utter dependence on the very beings I'd sworn to kill, I cried until exhaustion took

~ ☾ ~

me and nightmares replaced the horror of my reality.

*****

The Abyss called to me, begging me to return. Silence rose, and the iron chains of destiny bound me. In the distance, the fading memory of my life dimmed to darkness. Suspended in the familiar calm, I waited to hear my own shallow breaths, knowing that my breathing would stop, and the screaming would begin. The screams of a woman tormented, a woman standing on the precipice of life, poised to lunge into the utter blackness of death. My screams.

"VITTORIO! PLEASE!" I howled.

Searing pain burned my throat, threatening to consume my entire body.

"*Help me.*" My cry slashed through the darkness.

Death lingered in the shadows.

The sound of my racing heart pounded in my ears. The little bit of air that passed to my lungs ripped through my throat, fanning the flames.

I tried to raise my hands to protect myself, but he stopped me.

"Lucia, drink. It will help." Coldness hardened his voice. He wasn't as calm as usual. Something was wrong. "*Drink.*"

He touched my lips. Liquid as thick as honey and just as sweet dripped into my mouth, coating my tongue and throat, soothing me as it stopped the burning. I moved my tongue, trying to recognize the flavor and feel of the elixir.

My mouth latched onto his forearm. An eager moan slipped from my lips as my teeth cut into his flesh. I tore open his skin, and my mouth flooded with his blood.

He lurched away from me, and I jerked him back, sucking as hard as I could. I wasn't finished. I was greedy. I wanted more, *more*. I wanted it all. *Give it to me!*

"Easy, Lucia. I'm not going anywhere." His deep, sexy voice added to my pleasure. The way my name rolled off his tongue excited me. His accent always made everything sound sexier than it was. I wanted to yank him down on top of me and make love to him.

I remembered the last time we made love, the sound of his breathing, the smell of his body, the taste of his kisses, the

~ ☾ ~

feel of him inside me. It all came back to me, all at once. I sucked harder and faster.

My hips moved, wanting him on top of me. I wanted to let go of his arm and pull him down, but I couldn't. I couldn't take my mouth off him. He tasted divine. I couldn't waste even a drop of him. I had to have all of him. I needed him.

I sucked until my jaw hurt. My cheeks barely worked. My tongue was raw from licking his open flesh. I couldn't stop myself. My drinking slowed, but didn't stop.

I began to orient to my surroundings. There was no way I could have pulled him down on to me. He wasn't in front of me at all. I was lying against him, comfortably cradled in his arms, my head resting on his chest.

This time my satisfied moan was softer than the last one. I could barely drink another drop. My grip loosened. His arm pulled away from my mouth, and I let it go, dropping my hands to my lap, exhausted. "Vittorio?"

"Yes, *cuore mio*?"

"I don't feel good."

"No. You won't for a while. Go to sleep."

"What? Why don't I feel good? I'm too full."

"It's the process. It takes time. You'll feel better when you awaken."

My stomach gurgled, my throat burning again. My body hurt everywhere, like thousands of needles jabbing into every inch of me. "Vittorio, help me. Make it stop. *Please*." Tears seeped from my tightly closed eyes. As I rolled onto my side, he followed, wrapping his arms around me.

A monstrous groan ripped from my chest, I felt like I was going to vomit, violently. My stomach churned. I was afraid I'd have diarrhea and vomit at the same time. "Vittorio. *Help me.*"

"You'll be fine, Lucia. This will pass. Then you'll sleep."

"Why is this happening? Why did you let this happen?"

"It's the only way." He squeezed me tighter.

As wave after wave of nausea subsided, torrents of excruciating pain rolled over me. Needles pricked at me, harder and harder, deeper and deeper, making it impossible to relax. A fire raged in my throat. I thought for sure I'd be

~ ☾ ~

engulfed in flames. Sweat poured off me. I cried, begging for
sleep to take me, begging to die.

He didn't respond to my cries, just held me tighter against
his chest as he kissed my head. His sweet breath felt good
against my flaming body. I inhaled as deeply as I could,
smelling him. Even with the pain and nausea, his scent was
wonderful. He smelled of the vineyard: like the outdoors, like
sun-kissed grapevines. Between the waves of agony I knew I
wanted him, needed to have him. I was ravenous for him.

Finally, my body stopped. Everything just stopped. The
convulsing, the nausea, the needle pricks all stopped. Even
my desire for him ceased. I felt nothing. I lay there unable to
move, or open my eyes, or even breathe.

My inability to breathe frightened me. I tried to inhale. No
air moved. I listened for the pounding of my heart. It should
have throbbed loudly. But my heart didn't flinch.

Did I die?

"You did not die, Lucia. You will be fine. *Sleep*," he
commanded. His presence moved inside me, but it wasn't the
one I had come to recognize and love. Not the desirous
passion I longed to feel. This was the other one, the one that
frightened me, the powerful one that could crush me,
stamping me out with just a thought.

*Why is that one back? What have I done? Why has he
become that one?*

"*Go to sleep.*"

The need to obey him overwhelmed me. Those words
invaded every cell of my being, giving me no option but to
comply. I simply relaxed against him and slept.

My eyes opened to the darkness of a cave. It was pitch
black, yet I saw everything. Each speck of dirt on the ground
was clearly visible. The carvings on the wall twenty feet away
were plain as day. Feet stomped near me, and I turned in the
direction of the sound. Ants moved. I watched and listened,
astonished, as they marched to their holes.

Vittorio's breath breezed across my neck, bringing my
attention back to him. When I rolled over, my movements felt
odd, out of order, as though I was moving too fast.

~ ☾ ~

The sight of his face thrilled me. The green and gold flecks of his eyes shimmered while his hungry smile flashed in the darkness. Wavy brown hair fell softly down his neck.

I wanted him. I ripped his shirt open and tried to pin him to the ground. But he pushed me onto my back and pressed his lips to mine, kissing me with such fervor I thought he might crush my lips. He undressed me and was on top of me in seconds.

We made love on the dirt floor of the cave, and, for the first time, I was not worried about anything. All I could do was enjoy him. He was perfect. Enveloped in his aroma, I closed my eyes to better savor it. His kiss tasted as sweet as a grape just plucked from the vine on a sunny autumn day. His calloused hands moved across my body, punctuating my rapture.

Our bodies shuddered with ecstasy as we climaxed together. His breath fanned my face, then my chest as I arched my back in his arms. "*Vittorio.*" We shared the most beautiful experience of my life. I wanted it to go on forever.

But it ended, abruptly.

Pain shot from my throat straight to my heart when his teeth ripped through my neck. I screamed and tried to push him off me. "Vittorio, *no. Why?*"

He did not answer immediately. Instead, he drank in long, slow swallows. He only took a few sips of me, but it was enough. Lifting his head, he stared into my eyes. "You are mine. I am your creator. You are my child."

My mind raced. *What is he saying? What does he mean? What could this...Oh God.*

"You created me? *You created me?*" Panic gripped me.

"Yes." The answer was absolute. No going back. No way to reverse courses.

"I'm a vampire?" I screamed and I shoved him off me.

Standing in the dark cave, naked and shaking, unable to accept what he had said, I listened to my soul howling its angst.

Then I crumbled to my knees, unable to bear the weight of eternal damnation.

~ ☾ ~

CHAPTER SEVENTEEN

"Lucia. *Lucia.*"

"No. *No.*" I shoved at the hands pawing at me.

"Lucia, wake up. You're fine." The fragrant scent of gardenias filled the air. *Elizabeth.* "You were dreaming."

I lay gasping, sweat pouring from my body. *That wasn't a dream.* It was a fantasy, a very dark fantasy. Vittorio's aura had opened to me, shown me his deepest desire- to create me into a vampire. *Father was right. I can't trust him.*

"You're safe, really." She moved to hug me.

"Don't touch me." I crawled backward on the bed to the headboard and hugged my knees into my chest.

She put her hands up. "Okay, okay." She glanced to her left.

Alexander and Peter stood behind her. No one moved.

"What do you want?" I peered at them through a curtain of hair. Could I trust any of them?

"You screamed. We came to check on you." Elizabeth folded a leg and sat at the foot of the bed. "What were you dreaming?" Her eyes shifted, and Alexander placed a hand on her shoulder.

"Nothing. I don't want to talk about it." I didn't know how to explain what I'd seen, that I'd glimpsed into Vittorio's soul, seen his deepest desire. He wanted us to be together as intensely as I did, but for what reason? Did he love me or did he want to control my power?

"You're safe. I promise you. You're safe with us." Alexander squeezed Elizabeth's shoulders, though his gaze didn't leave mine.

"Where is he?" I was still open to him, reaching for him, reaching but not touching. I couldn't figure out how to shut it

~ ☾ ~

down, how to pull back. A part of me wanted to be with him. Actually *needed* to be with him.

"Gone. He and Bruno left," Peter said.

"Where?" How far would my own spirit travel for him? When would I feel him again?

"He hasn't decided. Bruno's trying to calm him down. To bring him back." Peter stood at the edge of the bed. "You know about Bruno, don't you?"

I didn't respond, too overwhelmed. *What have I done? Peter.*

"He has the ability to influence other vampires."

"To an extent," Elizabeth added. "He cannot make them do something that is completely beyond their capability or their own conscience."

"Right. He can't make a vampire kill someone unless that vampire is already headed down that path." Peter paced the length of the room, bending to inspect the couch lodged in the wall. "He'll stay with Vittorio and help him through this... situation."

"He told you?" Shame washed over me. I couldn't bring myself to look at Peter. I was the reason he hadn't received salvation. He and Bruno. If I'd taken Vittorio to The Light, neither of them would have been created vampire.

"He couldn't keep it from me or Bruno. We're his children. Our bonds are very strong. This sort of emotion can't be hidden." He ran his hand over the mantle jutting out above the fireplace.

I should have known. "I'm so sorry," I mumbled, choking back tears. He hadn't been given the chance for redemption when he was human. Now, when his chance came, it would most likely be at my hand.

He sat on the bed and pulled me into a hug. "This will work out. I promise you, some way or another, it will work out." He held me long enough for me to pull myself together.

Once my sobs had subsided he pushed me away from him. "This is so unlike you. I'm not sure how I feel about it." I glanced into his face. He looked grayer than usual, and the dark lines under his eyes dug further into his skin. "I'm not prepared for you being all mushy. I'm used to you barking

~ ☾ ~

orders and telling me you hate me. This is...hard to take."
That familiar cocky smile snuck across his lips.

I swiped at tears on my cheeks. "I don't really hate you."

"Are you sure? I sort of enjoy your venom." He raised an
eyebrow and the smile plastered itself in place.

"Yeah." I sniffled.

"In that case, you should know that the plan for today was
to get a tree. We still need a tree, so let's get a move on." Peter
smacked my leg.

"A tree?"

"Oh, yes. A Christmas tree." Elizabeth slipped off the bed
to stand beside Alexander. "Get dressed and meet us
downstairs. Dress in layers. We're traveling north." She
pulled Alexander toward the door, and they left.

"It will be fun. And you could use a little fun," Peter said,
heading toward the door. "I'd close it, but he smashed it into
the wall when he left. If I pull it out..." He peaked behind the
door.

"Don't bother. I'll change in the bathroom." I blew out a
breath and headed for the closet.

*****

Alexander and Elizabeth sat inside a Range Rover parked
in front of the house. Peter waited for me beside the truck,
leaning against the door and tapping his cell phone, looking
like a model even in a flannel shirt over a thermal, jeans, and
workman's boots. His blond hair moved in the wind.

"Has he contacted you?" I pulled on my gloves.

"Don't worry. Bruno will bring him back."

Just what I wanted to hear—my husband required
'influencing' to return to me.

I hurried past Peter into the back seat, afraid I'd crumble
to the ground if I looked into his blue eyes.

The outside of the house was styled like an old Victorian
with a steeple on the left side and a wrap-around porch. The
windows were large, but not even half the size of the ones in
the back. I had a feeling the front and the back of the house
didn't match at all. The garage sat off to the right with a blue
mustang parked in front.

"Whose car is that?"

~ ☾ ~

"Bruno's." Peter glanced toward the mustang. "The girls love fast cars." He waggled his eyebrows.

"Even vampire girls?"

"Especially vampire girls." He sat back, resting his left ankle on his knee.

I rolled my eyes. One thing was for sure. Boys were boys no matter human or otherwise.

Trees lined the drive like a fortress wall, making it nearly impossible to find the exit to the road. As we bumped along the unpaved drive, winding our way to the end, I imagined Sleepy Hollow and the Headless Horseman riding up the path. The sound of the trees scraping along the roof of the truck added to the creepy effect.

"How long is the driveway?" I asked once we reached the road.

"About a mile," Alexander answered as we pulled out of the drive and headed north. "It will take about an hour to get to the forest. Then we'll hike a short distance to find our tree."

"So we're not going to a tree farm? Is it legal to just cut down a tree anywhere?" I asked.

Peter smirked when a message appeared on his phone. "We're going so far into the woods, no one will notice." He didn't look up from his phone, just continued tapping away.

"Did you bring a saw?" I could just see us going all that way and then having a *Christmas Vacation* moment when we realized we had no way of cutting down the tree.

"Are you kidding? Of course we have a saw. Not that we wouldn't get a tree without one." Peter finally looked at me, a sly smile playing across his face. I couldn't tell if it was my question or whoever he was texting that amused him.

I sat silent for the next thirty minutes, concentrating on the Christmas tunes coming from the radio and trying not to think about what had happened last night or the nightmare that followed. Where had Vittorio gone? And would he return?

Peter's rapid-fire texting drew my attention. It took all I had not to beg him to tell me where Vittorio was. I rested against the window, watching the scenery fly by, wishing I

~ ☾ ~

had the telepathic link to Vittorio. Peter grinned as he tapped the screen. A picture of a blond beauty appeared on the display.

"Who's that?"

"Angela." He hummed a couple bars along with the radio.

"Who's she?"

"A friend." His tone made it clear she was more than a casual friend.

"Does she know...about you?"

"Yes. She's one of us." He glanced at me for a second, grinned, and went back to texting.

"Does she know Vittorio?"

He tucked the phone into his shirt pocket, slid across the seat, wrapped his arm around me and squeezed. "He'll be back."

I frowned, not quite sure I believed him.

When we reached the forest, we turned off the main road onto a barely passable dirt lane and drove into the woods for another forty minutes, stopping in front of a grove of giant pine trees. "We'll walk from here. Keep your eye out for a tree," Peter said.

This experience was far different from all the others I'd had. I was used to going to a tree farm and either picking out one to cut from a row lining the field or choosing one from the freshly cut trees near the parking lot. I had never actually driven into the forest to find a tree. Judging from the excitement, this was a competition. I leaned against the truck and watched as they gathered together to plan the selection process.

"Okay, we need something big, about ten feet tall and at least five feet wide." Elizabeth's hands spread out in front of her. "I don't care as much about the shape. It doesn't have to be perfect, but I have to be able to shape it into perfect, so no gaping holes. I want to hang as many ornaments as possible, so no super-tight branches either." She rested one hand on her hip and waved the other toward the trees.

As she described what she wanted, I realized she was giving them their running orders. She was clearly going to kick back and relax while they hunted down a tree. They

~ ☾ ~

rolled their eyes and Alexander silently mimicked her speech.

"Elizabeth, why don't you consider—" Peter began.

She shot him a look of daggers. Apparently, making suggestions was not acceptable. "I just told you what I want. I don't need to consider anything else." Her Greek accent made her fast retort slightly difficult to understand. "Okay, off you go." She waved them away, grabbing my hand and pulling me in the opposite direction from the grumbling tree crew. "Come on, Lu. Let's spend some time together."

"Is this how it is every year?" I asked, laughing at the idea of her ordering them around.

"No, usually I go with them and crack the whip. This year I'm giving them some freedom." She chuckled. "They really are good. I've only had to send them back a few times."

We walked through the pine needles and leaves. The forest smelled mossy, and the brisk air nipped at my skin, but under the trees very little snow lay on the ground.

My mind wandered to Vittorio. Where was he? Would he forgive me? What would I do if he didn't?

Elizabeth hooked her arm through mine. "Stop worrying. It will all work out according to God's will. You have to believe in that. We have, and it finally brought you to us."

I blinked and nodded, unable to convince myself.

"*Stop*. You'll only scare yourself," Elizabeth said, squeezing my arm. "Let's talk about something different, something to make us happy. We should enjoy our time together as much as possible. What do you think of your wardrobe?" The pitch of her voice climbed as if to coax a positive answer.

"Oh, I love it. You did a wonderful job. These boots are great." I paused, striking a pose to model them for her.

"I was a little worried, but I feel good seeing you dressed in my selections. You know, I'm sure Vittorio would love you to model the more delicate pieces of your wardrobe." She eyed me with a devious smile.

The now familiar warmth rose in my cheeks as I considered my lingerie drawer. Until last night, I was sure he wanted to see me in one of the skimpy items. Now, I wasn't so sure he'd ever want to see me again. Period.

She flashed a knowing smile. "Let's head back. I hear

~ ☾ ~

Alexander arguing with Peter. I think they may have found the tree."

We turned back in the direction we had just come.

Sunlight streamed through the green tree branches, lighting our way. The crisp sent of a recent snowfall draping the evergreens filled the air. There was no breeze under the pine canopy, which kept the wintery air tolerable. The giant trees towered high above us. I glanced up to see how high they went when something moving through the branches caught my eye.

I stopped walking. "What was that?"

"What?" Elizabeth's gaze followed mine into the trees.

The most horrendous stench of sweat polluted the forest, like a whirlpool of funk. "*Oh, no.*" I knew what had moved above me. I just didn't know who it was.

Elizabeth picked me up and ran. She whizzed through the trees, moving further into the forest, my weight not slowing her in any way. "Where are we going?" I asked.

"To meet the men," she answered. "I've alerted Alexander, and they're coming to us."

We'd only gone past a few trees when a vampire twice her size jumped onto Elizabeth's back, forcing her down. His fangs extended from his mouth as he lunged for her neck. She fell, tossing me into the air. I crashed against a tree and rolled into the dirt. As I scrambled to my feet, a cold, hard hand gripped my shoulder, pulling me off the ground. Fingers tore through my clothes, digging into my skin. I cried out and tried to break free, pounding against his dirty hand and fingers.

"Gotcha! Now The Master will give *me* the reward." The repulsive stench of sweat filled my nostrils. I choked for air. Pain shot through my shoulder and down my arm. Tears formed in my eyes. Between the pain and the smell I thought I was going to pass out.

Elizabeth fought with two vampires. She looked like a demon with black, angry eyes. Blood oozed from cuts on her face, neck, and chest. She growled through descended fangs and hunched, springing on one of her attackers, biting into his neck and tearing through him to the bone. With only her

~ ☾ ~

hands, she ripped his head from his shoulders. His body dropped to the ground. As she threw his head down, the other vampire jumped on her back.

"*Elizabeth!*"

My captor laughed as we watched his comrade bite Elizabeth's neck. I was so worried about her that it wasn't until I found myself suddenly suspended from a pine bough that I realized he had launched us upward into the trees. He jumped from branch to branch like an orangutan carrying a doll.

"Peter! *Peter!*"

"He can't save you. He's busy!" He laughed. Frizzy brown hair covered his head and filth caked his unshaven face.

There must have been another group attacking the men. Another well planned assault. We'd never get out of this with only the three of them and me. I wasn't ready. We needed Vittorio and Bruno.

He settled on a tree limb and ripped my jacket open, his crazed eyes fixed on my bloodied shoulder, leering at me in the way a junkie would regard a crack pipe, fangs dripping with saliva. "I was sent to get you for Samuel. But *I'm* thirsty."

That lecherous grin was more than I could stand. I punched him in the face and neck, each movement growing more frantic when he didn't even flinch.

"Peter! *Help me!*"

Lucia, focus. You have to focus. Father's stern words sounded in my head.

"*I can't.*"

The vampire looked at me like I was crazy. "What?" His eyes were the reddest I'd seen with very little trace of any other color in them.

Lucia, calm down, Father commanded, with a voice so cool and collected that I had no choice but to relax. *You have him where you need him. Concentrate. Think about The Abyss. Imagine it crushing you. Envision your own death.*

I tried to envision my death, but seeing it terrified me. I couldn't stand the feeling of being crushed or the inability to breathe. My throat tightened just considering it. Even with

~ ☾ ~

his encouragement I still could not summon the image. *I can't.* I can't.

Do it. Anger rippled through Father's voice, and he sent it to me with full force. *You have no choice. You* must *do it.*

I closed my eyes, trying to steady my nerves. Fear pulsed through me as I considered what could happen. *What if this vampire kills me?* I opened my eyes in time to see the vampire's eyes roll back as he lowered his mouth to my neck.

"Look at me." The words were little more than a shaky whisper.

He turned his head to the side and exhaled. His breath was awful. My stomach turned, but I fixed my attention on the vampire, fighting past my fear, and *it* happened. The Abyss appeared. The silent blackness descended upon us, and his scream held all the horror of someone being tortured. It rang in my ears as he released me, sending me spiraling to the ground.

Falling from the tree I bounced off the lower branches, wincing with each contact and trying to shield my face from being whipped by the thinner ones. Finally, I smashed into the ground.

Though sore and tired, I realized I'd done it. I'd called The Abyss, used it to defend myself. I wasn't defenseless.

My elation ended when I looked up.

My attacker plummeted downward, arms flailing, pathetic cries announcing his impending arrival.

"No. Damn it." I hadn't killed him, hadn't finished the task. With the wind knocked from my lungs, I couldn't get my feet under me, couldn't move out of his way. Every muscle in my body cramped, and I held my breath, waiting for him to crash on top of me.

A blur of color flashed, sending a gust of wind over me. The scent of sun-kissed grapevines whooshed above me as Vittorio collided with the vampire, slamming him to the ground several feet away.

I watched in awe as Vittorio dismembered my attacker, his fangs protruding, eyes narrowed to ferocious black slits. A low, inhuman growl vibrated from him when he ripped the head from the vampire's shoulders, biting into his flesh. He

~ ☾ ~

pulled the vampire apart, crushing his heart in one fist.

It was the first time I'd ever seen for myself what he was capable of. The savagery in him. The strength. The blind power.

Vampire.

Blood soaked his clothes, face, and hands. He roared at the heavens. A brutal howl of rage.

I couldn't look away, couldn't feel disgusted. I felt only one thing. Sorrow.

The drum beat within me, deep and steady. Its familiar rhythm called to my heart, challenging me to bring The Abyss. To take Vittorio to The Light. Set him free.

I can't. Not yet.

I wasn't ready. I couldn't control the power, hadn't finished the job with the young vampire. I'd never be able to save him, not in this state.

And...he was *mine.*

The beat silenced.

When he turned toward me, his empty, soulless eyes reminded me of Samuel. Blood dripped from his mouth and hands, and his whole body quaked. The excitement of the fight showed all over him. He stalked toward me, his breathing fast and rough.

I backed away, scooting along the forest floor. "Vittorio?" I backed into the tree. "Please, Vittorio, stop."

I wasn't ready to let him go, but I wasn't willing to become like him either.

He picked me up and whisked me away, moving more quickly than I'd ever seen him move. I didn't know what he would do, but I wasn't going willingly. I tried calling The Abyss to me once again. I heard myself breathing, heavy and raspy breaths. I began to feel like I couldn't breathe, like the blackness would crush me.

"Lucia, stop that." He squeezed me. "I'm trying to save you. Now is not the time to practice."

"Sorry," I mumbled, instantly losing my grasp on The Abyss. "Are you... should you be with me?"

"Yes," he answered as he ran through the forest with me in his arms. His stony response wasn't reassuring.

~ ☾ ~

"Are you sure?" My voice cracked when I asked. I tried to look at his face, but the cold wind blasting me as we moved made my eyes water. Through the tears, I saw the blood drying on his face, his fangs still visible.

"I'm fine. I won't hurt you." His tone was curt and angry.

"You don't have to carry me." I tried to wiggle loose.

"You'll slow us down." His pace quickened. The Range Rover came into sight, and parked beside it was an identical truck.

"What about the others? Is Elizabeth going to be okay?"

"Alexander is with her. I don't know how she is. Peter and Bruno are helping to defend her. They're causing enough of a distraction that Samuel won't realize he's lost you again. They'll meet us back at the house." He opened the driver's side door of the truck and helped me inside.

I wasn't ready for any of them to die because of me. And I wasn't ready to be left alone to figure out how to master my powers either. "Are you sure we shouldn't go help?"

He gunned the gas, peeling the tires and kicking up pine needles, dirt, and rocks as he went. "They will be fine without us."

We drove in silence, making it back to the house in half the time it took us to get to the forest. His attention remained on the road, and he didn't say another word until we turned down the driveway. "According to Peter, Elizabeth's badly injured but she'll recover with help." The car raced up the drive, Vittorio scanning the property the whole way.

A sigh escaped my lips. "Good." Until that moment, I hadn't realized I'd been holding my breath, praying she'd make it. Praying they'd all make it. "How many were there?"

"It seems there were nine total, including Brian." He lifted me out of the car, carried me inside, and placed me on the couch. His fangs retracted, and he took off his blood-soaked jacket and sweater as he walked to the kitchen to wash his face and hands.

I was sore, but pretty sure I hadn't broken anything in the fall. I did have some cuts, including a small puncture wound on my neck from the vampire who'd attacked me.

Gingerly, Vittorio helped me out of my sweater, exposing

~ ☾ ~

cuts in my shoulder and marks on my arms and back where bruises would soon appear.

"Vittorio, I can take care of myself."

He ignored my words, moving to examine the cuts, then he cleaned and treated them with an antibiotic ointment, not saying a word. His gaze never met mine, even when he worked on my face. None of the familiar sparkles flickered in his hazel eyes, but they weren't bottomless pools of black, either.

I tried to keep my mind off my desperate need to hold him. "How do you think they knew where we were?" I finally asked, unable to bear the silence.

"I don't know. I think Samuel knows where the house is. We may have to relocate. We'll discuss it when everyone gets back." He prepared the last bandage.

"Where?"

"We have a couple other homes in the U.S. in California, Texas, and one in Boston, which we can't use just now. We have homes in Italy, England, and France, too."

Of course we couldn't return to Boston. I couldn't risk the police catching me.

"You're all set. You should probably go change." He grabbed the ointment and dirty gauze and walked out of the room without another word. The door down the hall opened then clicked shut, and he was gone.

I stared after him, realizing that I hadn't felt *him*, his very being. He hadn't used it to reach for me, hadn't tried to touch me at all. He cared for my injuries like any emergency room doctor would have—with a cold, clinical hand.

I trudged up the stairs to change, feeling as though my heart was made of lead and weighed a thousand pounds.

When I returned to the living room, Elizabeth had taken my place on the couch.

She clung to Alexander, feeding from his wrist, wearing the most haunting expression. I'd never dreamed she could look so much worse than the gray day appearance. Her skin had withered, as though she was shriveling in front of me. Dried blood caked her clothing, face, and hands. Her black,

~ ☾ ~

empty eyes bulged and the dark circles beneath them grew darker.

"Lucia, leave the room." The expression on Alexander's face was a mix of worry, anger, and desperation. His fangs made him terrifying.

"It's not safe for you now. Elizabeth is too weak," Vittorio said, fangs protruding again. He stood beside Alexander, watching Elizabeth.

Peter and Bruno were positioned on the opposite side of the couch, fangs extended.

They stood like four sentries, waiting for something to happen, prepared to do whatever was needed.

Elizabeth swallowed greedily as she drank from Alexander. Her frantic, grating breaths raked the air. Her eyes darted around, flitting from face to face until she found me. The now crimson glow within them mesmerized me, pulling me into their depths. She stopped drinking and pushed Alexander's arm away.

A wave of urgency swamped me. Her desire, her need, rolled over me as her soft voice floated in my head, trying to persuade me to give myself to her. *Come to me, Lucia.* Sultry, hot, inviting, the voice wrapped around me, calling to me, like an old friend offering the promise of love, of friendship, of pleasure. Underneath the façade of gentleness was a desperation so potent it nearly consumed me.

I was drowning in her distress. For the first time since I'd met her, I was afraid of her.

She tried to rise from the couch but the others were on her before she could lift herself. In a blur of movements, they restrained her. Alexander yelled at her in Greek then turned to me. "Get out, Lucia! *Now!*"

I ran from the room in a fit of panic, unsure of where to go, but wanting to hide from all of them. I bolted down the hall and into Vittorio's study.

~ ☾ ~

CHAPTER EIGHTEEN

I leaned against the door, standing perfectly still and listening, my heavy breathing the only noise in the room. Sounds of wrestling came from the parlor. Occasional screams from Elizabeth, followed by angry commands from Alexander or Vittorio, combined with the noise of her struggle. It wasn't until there was only silence that I calmed down. Not until that moment did it occur to me that the room was pitch black; not even a sliver of light slipped under the door.

I fumbled along the wall until I found a switch. A crystal chandelier sent a soft glow about the center of the room, leaving the corners in darkness. Long drapes covered enormous windows, making it impossible for any natural light to sneak past. The room smelled of Vittorio. I closed my eyes and inhaled. His scent always made me feel safe, like he was there with me.

Across from the door, a leather captain's chair sat behind a large mahogany desk, empty save for the computer on one side. The chair obscured a painting on the wall, forcing me to walk across the room to examine the portrait. Of course, it was me. As much as I did not care to see myself, I had to admit, I didn't look that bad in the low light. The chandelier's crystals cast an iridescent shimmer on my painted likeness, making the portrait appear as if it was alive.

The wall to the right was one giant bookcase, filled with thousands of books. *How long has he lived here that he's amassed a library this size?*

There were books about different countries—England, France, The United States. Interestingly, there were a few books on re-incarnation. There were shelves of books in

~ ☾ ~

Italian. He had a number of my favorites including *The
Betrothed, The Decameron,* and *The Divine Comedy.* Some
of the books were very old. I thumbed through *The
Decameron* and realized immediately that it was my original
copy from Italy. However had he gotten his hands on it?

I studied the books in this section of the case, only to
discover another surprise hidden in the back corner of the
shelf. The dusty little book was ragged and worn, with dog-
eared pages and smudges. The title was gone, erased by time
and years of use. I held it in my hand, almost afraid to open
it. My memory flashed to the day I had given it to Vittorio,
our first anniversary.

I had wrapped it in one of my kerchiefs and tucked the
package into my pocket. When he came home for supper I
hinted teasingly to him until he finally chased me out into the
garden to get it. That night, he read the poems to me in bed.
He read them so often he practically wore out the letters.

I turned on the reading lamp and sank into the corner
chair, flipping to the first page. The note I'd written was
barely visible. *"To Vittorio, with all the love my heart can
hold. Lucia."*

The poems were mostly by Petrarca, but there were others
by de Medici, Boccaccio and Dante. He loved this book,
quoting from it when the mood struck, using it to lure me to
bed on many nights.

This reminiscing was foolish of me, only making my desire
for him stronger. My need to be in his arms, to feel him
holding me, to kiss him, swelled. I dug my nails into the
palms of my hands and forced myself out of the chair. I
tucked the book away, pulling myself back to the present,
back to my reality.

A drafting board and an easel displayed works in progress
on the opposite side of the room. Curiosity got the best of me,
and I walked toward the drafting table where a huge old book
sat atop a map of the east coast.

A few loose pages hung unevenly from the cracked and
tattered leather binding. The inscription on the small gold
plaque attached to the front read simply: *Lucia.*

I carried the book to the desk and pulled out the chair. The

~ ☾ ~

first page was a sketch of me. I recognized Vittorio's work immediately. Wild, brown spirals surrounded my head. The expression was hard to describe, a combination of seduction and power, nearly divine. My eyes were striking. They popped off the page as if they were three-dimensional.

I fanned the pages and noticed the different scripts. More than one person had written in the book, dating and marking each entry in order. I flipped back to the beginning and read the first page written in Vittorio's perfect Italian penmanship: *1760. The Search Begins. Alexander and Elizabeth have convinced me that Lucia is coming for me. I am learning to sense her. They believe that she is just a child at this point.*

As I read, the air around me moved and the sound of footfalls surprised me. "Who's there?"

"I am." Vittorio's deep voice came from the corner. He sat in the chair, legs crossed at the ankles, elbows resting on the arms. The lamplight barely illuminated his face, keeping his expression hidden.

My heart leapt at the sight of him.

"What is this?" I pointed to the book.

"We documented our search for you, starting at the very beginning when Alexander and Elizabeth found me." He didn't even glance in my direction. "We've tried to discern any patterns that have occurred, any changes in your abilities. We also recorded any stories about you and vampires that came in contact with you throughout your lives." His words fell between us like stones, cold and emotionless. "We have kept record, as best we could, of your families."

I licked my lips and sweat coated my palms as I glanced at The Book. Almost everything I could ever want to know about the last two hundred and fifty years lay here at my fingertips. I had only to read The Book to know everything. I turned the page, my body quivering with excitement.

His hand came down, pinning mine beneath his palm. "I am only going to show you the things I think you need to know. I don't want you to read anything else until you have experienced your own memories of each lifetime. You *must* learn for yourself before you read what we've learned."

~ ☽ ~

"*Why?*" My fingers tightened over the edge of the pages. "What difference does it make if I learn your views before my own? In fact, it might even prepare me for the memories." God knew I needed all the help I could get. I tried to tug The Book toward me, but was unable to budge it.

"Learning our views prior to understanding your own perspective will confuse you." His face, only inches from mine, was beautiful, but behind his eyes loomed a pain like I'd never seen. I wanted to touch him, to soothe the hurt away.

"We reacted to certain things, intervened at times and developed theories along the way that may or may not have been correct. We may have thought that events were occurring in a certain way for the wrong reasons. There were times that we did not understand what had happened to you until two lifetimes later. You *must* learn about your past and how it will influence your destiny from yourself." The soft glow from the chandelier softened the steely expression on his face. "In the end, you can read the whole book, but not until you have experienced all the memories for yourself. Do you understand?"

After a long moment, I reluctantly agreed. "Alright. But do you really think I'm going to remember every lifetime?"

"We've surmised that you only remember the ones from our... only from the time you met me to the present." His hand closed around mine, like an involuntary spasm, and he loosened his hold. "Promise me that when we finish here this evening, you will not search for this book." His voice was low, his tone clear. I wanted to reassure him. I honestly did, but I felt an urge growing inside me. Still, I murmured, "I promise." I hated the thought of upsetting him, yet I was already completely enthralled with The Book. The prospect of learning everything I needed to know in a few short hours without having to witness my lives and The Abyss for myself made my head spin. I could barely think of anything else.

Our relationship already teetered on a precarious ledge. I needed him to trust me, to believe in me. I needed to think of him, of his worries, his desires, not my own. "I promise," I repeated, more firmly.

~ ☾ ~

He sighed and opened The Book, flipping pages fast enough to whip the deliciously scented air into a breeze. The smell of him streamed around me, and I nearly melted onto the floor.

"Here, Lucia. These are a few entries from Danvers in the 1700's written by Elizabeth. These will give you a clear picture of the power Samuel has and the lengths he has gone to when trying to possess you." Vittorio slid the book in front of me.

I was almost too afraid to look at it...but not quite.

1781—entry number five—We are struggling to restore peace to Danvers since Samuel and Brian departed. We have destroyed four fledglings but believe that at least two others still exist. Vittorio has managed to control his rage long enough to assist with the cleanup.

Lucia's family has been massacred, not a single soul survived the attack. Samuel himself slaughtered her husband, leaving her sister and nieces for Brian and the fledglings. Her parents are nowhere to be found. We believe he took them to torture. Alexander has altered most of the memories, allowing the townsfolk to believe that a fire burned the homestead, killing the entire family. I was only able to help with a few survivors as I have spent most of my time hunting the revenant fledglings.

1781—entry number six—Vittorio hunts Samuel and Brian. We believe they fled north of the border to Canada. The day after his departure, six more fledglings appeared. We have managed to destroy five of them, but fear there may be another batch of them set to rise tomorrow.

1781—entry number seven—This morning we found the sixth fledgling. We persuaded him to tell us the resting spot of the others. We found four more before they could rise. The vampire-child told us his master would create more as he needed them. He said he and his brother were created at the same time, each feeding simultaneously from Samuel's wrists. How can this be? What kind of power does he have? We will leave Danvers tonight to meet Vittorio in Quebec.

Vittorio stared down at the book, his jaw set, eyes dark, the anger within them seething just beneath the surface. "We

~ ☾ ~

didn't meet Samuel until 1857 in Texas. He managed to evade us for many years. Prior to our meeting, we learned quite a bit about him from vampires who knew him and from having to clean up after his attacks. He has always been the same ruthless and bloodthirsty vampire he is today. We believed that Samuel's knowledge of you began back around the time Elizabeth and Alexander found me."

"Why were they looking for you? How'd they know about me?" What had ever possessed them to chase after a Pharo?

Our eyes met, his gaze piercing. His right eyebrow twitched once then went still. "Love." There was a dare in his expression, jaw jutting forward in challenge.

I chose not to take the bait. We didn't need another fight. And, frankly, I was more interested in the contents of The Book than having a go-around with him. I blinked and glanced down at the pages between us.

"They had been following the trail of art I had left. Eventually, Samuel used the same trail to track us." An angry undertone ebbed in the last sentence. "Apparently, he's known about you for many years." His angst, like a hard cold sheet of metal, filled the room.

I crossed my arms over my chest, feeling alone, isolated from him.

"Has he hunted you forever?" He leaned closer until his breath rustled my hair.

I edged away from him an inch or two, looking up into his face. "No. I've hunted him. It's only been since your existence that the tables have turned."

A smile twisted his lips, showing his fangs. "So it was me. Or rather, it *is* me. I'm the one who puts you in danger." He grunted out a harsh chuckle. "And all for love." He leaned on the desk, scowling at the floor.

"Vittorio—" His rage whipped around me, cold and cutting, and I stopped speaking.

He flipped the pages again. A growl rumbled from deep in his chest. "We first encountered Samuel in Texas. We were so close to you. We were just about to save you when..." Vittorio gripped the desk, and the wood groaned beneath him. "We missed our chance because of him." He turned the pages in

~ ☾ ~

The Book to a new entry. It was in the same script as the last one, indicating that Elizabeth had written it.

1857—entry number one—We have missed her again. We nearly lost Vittorio in this battle. Samuel has made obvious his strategy. He will try to kill Vittorio in advance of taking Lucia. If Cesar and Ramon had not arrived in time, all may have been lost. They attacked Samuel, chasing him into Mexico. I was able to rescue Vittorio. He required an immediate feeding and has not forgiven himself for taking the life of the sheriff in order to save his own. Alexander and I fed him throughout the night and he is recuperating.

The next entry had been forced into the paper. The words were embedded into the pages below. The penmanship had changed. Vittorio had made this entry.

1857—entry number two—Damn him! Damn them all! She is gone again. Again, we have missed her. This time I heard her voice. I heard her crying as she died. She screamed my name! Screamed for me to save her—and I did not! I let her down again! I am not good enough. I cannot endure any more of this! God, take me from this wretched life! Stop this torture! I should have known Kerina was his spawn. Devil that she was. Only one so wicked and evil as Samuel could create her. How did I not see that he was so like her? I will enjoy the day I destroy him.

I re-read the words two or three or four times, unable to absorb their meaning. They whirled in my head, moving too fast for me to understand. How did *I* not know? Was I so blind that I didn't see the obvious? "You're his...his descendant?"

"Yes."

One simple word and the last shred of trust I had in him crumbled, like an earthquake destroying everything I ever knew. "How? *How* is this possible?" The words blurred on the page as my mind spun through all the possibilities. "No wonder he knows where we are. No wonder he's always right on my heels. It's *you*, your connection to him. He reads your thoughts." My chest tightened. The ache called, a low throb building higher. How could I have been so blind? I should have sensed this connection, should have noticed the link.

~ ☾ ~

"Lucia, I am able to Guard. He cannot know my thoughts," he said, annoyance in his voice.

"How can you know for certain?" I wasn't strong enough. If Samuel found me, I wasn't ready. If Vittorio gave me over to him, I'd be... I didn't control my power. It controlled me. The beating drum pounded within me. I swallowed. *Breathe, Lu. It will be fine. He won't betray you. He can't.*

His eyebrow arched, and he pursed his lips. "I've known of my connection to Samuel for more than a hundred years. I've mastered my own thoughts, especially where you are concerned." He walked to the bookshelf, straightened a few of the books. "You're afraid."

Breathe.

"You don't trust me." He sighed.

Deep breaths. Rapid beats. The sizzle along my skin.

"Lucia, I have never betrayed you. Not in all these hundreds of years have I ever revealed a single detail of your existence to him." He faced me. "I was serious. I never wanted to hurt you." His face softened, though the pain behind his eyes remained. He glanced down at his feet. "I've safeguarded you, even avoiding my own redemption to ensure he never touched you."

The ache pounded. "He told me he should have killed you himself, but that he'd been foolish. He hadn't realized that you were the reason I'd lost interest in him."

"He's tried." A smirk crossed his face. "He has certainly tried. In Texas he nearly killed me. If not for Elizabeth, he would have."

My stomach tightened. If Samuel could have destroyed Vittorio, he'd have sent him into The Abyss, giving him the same opportunity that I could give. Death is death. Once it happens, the soul has only to decide to meet The Light.

But for some that decision doesn't come easy. Some souls require an escort, a Pharo, someone to deliver them through The Abyss. Some souls fear The Light.

He came back to the desk, motioning to The Book. "Turn the page. Read on." The air between us grew heavy with solemn desperation. "Learn who I really am."

1857— entry number three—Vittorio is uncontrollable.

~ ☾ ~

His anger has turned him into a demon. After destroying ten fledglings, bloodlust overcame him. He killed four women, snatching them from the arms of their husbands. I fear he may be lost to us forever. We have left Texas, fleeing to Mexico.

1867—entry number four—It has been ten years since Lucia's last death. Wherever she is now, she seems to be having a happy childhood. Vittorio has seen a few of her dreams. Some have been memories that he had forgotten. He is only at peace when he sleeps. His waking hours are torturous for everyone. Peter is healing from the fight they had the other day. Vittorio has refused to allow Elizabeth or me to help heal him. His guilt is overwhelming.

1870—entry number one—We have traveled to South America with Cesar and Ramon in hopes that Vittorio will find some peace. His eyes are nearly claret; very little hazel remains. It seems his hatred of God is breaking down his soul. Cesar knows a priest who will try to help Vittorio. A vampire-priest. Alexander and I agree that now we have heard everything.

1879—entry number one—Alexander and I have been able to feel Lucia much more than Vittorio. We have felt her joys and, lately, many sorrows. We still are not sure of her whereabouts. Although Father Guillermo has worked daily with him, Vittorio makes little progress. If left alone, he wanders the streets terrorizing the locals. We fear that Vittorio will lose his connection if he cannot overcome his anger.

*1884—**Lucia! Where are you? Please come to me! Please!***

The desperate, angry lines ripped through the paper.

*1894—**I feel her. She calls to me. In my sleep, her beautiful face appears. Eyes so green. Soft, flowing curls. She calls to me to find her. The Vampire Goddess, My Goddess.***

I read the last lines a couple times. *Goddess?* "Vittorio, what—"

He loomed in front of the desk, his hair hanging in his face, his eyes, black as night. "You made me the monster I

~ ☾ ~

am," he snarled. His lips pulled back in a vicious display of fangs.

"It's not true." Tears rolled down my cheeks. "Vittorio, I never meant—"

"You never meant what?" He leaned forward, stopping only inches from my face. "To condemn me? To leave me as a monster feeding from innocent humans? To selfishly let me chase you for three centuries, terrified that Samuel would possess you?" His face twisted with rage, and he slammed The Book shut. "No, you didn't. All you thought was to leave me alive. So *you* could play God."

In the blink of an eye, he was across the room. The chair, lamp, and table flew through the air, smashing to the floor. The bookshelf tipped forward and an avalanche of books tumbled downward. His ice-cold presence burned my skin. "You are not God! You had no right to judge me! No right to refuse me redemption!" A demented look of hate poured from his eyes. Saliva dripped off his fangs.

"I didn't. I didn't, I swear." I sobbed. "Vittorio, please." I backed toward the opposite wall. Energy pulsed along my skin. I bit my lip, unsure if I should try to bring my power to the surface or hold it back.

"You *will* bring me to salvation!" His roar sent me tumbling further backward as his aura expanded to encompass every free inch of the room.

Deep within, the pounding demanded my attention. My heart beat a steady rhythm, matching its cadence. Blood pulsed through me, zooming through my veins, sizzling as if to set my body aflame. The Abyss waited, ready for me to call it, ready for me to unleash it. I inhaled.

I could free his soul. I could bring him to The Light.

I pushed my light out, away from me, into the space between us. I hovered, split from myself, vulnerable to him, to anyone. Nothing protected me. My breathing sped. *I must go back.* I retreated back into myself. *No. No. I can do this. I can free him.* I thrust forward reaching for Vittorio.

He growled, crouching atop the pile of books, hands balled into fists.

The moment I touched him, his head snapped up. His eyes

~ ☾ ~

glazed with unshed tears and he shoved me back.

"Goddess, let me feel your power!" He stalked toward me, grabbing my wrist and jerking me into his embrace. "Vampire Goddess, show me The Light." His unrelenting aura crashed against me, challenging me. "*Show me.*" His rage flared.

His resentment broke my heart.

Wild and angry, his essence churned in the room, coiling around us like a snake, squeezing tight, tighter. I winced. He snickered. "Some goddess."

My aura pulled away and rose, moving above his. I closed my eyes and saw *it*. The Abyss. I called it to me, brought it into the room.

Utter darkness descended around us.

Power hummed along my body. My spirit surged, spinning around him, thawing his icy heart and weaving our bodies together, entwining our very beings as one. The hot energy within me streamed out, soothing his wild torrent.

The room vanished.

In the background, I heard the screaming. My own pained, sorrowful cries merged with his until I could no longer tell one from the other.

The Light appeared so far away, yet closer than it had been. I pulled him, carried him toward it.

Vittorio, here is your chance. Come to The Light, my love.

~ ☾ ~

CHAPTER NINETEEN

We coasted in the blackness beckoned by an illuminated pinprick in the distance. I willed us toward it, toward Father and Mother, toward eternal salvation.

Vittorio's screams held the horrors of his existence. Every life he'd stolen flashed in front of us. Each soul he'd cast into shadow clawed at him. He clung to me, like a frightened child holds his mother, immersing himself in the safety of my power. And I held him as close as I could, unable to shelter him from the pain, hoping only to ease his transition, knowing that soon it would all be over.

The brilliance of The Light radiated, welcoming us. We moved closer, reaching for eternity, ready to bask in The Splendor.

"No!" A voice boomed, and I stumbled.

"Arturo, wait!"

"Mother?" I called out, scrambling to gain my bearings.

"*Filomena*, she cannot. I will not allow her to damn her own soul for his."

"*You'll hurt her!*"

"*She will survive!*"

The force that hit me was too powerful to fight. I fell, plummeting backward, away from The Light, deeper into the darkness. I struggled to right myself, to get us back to the path. Father's presence appeared above me, blocking the way, rising over us.

"Father, please?"

"No, Child. Samuel waits. You must bring him first." He moved toward us, guiding us away from The Light.

"*Please, Father*. Don't do this. Let him go."

"No. His salvation ends yours." His presence, more

~ ☾ ~

powerful than I remembered, forced us backward.

Vittorio screamed. The memory of Bruno's creation stayed fixed before us: the taste of Bruno's blood, the sound of his heart slowing, wet, weakened beats, the last rise and the final fall of his chest as he heaved a shallow breath. The sound of redemption being ripped from his fingers.

"Vittorio, look at me," Father demanded, his voice resonant and calm. "Look at me."

When Vittorio lifted his face, clear tears streamed from glittery-hazel eyes down his bronze cheeks, his skin tanned as if he'd just come from the fields.

"She would die for you. Would you do the same for her?"

"Father?" I pushed Vittorio behind me. "Father, it's not the same."

"Quiet, Child." He scrutinized Vittorio. "She just tried to free your soul. Would you do the same for her?"

Vittorio hesitated. He stared at Father, trembling, not speaking. His aura remained tight within him, his fear acting as a blockade. What little sense of him I had retreated further from me.

Father's shoulders broadened. His power tested Vittorio, probing, prodding him for an answer, a reaction, any response.

Vittorio simply retreated deeper within himself.

"I feared this would be the case." Father glanced at me. "You cannot free his soul until you bring Samuel. And you cannot trust this vampire. He hides from me because he wants you."

He turned to Vittorio, leaned close to him and, in a low rumble, warned, "I will hunt you, vampire, to the end of my days. I will make you pay if you doom her."

Vittorio did not respond, not even with the slightest stirring to indicate he was alive.

"Go back, Child. Find Samuel. Do what you must. Then come home." He turned from us and walked toward The Light, leaving me with a catatonic Vittorio and the realization that I was truly alone in my hunt for Samuel.

I went to Vittorio and held him, hoping to coax him back to me. "Will he even be able to speak when I take him back?"

~ ☾ ~

I'd never returned anyone to their body after taking them into The Abyss.

"He will be as he was. Angry. Hungry. A danger to you," Father answered without turning, his voice fading into the blackness. "Hone your skills. Defend yourself."

I knew full and well Vittorio was a danger to me. The glimpse into his heart told me what he wanted.

God help me.

"Isn't there someone else who can do this with me? Anyone?" I stepped away from Vittorio and ran to Father. "Please? I'm afraid." Nothing could have been truer. I didn't remember how to fight or kill, and I didn't want to be a vampire. I clung to his hand, tears brimming in my eyes. "Father, you can't leave me to do this alone."

"There is no one. Only you can do this. You are the only one who knows how Samuel came to be. That is the key to his destruction."

"But I don't *know*. I don't *remember* the answer. I don't know my *own* abilities. At least tell me how my power works." I clutched his wrists, tugging as if to pull the answers from him. *"Don't send me away like this."*

"I cannot answer your questions. Your powers differ from mine, from your mother's, from any other Pharo's. We must each master our individual gift." He wiped the tears from my face. "Lucia, this is your fate. You did this...to all of us. You must fix it. There is no other way, my child."

An explosion erupted behind me, heat rushed along my back, shoving me into Father.

"How can I free her soul?" Vittorio's voice echoed in The Abyss. "I am not a Pharo. *I am a vampire. One of The Damned!*" he shouted, his hands rising in fists of anger.

"Vittorio." Father pulled me into his embrace, away from Vittorio. "She cannot defeat Samuel without you." His calm demeanor swept out, diminishing Vittorio's rage and slowing my racing heart as we returned to Vittorio's side.

"Father, don't."

"Lucia, he must understand." Father rested his hand on Vittorio's shoulder. "She willingly gave her Light to you. It compromised her strength, her memory. If she opens your

~ ☾ ~

path to redemption without first defeating Samuel, she will never be able to destroy him. But *he* will be able to capture and enslave her, condemning her for all eternity. Are you willing to fight with her? To die with her?"

Vittorio's face distorted, his anguish so evident, so raw. "Arturo, she condemned me. She forced me to suffer for her own selfish desire. Why would I die for her? Have I not suffered enough?"

"Yes, you have suffered. But if you don't help her, if you allow her to bring you to The Light, the piece of her that stays with you will be tormented. It will try every way to reach her. Your eternity will not be a heaven, but an actual hell within it."

Vittorio looked down at me. "Why? Why did you do this?"

I didn't respond, knowing the answer would not please him, just as it hadn't pleased Father.

"Answer me, Lucia. Why did you do this to us?" He tilted my face to his.

I blinked, and tears rolled downward. "I loved you. I couldn't risk losing you forever." He had been right. I was selfish. And now we would both pay for it.

"How did you do it? How did you even think of it?"

"I don't know. I just gave it to you, to protect you, to keep you safe, to keep others away from you." I watched as he listened, and I knew the moment he understood. Recognition flashed across his face.

"You marked me for your own." His aura stormed around me, hot and cold all at once.

I swallowed. "Don't be angry."

"You marked me...so that no other Pharo would touch me. Is that correct?"

I squeezed his arms. "Please, don't be angry." This was not the place for Vittorio to lose his temper. Father would not tolerate it. He'd risk everything to keep me safe, even if it meant hurting Vittorio.

"Her Light also makes it nearly impossible for anyone to kill you." Father's gaze moved over and beyond us. His head bowed as though responding to some other conversation. "No Pharo would risk condemning another, thus none would

~ ☾ ~

harm you. And no vampire alone is powerful enough to extinguish a Pharo's light."

Vittorio's chest rose and fell with deep, heavy breaths. "You realize that you're the one that makes Samuel hunt me? You are the one that has endangered yourself, not me. I didn't know what you'd done, or what it meant, or what Samuel thought." His tone grew harsher. "All these years, I've been a homing device. Samuel need only know where I am to know that you'll be near."

"I'm sorry. I never meant..."

"I know. I know. Love did it." He spit the words, turned away from me and glanced into The Abyss. His memories spun around us, like a million movies playing on a giant black screen. The low moans of other souls cried out to him. He paced, and his aura, strong enough to protect him from the horrors surrounding us, moved with him.

"If it's any consolation, her mother and I have had to endure seeing your mark on her neck in every lifetime since she gave you her Light."

"I noticed it, too, in the hospital. Why is it there?" Vittorio asked, turning from the memory of Peter's creation.

"She allowed the scar to form. She allowed you to claim her."

I sighed. "Let's go. I need to get back. I've got to find Samuel and destroy him so that you can..." I waved a hand at the speck of light in the distance. It was clear that I wasn't getting any help from Vittorio or Father. "...be free." Free to enjoy salvation, free of me.

"Kerina killed Max and Elsa. Weren't they Pharos?" Vittorio asked, ignoring me. "I thought a vampire alone couldn't kill a Pharo."

"Yes. But they had done their duty. They awakened the sleeping Pharo." Father motioned to me. "In three thousand years she never strayed, but then you came along." He grimaced. Even Pharos hated to admit when their wives were right. "And the moment your mother, Serafina, gave birth to you, Filomena said we'd have a problem when Lucia arrived. Filomena swore she felt you calling for Lucia with your first scream. She was right. Since 1629, Lucia has strayed from her

~ ☾ ~

course." His dark brown gaze flitted to mine.

"Enough, Father. This is pointless. Let us go." I walked back to Vittorio.

"We must kill Samuel." Vittorio stepped away from me. "That is her destiny. Not me. Samuel."

"Yes. That is the only way to resolve this. Vittorio, you must teach her about Samuel and vampires. Let her practice on your family. She will need to be stronger than she is now or he *will* capture her."

I huffed. "I'm standing right here. And I'm tired of being ignored."

"Yes, and you're too weak to do this alone. You must feed your Light." Father raised his eyebrows. "You've asked for help. I'm doing my best." He glanced toward Vittorio.

"Fine. But he's not—"

"Feed her Light? How does she do this?" Vittorio interrupted.

"She needs to destroy a vampire."

"She will get stronger with each death. Correct?" Vittorio asked.

"Yes. With each soul she delivers, with each visit to The Light, she will strengthen her powers."

"Good. She'll practice then we'll find Samuel. Let's go." He turned to me.

"Vittorio, be alert. She doesn't have the capacity to recall her past experiences at once. Her memories come to her in pieces, causing her to make the same mistakes in each lifetime. History continues to repeat itself."

"We noticed this. Her memories are systematic." He glanced down at me.

"What does that mean?" I asked.

"They come to you in order of each lifetime, and I don't know if you even remember every detail or just the important pieces. I'll teach you what I can, but you'll have to remember how to control your abilities." His eyes gleamed, my light within them beckoning to me. "I can't explain that to you."

"Go. Practice. Master your powers, Lucia." Father kissed my cheek. "Unlock your memories and learn all that you can."

Then he turned to Vittorio, placing a hand on his arm.

~ ☾ ~

"Vittorio, I've always loved you as a son. Today, I give her to you, again, because she needs you. But have no doubt, if you hurt her, I will come for vengeance."

"I know, Arturo. I expect nothing less."

"Lucia, take him back."

"But..."

He held up his hand. "Find Samuel together."

And with that command, Father left. The path to The Light vanished. All the horrors of Vittorio's existence surged forward. The Abyss held us. Cold, deep, and black, it spread out around us, howling its anguish.

Vittorio screamed. His breathing labored. His heart pounded.

Calm, Vittorio. You're not staying here. Calm.

*****

Something cool touched my forehead. The aroma of licorice, spicy and sweet, filled my lungs. I inhaled the comforting scent of Alexander.

"She's waking."

"Good. Maybe she'll be able to pry herself loose from his death-grip," Bruno said. "I wouldn't be surprised if he's broken her arms and ribs, even her back."

"Stop trying to move him. You'll hurt them both," Alexander warned. "Peter, let Elizabeth know she's coming around."

Stabbing pain shot from the back of my head to the front. I moaned and tried to reach up to relieve it, but my arms were stuck.

"What happened?" My voice cracked from my scratchy throat.

"We were hoping you could explain." Alexander wiped the cold cloth across my forehead again.

I opened my eyes, squinting into the light. They'd carried us to Vittorio's room. We lay on the bed with Alexander and Bruno holding cold compresses to our heads. Vittorio's head rested on my shoulder, his face hidden against my neck, arms clasped tight around me. I tried to move and found I couldn't. "I'm stuck."

"We can't get you free. Whatever you did, he's out for the

~ ☾ ~

count and not letting you go." Bruno removed the cool wet cloth from Vittorio's face, leaving a damp spot on my blouse.

I wiggled, trying to free myself.

"Forget it you're..."

Bruno's sentence trailed off as Vittorio sucked a full breath into his lungs and rolled onto his back, taking me with him. I landed sprawled across him, arms still stuck at my sides.

"Well, at least we know he's alive," Bruno said.

"Vittorio?" I said. He made no response. "That's it. Everybody take a limb and pull."

"It's not going to work." Bruno sighed as they all climbed onto the bed and grabbed an arm or leg. "We've already tried pulling you out."

"If we break him, you're taking the blame," Peter said.

"Why not?" What did it matter if he blamed me for one more thing?

"Okay," I said. "On three. One, two..."

"What are you doing?" Vittorio demanded, clinching his arms and legs around me even tighter.

"*Vittorio, you're crushing me.*"

He loosened his hold, but didn't let me go. "What's happening?"

"We're trying to help her," Bruno said. "You're squeezing her to death."

Vittorio tilted his head to glance at me. His body instantly relaxed, and he rolled us onto our sides. He ran his hand from my shoulder down my arm, along my leg, and a charge of excitement ran along my skin beneath his touch. "Did I hurt you?" Pushing me onto my back, he gently moved his hand across my ribs as he watched my face. My pulse jumped, heart sputtering, and I swallowed, trying to hide my body's reaction to him. "Do you have any pain?"

I shook my head.

"You're sure? Your back, any pain there?" He scooted closer and slid his hand beneath me, fingers probing each vertebra.

My breath caught in my throat, holding his scent deep within me. "I'm fine."

"What about your head? Does it hurt?" He gently tucked

~ ☾ ~

his fingers into my hair, caressing my scalp.

I closed my eyes so I could concentrate on answering the question. "My head hurts a little. But I'll live."

When I opened my eyes, his gaze captured mine. Green and gold flecks sparkled above me. His aura briefly touched me then pulled away, vanishing faster than it had arrived. "You need to practice." He rolled to his other side and stood.

I scooted off the bed to stand opposite him, trying to dampen the almost crushing disappointment of having to leave that bed and his embrace.

"It seems an explanation is in order," Alexander said, standing beside me.

"You think you could tell us what happened?" Bruno asked. "We just found the two of you squeezed together on top of a mountain of books with a thousand-pound bookshelf crushing you, a chair embedded in a wall, and a six-foot chandelier shattered on the floor."

"Not to mention the fact that Vittorio went into some death-sleep trance," Peter added, sitting at the edge of the bed.

Vittorio swiped his hand through his hair, sending a cloud of dust into the air. "She took me into The Abyss. I saw The Light."

His matter-of-fact explanation left everyone in awe. All four of them moved closer, eyes-wide.

"But...you're here. She brought you back," Elizabeth said.

"Yes. She must destroy Samuel before setting me free or she'll condemn herself." Vittorio unbuttoned his shirt, turning toward the closet.

"Actually destroy him? She has to face-off with him?" Bruno asked, his voice rising an octave and his accent deepening. His mouth hung agape and he looked from the closet to me and back as if waiting for someone to yell "April Fool's."

"Yes." Vittorio walked back into the room, pulling on a clean shirt. He tucked the gold cross hanging from his neck beneath the fabric and finished with the buttons.

"Impossible. She'll never be ready." Bruno stood to pace. "Even if we trained her all day, every day, she wouldn't be

~ ☾ ~

ready in this lifetime."

I scowled at Bruno. "*Hey*. I got Vittorio into The Abyss. And I called it to me in the forest. It's not like I'm completely incapable."

Peter scratched his head and slid his hand down over his neck, squeezing as though he was trying to work tension from it. "You hardly even notice when one of us is standing beside you. Your memory is atrocious. You should remember some basic facts from previous lives, like the fact that you have used your power to kill many times. You've used it in every lifetime since I've existed. Do you have any memory of that?"

I frowned. "No." I may not have been incapable, but I was far from knowing my own history or even remembering what it was like to actually kill someone with my power. And, unfortunately, the only vampire I could notice without trying was Vittorio, and that only happened when he let me. I hated to admit it, and wouldn't say it out loud, but Bruno could be right. I swallowed back the lump in my throat and bit my bottom lip.

"She hasn't experienced any of those memories," Vittorio said. "For whatever reason, her mind has not allowed her access to that information."

Bruno leaned against the bedpost. "Just the same, she doesn't remember enough to keep herself from getting hurt. She can't even control her aura. She's been buzzing all of us." He waved his hands in the air above his head. "God knows who else she's spending time with."

Buzzing them?

"She doesn't know the first thing about Guarding, Vittorio," Elizabeth said. "She must master this at once. He's constantly searching for her. She may be signaling him herself." Elizabeth stood beside Alexander. She had pinned her long hair back in a bun, and washed her face, but she still wore the bloodstained clothes from the fight in the forest. She appeared tired and literally drained. Her cheeks were hollow; her skin was not as white as usual. She also still looked hungry.

I shuffled to the side, putting Bruno between us.

"Why doesn't she remember? What has happened to her?

~ ☾ ~

Why is she so weak?" Alexander asked, pulling Elizabeth close to him.

"The Book. *I want The Book*." I dashed around the bed headed for the study. I didn't need to remember when all I had to do was read what had happened.

Vittorio blocked the doorway. "You promised."

"But..."

His presence around me shifted and cooled, concentrating entirely on me. His commanding power dominated my every thought and feeling. Just as he had done last night, he held me imprisoned in his essence, only this time he was not sharing memories. He was not protecting me from his emotions. He reached inside me, straight to my heart. "Promise me, again." His voice resonated inside me, paralyzing me with fear. Another side of him I didn't know.

"I promise," I whispered.

His hold over me changed, softened, and he moved toward me. "You must remember certain things for yourself to ensure your own understanding. We did not know Samuel was your destiny. We thought *I* was your destiny. Our theories may make it more difficult for you." He plucked plaster from my hair before looking past me to the others. "All of her challenges stem from the fact that she gave me a piece of her Light."

A collective gasp sounded then silence filled the room. The tension escalated. No one moved until I turned to look back at everyone and attempted a smile. I suddenly thought I knew exactly how a lamb felt in a den of wolves.

"Well, she'd better start practicing now." Bruno folded his arms over his chest then unfolded them in a huff. "She's a risk to everyone, a beacon burning in the midnight sky, screaming for Samuel to find." He left the room on that note, mumbling something about Samuel, and Brian, and training until I was blue in the face.

Vittorio laced his boots and pulled on his coat and gloves, "Freshen up and meet Elizabeth in the parlor. She'll resume your lessons tonight. Peter, Alexander, come with me. I want to run a sweep of the property."

"I'll see you downstairs." Elizabeth squeezed my hand as

~ ☾ ~

she walked by.

Boot Camp was about to begin, and I had no way out. I'd been drafted into the Redemption Army and my drill sergeants were a group of lost souls struggling not to kill me.

~ ☾ ~

CHAPTER TWENTY

The scene in the living room surprised me. Elizabeth sat on the couch with her feet up, directing ornament placement.

Bruno perched on a ladder, four glass ornaments dangling from his fingers. "Really, I don't think you're so injured that you can't hang these ornaments yourself."

"There's no reason to be short with me. You know I like the tree to look beautiful. I decorate it for you boys." She pulled another ornament from the box on her lap.

"That's fine. But you're acting like the supreme commander with the decorating." He plopped a little elf onto a branch, tossing a sideways glance at Elizabeth.

"I am not." She pointed to the top of the tree. "No, to the left."

Bruno muttered something and moved the delicate figurine.

I laughed. This was not what I'd expected for Redemption Army Boot Camp.

"Lu!" Smiling, she waved me over to sit beside her. "We can watch Bruno trim our tree."

Her smile faded somewhat as she looked me over. I wasn't sure if she was deciding to eat me or ignore me. She looked from me to Bruno then back to me then back to him again.

"She'll be fine, Lu," Bruno said, encouraging me to sit with her.

I sat beside her, praying he was right.

"I'm fine. I apologize about earlier. I wasn't feeling well." She reached for my hand.

I let her touch me, not wanting to make the situation worse than it was. "I understand." Her hands were cold, but her touch was gentle, tentative. I squeezed her hand and smiled.

~ ☾ ~

"No, no. Bruno." Elizabeth turned to him. "That star goes higher and to the right." Bruno moved the ornament to a new spot. "No, a little higher," she said, pointing. He moved the ornament again, and she paused, evaluating its placement. "Perfect." He rolled his eyes and huffed.

I laughed out loud. This was priceless. Just hours ago they ferociously fought for their own lives and mine. Yet here he was climbing up and down ladders to move delicate ornaments all around a tree for Elizabeth. He made a miserable face at me. I laughed even harder.

Bruno glared. "Knock it off or I'm going to hang you from the tree."

"Why don't I just help you?" I grabbed a couple ornaments and climbed the ladder on the opposite side.

"Lu, has Vittorio explained *anything* about guarding, yet?" Elizabeth asked.

"Not a thing." I placed a tiny glass ball on a branch. "Care to enlighten me?"

She paused, handed me up a couple more ornaments, then answered, "Yes. I will explain it. However, Vittorio will practice with you." Her tone hinted at something. Tension? Nerves?

She reached for another box, opened it, and began inspecting the ornaments. As she explained the concept of guarding, Bruno and I moved up and down the ladders, hanging ornaments. Between his speed and my concentration on Elizabeth, he easily hung twice as many as me.

"Guarding is the art of concealing your presence and thoughts," she began. "We all feel your presence. Lately, it runs rampant when you sleep. None of us hears your thoughts, as that is not a gift any of us possess. And, although you and Vittorio have a bond, it is different from vampire bonds and doesn't allow for the telepathic connection. But there are vampires who have the ability to hear anyone's thoughts."

I stopped on the ladder, concentrating.

"Most times we can tell when someone is listening to our thoughts. We feel their presence inside us. It's like having someone read the newspaper over your shoulder. They don't touch you, but you can feel them hovering. Once we sense

~ ☾ ~

that someone is there, we guard."

She glanced toward the window. "The one time a vampire can be forced to stop guarding is in the creator-child relationship. The creator can force the child to allow access. It's not a kind thing, but it's necessary in the beginning. Once they are mature, it's much easier to leave them alone. Very few children are able to guard from their creators. Alexander cannot guard from me, and neither Peter nor Bruno can guard from Vittorio." She turned to face me. "It takes time to become proficient at it. You'll have to practice. A lot. That is, if you'll even be able to do it."

I sat on one of the ladder rungs. "You think I might not be able to guard?"

"It's a difficult task to master, a rite of passage for vampires. *I* believe you can do it, but in case you can't, I wanted to mention it."

Somehow, I felt like I'd returned to school—not college, nothing fun like that, and worse than high school. Between the guarding practice and trying to control my abilities without maiming or killing one of them, I just knew these next several weeks were going to be a barrel of laughs.

"First, since no one hears your thoughts, we'll work on sensing the foreign presence. You must clear your mind and listen with your heart. Can you tell when Vittorio is near you?"

"Not always. I can sense him if he...well, if he forces me to notice him. And I can sense him when he's angry." Unfortunately, that was a mood I was becoming very familiar with.

"That's no surprise." Bruno moved the ladder to the back of the tree. "You'd have to be dead not to notice that."

"Okay. Your first assignment is to recognize when Vittorio is near. Once you learn to realize when someone is close to you, you can learn how to guard. I can't explain the guarding part until you learn to sense him." She rummaged through a big box. "Ah, here it is." She unwrapped a wad of tissue paper to reveal a lovely angel, draped in ivory lace.

"Let me try to sense you." I placed a tiny horn on a low branch of the tree.

~ ☾ ~

Moving the angel from one end of the mantel to the other and stepping back to admire its placement, Elizabeth didn't miss a beat in our conversation. "No. You must practice with Vittorio. You have a strong bond with him. It will be easier for you."

"Easier doesn't matter. I have to master it." I stacked a couple boxes on the floor and took a few more ornaments to the tree.

"To start, easier is best. Your aura is comfortable with his. It knows him, is drawn to him. Tonight, you will practice with him. Once you've mastered recognizing his presence, then you will practice with others. Sensing him is not the same as recognizing that he's standing beside you. It's quite different. You're going to feel his presence.

"When Alexander listens to my thoughts, I feel his presence inside me. I know it's him. He is comforting to me, just as I am to him. If I meet someone else who can hear my thoughts, I know right away that it is not Alexander, but an intruder. I feel a stranger inside me. Does this make sense?" She returned to the big box and retrieved three more angels of varying sizes.

"Yes, but Vittorio and I don't hear each other's thoughts."

"No, but you sense each other. Your spirits need each other. It works very much like a creator-fledgling relationship." Skirts were fluffed and hair and halos were straightened, and, in less time than it took me to process what she'd said, the mantel was covered in pretty little angels.

I didn't ask, but I wondered, in this situation, which of us was the creator and which was the fledgling.

The next box Elizabeth opened revealed candles and holders. She placed one of each on the end tables and arranged at least a half dozen pillars of varying sizes on a mirrored tray on the coffee table. "You should ask him what it feels like when you send your aura to him. Ask him what it feels like for him when he comes to you. Ask him to tell you when he's there so that you can practice becoming aware of his presence. He has practiced reading your feelings for hundreds of years. He should be able to help you understand."

~ ☾ ~

"How has he practiced?" *Hundreds of years?* Why did I
always feel like the vampires had the upper hand? And had it
always been this way, even before Vittorio?

"He has always had the ability to sense your feelings. I
imagine it started when your bond was forged during your
first life together. You have probably always felt his presence,
but never realized it." She smiled.

*****

We were lounging in the parlor when Vittorio and the
others returned. Bruno and Elizabeth had carried all the
boxes back to wherever they'd come from once we finished
decorating. The tree looked like it had emerged straight out of
Macy's Christmas catalogue, decorated from top to bottom
with ornaments and garland. The only lights in the room
came from the tree and the TV, casting a festive glow about
the room.

"Did you find anything?" I asked.

"Yes, on the outer edge of the property. Some tracks and
new foul scents. They know where we are. I'm certain they
followed you from here this morning. There wasn't a new
trail, so they have not returned." He glanced around the
room. I had the distinct feeling he was listening to something
else. I followed his gaze across the room to catch sight of
Peter and Bruno. Both faced the TV, but it was obvious to me
that neither paid any attention to the show. They were clearly
deep in conversation with each other and Vittorio.

"What are you discussing with them?"

"Nothing. No need to worry." His dismissal did not sit well
with me. "We'll need to leave in the morning. We probably
have a couple days until Samuel returns." Vittorio's voice was
that of a general advising his troops, firm and confident.

"Where will we go?" I asked. "I can't just run. He'll find
me. Besides, I need to train and then deal with him." I threw
the magazine I had been reading onto the end table and
unfolded my legs so that both feet were planted firmly on the
floor. "Let's stay and fight."

Vittorio's voice never wavered from that authoritative
tone. "We can't stay. You're not ready. I think we'll go to
Texas. We can easily get there in a couple days, driving

~ ☽ ~

straight through. We can slip over the border into Mexico, if need be." He stood near the doorway, surveying the parlor, but his aura filled the room.

"Are you sure about that?" Massachusetts to Texas seemed a lot farther than a couple days to me.

Peter and Bruno laughed. I even heard Alexander chuckle from one of the other rooms.

"Oh, yeah. We'll get there in a couple days." Bruno pulled the handle on the recliner. "I didn't recognize any of the vampires with Brian," He tucked his hands behind his head and crossed his ankles, looking at Vittorio. "The two that fled with him were petrified when they saw what you did to the one who attacked Lucia. Even Brian seemed frightened."

The terrifying image of Vittorio ripping the vampire-child's heart from his chest flashed across my mind, followed by his enraged, blood-soaked face. The vision of him stalking toward me, like something from a horror movie, stayed fixed in my mind until he spoke again.

"The others were very new children. They didn't appear to be more than a day or two old," Vittorio stated. "I don't think they had even fed for the first time. I wouldn't be surprised if Samuel destroys them. He won't be able to control them if he forces them into battle without allowing them to hunt."

"He continues with his usual tactics," Peter commented as he flicked through the channels on the TV, finally settling on *It's a Wonderful Life.*

"It's curious that he hasn't altered his strategy." Alexander glided across the room and poured himself onto the couch with Elizabeth. They lay cuddled together while we discussed the attack. "He always challenges us when Lucia has been available to him elsewhere. I can't understand why he hasn't tried another method."

Vittorio's eyes narrowed. "He still hopes to kill me and escape with Lucia. It's the only logical explanation for his behavior. He knows, full and well, that I will not allow her to be taken from me, and if he manages somehow to capture her, I will hunt him to his death."

"What do you mean, Alexander?" I leaned forward to see him. "Vittorio wasn't with us today."

~ ☾ ~

"He was in the forest. Hunting." Alexander smiled at Elizabeth, and she snuggled in closer to him.

I glanced at Vittorio.

He raised an eyebrow. "I was hungry."

"We never should have been in the woods searching for that stupid tree," I said.

"Hey. The tree looks great." Bruno stood to adjust an ornament.

The simple gesture brought Elizabeth off the couch to move the ornament Bruno had touched. We all watched and waited until they'd completed their argument over the tree decorations.

Eventually, Alexander retrieved Elizabeth. "Elizabeth, you've been away from me for long enough." They settled back on the couch, and Bruno plopped back into the recliner beside Peter, who remained entirely too interested in the movie.

I paced the floor in front of the tree, hundreds of questions forming in my mind. Why would we wait until morning to leave? When were we going to practice? What was Samuel's strategy? What was our plan? When were we going to attack? What if he attacked us? How long would we run? *What if I don't master my powers?* "Vittorio..."

"Calm down, Lucia. Samuel will not attack us here."

"How do you know? Why wouldn't he? What's stopping him?" I walked the length of the room, every possible worry spinning through my mind. We could be attacked right here in the house. And then what? "You seem to think you know him so well. If you really knew him, wouldn't you have destroyed him by now? You don't know him. You can't predict." I wasn't ready. They knew it, I knew it. And I'd bet my life that Samuel knew it, too.

"I do know him. You forget where I came from." He folded his arms across his chest and leaned against the doorframe. "Samuel did not always know about me. He couldn't find you in your first few lives following my creation. It wasn't until I began searching for you that he noticed *me*. The power between you and me draws and repels him. It allows him to know where you..." He motioned to me then himself.

~ ☾ ~

"...where *we* are. But when we are together, he is cautious."

He left the room, and a loud bang came from down the hall. Sounds of books being shuffled and tossed about followed. Then he returned to the parlor, carrying The Book.

Vittorio sat on the love seat, one ankle propped on his knee, The Book balanced on his leg. "I didn't understand it until your father explained what you'd done."

I stopped pacing and glanced at him. *My Light.* I knew when I'd given him the little piece of me that he'd be easy to find, an obvious mark. But I only thought other Pharos would notice him, not maniacal vampires.

"Do you think Samuel knows why he is aware of you?" I asked.

"No. I think if he did, I'd be his primary concern, not you."

He shifted on the couch, his hand landing on The Book. And the shiny gold plate attached to the leather cover captured my attention. Desire flared within me. So many secrets lay hidden in its pages. Answers to questions I hadn't even thought to ask. A wild urge to pluck it from Vittorio's lap and read every word rose within me. But to try was insanity. He'd never let me have The Book.

I tore my gaze away and found Vittorio watching me. I instantly knew he'd felt my desire. But his face held no expression—not anger, not disappointment, nor even interest.

I turned to the tree as my promise not to search for The Book, not to read its contents until I'd experienced the memories for myself, played in my mind. Could he trust me to keep that promise? *Can I trust myself?*

A bell rang from the television, and a little voice announced something about angels getting their wings.

Tis the season. I flicked the little bells on the tree, making three or four of them ring. *There, wings all around.* I paced again.

"Lucia, come, sit. You're needlessly worrying." Vittorio held his hand out to me.

I wanted to go to him, to let him hold me. But I knew his motivation was not to love me. It was only to be redeemed. I stayed by the tree.

"I need to practice guarding." I glanced at Elizabeth. She

~ ☾ ~

and Alexander were lost in each other, oblivious to what went on around them.

"Come." He motioned for me.

I bit my lip.

He patted the spot beside him.

I gave into my weakness and joined him on the love seat, cautious about keeping enough distance between us so as not to melt into a blubbering puddle and beg him to forgive me, to love me again.

His arm rested on the back of the couch, his fingers just barely touching my shoulder. My breath hitched. "Your light is a magnet, pulling Samuel to you, to me. He so desperately desires your power that he has made missteps, proving that his obsession for you is his weakness. He has made enemies of humans, some of whom have stood to fight and run him out of towns. He would love to possess you, but when you are with me, your power is magnified."

"How?" I peered at him from the corner of my eye. Stubble shadowed his chin, and his tongue moved across his lips, leaving them glistening. I bit my lip again and tried not to stare at his mouth.

"As your father said, your Light wants to go home. When we are together, it's so close to being home that it flares like a supernova." His thumb moved back and forth over my shoulder.

"How do..." My voice cracked. I cleared my throat. "How do you know? Do you feel it?" *I* felt it. I hadn't understood it, but now that I thought about it, I knew what it was.

Now he lightly strummed three fingers across my shoulder.

Deep within, the drumming pounded, low and steady. My heart raced, keeping perfect rhythm with it. I coughed to cover the excitement bubbling inside me. "Excuse me. I had a tickle."

"Yes. My heart tries to match it, but can't. If I were human, I'd think I was having a never-ending heart attack." His hand passed over my shoulder once more then he rested his arm on the back of the love seat. "Relax. There's no need for you to be so anxious."

~ ☾ ~

"When you saw her father, did he explain anything about her eyes?" Bruno asked. His eyes nearly popped out of his head. "That glow- it's like they're radioactive."

I turned to Vittorio.

He smiled. "It has to be her Light. This is what they looked like in The Abyss. They're a beautiful shade of green." He brushed his fingers along my cheek.

Heat raced across my skin, and my heart no longer matched the thrumming. It beat faster, louder than the aching beat within me. "I need sunglasses." I closed my eyes. *Breathe, Lucia. Stop acting like a teenager. Think of the situation at hand. Not him. Samuel, not Vittorio. Samuel. Samuel.*

"We'll find some tomorrow. But, for now, let me show you something more." Vittorio opened The Book.

The Book. The Book. The Book.

I slid closer to it, wedging myself beside him and sitting on both my hands in an effort to keep from snatching it away from him. I wasn't sure if I wanted to possess The Book or him. I balled my hands into fists, hoping to keep them beneath me.

"Vampires already fear you. They believe you will kill anyone in your path. You have quite a reputation. Elizabeth wrote this entry. Roger was a young vampire, maybe fifty years old." He flipped the pages until he stopped on a page titled: 'The Legend Continues.'

1895—entry number six—Roger is incomprehensible. He has been gibbering for nearly four days, babbling endlessly about The Goddess. She appeared before him, more alluring than any creature he'd ever seen or imagined. She called him to her, luring him closer and closer with sweet enchantments and promises of love. He wanted nothing more than to touch her, to feel her in his arms, to taste her. When he was within striking distance, her mood altered with a force so powerful he cowered at her feet.

Angry and vengeful, she demanded to know where Vittorio was. "Where is he?" Her voice crashed around them as if descending from the heavens. "Tell me where he is."

He insists he saw his own death in front of him.

~ ☾ ~

*Blackness, bone-chillingly cold and empty, surrounded him.
He screamed and screamed for help, begging to be set free,
but she set the blackness onto him. It crashed down,
smashing him to the ground. He heard his own breaths,
ragged in his ears.*

"Where is he?"

*He didn't know what happened or why she stopped, but
suddenly she did. She bent to him, pulling his head back by
his hair. Her hypnotic glowing eyes enthralled him like a
master vampire's. "Find Vittorio. Tell him I come for him."
When she left him, Roger lay sobbing, unable to move,
paralyzed with fear.*

*Bloody tears had dried down his temples. She managed
to bleed him from his nose as well. He vomited blood for
hours until the sounds of his retching made us worry he'd
kill himself.*

*Her powers grow greater with each lifetime. This time
she killed three and left one to tell his story.*

I covered my open mouth. I really had been terrifying. But
several lifetimes later that power had all but faded.

Alexander kicked off his shoes. "You're considered to be a
myth, The Vampire Goddess, the woman with the magical
eyes who brings torment and death to vampires. There are
legends about you circulating. The reality that you exist is
probably the best-kept secret in all of creation. No one really
wants to believe it, which helps to keep you safe," he
explained. He and Elizabeth faced us, both expressionless, as
if they weren't having a conversation with every vampire's
worst nightmare come to life.

Vittorio adjusted the book in his lap, leaning toward me.
"Your legend has grown across the years with each lifetime
and every death you delivered. Vampires don't understand
who you really are. They believe that you are a goddess who is
sometimes angered by vampire antics, striking out, killing or
crippling vampires who misbehave. They don't know when or
where you'll appear, but, when you have surfaced, the sight of
you alone has struck terror in the hearts of many. In fact, we
have heard it said that warring vampires will wish your wrath
on each other."

~ ☾ ~

The Vampire Goddess.

The humor in that term struck me and I sucked my cheeks in, biting down to keep from laughing hysterically. By my estimation a goddess was beautiful, confident, powerful, determined even. Of all those things I could, perhaps, have been convinced that I fell somewhere in the pretty spectrum, not goddess-like, but not on the cave troll end either. But confident, powerful, and determined? *Nope.* In those qualities I was completely lacking.

Wouldn't a vampire be surprised to find me standing behind The Vampire Goddess curtain? Me with power that sort of worked, but wasn't very effective. Sure, I could knock you out of a tree branch or bring you to your knees, but you weren't getting to Heaven through me. No, sir. I snorted then covered my lips.

"Lucia," Alexander said. "If the truth about your existence became known, we would quickly be over-taken. Samuel would be only one of our worries. We have been lucky so far. Samuel is just as fearful that others will find and create you before he can. This is why he rarely has a mature vampire, other than Brian, in his clan."

"But don't all vampires know about The Pharos?" I asked.

Vittorio settled back against the couch, adjusting one of the cushions. "That, too, is considered a legend. You will have to ask your father to be sure, but it is possible that you are the only Pharo left to actually hunt vampires."

"I'll ask, if or when I see him." God only knew when that would be.

"If there are other Pharos, they are hidden, working mysteriously among us."

Mysteriously. Most likely, if there were others, they were doing what they were supposed to do, and therefore, weren't in any trouble. Yet another subject for me to ask Father to explain. *I should make a list.*

"Here is something that may interest you." Vittorio slid The Book onto my lap.

I pulled it to me, the tome heavy on my legs, and ran my fingers across the open pages. Excitement surged. Finally, I had it. I hugged The Book to me, crushing its pages against

~ ☾ ~

my chest, and inched to the edge of the couch.

Vittorio wrapped his arm around my shoulder and pulled me against him. Warmth encircled me, weaving through my hair, around my neck and arms, over my legs. *Easy, Lucia,* his voice purred in my head. *Release The Book.* Patiently he waited for me to comply. "Let me show you." He clutched my arm, his fingers playing along my skin like a harpist works his instrument.

I placed The Book back in my lap, but still gripped the edges tightly.

"Here." He pointed to an entry. "This is the one."

1902—entry number eight—Our three days of searching finally paid off. We found Samuel's lair, hidden in the basement of the foundry. Nineteen fledglings slept piled together like dead bodies waiting for a pyre. Sobbing humans huddled in a corner, terrified even to look in our direction. When Elizabeth approached them, a young woman screamed, pleading for her life, begging for mercy.

Elizabeth was able to calm her enough to learn her name was Helen and that her family had been taken hostage. Helen explained that the men had been killed, drained. Then Samuel drank from each of the women, tasting them, demanding to have "it".

"Give it to me! Give it to me!" He'd screamed the words, howling them louder than humanly possible.

"What do you want? What?" Helen's mother had begged.

"Damn you!" he shouted, shaking her so that her head bounced back and forth. He threw her to the ground when she no longer breathed.

Helen told us that the town folk had always known he was strange, but no one ever questioned him. Young men and women had gone missing over the years, only to reappear a generation later, denying their old identities. Samuel's father and grandfather had run a business from this same building for more than eighty years. Now, Samuel had returned to run the family store. She knew he had been the one, the same man, for all those years.

"I've seen him. He's vampire," she whispered, tears

~ ☾ ~

streaming down her cheeks. "Evil."

"What did he want?" Elizabeth asked.

"Power. He said he wants our power," Helen answered. "We have no power. We're poor. We have nothing." She sobbed. "Not even a mother or father anymore."

We did not understand why he took the family until we saw the little girl hidden in the shadows. With eyes as wide as walnuts and green as grass, she'd charmed him. Quietly sitting and watching, mesmerized by the adults' fear, she had watched the entire attack unfold, and now she watched still, tucked into a little ball in a corner on the floor.

Emma was her name. She could have been Lucia. She looked so much like her, but she was not.

"He's going to keep me until I grow up," she said. "Then he's going to marry me."

"How old are you?"

"Seven." She pushed her hair from her face. As sweet as she smelled, she did not hold any of Lucia's spirit. "He's going to keep all of us." She turned to the darkened room behind her. "One of us has the power."

Peter opened the door to find five more girls, not one of them older than nine years, all huddled together.

We freed the six girls and the four women, sending them off believing there'd been an accident at the building that killed their men. Then we staked and burned the fledglings, torching the factory, too.

But even with our urgings, Helen was too traumatized to forget all that she'd seen. Her reports of Samuel being a vampire weren't taken lightly. Some thought she suffered from a mental disease. But others, those who'd seen Samuel the night he stole the girls and women from their homes, believed. They hunted Samuel by day and hid in their homes, barricaded behind locked doors and windows at night.

He was forced to flee.

"Children? He captured little girls?" My eyes filled with tears at the thought of little girls being tortured because of me, losing their souls to him because of me.

"We found that he'd tried it a number of times, never getting the result he wanted."

~ ☾ ~

The idea of him ripping them from their beds, from their mother's arms, and talking to them, touching them, holding them, incensed me. The pounding rhythm built, faster, louder, deeper. "I have to practice. I have to destroy him." My fingers tensed and my nails dug into the leather binding in my hands. "He must die."

Vittorio pulled The Book from my lap. "Yes, and we will destroy him. When you are ready."

The sound of my breathing deepened, coming more quickly. Power prickled along my skin. Within myself, I saw The Abyss. Cold and dark, it churned faster, wilder. Energy hummed in the air around me.

Come to me. My own voice, soft and seductive, called it to the surface. Heavy, solid tension constricted around me. Distant screams echoed in my ears.

"Lucia, calm down. Now is not the time." Vittorio closed The Book. "*Cuore mio*, relax. Soon enough you will have your chance."

I glanced at his eyes and saw the reflection of my own. They glowed bright as two stars, greener than ever.

"It's late. You need to sleep." He stood and helped me to my feet. His aura blanketed me, soothing me, quieting the drum, pulling me away from The Abyss. "Peter, Bruno, you take the first shift."

"Elizabeth and I will be up to relieve you in four hours," Alexander said. "She needs to rest, otherwise we would be happy to take the first watch."

"Go, rest. We'll be fine." Bruno unplugged the tree, fading into the shadows. My confusion must have been evident. "We don't need the light."

"In fact, better that we don't have it. We see more clearly in the dark." Peter turned off the TV. "Rest, Lucia. You'll need your strength." He patted my shoulder on his way toward the French doors. "I'll take a walk around the outside." He vanished into the darkness.

"Good night, Lucia. Sleep well," Alexander said. "Come, Elizabeth. You too need to rest."

"I'd like a moment with Lu," she said.

Everyone froze for a quick second. Peter appeared in the

~ ☾ ~

doorway.

"I have something to tell her. That's all." She raised an eyebrow to Alexander.

"It will be fine," he said. "Vittorio, let's go clear a path in your study." He motioned for Vittorio to lead the way.

Elizabeth looked like herself. Beautiful, kind, non-predator-like. Gone were the crimson orbs. Big, brown eyes twinkled at me. She held out her hand. "It won't take but a moment."

I took her hand, quickly calculating how fast Vittorio and Alexander could make it from the study to my defense.

She led the way into the kitchen, ducking her head back into the parlor. "I just want to be sure that Vittorio is in his study." The house rattled when a loud bang heralded the return of the bookcase to the upright position. "Good. Alexander is keeping him busy."

She rushed to my side. "I found something hidden in your pocket when we carried you and Vittorio to his room." She smiled. "I took the liberty of removing it and hiding it in your lingerie drawer. I don't think he'll find it there."

"Thanks." I'd completely forgotten about the little book.

"It would be a wonderful Christmas gift for him," she said.

"Yes. It would be, if we were exchanging gifts. If we..." I didn't want to consider any *ifs*. There was no way for us to have any *ifs*. He didn't trust me. And, in all honesty, I didn't trust him. He knew what I'd done to him. Selfishly, I'd done it. And now, I knew that all he wanted was salvation. I had no choice but to give it to him, and, once it happened, I'd be alone to continue my work until God saw fit to allow my own redemption. I blinked hard to try to hold back the tears.

There was absolutely no point to considering *if*. I'd prolonged the inevitable for far too long. This lifetime would give me no option but to accept my calling and bring them all to The Light.

Elizabeth dabbed my cheeks. "Don't cry. It will all work out. Have no doubt."

"I know. I know." There was no avoiding fate. No matter how hard you tried, she always found you and took what was hers. I'd always known this would happen.

~ ☾ ~

Elizabeth hugged me. "Come on. Alexander and Vittorio are tired of cleaning, and Vittorio is becoming suspicious." She smiled. "I love when he doesn't know everything."

The men met us on the staircase.

"Everything all right?" Dust covered Vittorio's clothes and hair. He and Alexander looked as though they'd come from a construction site.

"Yes," we answered. Elizabeth giggled as she smoothed her hands over Alexander's chest. He grinned.

"Good. Good." Vittorio's left eye squinted slightly as he studied me.

I smiled. "I'm tired."

"Let's go." He motioned for us to ascend the stairs. "We should plan to get to St. Aloysius by seven, mass will start at nine so we'll need to be out of the church by eight to avoid suspicions. We'll leave straight from church."

"Very good. We should have plenty of time for prayers and meditation," Alexander said, falling into step behind Elizabeth.

"We're going to church?" I asked. "Do you think it's wise to waste time?"

They all stopped moving and I pivoted to face them.

"Not everyone has the type of relationship you have with the Lord," Elizabeth said. "Some of us need to pray."

"I pray, too," I said. "It's not like I have a hotline to him. And, remember, I've been avoiding his...expectations...requests...demands. I don't know what to call it. But I haven't been doing what he wants. That can't be good."

"Then a little time in church will do you good," Vittorio said. He studied my face, slowly blinking.

"You all actually go into church." I laughed and continued up the stairs. "Vampires in church."

"You know we go to church. You saw it in my memories." Vittorio stepped onto the stair directly behind me so his body grazed mine. "Have you forgotten what I've taught you already?" The words breezed through my hair, and his hand rested on my hip.

My heart sped.

~ ☾ ~

"Hmm?" His deep voice tickled my ear.
The scent of him filled my lungs. I closed my eyes to force back the desire that suddenly erupted within me. "No." I marched up the stairs. "Good night," I called from the landing and darted down the hall to his room.

~ ☾ ~

CHAPTER TWENTY-ONE

After a quick shower and a long search for the least sheer nightie in the drawer, I padded into the bedroom and surveyed the damage. The mantle jutting from the wall had been removed, and plastic covered the gaping hole that remained. A couch-shaped opening on the adjacent wall allowed for an unobstructed view into the hallway. Plaster littered the floor. A moment of trepidation crept over me. It hadn't taken Vittorio more than a few minutes to cause this much destruction.

"We'll have to do some home repairs when we return." He stood leaning against the bedroom door, which was still embedded in the sheetrock. "It's not the first time." He stepped away from the door, peeking behind it and inspecting the frame. When he gripped the knob, the hinges groaned, plaster cracked, and finally the door swung free. He sighed and pushed it into the frame, closing it securely.

When he turned toward me, my legs nearly melted. His tousled hair framed his face and hung down his neck. His eyes lit, and an inviting smile graced his lips. As he unbuttoned his shirt, the dark curls on his chest caught my attention.

I turned away, fumbling with the switch on the bedside lamp, no longer worried about the damage he'd caused. My desire for him made it nearly impossible for me to remember any of my worries.

"You're nervous. Or is it worried? You're getting better at masking your emotions." He walked toward the closet. "Though I think it's beginner's luck more than skill." With two quick thuds his shoes hit the closet floor. "By the way, I like your choice of sleepwear."

~ ☾ ~

Even from the closet his voice was a deep whisper, tickling my skin, stoking my desire for him. I crossed my arms over my chest and squeezed my shoulders, trying to diminish the clearly visible effect he had on my breasts.

He dropped his watch on the night table as he glided toward the bathroom. "So, Elizabeth has explained guarding. We should practice." It amazed me that he could project his voice in such a way that it sounded as if he was standing beside me. "You'll need to relax, let your intuition guide you."

I listened as he turned on the water for a shower. When the sounds of the spray turned to splashes, I knew he was bathing. I turned toward the bathroom, fighting a wild drive to peek at him. *Knock it off, Lucia. Samuel. Samuel. Samuel.* Even that dreaded name did little to cool my desire.

The water stopped, and I turned toward the bed, aching with need. I gritted my teeth and squeezed my eyes shut, trying to bite back my urge to go to him.

"If you're cold, get in the bed, *cuore mio.*" He leaned around me to pull the blanket down. The soft hair on his bare chest tickled my skin. His hand rested on the small of my back as he guided me toward the bed.

Heat pooled in my belly. "No. I'll sleep on the couch." I backed out of his space. "I'll just take a pillow, and I'll be fine in front of the fire." I clasped the pillow to my chest and walked around him. Maybe I should have slept in another room. But the truth was that I wanted to be near him, in his arms, even if I knew I shouldn't.

The heat of his gaze seemed to burn on my backside as I crossed the room.

"I think you're going to be cold. That little red number was not made for sleeping alone on the couch in front of a hearth that is clearly not capable of containing a fire."

"Then maybe you could get me a blanket." I raised my chin, hugging the pillow like a life preserver.

He licked his lips. "Or you could simply come to bed." He sat on the edge of the bed, shirtless. His dark chest hair formed a V down to his bellybutton where the trail continued into his pants. My eyes followed the path downward and heat rose up my neck to my cheeks. His hips pivoted.

~ ☾ ~

I looked at his face.

"Do you like my pajamas? I thought they were festive." He stood to model the silky red pants, turning a slow circle that set my body to burning.

"They are festive," I whispered, admiring his butt, round and muscular, just as perfect as ever. The pajama bottoms sat low on his hips, a black drawstring dangling in the front, giving a full view of his tight abs. My mouth watered.

"I'm glad you like them."

His teeth glinted when he flashed his smile. I would have been completely dazzled by him, if not for the guilty feeling that still sat in my chest.

"They go well with your nightie." He moved toward me with such grace, it almost seemed as though he hadn't moved at all.

"Where are the extra blankets? I'd be happy to get one myself." I shuffled to the side, holding onto my pillow.

"You're going to rip it." He pointed to my hands. "You're far too nervous. This isn't our first night alone. Not our wedding night." He stepped in front of me.

"I know that." I forced my hands to loosen, but my arms still crushed the pillow. The sound of down feathers disintegrating to fuzz squeaked inside the satin pillowcase.

He pursed his lips and cocked his head. "If you know, why are you so nervous?"

"I'm not. I am, however, very tired." I huffed and kept my gaze away from his face, his chest, the hair below his belly button, and those damn red pants. I examined the rip in the arm of the couch. *If I put a pillow over it, I won't even feel it when I'm sleeping.* "Vittorio, a blanket? Please?"

"You're cold?" He stepped closer, his scent reaching me first. "I can't have that. As your husband, it's my duty to care for your needs, whatever they are."

Warmth—no, it was passion. *Passion* washed over me, streaming like a running brook. It bubbled and turned, pouring over my neck and down my chest, teasing my nipples to peaks again then wrapping around my arms and legs. Soft, comforting caresses chased away my tension and anxiety, relaxing my body and mind, nearly wiping away the

~ ☾ ~

protective wall I'd begun building around my heart.

"Let yourself go. We belong together. As your father explained, we're bound to each other." He held me against his chest. "Let me care for you, *cuore mio*."

I wanted to. I wanted to let him have me. I wanted him to love me like he once did. I wanted him to take away all my worries, all my troubles. But I couldn't. I'd burdened him enough. I couldn't take advantage of him.

I stiffened in his embrace, unable to look into his face.

His arms tensed, and he held me to him. "Why do you fight me?" He kissed my temple. "Why do you resist what we both want?" His breath tickled my ear and I squirmed to avoid temptation. "What we both require." My fingers kneaded his chest muscles. "I feel your fear. I would never hurt you. How could I hurt you, when a small part of your spirit exists in me?" His mouth moved along my neck. He tenderly kissed the sore spot, working small circles. His tongue, wet and hot, lapped over my rapidly beating pulse. He closed his mouth over the vein, and I felt him suck, softly, soothingly. I moaned for him.

Lucia. His voice swept through my mind. *I want you, my love.* The tone seductive, powerful, primal. His desire, unbridled.

My eyes popped open, and I shoved him, breaking from his hold.

Panting, I backed away. "Don't touch me." I scraped the back of my hand across my neck. "You can't have me. Get out. I don't want you near me." I stumbled toward the opening in the wall, reaching for the couch to keep from falling. I'd leave if he wouldn't.

He stood perfectly still, but his aura circled, turning in the room, touching me, testing me. He bowed his head. "What have you dreamt?" Sadness hung in the question. "In your dreams, what have you seen?"

"Nothing. Just leave. I need to rest." I'd have sworn the room was an inferno. Sweat dripped down my neck and between my breasts.

"You cannot lie to me." He sat on the edge of the bed. "I felt your aura moving freely with mine, calling to me, wanting

~ ☾ ~

me to touch you. Until you panicked. You remembered something. What was it?"

I sat on the couch. "It wasn't a memory."

He stood.

"Stay on the bed. Don't test me, Vittorio. I don't want to call The Abyss, but I swear I'll do it if you come near me." Tears overflowed from my eyes and rushed down my cheeks.

He collapsed onto the bed. "You believe I would harm you?" He scrubbed his hands through his hair.

"You'd create me and keep me for your own." I picked at the hem of my nightie. Tears dropped onto my legs and rolled down my skin. "I'm not safe in your arms. I want you too much, but I want you to love me, not hurt me."

He didn't say a word, simply leaned forward, resting his face in his hands, elbows on his knees. The silence seemed to last an hour.

"I would never, never condemn you to this." His voice cracked. "I love you too much to do it." Pink tears glistened in his eyes when he lifted his face. "Never."

I sat perfectly still, wanting to believe him, to trust him, but knowing it was impossible. "I saw into your heart, Vittorio. I *saw* what you want. I felt your desire to claim me. You can't deny it."

"I cannot deny wanting you." His shoulders slumped and those tiny lines around his eyes deepened. "I cannot deny a fantasy of being with you forever in a way that eliminates all danger. The only world I can recognize where that is an option is one where you are no longer at all human or weak. One where my desires would not include your blood. You cannot hate me for wanting you. Just as I could never hate you for what you did."

I stared at him, unable to comment.

He moved to the door. "I'll sleep down the hall."

I sat on the couch, motionless. I didn't hate him. I could never hate him. But I didn't know if I could ever trust him either. I pulled the blanket from the bed and returned to the couch. How could I sleep in his bed without him?

~ ☾ ~

CHAPTER TWENTY-TWO

My dreams remained a rollercoaster of memories and nightmares, rolling from one vision to the next, never giving me an opportunity to understand what was happening.

*****

The soft glow of candles lit the church. Vittorio helped me from the pew as we stood to receive communion. We held hands, and mine fit perfectly in his. The rough spots on his palms, calloused from working the fields, were familiar, and I loved the way they felt against my skin. I smiled at him. He squeezed my hand as we walked side by side to the altar. We received the Eucharist and walked back to our pew together. I knelt in prayer, closing my eyes.

*****

When I opened my eyes, I was in his study frantically searching all the corners, in the drawers, the shadows. I climbed the giant bookcases, trying to find it. Where was it? Where had he hidden The Book?

I tore the room apart, desperately searching for it. My need dominated me. I had to have it. Desire raged in me. My heart pounded while I raced about the room, hunting for The Book.

As I stooped to look behind the bookcase, a key rattled in the lock and the doorknob clicked. I spun around to face him, ready to feel his wrath. But when the door opened, it wasn't Vittorio.

It was Samuel. His platinum hair hung loose around his shoulders. His cruel smile displayed long, sharp fangs. "I can teach you what you need to know." He entered the room, and murky mist obscured my vision. It wasn't until I felt his fingers knotted in my hair that I knew where he was. I tried to

~ ☾ ~

scream but his cold mouth crushed my throat.

Blood trickled down my neck when he lifted his head and spoke, "Lucia, you are mine." His voice was different, not the same cruel hiss from the hospital, but a familiar romantic whisper, soft and seductive.

I gasped for air and blinked at him.

Dark hair replaced the blond, falling in waves around his face. Vittorio's hazel gaze morphed to black and fastened on me, probing my soul. There was no denying him access. His presence inside me explored every corner of my being. "Vittorio," I whimpered. His fangs dripped with my blood as he lowered his mouth to my neck again. He drank from me, draining me to near death. My eyes closed to blackness.

*****

When I opened my eyes, I stood beside a carriage, wearing a long fur cape, heavy hat, gloves, and boots. The carriage, filled with boxes and tools, was harnessed to four large horses. As the sun set, the temperature plummeted.

I was tired and wanted to rest.

"No. You must train." Papa shoved my sword into my hand. "You must know how to defend yourself in the dark. Our enemies can see us perfectly in the shadows. You must learn to hear and sense them. They will move swiftly. If you are not prepared and driven to succeed, you will not survive."

"Yes, Papa," I said as I prepared for their assault. The sounds of cloaks flapping and feet on the ground were the only signs of their advance. The glint of firelight off my father's sword caught my eye in time for me to defend myself. But I was not fast enough to defend from both of them. Costin disarmed me and flattened me on my back before I saw him at my side.

"Again!" Papa yelled. I grabbed my sword and scrambled to my feet. It was the same outcome. "Again! We will do this all night until you defend!"

I prepared for the attack and again Costin bested me. Anger pulsed through me. I wanted to hurt him.

"Lu! Why? *Why* have you not altered your defense? How many times must we do this before you change your practice? Use your brain!" Papa barked. "Costin, you must attack. Once

~ ☾ ~

she is disarmed, continue. Since she refuses to change her defense, do not stop. We must make her try to defend herself with no weapon!"

My heart raced as I realized that they might actually hurt me. I stood trembling in the darkness, waiting for them to advance. When I heard them moving, I changed my strategy. I attacked Papa, disarming him, then I was able to defend against Costin. I swung the sword with all my strength. The blade sliced through his cloak, and his breathing quickened as he retreated. I ran at him, attacking as fast as I could. After disarming him, I jumped, knocking him to the ground and landing atop his chest, pinning him with the hilt of my sword against his throat.

In the darkness, his heavy breathing stirred on my face and his hands squeezed my waist as he tried to move me. "Good job, love. You were making me nervous."

My father reached down and helped me stand. "Good, good. Lu, you must always be prepared to change your plan. Your life depends on your ability to be flexible and think quickly. You must be prepared at all times."

*****

Clouds rushed overhead. Thunder clapped in the distance.

I stood outside, in front of the new Tempo building in Boston. Cold rain fell on my upturned face. Not a star shone in the heavens above me. The night sky turned black as The Abyss.

My reflection in the mirrored glass wall showed a woman I hardly recognized. Clad all in black, my pale skin showed in stark contrast to my clothing. My hair billowed in the wind. I felt powerful, unstoppable. The most beguiling smile appeared on my lips. My eyes glowed a deep green, lit by some magnetic force. I was irresistible, seductive, dangerous. Power pulsed through me like a current, drawing him to me.

"Come to me. Come to me, my love," I called.

I had a need, an all-consuming desire for him. The taste of his blood remained fresh in my memory. His scent clouded my senses. *I must have him.* The raw instinct to seduce him clawed at me. I wanted his blood. I was the Vampire Goddess.

My voice was not my own as my need for him possessed

~ ☾ ~

me. I didn't move my lips, yet that voice, sexy and angry, called to him, commanding him. *Come to me.* The sound was terrifying—my own voice, so deadly, so erotic, not at all like me.

I summoned The Abyss. The blackness surrounded me, roiling out from my body. But this time it did not try to crush me. I did not feel it taking me. No terrified screams sounded as I waited to die.

My voice boomed around me. "Come to me. Come to me, my love."

His aura stirred, finally coming. Slowly, unwillingly, he came.

My body swayed with the force of The Abyss as I controlled it, wielding it like a powerful weapon. I was its master.

My spirit expanded, making me stronger, its heat building, growing hot enough to swallow The Abyss, trapping the cold blackness within me.

I closed my eyes and inhaled, breathing in its power, allowing it to spread through me, knowing that this time I would free his soul.

*****

I pulled myself from my dreams, panting and trembling, understanding that the only way for me to truly master my power was to control my aura, both sleeping and awake. It was the doorway to The Abyss, not my mind as I had once believed. My ability was entirely spiritual.

I sat up and found Vittorio at the end of the couch watching me.

"What are you doing?" I wiped the blanket across my sweaty neck and chest.

His luminescent skin nearly glowed, even in the dark room. His body stiffened, his eyes darting over me, never settling. Fangs extended from beneath his lips. "You summoned me." The flat, toneless words fell between us.

I *had* summoned him. In my dream I called him to me, forcing his compliance.

He sat, silent and still, like a statue. No human could be so motionless. He didn't even breathe. "You're thirsty." In spite

~ ☾ ~

of his stoic posture, he couldn't control his tongue. His accent thickened, revealing his fear.

"I am not." I scooted back against the arm of the couch. A frightened vampire was a dangerous one.

"Yes, you are," he whispered. "You were very clear about it."

My heart pounded in my chest. I listened for the thrumming, expecting the ache to awaken, but it did not. The only beats came from my heart. Rapid, frightened beats. "Did you see any of the dreams?"

"Yes. All four," he said, still not moving.

I fidgeted, wrapping the blanket around me. "What do you think they mean?"

"Some are memories. Some dreams."

"I'm scared." I needed him, wanted him to hold me, wanted him to want me.

"I know. I feel it. Your spirit flashes colder and colder."

"You're afraid of me, too." I hugged my knees to my chest and rested my chin on them. "I sense your fear. Your energy pulses. It's different than usual. Not smooth."

"You are terrifying." He stared at me, unblinking.

I swallowed the lump in my throat and kept my face turned away from him, unable to meet his gaze. A deluge of tears built behind my eyes, and looking at him would break the dam. I'd never dreamt he'd feel this way.

"I have not been summoned or forced against my will to do anything since I left Kerina. Not even she controlled me entirely." He finally inhaled. "While you slept, you came to me at first softly, seductively. You danced over me, teasing, offering yourself to me in ways we have not known since our life together."

I dared to glance at him. His eyes glistened, and I turned away.

"Then, when I reminded you of Samuel and your need to destroy him first, you changed. Your voice. Your soul...darkened. Such darkness I've never known," he whispered and wiped tears from his cheeks. "There is a shadow in you, on your soul. One I cannot understand."

"What was it? Did you see what it was?" I blinked and

~ ☾ ~

swiped my hand across my cheeks to stop my own tears.

"I don't know. It was too dark, too angry. I was afraid to look."

"Was it Samuel?" The only true evil I knew was him, and all I could imagine was that he had left his mark on me somehow.

He shook his head. "I can't be sure."

"What about the other dreams? What did they mean?"

"The first was your memory of our last Christmas together." He picked at a rip in the leather couch. "The priest was Father Di Giulio. Father Marcantonio died earlier in the year, and Father Di Guilio replaced him." He had always like Father Marcantonio better. It wasn't surprising that he remembered his death and subsequent replacement.

"What do you think the dream with Samuel meant?"

"I'm not sure. Obviously, you're still anxious about my desires. You imagined that I killed you, which is not much better than thinking I created you." He frowned. "But, more worrisome than you fearing me, you may have some link to Samuel, and he could be showing you what he wants you to see."

My heart pounded. Acid turned in my stomach. "I heard him in my mind, felt him. What if he *is* reaching into me?" I touched my neck, the invisible wound throbbing beneath my fingers.

"You need to control your aura. You can't let it roam to him or to me." The tone of his voice hardened. "You must destroy him before me."

"I know." I desperately wanted to crawl into his arms and sob. "I have to defeat him, Vittorio. This may be my last chance." My voice faltered.

"What do you mean?"

"Father said something about me being sent somewhere if I didn't accomplish it this time."

He studied my face, his brows slightly creased. "Do you remember where?"

"No." A heaviness weighed on me. "You're worried...for me. I feel it."

"Yes. It's getting harder to hide my emotions from you.

~ ☾ ~

You recognize my spirit almost as if it were your own." He sighed. "You need to rest. I believe that a sleep-deprived Pharo is a very dangerous one. It may be the reason you can't control yourself." He stood.

"Vittorio, wait." I wanted him to stay. I needed him. "Don't leave. What about the other dreams?"

"Well, the one at the Tempo building may have been a premonition of sorts. That obviously hasn't happened, but it is what brought me here. The other one...that was a memory. Did you recognize the language?" He stepped to my side. His fangs disappeared.

"No. It was barely familiar at all."

"Romanian. You lived in Romania during your second life." He scooped me into his arms. "There is no point in my sleeping elsewhere. You will simply call me to you." His voice was tenuous, his aura cool and fidgety, as though it trembled.

"I'm sorry." I slid my hand over his shoulder and cuddled into his arms. "I don't want to hurt you."

"I know. You've avoided this for centuries." He carried me to the bed. "I don't want to hurt you either. We seem a well-matched pair, and to separate us does not help matters." He pulled the blanket from around me, draping it over us, and settled down beside me. "Of course, we have Bruno to help me maintain control. Your control is a concern we must master."

I nestled into his arms, twining my fingers through his gold chain and cross. "What will he do?"

His arm slid over me, and I pulled his leg across mine. He nuzzled his face into my hair, inhaling a deep, slow breath. "His influence will keep my desire for you contained." His presence tempered, and the fidgeting stopped. Its movement became fluid, moving freely once again.

"I don't like that you fear me so much."

"I cannot help it, Lucia. Your power is awesome. And that shadow within you is like nothing I've ever seen." He squeezed me tight against him.

What had I done? What was this stain? "What if it's so evil that you can't forgive me?"

"I love you. I will always love you. It is not up to me to

~ ☾ ~

forgive your sins. You know that."

I sunk into his embrace, praying that whatever evil I held within me would be, could be, forgiven.

~ ☾ ~

CHAPTER TWENTY-THREE

I awoke at 6:10 in the morning, exactly. I knew this because of the annoying ringing coming from the bedside.

"What is that?" I pulled the blanket over my head.

The ringing grew louder.

"Vittorio?" I reached over to his side of the bed. Empty.

I rolled over, and my hand shot out toward the noise, fumbling for the alarm. I finally gave up and looked at the nightstand.

There, in front of the alarm clock, was a package. It looked just like all the others he had given me in our past life together. Anticipation made my hands unsteady as I placed it on the pillow in front of me. There hadn't been any other gift that ever brought me such happiness. A tear leaked from the corner of my eye.

The alarm clicked off.

"Are you going to open it?" Vittorio climbed onto the bed beside me and kissed my cheek.

I nodded, unable to speak.

He smiled. "What if it isn't what you think it is? You might be wasting these tears." He caught one on his finger.

I sat up, placing the little package in my lap. The wrapping was exactly the same: a kerchief tied with white ribbon to form a pouch. I plucked the ribbon and the fabric fell open, revealing exactly what I knew would be there. Six chestnuts, two figs, and a piece of Italian chocolate.

I tried not to cry, but the attempt was futile. This was the Christmas gift he'd given me every year since we'd begun courting. He traveled into town to buy the chocolate and ribbon, picked the chestnuts and figs from our farm, and let Mama pick the kerchief.

~ ☾ ~

"For more than three hundred years I have thought about your response to this gift. It was the same each Christmas. And for the life of me, I cannot figure out why chocolate, nuts, and fruit make you cry." He beamed.

"It's the kerchief," I said as several more tears rushed down my face.

We both laughed.

"As I recall, you are supposed to wear the Christmas kerchief to church today." He pulled me into his arms.

I laughed. "I don't think it's big enough to contain this." I held a handful of hair out from my head.

"Oh, you could manage..." He ran his fingers through my hair. "...if your mother was here, giving you the look." He narrowed one eye the same way she always had when she lectured me about the kerchief.

I kissed him and giggled.

"I never quite liked the kerchief. It always held you back, forced the curls to try to behave." He sighed with obvious contentment. "No. No kerchief today." He fanned the long tresses out behind me. "*Buon Natale*, Lucia."

His presence, so gentle and happy, moved through me. And my aura opened to him, meeting his, holding him close. He closed his eyes and inhaled deeply as I danced around him, impassioned and excited, finally both controlling myself and sharing the moment with him. I reached within him and tickled places long in need of attention. He moaned, and his fingers squeezed my thigh. A squeak of pleasure slipped past my lips.

I couldn't keep it up for long, and, suddenly, my control ended. The feel of his excitement and pleasure caught me off guard. As fast as it came, it vanished. The heated sensation that zoomed along my skin ceased, replaced by a cold rush.

I shivered, and so did he. I couldn't hide my disappointment in myself.

He opened his eyes and smiled. "No, don't feel badly. That was wonderful. The best gift I've ever received." He kissed my lips. "Soon, *cuore mio*, you'll have complete control. And then..." He growled into my ear, and I squirmed against him.

Cheeks flushed, his head rested on the pillow beside mine.

~ ☾ ~

"So you liked that?" I smoothed my fingers over the stubble on his chin.

"Hmm. Yes. Very, very much. I haven't had—"

"I have a gift for you," I interrupted. "Do you want it?" I bolted up.

"A gift? When did you get me a gift?" His surprise thrilled me.

I grinned from ear to ear. "Never mind when. Do you want it?" I batted my eyes at him.

He hesitated. "When?"

I giggled. "I guess you don't want it. In that case, would you like a fig?" I bit into a fruit and offered him a bite.

He frowned at the fig. "I want the gift. What is it?"

"Oh, I'm not telling. *Mmm.* This fig is so sweet. Are you sure you don't want a bite?" I held it to his lips.

He pushed my hand away. "No fig. What is it? Tell me what it is." His face lit like a child's on Christmas morning. His presence whooshed around me, uncontained and eager.

I laughed.

A memory flashed through my mind of him trying to get me to tell him about a birthday surprise. He badgered me for days, finally resorting to chasing me around the kitchen until he'd caught me, pinning me to the table and offering to pleasure me in any way, if only I'd tell him. We both laughed at the memory.

"You never have been able to handle a surprise." I grinned at him. "Let's eat this last fig, then I'll get your gift."

"*No, no, no.* I can't wait. You have to give it to me now." He pulled the fig from my fingers so quickly I had no time to fake a squawk. He wrapped my gift back up, tied the bow, and placed it on the nightstand. "Okay, I'm ready." He tried shooing me off the bed.

I checked the time. "I don't know. Maybe we should wait until after church. We could both use a visit with God." I stretched and sighed. "Let's get ready. Take a shower. Get dressed. Have breakfast."

"I can't wait. You have to give it to me. Where is it? I'll get it." He was off the bed, opening drawers on the nightstand and the desk, paying no attention to my halfhearted attempts

~ ☾ ~

to redirect him. When he came up empty, he darted to the closet.

"Stop!" I jumped out of bed and ran to the closet, blocking his way. He managed to open the door in spite of me plastering my body against it.

"So, it's in here." He looked over my head into the closet.

I tried desperately not to think of the lingerie drawer. I didn't want to give it away, but, the more I tried not to think about it, the faster it became my foremost thought. Energy raced around us. His aura coaxed mine, caressing and teasing until a huge grin appeared on his face as he looked from my face to the drawer.

"You wouldn't!" I put my hands on his chest and pushed. He didn't budge. "It's not fair to use your superhuman strength."

He took one step backward but still held on to the doorframe. "I have to have it. I can't wait. Please, let me have it."

The sound of his pleading thrilled me. I loved that my powerful, fierce vampire was begging me for his Christmas gift. I reveled in the moment. "I don't think so. I think you should wait until after church like a good little boy. Now, go get ready." I gave him another push.

"I can't." He grinned at me, let go of the doorframe, and slid his hands down to my waist.

"Don't you dare." But it was too late. He picked me up. I knew what he was doing, and there was very little time to stop him. "Vittorio. You're not fighting fair."

He held me close, pinning me against the wall. I instinctively wrapped my arms and legs around him. His hands were on my thighs, sliding toward my bottom, and his mouth moved along my neck. "Please, give me my gift," he begged between kisses. "Please."

I thought about not giving in to him. I enjoyed his tactics. Why give in? How long could I get away with it? Not long, was the answer. But he kept kissing and squeezing me, and I hung on, hoping for more. Then he warned, "If you wait too long, I'll get it myself."

"Oh, fine." I knew it couldn't last. "You're incorrigible. Go

~ ☾ ~

back to bed, and I'll get it for you."

He put me down and backed away from the closet, smiling like the Cheshire cat. He always won. No matter how hard I tried, he always beat me.

I went into the closet, but before retrieving the gift, I peeked out at him to be sure he was on the bed. He sat on the edge, waiting. "You'll need to get *in* the bed."

Laughing, he slid backwards, propping himself up against the headboard. He cocked his head to the side and raised an eyebrow. "Will this do?"

"That's fine." I went back into the closet to find the gift. I pulled the book out of the drawer, using a T-shirt to wipe it down, removing any dust, then rummaged through the drawer and pulled out another nightie. I wrapped the lacy little number around the book and came out with it behind my back. "Close your eyes," I said, climbing onto the bed.

I sat beside him, enjoying the sight of him. Even in the early morning light he was beautiful, like an angel. I watched the perfect muscles of his chest rise and fall with each breath. The temptation to touch him was irresistible, and I ran my fingers down his arm from his shoulder to the curve of his elbow.

"I thought you were giving me my gift," he said without opening his eyes.

I placed the small book in his hands. "Okay. You can open them."

When he opened his eyes, they were the most dazzling they'd been since I first saw him. The gold and green flecks shone, sparkling like tiny crystals. I gasped at their beauty, unable to look away. He was not holding me, not forcing me to him. In that moment, I knew he had no control over me. It was my own heart holding me, and I thought it would burst for all the love I felt for him.

He touched my cheek. "*Cuore mio*, you do the same thing to me."

My cheeks flushed, again. "Open your gift," I whispered.

He looked down at the bundle in his hands and grinned. "I like the gift wrap." As he unfolded the nightie from the book, I watched his face. His smile sent heat waves through me. I

~ ☾ ~

knew right away he loved it. "I wondered where this went. I tried turning that study upside down to find this last night."

"With Alexander?"

"Yes, while Elizabeth had you in the kitchen."

I laughed. "Was Alexander helpful?"

"No. In fact, he was in the way the entire time, babbling about some encyclopedia." He thumbed through the pages. "I loved this book the first time you gave it to me. I love it just as much now," he said, stopping on a page. "Vidi Madonna Sopra Un Fresco Rio," he read at the top of the page. Casting me a quick smile. "I Saw My Lady by a Cool, Fresh Stream." He recited the de' Medici poem, using the exact intonation he'd used so many time before:

> *I saw my lady by a cool, fresh stream*
> *Among green branches and gay ladies stand;*
> *Since the first hour when I felt love's hot brand*
> *I never saw her face more lovely gleam.*
> *This sight fulfilled in part my fondest dream*
> *And over my soul put reason in command;*
> *But when I left, my heart stayed at her hand,*
> *My fears and grief the greater came to seem.*
> *When now the sun bent downwards to the west,*
> *And left the earth in shadow and in night,*
> *Then my own sun was hidden from its ray.*
> *The setting sun more sadness brought at best.*
> *How all too little lasts this world's best light!*
> *But memory does not so soon fade away.*

Hearing him read the beautiful words made my heart swell. It reminded me of all the nights we cuddled into bed and he read to me.

"Thank you, love," he said, kissing my lips and hugging me tight.

"*Buon Natale*, Vittorio."

*****

We drove to church in two identical black Mercedes. Bruno rode with us, and Peter rode with Elizabeth and Alexander.

"It's 6:48. Are we going to make it?" I asked.

~ ☾ ~

Laughter rang out from the backseat.

"Yes, we'll make it." Vittorio smirked.

We pulled onto the road to head into town and immediately began driving at warp speed. The trees blurred past us as the Mercedes hugged the road.

I leaned over to check the speedometer.

Vittorio squeezed my leg. "Don't look. It will only make you nervous."

He was probably right. I glanced in the side mirror and saw the other Mercedes hot on our trail, tailgating. The other car drove so close to us that I couldn't see the front of the vehicle. My breath caught in my chest.

He gave me another squeeze. "It will be fine. Don't look in the mirror either."

"Maniacs," I said. Vittorio and Bruno both chuckled. "How do you drive like that?"

"It's just one of the many attributes of our kind," Bruno said, clearly delighted with this talent. "You know: better reflexes, quicker responses, faster thinking. Just better all around."

I rolled my eyes. *Better all around aside from the damned soul issue.* "Are we going to a church where you typically attend mass?"

"Yes. Whenever we occupy this house we attend services here. Father Gregoire will probably serve the 9:00 mass," Vittorio answered.

"Has he ever commented on the fact that none of you ever seem to change?"

"Father Gregoire is ..." he paused then glanced at me. "He is a friend. We've known him for many years. The priests at St. Aloysius have been kind to us. Father Gregoire knows who we are, like Father Gabriele knew me."

"Does he know about me?"

"Yes. He's helped me hold on while I searched for you. There were times in the past fifty years when I thought I'd go crazy waiting for you. Father Gregoire helped me through some very dark hours." He adjusted the temperature, then the stereo. A jazzy 1940's rendition of White Christmas began playing.

~ ☾ ~

We took the back roads into town. When the car pulled onto the main road Vittorio slowed down, driving only ten miles over the speed limit. We pulled into a spot at the church with three minutes to spare.

"If we had driven the speed limit, how long would it have taken us to get here?" I asked as Bruno opened the car door for me.

"I have no idea. We've never tried it."

I believed him.

Vittorio held my hand as we walked to the church. The familiar feeling of his calluses against my palm comforted me, reminding me of the many times we'd done this in our first life together. I tucked my thumb in and scratched at a callus. "You still have these?"

He nodded, but didn't say a word, only briefly turning his attention from the church.

St. Aloysius's church was a brick building with a tall steeple, five peaks, and three wooden doors; the two on either side were single doors with the main entrance in the middle consisting of a set of double doors. The concrete steps leading up to the entryway were newly replaced. The earth around them still waited for landscaping.

The scent of incense and burning candles drifted in the air with surprising intensity.

Father Gregoire stood in front of the church, surveying the mason's work, oblivious to our arrival. His white hair moved in the wind while his coat flapped about him.

Vittorio pulled me closer, his pace slowing. He didn't take his eyes off the priest. Peter and Bruno fell into step around us with Elizabeth and Alexander flanking them.

"Good morning, Father," Vittorio said.

"I see you've brought the family," Father Gregoire replied, not turning from the steps. "Who is this with you?"

"Merry Christmas, Father," I said. Nervous energy stirred within me, and my hands were unsteady, as though I'd consumed too much caffeine. The ache within me beat softly.

"Father?" Vittorio pulled me against his body. His aura wrapped tight around me, forcing my own to remain still and silent.

~ ☾ ~

I inhaled, but couldn't get a clean breath. The smell of incense choked me. Vittorio turned me, my face to his chest, and whispered, "Take a deep breath. Remember The Abyss. That is your objective."

I nodded. The drum beat louder, the rhythm low and steady. I listened, forcing my heart to match its call.

"Father? Who came to you?" Vittorio asked.

Father Gregoire laughed. The short chuckles grew to a deep belly laugh and onto hysterical giggles. He bent over, clutching the handrail. "Who came to me?" he repeated, snorting and gasping.

As the giggles died down, his sobs grew louder. "I am an old man who spent his whole life ministering to the sick, guiding God's people. Now look at me!" He spun to face us with such speed that I didn't see him move. One minute he was hunched over and the next he stood only inches from us.

Red eyes, dark, almost a black-red, punctuated his wrinkled face. Bloody tears ran down his cheeks and two short fangs dipped below his top lip.

"I can't even go into God's house." He sobbed and slumped to the step.

The pounding beat called to me. I tried to slip from Vittorio's hold.

"No, Lucia." He tightened his grip on me.

"He needs to be free. I can't watch him suffer," I said, my heart breaking for the priest.

"He is not ready. He is confused. We need to learn what we can from him." Vittorio's presence darkened. His sadness draped me, sinking into my heart like a leaden weight.

"Let me help him," I said.

"Father, you know you can enter the church. You're a good man. God would welcome you home," Vittorio said.

"I can't. I can't let him see me this way," he cried.

Bruno sat beside the priest, and Father Gregoire turned to him. A slight grin formed on the priest's lips.

"How do you do it, Bruno?" He reached out to touch him.

"It is my gift. And I'm happy to share it with you, Father." Bruno hugged the priest.

For the first time since I'd met him, I saw how powerful

~ ☾ ~

Bruno was. His influence over the priest calmed him, quelling his fears, encouraging his fortitude to hold on a little longer.

Father Gregoire removed a handkerchief from his pocket and wiped his face.

"We'll enter together," Bruno said.

"Yes." Father Gregoire swallowed, wiping away more tears as they trickled down his cheeks. "With you, I can do it."

"Father, who came?" Vittorio asked.

"The redhead. I don't know his name. A Scotsman with a terrible odor. He talked about Lucia, demanded to know where she was, that I tell him when I see her." He stared at me, and behind his eyes I saw his innocence swallowed by the devil within him.

"Father!" Bruno demanded.

"I'm sorry. He made me. I can feel him inside." His hands twisted in the fabric against his chest.

"What happened?" I asked. "What has he done?" My aura jolted as my heart flew into an uncontrollable panic, no longer able to keep calm and beat the steady rhythm.

"Easy, Lucia. Keep your wits. Now, more than ever, you need to be attentive." Vittorio's presence seemed to solidify like a wall, bearing down on mine, restricting its ability to escape. "Brian commands him."

"What do you mean? Isn't Bruno doing his thing? How is Brian interfering?"

"It's complicated. Brian is his master. Bruno is influencing Father Gregoire, but he can't influence Brian because he's not here. He's using his telepathic connection, which Bruno can't touch." He looked around.

Alexander appeared at Vittorio's side. "We've checked the perimeter. They're not on the outside, and I don't believe they are in the church. However, they are not far. Their trail is still fresh."

"When did he come to you, Father?" Bruno asked, his soft, lulling voice drawing Father Gregoire's attention back to him.

"Two days ago." He answered calmly.

"Have you fed?"

"No," he mumbled. "I cannot. I cannot bring myself to do it." Tears flowed again. "God help me."

~ ☾ ~

My heart ached to see the priest in such a state of shame and fear. "Vittorio, I have to help him."

"Not yet." He turned me away from the priest. "Where is he, Father?"

"I don't know. He didn't tell me."

"Reach for him. You are his child. You can find him," Vittorio said.

The old priest looked at Vittorio, confused and scared. "How?"

"Vittorio, you know that goes both ways. Father will call Brian to her." Peter pointed toward me.

Vittorio's features hardened and he very clearly issued an order as all his attention remained centered on Father Gregoire. "Bruno, help him."

"But, Vittorio—"

"*Now.*" His voice, nearly a growl, gave away the fact that his patience was waning. "We need to know where he is."

Bruno turned to the priest and smiled. "Father..." His deep, gentle voice turned coaxing.

Father Gregoire's face drooped, his eyelids sagged, and he slumped forward, sleeping in Bruno's arms.

"I'm not sure if Brian's an idiot or a genius. His permanent lair is not with Samuel. I couldn't quite get the location, but it's back in Rhode Island," Bruno said.

"Fine. Carry him in," Vittorio said, scurrying me up the steps.

"He could be living near my family." The idea of it horrified me. They weren't safe. He'd hurt them, use them to get to me.

"Your family is safe, Lucia. Your parents left, returning to The Light." Vittorio wrenched open the door, pausing for a moment to scent the air.

"What about Michael? They could capture him." What would I do if he was created Vampire? Guilt stabbed at me. *My God.* How many other innocent men had I condemned because I'd avoided my duty?

"We'll worry about Michael after." Vittorio ushered me into the church, glancing over his shoulder with steely eyes.

The building stood empty and bitingly cold. Peter went to

~ ☾ ~

the thermostat, and the pipes began ticking and clicking as the heating system rumbled to life. The combined scents of incense, flowers, and furniture polish reminded me of every church I'd ever entered.

Sunlight streamed through the stained glass windows, illuminating the interior of the building. Rays of blue, red, green, and gold shone down on us. Candles burned beneath statues of Mary and St. Aloysisus as they stood watch from the front of the church. Beautiful depictions of the Stations of the Cross adorned the far aisles and an ornate crucifix hung above the altar.

I followed Vittorio up the center aisle, stopping halfway and entering a pew. He left my side, returning to the back of the church. When Bruno placed Father Gregoire on the altar, the priest roused and began weeping.

"Let Father kneel at the altar to say his prayers." Vittorio stood in front of the glass wall dividing the children's room from the rest of the congregation. He peered into the unlit corners of the tiny soundproof room, inspecting every nook.

Alexander and Peter each sat near the back of the church, on opposite sides. Elizabeth stationed herself at the front, near the side door on the left, and Bruno stood directly behind the priest.

I bent to lower the kneeler, making the sign of the cross at the same time. I needed some time with God to discuss my destiny and I didn't want to waste even a second of it.

I bowed my head and barely finished The Lord's Prayer when Vittorio returned to my side.

"Lucia," he whispered. "In a few minutes you must free Father Gregoire." He watched the old priest, whose head bobbed as he cried and prayed.

"Why didn't you let me do it outside?" I said in the same low voice.

"Because he needed time to clear his conscience. I couldn't let him...."

I squeezed his hand. "Vittorio, you must know that the trip through The Abyss provides time for that. Don't you understand?"

"Yes. I know. But the sins he carries are not only his own.

~ ☾ ~

He has the weight of so many souls in his heart." He stared down at the kneeler for a second. "My sins alone may condemn him." He glanced at me. "He's a good man."

So are you.

Alexander appeared at the pew. He glanced at Father Gregoire then back to us. "The organist is in suppression." He spoke so softly, I had to strain to hear him.

Father Gregoire's head turned at the words, but he remained kneeling. His sobs grew louder, wracking his body.

"What happened?" Vittorio asked.

"I did not drink from her." Father Gregoire rocked back and forth, hugging his arms across his chest.

"No, he didn't. She bears Brian's mark," Alexander said.

The priest sat back on his heels, resting his head on the rail. "He made me bring her to him. She saw him, and he took her. *Oh, God.* Her screams. The fear." He wailed his agony.

"What is suppression?" I asked.

"It is part of the creation of a vampire. The point between the fledgling drinking of the master and awakening as a vampire." Vittorio slid back in the pew, never losing sight of Father Gregoire. "How much longer?"

"A day, no more. She still looks dead," Alexander answered.

"There is another in the sacristy. A man." Elizabeth slipped a set of rosary beads over my head. "Wear this. Fledglings always fear religious symbols. This will give you time."

"I can't wear..."

She caught my hand. "Yes, you can. You must." Her dark brown eyes had gone completely black.

I let the beads drop to my chest.

"So much for practicing, Lucia. You must succeed in this." Vittorio led the way to Father Gregoire.

"I know." *Please God, let me do it. Please, let this work.*

I wiped my sweaty palms on my trousers and rocked back and forth beside Vittorio. The sound of my own hyperventilating blocked all other noise. Vittorio's lips moved, but I didn't hear anything except my breaths rushing in and out of my lungs.

~ ☾ ~

I concentrated on his shoes, trying to calm myself.

"Lucia, look at me." His soft voice cut through the noise in my head.

I looked up. His lips didn't move, and yet he soothed me. *Calm,* cuore mio. *You have done this many, many times in the past. You can do it again.*

His hands rested on my neck, his face only inches from mine. Gently caressing me, his presence within me moved slowly. He tenderly kissed my forehead. "You will provide Father with freedom from a hell he does not deserve."

"Okay." I nodded. "Okay."

He stepped back, and my gaze met Father Gregoire's. He trembled and quickly looked away. Bruno squeezed his shoulder.

"Prepare yourself. You will not have much time when Bruno releases him," Vittorio said.

"What?" I licked my lips and swallowed. One thing I needed was a little bit of time.

"You must free him immediately." He walked me back up the center aisle about fifteen feet. "Once Bruno no longer influences him, he will want you. You must work quickly."

"I'm not ready. I...I...need..." My stomach flipped. *Breathe. Just breathe.* I fanned my hands in front of me, partly to calm my nervousness and partly to dry my sweaty palms.

"You must gather all your strength." His hands gripped my shoulders. "Rally to the call. Feel the aching beat. Set it loose. Let it lead you."

I studied his chiseled face, the gray skin tone, dark, hazel-black irises, and long fangs. His brows crinkled and stress lines formed at the corners of his eyes. He loved this man.

"Please, Lucia. Take him to The Light."

"Of course."

He kissed me again and walked to the altar. "Come, Father." He held out his hand to assist the elderly man up from the floor.

Bruno stepped behind the priest. "You're sure about this?"

"Yes. She's ready."

They held the priest, each with a hand on a shoulder and one clamped tight around his wrist.

~ ☾ ~

"As soon as you're ready, Lucia, I will release him," Bruno said.

"I know. I need a minute." The second hand on the clock above the door ticked, tapping an even rhythm and becoming the focal point I needed. The tick-tock blocked out the sounds of the heating system, Father Gregoire's whimpers, and the noises from outside the church.

I closed my eyes and reached within myself. Deep inside, the ache pounded, waiting to be called. I turned to face them, knowing my power was ready to be unleashed. "Let him go."

Vittorio pulled the priest from Bruno's grip.

A split second of silence held us all quiet, then Father Gregoire lunged.

~ ☾ ~

CHAPTER TWENTY-FOUR

*"Amor, accesso di virtu, sempre altro accesse, pur che lo
fiamma sua paresse fuore."*
~Dante
Love, unkindled by virtue, always kindles another love,
providing its flame shines forth.

He leapt through the air, practically levitating above my
head. The overwhelming scent of incense choked me. I dove
out of his reach, coughing.

Vittorio crashed into him. "Lucia, *now*!" He struggled with
Father Gregoire, whose cackling laughter grew louder and
louder with each passing second. "Don't make me hurt him!"

"Come here, Lucia," Father Gregoire said, his scratchy
voice singing the words. "Come, pretty." He smiled and
crooked his finger at me.

Vittorio pinned him to the wall, holding him so tightly that
I heard his bones breaking with audible cracks. Vittorio
grimaced.

"Oops." Father Gregoire giggled. "You've hurt me, Vittorio.
Naughty boy."

"Lucia! What are you waiting for?"

I didn't know the answer. This was truly the most pathetic
sight I'd ever seen. If anyone didn't know what was
happening, they'd have thought a young, muscular man was
beating the hell out of an elderly, mentally ill priest.

And yet my powers didn't surface.

"I can't feel anything. I can't do it."

The priest laughed. "She can't do it. She's not really the
Goddess, is she?" He smacked his lips. "I'm thirsty." He
turned his head and bit Vittorio's wrist.

~ ☾ ~

His teeth broke the flesh, and, as soon as blood began to spurt, he latched on to Vittorio's arm, sucking savagely.

The ache flared. The beat pulsed, drumming hard and fast. Energy surged through me, vibrating along my skin.

My power flew rampant through the building, blowing by us like a windstorm, tossing hymnals and prayer books in every direction. Candles flickered then snuffed. The holy water sloshed from the basins at the door and sprayed me. I squinted and blinked, trying to shield my eyes.

Father Gregoire released Vittorio's arm. "What is that?" he demanded, turning his head after the rush of air.

Books pelted us, and he growled.

"Focus, *cuore mio*. You can do it." Vittorio's deep, calm voice encouraged me.

I tried to regain control of the maelstrom bounding through the church, afraid the walls would collapse on top of us if I didn't.

Focus. Focus. Focus. I can do it. I can do it. I can do it.

I closed my eyes and listened to my heart, trying to slow the frantic beats. I squeezed my eyes shut and concentrated. Once my heart beat in perfect rhythm with the low rumble of the drum, I knew I could handle this.

My sudden diligence acted like a vacuum, drawing my aura back into me with such speed that the resulting silence was like a sonic boom, slamming the vampires into the floor.

I welcomed it back, brought her to me where she belonged. It took only a second for the rush of power to fill me.

The Abyss had arrived. The cold shifted, no longer hovering around me as an empty void. It spilled forward, corralling the vampires together.

"*Lucia!*" Vittorio howled.

My gaze met Father Gregoire's, enchanting him, pulling him to me.

His jagged breaths rattled in my ears. His screams exploded in the darkness.

We stood together in The Abyss.

It came for him, forcing Father Gregoire into my arms. He no longer laughed or sang. He barely breathed as he hid his face in my chest, mumbling some prayer, begging to be forgiven.

~ ☾ ~

Millions of moments in his life flashed around us. Very few of the scenes did not relate to his calling as a priest. A couple from his young life before the priesthood flickered by: one with a girl in the back of a car, one with an older man, his father scolding him for lying to his mother, and several of him sipping whiskey from a flask during seminary. All of them seemed so minor to me, yet they'd weighed on his conscience all these long years. He cried.

The next scenes were confessions he'd taken and absolutions he'd given.

Scene after scene of a man, woman, or child whispering sins to him. He asked questions, trying to gauge the level of repentance in each one. Then he doled out the penance: prayers for each and some effort on their part to make the situation better.

Children, confessing their sins in preparation of receiving the sacraments of Communion and Confirmation, were dealt with gently. He worked hard to make them see the errors in treating others poorly, in lying, cheating, or stealing. He listened to all, cared for each one of them, welcoming and encouraging his congregation to listen to their consciences and do the right thing.

He forgave adulterers, requiring commitment to honor thy spouse; liars needed to make amends, to tell the truth, to correct the problem; murderers, and there were a few, did not always repent. Even the ones in prison sometimes refused to accept responsibility, cursing the priest and the victim.

"Will He forgive me, Lucia?" His voice startled me.

I squeezed him. "You will see Him soon."

Memories eddied like a whirlpool, until one finally stopped in front of us. "I tried to do my best. I couldn't turn my back to Vittorio," he said.

I watched it unfold, unable to look away.

As a young priest, Father Gregoire met with Vittorio in a small, dimly lit room. They sat facing each other, a small end table off to one side holding a burning candle, a picture of Christ, and a box of tissues.

"When did this happen?" Father Gregoire asked in the memory.

~ ☾ ~

"Many years ago now, Father," Vittorio answered. "More than a hundred." His head bent toward the floor, his attention never settling on one spot.

The priest scratched his head, then smoothed his blond hair. For a long while he didn't say a word, just watched Vittorio.

My husband squirmed, clearly uncomfortable with the silence. His jaw set, and the muscles rapidly pulsed. Still, his gaze didn't meet the priest's.

"What have you done since?"

"What do you mean?" Vittorio looked at Father Gregoire. There were no sparkles in Vittorio's eyes. The hazel ring around his irises was flat, completely lifeless. Tiny lines etched his skin at the corners, and a frown turned his lips downward.

"Have you seen him? Heard from him?"

"Yes, I check on him when I can. I—I keep tabs on him, make sure I know what he's doing."

"What about the link you told me of, the one you have with Peter and Bruno? Don't you have that with him?" Father Gregoire studied Vittorio.

"Yes, Father. But I don't often use it."

"Why?"

Vittorio looked away again, his lips pulling into a straight line. "I don't want to...I fear I'll kill him if I know what he did with her. And, if I use the link, I'll be tempted to search his every thought for information."

"Is that the only reason?" The priest leaned forward in his chair, moving a Bible from one hand to the other.

Vittorio swallowed and blinked hard then barely shook his head.

"Well?"

"I mean to punish him."

"I don't understand."

"By leaving him unable to feel me, he is alone, isolated." His fangs descended.

"You want him to fear you." Father opened the Bible and thumbed through the pages.

"Yes." Vittorio seemed lost in his thoughts, not noticing the priest.

~ ☽ ~

"Do you think he does?" He placed the red ribbon on the page to mark his spot.

"I know it is so."

Father Gregoire rested his hand on his chin. His expression remained intent, thoughtful, but not harsh. "Are you pleased with this?"

"I try not to be, but I am. My jealousy consumes me at times. It is like a black monster gnawing at me. I dream of killing him." Vittorio's angry voice rumbled from deep in his chest.

"But you could have done so, and chose not to," Father Gregoire said.

"*Yes.*" Vittorio stood, pacing the room.

"Why?"

"To punish him. To make him suffer as I have suffered." He walked the length of the room, taking long, quick strides. "To make his days last an eternity."

Father Gregoire bristled at the speed of Vittorio's movements. "Vittorio, you're making me nervous."

Vittorio immediately sat in front of the priest, and retracted his fangs. "I'm sorry. I won't hurt you, Father. I'm strong enough to control my emotions."

"I think we've gone far enough today. You will pray the same as yesterday." He handed the Bible to Vittorio.

"And tomorrow? You will see me again?" The question was a plea.

"Yes. Tomorrow at four o'clock." Father Gregoire stood.

The scene faded away, and Father Gregoire fell against me. "I forgave him for the creations, the anger, the deaths, the vengeance. He has had so many dark moments. And I forgave each one."

We moved toward The Light. Its warmth bathed us. I inhaled a deep, fulfilling breath and pulled us closer to the beauty awaiting him.

A soul appeared, holding a hand out to us. Father Gregoire let go of me and leaned into the open arms waiting for him.

A burst of love thrust forward, rolling over me, around me, through me. A roar of happy cries sounded from The Light. I peeked beyond the presence at the threshold. Hundreds of

~ ☾ ~

souls danced around Father Gregoire, welcoming him, showering him with affection.

The Light. It shined right through the being at the entryway, radiating such love that I was overcome. Tears filled my eyes. I'd forgotten what it was like to save someone from the fires of hell.

It wasn't just the priest's gratitude that filled me with joy. It was the love of all the souls, thankful that I'd delivered another through The Abyss. Every lost soul returned was one more to help fill the chasm, strengthening The Light, weakening our enemies, and allowing good to triumph over evil. Every lost soul returned strengthened the Pharos.

Now I remembered where my power came from.

Lucia, thank you, child. Go. Bring more of them home. We need them all.

Yes, Father.

Finally, I understood what it meant to be a Pharo. I knew my destiny of bringing Vittorio and the others to The Light was a gift, not a punishment. I was humbled to be so honored.

The Light slipped away, leaving me hovering in the darkness of The Abyss, isolated and yearning for its acceptance.

"Lucia."

I opened my eyes, but found myself blind. "Vittorio?"

"I'm here." He held me close, softly kissing my cheeks and forehead. His body trembled.

"What happened? Why are we on the floor?" The others huddled around us. Elizabeth cried in Alexander's arms.

"It happened so fast. You both dropped as though you died." Vittorio squeezed me tighter. "But you're back." He kissed my lips this time.

"My soul left my body. So did his." I glanced to the left. Father Gregoire lay beside us, dead.

Sadness hung heavy in the room. "He was a good friend," Vittorio said. "You saved him."

I slid my hands around his back. "I know."

I had saved Father Gregoire. But to do it, I killed him. The reality of what I had done overwhelmed me. His soul was free

~ ☾ ~

JORDAN K. ROSE

for all eternity. I had brought him through the horrors of The Abyss, led him to The Light, and helped him gain redemption.

But to be redeemed, he had to die. And his death came at my hand.

My stomach churned. My eyes watered. And my mind and heart revolted against the true and full understanding of what I was. I had killed someone, innocent save for being created a vampire.

To kill someone, to stop a heart from beating, or a brain from forming a thought, it was more power than I wanted, more power than anyone should have. And I did it without using a weapon, without even raising my hands.

My will alone forced his spirit to The Light.

My mind reeled. Vittorio had been right. I was more powerful than I knew.

Without thinking about it, by just following my heart, my instinct, my destiny, I commanded a power I didn't fully understand.

I was a vampire slayer, once again. I was the Vampire Goddess.

Vittorio brought us both to our feet. "There's no time to grieve. You must take the other two."

I wobbled and leaned against the wall, unable to see more than an arm's length away. "I can't see a thing."

"I'm not surprised."

His voice came from the distance. Then the sound of something slumping in front of me drew my attention.

"What are you doing?"

"We've brought the others to you."

"Why aren't you surprised that I can't see?" I turned my head, following the sound of their movements.

"Your eyes are no longer glowing like they were. I'm pretty sure that your eyes glow when you command your powers, giving you the ability to see in the darkness of The Abyss. Now, in daylight, you must adjust." He took my hand. "One more trip. We don't have much time." He ushered me to the front of the church, one arm wrapped around my waist.

Blindness disoriented me. I leaned into Vittorio's arms,

~ ☾ ~

needing him to help me balance. "I can't even see them."
With one hand I clung to him, keeping my other hand in front
of me for the moment when I would come in contact with
them.

"They aren't conscious so you don't have to worry about
them attacking. Feel for their souls. That should help you."
Vittorio placed my left hand on a railing, keeping his other
hand firmly around my waist. "Peter, Bruno, go with
Alexander and Elizabeth into the sacristy."

"What for?" Bruno asked.

"I'm afraid that it might be easier for her to sense us and
not the fledglings. She might—"

"You need to go, too," I interrupted. "I'm easily drawn to
you. It's not safe for you to stay either." I'd already attacked
him twice. I couldn't risk a third time. Now that I'd actually
delivered a soul, I might not be able to stop myself from
taking him.

"No. I don't want to—"

"Go. My powers are rising again and I can't guarantee my
control yet." I turned toward him.

My aura revolved around us, picking up speed with each
pass. I tried to steady it.

But it was too late. The Abyss descended. "NOW!" I
shouted at them. The sound of their footsteps rushing from
the room followed by a door slamming told me I was free to
begin my work.

The Abyss lifted me to new heights, making me stronger,
more powerful than I could have imagined. The air crackled
with the current of electricity. Heat flared across my skin. I
inhaled, a deep and fulfilling breath, the last breath we would
take.

Then the screaming began. Their souls' screams for mercy
didn't stop me. Wielding The Abyss like a samurai warrior
works a sword, I sent the blackness crashing down, its weight
crushing them. As The Abyss rolled over them, taking them,
their voices quieted.

Silence rang in my ears, loud and clear. Cold air blew into
the church and the sun shone through the shattered windows,
gently heating my face. I basked in the rays of sunshine,

~ ☾ ~

reveling in the fact that I'd just delivered two more souls to The Light.

"You know you will see them again," Vittorio said as he entered the room, his tone deeper than usual.

I turned toward his voice. "Are you talking to me?"

"Yes."

"See who again?" I sat in the nearest pew, suddenly very tired.

"Them," he answered, picking me up.

"Aren't they dead?"

"You sent them into The Abyss, alone."

"What does that mean?" Peter asked.

"Are we using the dumpster out back?" Bruno asked.

"Yes. I don't want to burn them in church," Vittorio answered as he carried me through the building, his sadness for the loss of Father Gregoire and the damage done to the church obvious.

A gust of cold air whooshed around us. "What did you mean?" I squeezed my eyes shut against the sunlight and tucked in closer to his chest.

The smell of burning trash assailed my nostrils. Heat emanated from the dumpster.

"Won't someone notice the bodies?" I asked.

"The bodies will be disintegrated by the time anyone arrives. Vampires don't take long to burn," Vittorio explained. "When the parishioners arrive and find the mess inside and the fire out back, they'll think vandals broke in."

His essence pulled away from mine, and he was silent for a moment before whispering, "Amen."

"Let's go," Peter said. "We don't have a lot of time."

We pulled out of the parking lot and zoomed toward the highway. Wearing Peter's sunglasses helped a bit, but my eyes remained sensitive.

"Vittorio, explain what you meant—that I'd see them again," I said through a yawn.

"You left them in The Abyss. You didn't take them to The Light," he answered as he took the turn onto the highway. "When you took me to The Abyss, when your father was with us, I saw the souls there. Some chose not to go to The Light.

~ ☾ ~

Others were there waiting for a chance to be taken. They will wait."

"How do you know that?" I asked, a pit forming in my stomach.

"She was still standing, when I came back into the church." Peter said from the backseat.

"Yes. Gone for only a few seconds. Conscious the whole time," Vittorio adjusted the rear view mirror.

"What do you mean? Do you think I'm going to pass out with every trip into The Abyss?" How the hell would I keep myself safe? What if I came back from The Abyss to find a vampire feeding from me? Would I sense an attack on my body while my soul was traveling away from it?

Peter leaned into the front seat. "Do you think she'll be able to do the whole job more quickly at some point, possibly remaining consciously here on this plane while gone to the other? Do you have any recollection of this, Lucia?"

I shook my head. "None." Nothing at all came to me. I didn't have a memory of any trips through The Abyss other than the ones I'd taken in this lifetime.

"It seems a fair assumption that once she masters her skills, she will be able to defend her physical body while in The Abyss," Vittorio said.

The car accelerated up the on-ramp. He flew across four lanes and sped down the highway.

"Don't you know how to drive at normal speeds?" I mumbled. The road blurred by me.

Two souls sat in purgatory, waiting for a chance at redemption. I'd sent them to be punished by not finishing the job. A guilty pang stabbed in my gut. My job was not to punish any soul. I was to deliver them through The Abyss, not leave them in limbo.

"You will see them again, Lucia. They will come to you. Then you can help them," Vittorio said.

I nodded, swallowing a lump of emotion. "It's terribly cruel, what I did."

"It was unkind. But you did not know." He adjusted the temperature in the car.

I sat, silent for a long while, fighting back tears. Finally, I

~ ☾ ~

admitted, "I enjoyed it. In that instant, when they screamed and cried, I enjoyed killing them." My mouth was suddenly dry. I tried to swallow, but couldn't. "I wanted them to die. I liked feeling their fear."

Peter's anxiety glutted the car.

"I'm sorry," I choked out.

"Go to sleep, Lucia. You've expended a lot of energy. Rest. You'll feel better when we arrive in Mystic." But even Vittorio could not hide his fear. I sensed it, bubbling within him. "Tilt the chair back and rest."

It was a command, and although I knew I could refuse, I wanted to obey. I wanted to forget this revelation, that I actually liked the grimmest aspect of my destiny.

~ ☾ ~

CHAPTER TWENTY-FIVE

I closed my eyes and gave into exhaustion, allowing my own memories to flood my mind.

*****

The faces huddled around the fire with me were all familiar. Costin, Iosef, Anton, and Papa finished their breakfasts. The rising sun cast an orange glow on their bleak faces. I pulled my cape tighter and crouched lower on the log.

"With the attack last night they obviously know we are coming. They are waiting for us." The smoke from Papa's pipe encircled his head, creating a halo above him as his brows knitted together in concentration. "Our enemies are weaker during the hours of the sun. If we arrive at their nest in the next two hours we will be able to use the daylight to our advantage.

"We will travel through the valley along the river to the fortress. When we are close enough, we will leave the horses and carriage and walk the final distance. However, if we are attacked, we must be ready. Lu, you must pay attention."

"Yes, Papa." Tension drilled into my muscles. After last night's brazen attack on our camp and my inability to defend myself, I'd hardly slept. Even cradled in Costin's arms, I barely closed my eyes for even a moment.

"We will enter the fortress with our equipment in hand, taking only what we can carry. There will be no time to unpack once we pass the gate." Papa's eyes narrowed, and he puffed another drag from his pipe. "A fate worse than death lurks in this place. We must remember our oaths. If any one of us is taken and fed upon it is the duty of those remaining to kill the victim. We cannot allow each other to be created into vampires. Do you understand?"

~ ☾ ~

We did. We all knew the dangers ahead, and what we might need to do to protect one another.

"Let us reaffirm our oaths."

One by one, we swore our allegiance to the group and the cause. Costin grimaced when he swore his loyalty. It would kill him to have to complete the duty, if I was captured, but he needed to keep his word. He couldn't let me be created. I couldn't be turned into one of those abominable creatures, damned to roam the earth for all eternity, draining the life from others. Just as I wouldn't let any of them become one of Satan's henchmen, they could not let it happen to me.

We packed the rest of our supplies and mounted the carriage. In utter silence we rode to our destination. The sun rode high into the sky with no sign of the creatures. We abandoned the carriage about a mile from the fortress and hiked the rest of the way. Around my waist I had strapped my sword, four wooden stakes, and a scythe. I carried my torch and a shorter knife in my hands. My crucifix lay exposed on my chest. We were all geared with the same tools, and Papa also carried holy water.

We entered the fortress quietly through an unlatched iron gate. The Great Room was empty save for a few chairs surrounding a long table at the far end. Gray walls ascended some twenty feet above us. Sunlight streamed in from windows on the eastern wall. Four doors led from the room, two to the left, one straight back behind the table, and one to the right. We headed for the door in the back of the room, knowing it would eventually lead us below ground.

The overwhelming stench of the vampires nearly knocked me down.

I smelled death.

The odor of decaying bodies polluted the air, mixing with the stink of a farm, something like a pig trough. A spicy-sweet, pungent scent flooded my nostrils, burning and gagging me all at once as it intermingled with a flowery smell. The cloying odor caused me to imagine thousands of flowers shoved all around my body, suffocating me.

I choked, trying to catch my breath. All the air seemed to be wrenched away from me, replaced by a thick, heavy film

~ ☾ ~

impossible to break though. I couldn't get air into my lungs. The sounds of my gasps shattered the silence.

"*Lu*," Papa growled. "Pay attention. Do not lose sight of your task." His anger brimmed and it was clear he was afraid something would happen to me, just as he'd feared last night, but I couldn't help myself. The disgusting miasma staggered me.

"What's wrong?" Costin whispered in my ear.

"Can't you smell it? The stink of the monsters?"

He held his torch over us. "No. It smells like it always does: moldy, like rot."

"I smell different odors. I can smell different vampires," I whispered.

"What do you mean?"

"This place reeks of three distinct beings," I explained, realizing that I could count the number of vampires by the scent associated with them. "I know there are four of them here."

"*Quiet.*" Papa's cape flapped as he whipped back to face us.

We crept around a corner, barely able to see more than a few feet ahead. The fuzzy light of our torches did little to cut through the darkness of the wide corridor.

Something shot behind us in the shadows. A woman's laugh echoed in the cavernous passageway. Seconds later a door slammed down the hall. Quickly, we turned, waving the torches at the empty darkness. My heart raced.

"Artur, should we split up?" Anton asked Papa.

"We stay together." Papa led the way around the great hall, an endless walk sloping downward into the earth.

As we rounded a bend, we came upon two enormous doors. Papa moved the wooden latch back; Anton and Iosef pushed the doors open. Hot, blinding light poured onto us. Torches flamed on each wall, on tables, and from the ceiling. The smell of burning oil mixed with the odors permeating the air.

I shielded my face until my eyes adjusted. When I lowered my arm, the most striking creature stood before us, waiting in the middle of a giant old ballroom.

Tall, with broad shoulders and white, nearly glowing skin,

~ ☾ ~

his features were perfect, as if he'd been chiseled from marble. Long black hair hung past his shoulders and his eyes burned red like roses—no, like blood. They were the color of blood.

I couldn't look away from him. His eyes bewitched me. It wasn't until he smiled that I was able to break his hold on my consciousness.

The flash of his blindingly white teeth caught my attention. My gaze moved from his eyes to his mouth. His dark beard and moustache were trimmed close enough to accentuate his strong jaw line. His lips curved into a sensuous smile, and his fangs protruded. He was terrifying and beautiful all at once.

Secretly he called to me, *My sweet, come to me.* When he held out his hand, inviting me to him, his fur cape swayed, sending that sickening spicy-sweet scent to me. It swooshed into my nose, causing me to keel over, gagging.

"Lu, what's wrong?" Papa demanded, his attention focused on the beautiful creature.

Costin put his arm around me and helped me stand.

Come to me, the creature beckoned though still lips. I felt myself being pulled toward him, wanting to go to him. The desire to be in his arms burned me.

"He calls to me." I could barely breathe the words without rushing to his embrace.

"Don't go to him. Stay with me." Costin held me tight against him, wrapping both his arms around me. I turned my face into his chest and smelled him, the strong musky scent of my husband.

I knew I should stay with Costin, but the creature called me. I ached for his touch, wanted to fall into his arms, needed to have him.

"There are three that I see." Papa's hushed announcement was barely a whisper.

"Yes! That's right. There are three of us," a woman's voice called.

I looked past the vampire standing nearest us to see a petite woman sitting on a throne. Long, thick black hair hung down her back. She was stunning—flawless skin that seemed

~ ☾ ~

to glow in the torchlight, big, crimson-colored eyes, and the same perfect smile as the man. Sharp fangs extended from her open mouth. She was barely dressed, wearing only a toga. A nearly transparent toga. Every man in the room noticed when I did, their attention fixed on the female vampire as if drawn by a silent mating call.

"My love," she purred.

"Yes, mistress," the gorgeous vampire answered as he leered at me.

"Get her for me. I want to feed." She flipped her hair off her shoulders, tilting her head back. Her silky, black mane fanned out behind her in the most mesmerizing way. I could almost hear each strand slip into place.

"Of course, Elisabet," he answered. "Anything for you." The deep rhythmic tone of his voice captivated me, leaving me frozen, wanting to hear more.

With movements as smooth as running water he glided toward me, throwing my men aside with just the wave of his arms. They flew through the air, crashing into the stone walls and tumbling to the floor.

Between one breath and the next he stood over me, caressing my cheek with the back of his hand. I was vaguely aware of his fingers untying my cape. The fur slid down my back, and he masterfully unbuckled my gear belt, letting it too drop to the floor. His arms moved around my waist, pulling me against his hard body.

My sweet. His voice invaded in my mind.

He compelled me to slide my hands up his muscular arms. I paused to squeeze his biceps. His hands began moving; one slid up my backside while the other traveled up from my waist to my breast, and he squeezed. I gasped with desire. He *made* me want him.

"Relax for me, my sweet." I lay in his arms, tilting my head back, yielding to his commands. "Let me taste you, my love." He leaned over me, inhaling my scent from my breast to my neck, finally stopping, his lips poised above mine, barely touching me.

His fang nicked my lip, and a tiny droplet of blood seeped from the cut. His breath caught in his throat, and his grip

~ ☾ ~

tightened, holding me more firmly to him. He sucked my lip into his mouth and moaned. I felt him hard against me and I liked it. I ground my body against his, aching for him to take all of me.

"Alexandru! Bring her to me!" the woman screamed. Her shrill voice bounced off the walls.

He released my lip, and his head jerked up. "Yes, Elisabet, my love." He thrust me away from his body and spun with me in his arms to move towards her.

Secretly he spoke to me. *You are mine.* I felt the claim inside me as though his hands were touching me. "It's time to fight, little one."

The soft reminder snapped me from my lethargy.

"No! Papa! Papa!" I thrashed about wildly, trying to break free of his hold.

He leered, and his sharp teeth gleamed in the torchlight.

"*Lu!*" Costin screamed as he ran toward us.

*****

You can't trust them, Lucia.

The words slithered through my mind like a snake winding its way to a cool, dark hole. No rush, just a steady crawl toward the opening.

Instinctively I backed away, hiding within myself.

You can't trust him *either.*

This time the voice hung inside me. A bleak, heavy fog blanketed my soul.

My own light struggled to stay lit.

Deep within, the ache pounded.

The shadow consuming me flinched, but didn't leave. It weighted down, a burden meant to crush me. I was suffocating. The putrid, acidy odor filled my nostrils, burning my lungs.

My heart beat faster, matching the angry beats of the drum.

Come to me. Don't fight me. The shadow crept toward my flickering light, and the beating drum thundered.

My aura flared like the sun, leaving no part of me in darkness.

The shadow vanished.

~ ☾ ~

*****

"Lucia." His scruffy chin nuzzled my ear. "*Cuore mio*, you're not in Romania. It was just a memory."

I opened my eyes. Vittorio lay beside me on a bed, his body curved around mine.

"Did you see him?" My breaths came choppy and rough.

"Yes. But you must understand: everyone has a dark side. We all walk a path with many twists and turns."

"He doesn't have any light, Vittorio. He is pure darkness. Only shadow remains in him." Sweat rolled down my neck.

"How can you say that? Alexander is a good man. He's made mistakes, but his heart is good." He folded the blanket back from my chest. "I know what you saw was upsetting, but you have no reason to fear him now." He lay beside me propped on one elbow. "They both care for you." He hadn't seen. Samuel came to me right under his nose, and he hadn't seen it.

"Samuel. It was Samuel I saw. He spoke to me. He wants me."

"You saw him?"

"It wasn't so much him, but the darkness. He *was* the darkness." I sat up, hugging my knees to my chest.

He sat up, too, leaning close to me. "Did he call you to him?" He touched my chin.

"He told me not to fight him." I glanced at Vittorio. "Do you know more about him, about me and him?"

"I know bits and pieces about what he's done in the past three hundred years, but nothing more, nothing about how he came to be. He's kept that secret very well."

"Father said I was there when he was created. I know something. We have to figure out a way to unlock my memories or I'll never defeat him." I couldn't fail again. I didn't want to end another lifetime running away from him. I wanted to meet my destiny and move *on*.

"You have to control your aura."

I flipped the blanket back and stood beside the bed. "Enough with the 'control the aura' speech. I didn't go to him. He came to me."

"You are powerful enough to block him, if you truly desired."

~ ☾ ~

"What does that mean?"

"He sired Kerina and, therefore, should be able to communicate with me, and Peter and Bruno, telepathically. However, I do not allow him access to me or my own. You are more powerful than I am. You should be able to block him as well." He scooted to the edge of the bed and bent to pull on his shoes. "You're not focused enough."

"Did it ever occur to you that I might be as focused as humanly possible?" My temples throbbed. *Focus?* I was focused. Along with angry, irritated, and terrified. I gritted my teeth and paced. "And, right now, I do not need to be more *focused*. Right now, I need to get back on the job or I'm heading to some hellish prison that I can't even fathom because I can't possibly understand a fate worse than the one I'm currently living." I turned away, balled my fists, and screamed in frustration. Vittorio remained still, unmoved by my tirade, though he did manage to blink, slowly. His lack of response only added to my irritation. Everyone should be angry right now. "*They* killed me, didn't they?" I jerked my finger toward the bedroom door, figuring Elizabeth and Alexander were somewhere on the other side.

He didn't answer, just sat on the edge of the bed watching me, his hands folded in his lap, ankles crossed, head tilted down. His hazel eyes sparkled as they followed my movements.

"Tell me." I bit my lip, waiting for him to confirm yet another rotten detail of my past.

"First, you are not human. You have probably never *been* human. You may have a human figure, but you are supernatural, sent by God."

"Don't change the subject. And, if that was some sort of compliment, I didn't like it. 'You're pretty' would have worked better. Tell me what they did."

"*Cuore mio*, you must remember that everyone changes, even a vampire. Alexander and Elizabeth have learned from their mistakes, repented, and sought God's forgiveness."

"Tell me. Don't make me wait to learn for myself." I turned away from him, not wanting him to see the tears leaking from my eyes. I'd trusted them both. Relied on them for my safety.

~ ☾ ~

How could I have not realized who they were?

Two vampires I should have destroyed without hesitating had managed to endear themselves to me, tricked me into caring for them. They'd probably fought over me then drained me dry in a feeding frenzy.

"Lucia." He came to me, held me as he tilted my face toward his. "This is why you must let your memories unfold. What happened in that lifetime is not what you think. Elizabeth and Alexander care for you. They are not the same vampires you knew in your past life." He wiped the tears from my cheeks.

His aura moved around us, trying to comfort me, trying to help me understand. Gentle and persuasive, he surrounded me in calm.

As the anxiety faded an opportunity became obvious. They knew what happened in that lifetime.

"Where are they?"

"I sent them away, to do some negotiating with a possible ally."

I pushed out of his arms. "Why would you do that?" How could I get answers from them now?

"I saw your dream. I know your heart. You will regret seeking vengeance on them without knowing everything." His eyes darkened, suppressing some of the hazel specks.

"You don't know me. *I* don't even know me." I glanced out the window.

Night had fallen. But I'd known that without seeing the dark sky. Vittorio's perfect, luminescent skin told me that the sun had set some time ago.

"You forget what we share," he whispered. "I know you better than you know yourself. You hold the answers to your own questions. Their perspective will only anger you more."

I rapped my knuckles on the windowsill. "How can you?" I turned toward him and glared. "How is it that you know me better than I know myself?" *Everyone* seemed to know more about me than I did.

"You come to me. Your aura seeks its missing piece. I can't give it to you, not until the end. This is why you must control yourself. You must not rely on me to do it for you. I may not

~ ☾ ~

always be able to. And I may challenge you in the end. You cannot let me know your weaknesses." He exuded that suave confidence that was so familiar, slowly blinking, taking in my every move.

I didn't understand. I didn't want to admit that understanding how my aura worked was still something I had to learn, and I didn't have to. My ignorance was clear as day.

He pulled on a shirt and fastened the buttons without looking down. "I am not something extraordinary. At one time, I was a simple man who lived a good life and loved his wife." His accent thickened. "Now I am a vampire. But my soul is still that of a simple man. I fear death, just as any other soul. I want redemption. God knows I want it more than anything else. But I will not run to my death. Fear makes me fight to live. Hundreds of years of fighting death make me run from it. You will need to control yourself to have the upper hand with me."

I was going to have to kill him. I knew it. He knew it. But my heart couldn't accept this fact. It crumbled inside me. "Why is this happening now? Why didn't I find you twenty years ago? Why didn't I awaken to this destiny sooner?"

"As far as we can tell, you manage to remain oblivious until about the same point in each lifetime. Then, for whatever reason, your aura becomes alert and you are no longer able to ignore your fate."

"Every lifetime is the same?" I looked out the window at the yard. A floodlight illuminated the back of the house. Giant pots draped with plastic sat on a tiled patio. Covered furniture lay stacked along the wall. I turned back toward the room.

"Yes." He watched me, sent his aura to move around me, touching me, holding me. Again, he was a comfort, one I wasn't sure I could live without.

"Do I die at the same time in every lifetime?" I didn't let him know that I knew what he was doing. When I thought about it, I realized I had always felt him near me, always had his attention.

The slight nod of his chin was his only response.

"When?" My throat tightened. I held the breath I forced into my lungs. *God, what if it's tomorrow?*

~ ☾ ~

"April. The eleventh," he whispered.

"The day before my birthday. That's the day I died in our lifetime." I now knew the date of my impending death. In less than five months I was going to die. Tears filled my eyes again. Dead.

"Lucia." He came to the window. "We have only a few short months to break the cycle. And there is much to be done, many memories to unlock, pieces to fit together. You must determine Samuel's weakness and use it. You must learn to be consistent in using your powers. And to do those things, you *must* control your aura. Try not to think about dying." He pulled me close to him and kissed my forehead. "For what it's worth, if it comes to it, you've done it before. You can do it again."

"Thanks for the vote of confidence," I mumbled into his shirt. "But, remember, if I don't destroy Samuel and kill you, Father said I might be sent somewhere else, never to return."

Where? Where could I go? An eternity of purgatory wasn't punishment enough? Losing the man I loved to my sworn enemies then being forced to kill him wasn't enough?

"You won't fail this time. You will destroy us both." He breathed the words into my hair, and I felt his spirit crash against him, like a flash exploding within. And just as quickly, it cooled.

I blanched. The promise of success in his tone was meant to be encouraging. *Yet, how does one take solace in knowing your soul mate plans to ensure you succeed at killing him?*

One way or another, he would make sure Samuel was destroyed in this lifetime. Then he'd die. And he'd do it to save me.

Vampire or not, I loved him and I knew beyond anything else that my love for him was my curse. It blinded me to the danger he posed, weakening my resolve. I rested my cheek against his chest. "When do you feel me? Only when I'm aware, or do you feel the connection sooner?"

"I always feel you. In each lifetime it's always a subdued call, but it's there."

Something had to be preventing me from killing Samuel and keeping Vittorio alive. Why couldn't I just kill the one and have the other?

"Something must have happened in our first lifetime. Something triggers my awakening." I slipped my hands beneath his shirt and slowly worked them up and down his back. The taut muscles relaxed more and more with each pass of my hands over his smooth skin.

"Yes, I agree. But you don't seem to remember." One hand knotted in my hair while the other caressed my back.

He was right. Nothing stuck out in my mind. No memory that would lead me to understand why I always realized I was a vampire hunter five months prior to my death.

His heart beat against my cheek, and I smiled. Strong and steady. I took a deep breath, inhaling his scent. Memories flooded my mind: racing through the grapevines with him hot on my trail, sneaking out my second floor window to meet him under the moon, making love to him under the midday sun, hidden in the southern field.

His heart sped.

"You saw that?" I asked without moving.

"Hmm. I think of that often." His arms tightened around me.

I pressed closer to him. "How did you see it?"

"You still have not reigned in your aura." He nuzzled his chin in my hair.

"But I'm awake."

"Yes, because I woke you. I pulled you from the memory and, apparently, ended Samuel's visit." His breath in my hair sent a spurt of excitement shooting through me. My energy spun hot around us. It rolled through me, settling between my hips. My legs nearly melted beneath me.

"What else? What other memories do you think of?" I made tiny circles on his back and listened to the quickening beat of his heart. He was mine, and I wanted him. If there was any absolute truth, it was that in this lifetime no man ever made me feel like this.

"I know what you're doing," he said.

"What?" I glanced up at him.

"I am not so easily seduced, even by my wife." He kissed my lips.

~ ☾ ~

"Would it be so bad?"

He inhaled. "It would be wonderful."

"Then let me have you." I blinked slowly, and curved my lips into a slight smile, still massaging his back.

"You must practice. Remember?" he whispered against my mouth. His heart pounded in his chest, forcing his blood to flow south, and his body responded.

"You want to, though." My fingers danced across his back. "I feel your heart, your desire, your..." I let my hand slide around his waist to his zipper.

"Of course I want to. I haven't made love to you in three hundred and sixty years. That's a long time to fantasize." He caught my hand and slid it back around him.

"I could make all your dreams come true." My hands slowly wandered lower to squeeze his ass.

He grinned. "Yes, you could." The green and gold flecks in his eyes glittered. "But we need to meet your destiny."

"Vittorio, I'm dying." I let the words hang between us for a few seconds. "You don't want me to die unhappy, do you?" I pouted.

He laughed. "You are tricky, my love." He kissed my lips then my neck. "I never want you to be unhappy." He forced me to relinquish my grasp on his backside, prying my fingers loose with amazing skill.

My smile broadened. I made an obvious show of taking in the sight of him. I licked my lips, narrowed my eyes, and blinked more slowly as my gaze moved from his handsome face down his neck to his broad shoulders and muscular chest, on to his narrow waist and lower, where it paused, happily admiring my work.

"*Signora* Della Caccia, you seem to like what you see." He stood in front of me, not flinching, not at all embarrassed by my roving gaze.

"You know that I do. And this time, I'm not afraid or inexperienced. I even remember what you like, *Signore*." I stepped closer.

~ ☾ ~

CHAPTER TWENTY-SIX

I should have known I wasn't going to seduce him. He always had much stronger fortitude than I. Of course, even knowing that would not have prepared me for ending up in the shower fully clothed.

"The least you could have done was undress me!" I yelled as he slammed the door behind him. "Or turn the water to hot!" I spun the knob as fast as I could but ice-cold water continued to spray me.

Vittorio cracked the door open. "You don't need any more heat." He shoved my suitcase into the bathroom and left.

I laughed. He was the one who didn't need any more heat, and my getting into the shower naked would have put him at a terrible disadvantage.

I stripped off my wet clothes and showered, spending a great deal of time maintaining an open energy flow and thinking hot little thoughts.

By the time I finished bathing and dressing, I was thoroughly wrinkled and starving, but a relaxing meal was not on the agenda.

An angry current boiled up the hall. I stood in the doorway of the bedroom, examining the tension around me. It wasn't just Vittorio that I felt. Even Peter and Bruno exuded a rage that seemed to vibrate through the house. The air pressure plummeted, squeezing tighter and tighter, making it difficult to breathe. Strands of hair caught in the static charge, waving around my head.

Inside me, the drum beat low and steady. A warning.

I braced myself in the doorway and clung to my aura, afraid to let her move away.

"How many were there?" Vittorio demanded, his voice

~ ☾ ~

carrying from the room down the hall, a living room, I assumed.

"At least twenty," a voice with a thick Southern drawl answered from the end of the hall then heavy footsteps moved away. "Brian's been busy. Not one of the fledglings was older than a month." The owner of the deep voice had moved further into the room with Vittorio.

"We should have known when we found Father Gregoire," Bruno said.

A low growl thundered, and all three auras vanished from me, leaving me cold and alone. I hugged my arms around myself and leaned against the wall.

"Did you destroy any?" Vittorio's voice dropped. A loud bang followed his question, and the sound of clicking accompanied footsteps on the tile.

"Two, maybe three," the stranger answered.

"That's it? You couldn't do better?" Vittorio snarled. "What have you been doing all this time? Obviously not sparring, not honing your fighting skills."

Silence followed, hanging in the air for what seemed like an hour.

I crept down the hall, careful not to make a sound, and peeked around the corner into the room.

The stranger stood across the living room in the threshold of the dining room with his back to me. His long brown hair hung loose past his shoulders except for the small amount at the top of his head, held back by a clip. He wore a torn black leather jacket, bloody jeans, and dark cowboy boots.

He and Vittorio stood face to face. Vittorio studied the stranger, the muscle in his jaw flexing the whole time.

"Drink. Heal yourself. Then go." They were orders, but something about Vittorio's voice changed. His anger ebbed a bit. I'd have sworn it was concern I heard.

One minute Vittorio's arm hung at his side, and by the next the stranger had Vittorio's wrist against his mouth, biting down then quietly drinking. I blinked, still surprised sometimes at the light speed movement of the vampires, too quick for my naked eye to follow.

Vittorio watched the man. His eyes weren't flat black, as

~ ☾ ~

I'd come to expect when he was angry. The hazel color stippled his irises.

Once the stranger released Vittorio's wrist he unrolled his sleeve and buttoned the cuff. "Go north. Let me know as soon as they've arrived. Peter will guard the west."

The stranger muttered something and turned to leave. Spurs on his cowboy boots clicked with each step he took. As he walked past the hallway, he glanced in my direction.

My heart hammered. The drumming sped. The dual beats pounded in my ears.

Big brown eyes met mine. His long thin nose had been broken. The gash on the bridge healed as he walked. Two fangs protruded from behind his full lips, and a deep cleft sat in the middle of his chin.

He nodded a greeting to me but kept walking. Peter followed, barely looking in my direction. The door slammed shut, then tires squealed in the driveway.

The pressure in the room eased. I finally breathed, drawing attention to my position.

"Come here, *cuore mio*." Vittorio opened a drawer in a large oak credenza behind the table, removing something shiny.

I entered the room. "Who was that?"

A giant wooden cross hung on the burnt umber wall above the fireplace. Its ends came to sharp points. Three white pillar candles burned on the mantel. A large ivory couch, cluttered with pillows, faced the glass doors out to the patio, while two uncomfortable-looking wooden chairs sat in the corners. The exposed ceiling beams had been painted black. To the far right, the room opened to a dining room, and beyond that lay the kitchen.

"Tomas," Vittorio answered me. "Here." He handed me a gold chain from which a plain gold cross dangled.

"Who is he?"

"This is his house." He glanced past me to Bruno.

I sighed. They were obviously having some private conversation, and I was beginning to hate that everyone else seemed to have a telepathic connection.

I slipped the cross over my head and dropped it into my sweater. "Is that it, Vittorio? You're not going to explain what

~ ☾ ~

just happened? I saw him bite you."

Vittorio's gaze fixed on me, and a flood of concern washed over me. He took a few audible deep breaths then spoke, "Brian hunts you separately from Samuel." He reached for the cross, pulling it from beneath the fabric to lie exposed on my chest. "Tomas caught a few of the fledglings feeding. He killed the ones he surprised, but was attacked by the others. He needed assistance to heal."

"Vittorio, you're worrying," Bruno said. He stood in the doorway to the kitchen, arms folded over his chest. "Yet she held her aura tight enough for Tomas not to notice her in the hallway. In fact, none of us knew she'd snuck in that far. She *is* ready."

Little wrinkles appeared at the corners of Vittorio's eyes. His hand rested on my neck. "There are some thirty vampires coming for you. Most are fledglings, which we four should be able to handle. But Brian is leading them, and if he has separated from Samuel, he is stronger than we realized."

"I should be able to handle one vampire." I relaxed and accidentally proved Bruno wrong. Overcharged energy zoomed around the room, blowing by us, knocking paintings from the wall, extinguishing the candle flames, and shoving me into Vittorio's arms.

He caught me and frowned. "*Should* is the operative word. We have about half an hour before..." He shook his head then sighed. "Let's just practice."

"I'm not attacking you or Bruno. Now would not be a good time to accidentally kill either of you." I stepped back, straightening my sweater and trying to smooth my unruly hair.

"No, it wouldn't. You'll practice controlling yourself," Vittorio said. "Bruno, you come at her from behind. I'll take the front."

"What? Wait a minute."

But they didn't. I ended up flattened, face down on the hard tile floor.

"What the hell was that?" I shouted as I rolled over to find Bruno seated on the couch and Vittorio standing where I'd last seen him.

~ ☾ ~

"Up. Again," Vittorio ordered, not moving from where he stood.

I pushed myself to my feet, and, as I wiped my hands on my jeans, they knocked me on my ass again.

"*What the hell?*" I shouted. "I'm not ready."

"Again," Vittorio commanded.

This time I didn't make it off the floor. They flattened me, pinning me down and holding me frozen. Bruno stood, grabbed my leg, and dangled me in the air. He swung me around and tossed me onto the sofa.

"No more!" I flipped off the sofa and crouched behind it. *What the hell is happening?*

The sofa flew across the room, and they stood in front of me, eyes dark, fangs descended.

"I don't like this." I stood, pulse racing. "I don't understand what I'm supposed to do."

"Use your power to stop us." Vittorio's presence moved around me, squeezing and jabbing me.

I batted my hands wherever I felt him, shoving at his invisible touches. "Stop that." The God-awful feeling of his cold presence burned my skin. A lump formed in my throat. "Stop it!" I screamed, swinging at his presence. My hair flew in every direction, blinding me.

"Make me." He moved faster, colder.

Bruno's presence spun around me in a fury, occasionally reaching out to touch me. They tormented me like bullies on the playground.

"Stop it!" I backed away.

They didn't stop. The freezing sting of Vittorio's touch prickled while Bruno taunted me, poking and prodding.

All the while, my aura raced about the room, uncontrolled and frightened. I couldn't calm her, couldn't coax her to me, couldn't even discern her location for more than a split second.

The rush of my energy screamed through the house, shattering the silence of the dim room.

Anger bubbled deep within me. They weren't letting me get to her. They wanted me scared. They were trying to hurt me, trying to confuse me.

~ ☾ ~

I stopped moving and closed my eyes, searching for my Light. In the distance, it flickered. Its flame leapt for me.

A steely blast pushed me away from the Light. But I reached, undeterred by the searing cold of their presence.

I can do it. I can do it. I can do it.

The little flame flashed, bursting forward, radiating from deep within me, heating my frozen core, and pulling my aura home to my body. My eyes opened and my power emerged.

I hit back, leaving scorch marks across both of their chests, arms, legs, and faces. My aura whirled around them, corralling them closer, forcing them to me.

Bruno's lips moved, but I couldn't hear a word. The sound of my energy moving thundered in my ears like a freight train speeding down the tracks. Vittorio nodded and stepped in front of him.

Suddenly, I was too hot. The heat that had comforted me seconds ago began to consume me like an inferno.

Vittorio reached for me, one hand sliding around my waist, pulling me into his embrace while the other slipped into my hair. His mouth bent to mine, and, with the slightest touch of his lips, everything stopped.

The untamed rush of energy bounding through the room slowed and hovered around us. The noise silenced. My pulse decreased to a steady beat, and I closed my eyes, tilting my head back as I waited for his kiss.

Sweet and tender, his soft lips soothed me, and I calmed my aura, holding her close within me.

"You believe your aura is separate from you," Vittorio said. "But it *is* you. You are it."

"How do you know what I think?" I rested my head on his chest, exhausted.

"When will you realize that when you command your power, I feel the call? You've done well tonight, but you must remember that *you* are your aura. Don't try to think of it as something trapped within or outside."

I leaned against him, unsure how I was going to acclimate to the idea that I was my aura or that she was me.

"Eat this." Bruno pushed a banana between Vittorio and me. "And this." He shoved a sandwich into my hand.

~ ☾ ~

"Peanut butter?" I asked, sniffing the bread.

"And jelly. Hurry up. We don't have much time. You need the nourishment to stay alert."

I did my best to eat the sandwich as fast as possible without choking.

"The fruit, too." He paced in front of the glass doors by the patio, rolling his shoulders then his neck, alternating with each step. His attention stayed fixed on the darkened yard. "We have to remember to feed her."

"I'm not a pet. I can fend for myself." I walked toward the kitchen.

He mumbled something under his breath, but I kept going.

I'd just finished my second glass of water and taken a bite of the banana when Bruno knocked me to the floor. "*Get down.*"

Someone flew through the closed window, glass exploding in a rain around us.

Bruno caught the vampire fledgling and dismembered him where he landed. More glass shattered in the back of the house.

Screams erupted. I crawled along the cabinets to the dining room, out of the line of fire. Bruno stood at the window, systematically killing each fledgling as, one after another, they dove through the opening as if programmed to leap to their deaths. He caught them by the neck, and with vampire speed he either plunged his fist through the vampire's chest to pull out its heart or twisted its head until he'd decapitated the foolish fledgling. I'd barely made it more than a few feet and he'd already killed five and was starting on the sixth.

Vittorio was a bloody mess. The bodies of four vampires lay scattered around him. Three fledglings clung to his body, each biting and clawing him. Others poured into the house, two and three at a time, running at Vittorio, piling onto him.

I grabbed the wooden cross from the floor and drove a pointed end into the back of one of the vampires. He screamed and jumped from Vittorio's back, reaching behind him to pull the wood out with no success.

~ ☾ ~

My aura pulsed. The drum pounded within me. I needed a few seconds to call my power. Even with my aura contained, I needed time to build my strength.

"*Bruno*," I yelled. "Bruno, do something."

He entered the room, two vampires clinging to him.

"Something's wrong. I'm unable to influence any of them." He tossed one from his back and sent him flying through a wall.

"Where's Peter?" I jumped onto the back of one of the fledglings.

"Right here." The vomitous stench accompanying the Scottish voice made me gag.

Brian stepped into the parlor, prodding Peter in front of him. The grin on Brian's face exposed every one of his teeth. "If you'd be so kind as to release my child, I'd be happy to give you back your...stepson." He laughed. "You have *stepsons*, in fact." He roared, his taunting laugh grating on my nerves.

He shoved Peter to his knees, one hand knotted in his hair. Blood pumped from Peter's neck, and his skin became grayer with each beat of his heart. "My child," Brian carelessly gestured to the vampire whose back I sat on. "Lucia."

I released the fledgling.

Calm, Lucia. You can do it. Remain calm. I held my aura tight as she surged to the beat of the pounding drum, begging to be released. "I'll take Peter."

"Of course." Brian shoved Peter forward, and he tumbled to the floor. "You really are lovely. Powerful, beautiful, enchanting. Your eyes are just...I can't wait to see them glow for me." He leered. "You'll be the perfect vampire."

"Call off your fledglings." I snarled, trying my damnedest not to breathe. The foul stenches coming from Brian and his fledglings sickened me.

"Oh, no." He snorted. "They will keep Vittorio under control. I'm taking no chances with him. I've figured out these other two." He pointed from Peter to Bruno. "But I'm still not sure what powers him."

"Where's Tomas?" Bruno demanded, dragging Peter away from the pile of ravenous fledglings.

~ ☾ ~

Brian smirked. "Dead, I'm told. My children were hungry." He waved toward the writhing mass of revenant vampires. "Lucia, did you know that even though human blood feeds us, vampire blood is far more potent? When we feed from each other, especially from ones as powerful as...Vittorio, let's say, we are stronger than if we feed from humans. And, if that vampire is well fed, then, *oh*." His eyes widened. "The possibilities are wonderful."

"They'll kill him." The sound of my racing heart pounded in my ears. If Vittorio died, I'd never be able to defeat Samuel, never see my parents again, and I'd be banished to some place I couldn't even begin to imagine. But, worse than all of that, my love would be gone from me forever. I blinked back tears, refusing to let Brian see my fear.

"That's the plan." Brian sat on the couch. "Then, if the other two don't join me, I'll kill them, too."

"If you want me, you have to let him live."

"*No*," Vittorio growled from beneath the pile of fledglings. His angry aura bubbled around me, throbbing in pain. He was already dying.

"*Vittorio*." I dropped to my knees, crawling toward the pile. Peter and Bruno dragged me back.

"My dear, you are in no position to negotiate," Brian said. "I have beaten Samuel out of his own prize, taken you right from under his nose. And now, I have the pleasure of beating Vittorio, too."

I kicked a fledgling in the ribs, and heard the bones crack, but he never stopped drinking. I'd forgotten what bloodlust did to vampires.

"How did you beat Samuel?" Bruno asked, restraining me against his chest.

"The same way I've beaten Vittorio," Brian answered. "Two powerful vampires, full of themselves, neither wise enough to pay attention to the little people around them."

He yanked the cross out of the back of the whining fledgling and tossed it to the floor.

"Bruno, you should know you cannot control vampires who are already under another's control. These mindless twits can't think on their own. By refusing them sustenance

~ ☾ ~

from anyone but me, I control all their thoughts." Brian petted the head of the fledgling cowering beside him.

Like a happy puppy the new vampire leaned into Brian's hand. The display turned my stomach. I couldn't imagine the way these poor vampire's lives had turned out, no control, no choice. Forced to do as he ordered like mindless killing machines.

"And what happens now that they've fed from Vittorio?" Bruno asked.

"You can be sure they will die. I am not as blind as Samuel. No fledgling of mine will ever be stronger than me. I'll make more." His smiled. "It seems a pity to waste them after such limited service. But it's for the greater good." He shoved the fledgling away from him.

He repulsed me. Just like Samuel, Brian had no respect for anyone. He didn't deserve to exist.

"How are you able to make them so quickly?" Bruno's dark eyes darted back and forth, scanning the room.

"By feeding from other vampires, of course. How else would I so quickly revitalize myself? Creating a vampire every night is exhausting." He feigned a yawn. "A master needs his nourishment."

"What about Samuel? How did you keep this hidden from him?" I asked.

"His obsession blinds him. He has no idea what I've been up to. But he's going to know. Soon enough, he's going to know." He laughed. "Come here, darling. Let's not waste any more time."

I stepped toward him.

"Lucia, *no*." Bruno grabbed me.

I turned on him and I knew what he saw.

My eyes glowed bright green. My skin burned his where he touched me. And a smile of victory graced my lips. He released me and stumbled backward, pulling Peter with him.

I spun to face Brian, sending my aura out like a harbinger, announcing the arrival of The Abyss. She coiled around me, blasting the remaining lights, leaving the entire house in darkness.

~ ☾ ~

CHAPTER TWENTY-SEVEN

Infinite blackness surrounded us as The Abyss descended. Dismal, yet eager, it rolled into the room, gripping every fledgling that remained alive in its long black tendrils, holding them suspended in emptiness. Paralyzed with terror, they stared at me, whimpering.

"Come to me," I called Brian.

He stood and walked toward me. "No! This can't be. You're not ready. Samuel said you're not strong enough." He tried to stop his feet from moving and bent over, grasping for the sofa that no longer sat behind him. His feet dragged him to me. *"No! Please, no!"*

His screams merged with those of his fledglings. Louder and louder they cried, begging to be forgiven, begging to be free.

Thousands of scenes from each of their lives flew past. One by one, the fledglings moved to The Light. Joyous voices sang as each one of them stepped into its welcoming embrace. Even the choir director and the organist from St. Aloysius met their arrival.

As each soul merged into The Splendor, my powers grew stronger. Waves of energy coursed through me. I felt more alive than I'd ever felt. I inhaled, pulling a satisfying breath into my lungs as I watched them all go. All but one.

"Please, Lucia. Please, don't leave me here." Brian reached for me, his hands twisting in my shirt, sweat beading on his brow.

"I want to know what you know about Samuel."

"I don't know anything. He never told me anything." His cheeks flushed nearly the same color as his hair. "He doesn't trust anyone, not even you." He wiped his face on the back of

~ ☾ ~

his hand and clung to me with the other. "Don't leave me here." Tears glistened in his green eyes.

I glared at him. Games. We stood in The Abyss, scenes from his wretched existence zooming by us, all the horrid detail of who he was and what he'd done, laid bare, and still he played games. "What do you mean, not even me? Why would he trust me?"

He didn't respond, just sobbed like a baby.

The Abyss wailed.

"*Please.*" Freckles stood out on his ivory skin.

"*Answer me.*" My voice boomed in the endless void.

He blubbered, not forming even one coherent word.

"Answer me or I'll leave you here to rot for all eternity." I pushed him to arm's length, holding him out to The Abyss.

"*No, no! Don't!*" He clung to my arm and tried to climb back to me. All the while, tears poured from his eyes.

"Why would he trust me?"

"He was there when you were created. He knows you, everything about you. He knows it all." His fingers dug into me.

"When I was created?" The words made no sense. *I* had been there when *he* was created. Wasn't that what Father said? Had I misunderstood?

"Yes," he whimpered. "Please, Lucia."

"Liar!" Even on the edge of hell with the promise of eternal peace at his fingertips, the vampire wouldn't show any honor.

I let him go, and he fell, plummeting downward, screaming the entire time. I turned my back to him, ignoring his pathetic cries. Anger washed over me. I would never know the truth. I could trust no one. I paced, trying to understand what I had to do next.

The gentle scent of rainfall came to me. "Lucia, you cannot condemn him for answering your questions."

I spun toward the voice, feeling betrayed.

Father appeared in The Light.

Mother waited behind him, her disappointment in me so obvious.

"He said Samuel was there when I was created. But you told me otherwise." I shouted the words at them.

~ ☾ ~

"We both told you the truth." Father moved toward me.

"I don't understand. How?" I stepped back.

"Keep practicing, unlock your memories. It will come to you. Do you understand now why you must learn from yourself? Why forcing information from others will only confuse you?"

I stormed away from him, anger boiling over. "I *don't* understand. Why don't you just tell me, Father? Why punish me?" What in God's name could I have done to deserve this?

"You are punishing yourself. You need only to remember." His aura wrapped around me. Love, unyielding and all-consuming, radiated over me.

"Why can't I just remember? Why is this happening?" My demand held none of the anger from seconds before. His essence soothed me, turning the questions into pleas for information. "How do you do that?"

"You are my child." He smiled. "A parent always knows how to comfort his child."

"You haven't explained my memory."

"I cannot. It is your memory. You must work it out. Understand, Lucia, that all things can be forgiven." He hugged me.

"You've been no help," I complained.

"Go, my child. Your husband needs you. Strengthen the bond. Let your love consume him. You've done well today. But your work is not complete and you need to connect more with the piece you've given away." He released me.

"Strengthen the bond? You want me to let him feed from me?" The idea of it frightened me. Even as I stood here knowing I could stop him, knowing I could defend myself, I was still terrified of letting him have me.

"There is more than one way to strengthen your bond to Vittorio," he said, kissing my head.

Brian appeared beside me, sobbing. "I'm sorry. I didn't mean all those things. I just wanted to…"

"Come, Brian. Tell us your story," Mother said, opening her arms to welcome the lost soul.

I watched as she guided him into The Light and Father followed them over the threshold. As quickly as it had

~ ☾ ~

appeared, The Light slipped away, leaving me hovering in The Abyss, confused and strangely excited.

*****

"Drink, Vittorio. Take what you need," Bruno said.

"He's not dead, is he?" Peter asked. "Why doesn't he feed?"

"Hold his jaw open," Bruno said.

Their combined distress frightened me.

I opened my eyes, but was blinded again. I crawled toward their voices, falling over the dead vampires piled around us.

"Where is he?" I asked. "I can't see."

"Here." Peter pulled me toward them. "He's not responding."

I touched Vittorio's face. He was cold. My hand slid to his chest. His heart didn't beat.

"Vittorio," I called softly, combing hair from his face.

He didn't move, didn't make a sound.

I pressed my lips to his and sent my aura into him, searching for the little piece of me that I'd given away so many years ago.

Deep within him, I found it. At first I thought it hid from me, but then I realized he held it protected from everything else around him, even his own desires. His aura curled around the little light like a hurricane glass protects a flame.

My aura moved around his, caressing it, searching for a way to unlock him, but I found none. He'd created an impervious fortress around my Light, barricading himself in with it. As impenetrable as the shelter he provided was, I had to reach him. He needed nourishment or he'd die.

"He's not dead," I said. "But he needs to drink."

"We've both offered. He's not responding." Bruno bit into his wrist again and placed it to Vittorio's lips. "Peter, hold his mouth open."

"No." I pulled Bruno's arm away. "He'll drink from me." My fear of him vanished. The need to save him took over. I lay beside Vittorio, slipping my arm under his neck, balancing myself on my elbow, one leg bent over him as I tugged at the collar of my sweater.

"Lucia, it's a bad idea. He's too weak to stop himself from hurting you." Peter leaned over my shoulder.

~ ☾ ~

"Help me with this sweater," I said, ignoring him. "Rip the collar so he can get to me." Part of me believed this was a bad idea, but I knew there was no other choice. He wasn't responding to them or to me. But I knew the Light he protected would have no ability to refuse my call. It would force him to awaken and drink.

"Let us find another human," Bruno said, standing.

"He needs *me*. Help me. There isn't a lot of time." The collar stretched as I pulled.

Peter tore the sweater down the front from the neck to the waist, exposing my black lace bra. "Nice. I can see in the dark."

"Shut up." I pushed my hair over my shoulder.

My aura moved, cradling Vittorio and me together. Warmth pooled within me as I rested my hand above his heart. "Vittorio," I whispered into his ear. "Come to me. There's no need to hide. Come back to me."

His aura stirred in slow, tentative movements, testing his surroundings. It pushed against mine, forcing me back from him.

"Vittorio, it's me," I whispered as my aura moved closer.

His eyelashes fluttered against my cheek, and he pulled in a breath.

"Drink, Vittorio. Drink and be well."

His lips grazed my neck, and he mumbled his disagreement against my skin.

"You can't hurt me," I reminded him and hoped my own doubt didn't show.

"It's still a terrible idea," he groaned.

But his fangs sank into my skin and his lips latched onto me. Within only a few sips, his arms wrapped around me and he rolled me onto my back. His mouth worked the wound at my neck, suckling and swallowing.

My fingers slid into his hair, holding him to me. He pinned me beneath him, separating my legs, his hips meeting mine. I wrapped my legs around him and ran my hand up his back.

His aura teased mine, coaxing me to flow freely with him. I moaned, and my breathing quickened. His hands moved. The one under my neck slid to my shoulder. The one at my waist

~ ☾ ~

moved upward.

"Vittorio." I caught his hand.

He mumbled, swallowed, and kept his hand on my ribs.

"Bummer," Bruno said.

I felt the heat race to my cheeks and wiggled beneath him.

Lucia. Oh, Lucia. Vittorio's voice whirled in my head.

How do you do that? I thought.

Apparently, you can do it, too. His thought answered as his tongue lapped my neck, working small circles around the puncture marks. *Your father's going to kill me when he sees what I've done.*

He sent me to you, so he's not allowed any room for upset. No longer able to resist temptation, I moved my hips against him. It happened involuntarily, and as soon as it did, I wished it hadn't.

"Wow!" It was a simultaneous exclamation, in stereo. I heard it through Vittorio's thoughts and out of Peter and Bruno's mouths.

"Shut up," I said. "Are you almost done?" I asked, acting as though I wanted Vittorio off me. But I didn't want him to stop. I hoped he'd hold me all night, hoped his mouth would stay latched onto me, tongue swirling until my mind was numb. I wanted to feel him thrust against me as hard as he was until finally he slid inside me. *God, I want to make love to him.*

As you wish, cuore mio. The words rushed through my mind as his hips pumped against my body. My skin nearly erupted in flames.

He let go of my neck. "You two can clean up, right?" He picked me up. "We'll be in Tomas's hidden room. When he arrives, he'll help you. Let me know if there's a problem." Without waiting for an answer, he flew down the hall, tapped a spot on the wall, pushed a panel aside, and descended the stairs.

"Fine," Bruno called. Then his voice dropped. "I told you Tomas wasn't dead."

"You were right," Peter said.

"Naturally."

~ ☾ ~

CHAPTER TWENTY-EIGHT

"Che dolce piu che piu giocondo stato saria di quel d'un amoroso cuore."
~Tasso
How sweet is the rapturous state of soft passions in a heart full of love.

I lay on the bed, watching Vittorio undress. His torn shirt had fallen off his body when he put me down. He unbuttoned his jeans, kicking his shoes off at the same time, then peeled the destroyed denim from his legs.

His hair, an untamed mess of waves, fell around his face. In the dim candlelight, his eyes gleamed. He licked his lips, and a soft smile appeared. My gaze wandered lower to a scar on his left shoulder.

"What's that?" I sat up to touch it.

He followed my hand as my fingers traced the jagged cut.

"It's from a fight with Kerina the night she took me." He pulled my fingers to his lips, leaving soft kisses on each knuckle.

"I've never seen it." I kissed his shoulder, letting my tongue slide over the raised skin.

"Your power is stronger." His breath hitched, and I knew that he was just as excited as I. "You can see things that were once hidden from you."

I slid my hand along his arm and pulled him onto the bed.

He lay beside me, waiting for me to make the first move. He didn't wait long. I pushed him onto his back.

"I want to look at you. What else has changed?" I asked, folding my legs under me. "What else haven't I noticed?"

He smiled. "Nothing that I'm aware of. Once I changed, no

~ ☾ ~

other scars were made but no old ones healed." His thumb picked at the calluses on his palm.

I studied his body, turning his arms to check for marks, running my hand over his chest, finding the little scar from the day he followed me off a cliff and into the river when I was fourteen.

"That day your little trick nearly killed me," he said.

"Did not." I knelt between his legs and slid both my hands down his stomach, over his abdomen to his hips.

He inhaled.

My hands moved down his left leg, starting at his hip joint, squeezing as I went, checking for changes. My fingers lingered behind his knee then massaged down his calf before starting on the right foot and working my way back up to stop inside his thigh.

My gaze met his.

"You're killing me now," he said, his hands making fists of the blanket.

I grinned. "I know." I wrapped my hand around his cock and made a show of checking him for changes. He closed his eyes and bit his lip, his chest rising and falling with each heavy breath.

I straddled his legs and let the ripped sweater slide from my arms. His hands rested on my thighs, squeezing and massaging while I reached behind and unhooked my bra. He slipped the straps from my shoulders and tossed it aside, never once taking his gaze from mine.

His hands roamed up my arms, rising to my shoulders, and sliding down my chest to cup my breasts, thumbs stroking over my hardened nipples.

I moaned.

He sat up with usual vampire speed, wrapping his arms around me, and pulling our bodies together. And I giggled at his eagerness. Then he kissed me.

His mouth moved along my neck, tongue working his way down to my chest. I rose onto my knees, positioning my breasts in front of him, and he kissed them both before taking one into his mouth.

I held him, running the fingers of one hand through his

~ ☾ ~

hair. His gentle yet insistent tugs on my nipple made me writhe against him. As he moved from one breast to the other, his hands worked the button and zipper of my jeans. He folded them down to mid-thigh then laid me on my back to pull them from my legs.

I grinned as he stalked up the bed on all fours, pausing only to lick or nibble me. His descended fangs actually excited me. I squirmed as he nipped my thigh. His sparkling eyes showed his excitement as his tongue worked the knick in my skin.

He stopped between my legs and kissed me deeply. Long, slow kisses that made my back arch.

"Vittorio, I want our first time to happen together." I reached for him.

He glanced at me and grinned. "Just like our wedding night. Although, I did get further this time." He crawled up to me.

I lay beneath him, panting. "Yes, you did."

He nuzzled my ear. "I've missed each delicious inch of you." He spoke the words in Italian, his deep voice adding to my pleasure.

He held his weight on his knees as he slid into me, lowering himself enough to move as deep as he could, pulling back, and sliding deeper.

We moved together just as we always had: in perfect rhythm, meeting each other's needs, desires, knowing exactly what made the other happy.

"I love you, Lucia."

I pulled his lips to mine and kissed him, sliding my tongue across his fangs, not caring about the tiny cuts. He plunged his tongue into my mouth, and I tasted him.

"You're bleeding."

"To heal your cuts," he answered, angling his hips to move deeper.

I sighed. He tasted wonderful, like fine vintage wine. As I savored the taste of him, my desire for him flared white hot.

He quickened our pace, and I rocked up into him.

"Let go of your aura, *cuore mio*." His presence surrounded me, moving over us like a silken wrap. His scent filled the air.

~ ☾ ~

"Let go and join me."

My aura hovered inside me, excited but tentative. She waited for something. "I'm not holding her."

"She is you. Relax for me." He kissed my lips. "Relax and let us both enjoy your pleasure."

"Hold me like you did the first time."

He balanced on one arm and hooked the other under my leg, bringing my knee up, never once breaking rhythm.

I closed my eyes as my aura burst forward, entwining with his.

Perfectly paired we merged as one, embracing each other like two pieces of the same being. Our joining together set free a rapture I'd never imagined.

My Light within him glowed, reaching for me, and, for a brief moment, I touched it, delving within him.

With absolute clarity I saw everything—his body, his aura, his dreams, and his nightmares. Every single aspect of him was laid bare for me to view. The visions whirled by me, becoming a blur, and yet I took it all in.

The sparkle of pleasure twinkled in his eyes. Beyond that, deep within him, love heated his core. His aura pulsed with excitement. His need to have me, touch me, to finally taste me, was met.

Being in my arms and holding me in his, telling me that he loved me and hearing me say I loved him, knowing beyond even a shadow of doubt that I understood his love had only ever been for me and that mine was solely for him, these were his deepest desires.

Without my love, he didn't care to live.

He thought his worst nightmare was Samuel capturing me and creating me into a vampire. That was before he'd learned what would happen if he went to The Light before Samuel was destroyed. Now, the idea that he could cause me to suffer had become his greatest fear.

The guilt biting at the edges of that vision stung. I couldn't bear the idea of him holding himself responsible for my actions. It was my fault that we were in this mess. I couldn't let him worry.

"Vittorio." I tried to soothe his fears and make him

~ ☾ ~

understand that it was my foolishness that put us in this situation. My aura wrapped tight around his.

"No, *cuore mio*. Do not try to take this away. I need it." His movements slowed, deepened. "I must remember how high the stakes are at all times." His lips met mine, softly kissing me. He pulled back barely an inch. "I could not be happier than I am now. Do not worry about the other parts of me. Let's just enjoy each other."

And with those words, heated passion washed through me, cresting like a river overflowing a dam. Vittorio moaned and released my leg. My back arched, and I called out his name, squeezing my legs around his hips as I held him.

He collapsed on top of me, his face buried in my hair, his arms and legs barely holding his weight.

His heart pounded in his chest, a strong, steady beat. And mine matched it, beating with the happiness I had waited to feel for more than three hundred and fifty years.

As much as I loved what was happening, I couldn't breathe. "Vittorio, you're crushing me." I barely had the strength to move my hands. I certainly wasn't moving him off me.

He laughed and took me with him as he rolled onto his back and settled in. "Like you always did, you have exhausted me, Lucia."

"Glad to know I haven't lost my touch." I folded my leg over his and snuggled into his arms.

His fingers twirled my hair. "How do you feel?"

"Fine. Why?" I glanced at him.

"Any different?"

I did feel different. Stronger. Almost like I felt when I took Father Gregoire to The Light. Joyful. "Yes. I feel alive, energized."

"Me, too." He inhaled a deep breath. "Better than I've felt since our life together."

I smiled. "Why? Why do you think we feel..." I cocked an eyebrow at him. "Did you know this would happen?"

"What?" He grinned, and in his eyes flecks of gold and green sparkled, twinkling like the stars. *Cuore Mio, my love, always.*

~ ☾ ~

You're not moving your lips, but I hear all your thoughts.

I didn't know. I thought it only happened because we were intimate. And you're not moving your lips either. His thumb traced my lips.

"All my thoughts? Are you going to hear *all* my thoughts?" This time my lips did move.

His grin widened, and he nodded.

"That's it." I sat up. "Guarding. Teach me how to do it. Right now. I'm not having you hear every single thought I have."

He pulled me back down. "Let me just enjoy you for one night. I'll teach you to guard in the morning."

"Fine. But as soon as we wake up, you're teaching me. *And* no holding anything against me for what I think all night. *And* no repeating anything you hear. *And* no asking me about anything."

He laughed. "What are you so worried about? I've always watched your dreams."

"Dreams, memories—those are one thing. But my personal thoughts—those are something else altogether."

They were. He'd know my deepest desires. He'd learn my darkest fears. *I* didn't even acknowledge those things. I did not want him bringing them up.

"Relax, Lucia. I won't pry." He rolled onto his side. "You do realize this is a two-way street." He slid his arm under my neck.

I looked at him.

He winked.

"You wouldn't stop me?"

He shook his head.

"Even from seeing things you don't want me to know?"

"No. I don't want there to be secrets between us." His leg slipped over mine. His arm draped across me, pulling me into the curve of his body.

I felt his aura's movements. He was restless, still in need of something. His aura paced. It moved slowly, but it moved.

I rolled onto my side and closed my eyes, trying to understand what he needed.

Sleep, Lucia. We need to rest tonight. Our work is only

~ ☾ ~

just beginning. His deep voice moved in my head.

I didn't sleep, not at first. Instead, I wandered through his thoughts, looking for the one that kept his aura from resting. And when I found it, I giggled.

"Stop that." He squeezed me.

I giggled again.

"If you're going to do that, then I'm guarding."

"No, don't." I sucked my cheeks in so another giggle wouldn't slip out.

Such a simple, tiny thing worried him. Something that seemed so obvious to me, he needed exact confirmation to accept as truth.

His worries for Samuel weren't as great as this one. Samuel, who was the most vile creature on the planet, who stalked me with plans to make me his vampire slave, but Samuel wasn't what worried Vittorio the most.

"I'm concerned. We have a lot to prepare you for."

"You're not that worried."

"Yes, I am."

"No. Not compared to this."

"Fine. How long do you plan to torture me? I wanted you to fall asleep first. But, if this is what you're going to do..."

I laughed.

"Fine. I'm going to sleep." He closed his eyes and became completely motionless. Even his breathing stopped.

After what we just did, he still wondered. The idea of it seemed ridiculous.

"Vittorio? Are you really sleeping?"

He didn't respond. But his aura moved closer, eager and tingling.

I grinned and closed my eyes. Then I sent my aura to him, whispering the words he needed to hear. *I love you, Vittorio.*

A quiet calm followed. His aura settled down, curling around mine for the healing rest we both needed. We drifted into sleep, sharing our memories, our dreams, and our love.

~ ☾ ~

ACKNOWLEDGEMENTS

I'd like to thank a few people who've made it possible for me to become a published author. Thanks to my parents who always told me to "try it" no matter what "it" was. Thank you Aunt Pat for helping with research on mental illness in the 1700s. Special thanks to my friend Cheryl and my critique partner Kat Duncan who had to hear every detail of backstory about Lucia and Vittorio. Thank you for asking me question after question and never telling me to leave you alone. Thank you, Steph Murray, Marlene Castricato and Donna O'Brien at Crescent Moon Press for believing in my story and connecting me with my editor, E. Walker. E., thanks for your hard work and wonderful editing of *Perpetual Light*.

Last, but certainly not least, thank you to my husband, Ken, for supporting every one of my many, many endeavors, for celebrating my successes and for helping me get over all the bumps in the road along the way. I love you.

Jordan K. Rose

After trying her hand at many, many things—from crafting and art classes, to cooking and sewing classes, to running her own handbag business, Jordan finally figured out how to channel her creativity. With an active imagination and a little encouragement from her husband, she sat down and began to write, each night clicking away at the keys with her black Labrador, Dino, curled up under the desk.

A few short years later she's entered the publishing arena with no plans to ever turn back.

Jordan's a member of Rhode Island Romance Writers, as well as RWA National, and the New England (NEC), Connecticut (CTRWA), and Fantasy, Futuristic and Paranormal (FFnP) Chapters.

She's currently working on the first book of the Eva Prim series. For more information about Eva, please visit: www.evaprim.com.

Find Jordan on her website at www.jordankrose.com.
Follow her tweets on https://twitter.com/#!/jordankrose
Friend her on Facebook at
https://www.facebook.com/jordankrose

CPSIA information can be obtained at www.ICGtesting.com
Printed in the USA
BVOW030626020312

284245BV00001B/30/P